Of Body and Bone

Book Three in Detectives Daniels and Remalla

J. T. Bishop

Eudoran Press LLC

Eudoran Press LLC

6009 W. Parker Rd. Su. 149, #205

Dallas, TX 75093

www.jtbishopauthor.com

Publisher's Note: This is a work of fiction. Names, characters, places, and incidents are a product of the author's imagination. Locales and public names are sometimes used for atmospheric purposes. Any resemblance to actual people, living or dead, or to businesses, companies, events, institutions, or locales is completely coincidental.

Author Photos by Nick Bishop and Mayza Clark Photography

Book Editing and Proofing by P. Creeden and G. Enstam

Cover Design by J.T. Bishop

Of Body and Bone/ J.T. Bishop -- 1st ed.

ISBN 978-1-955370-61-5

Paperback ISBN 978-1-955370-12-7

Hardback ISBN 978-1-955370-25-7

To Suzzie...

I know of no other person with your strength, sass, and enduring spirit. We are so lucky to call you sister, aunt and friend. Love you and I'll be looking for those pennies.

Other Books by J. T. Bishop

The Red-Line Trilogy

Red-Line: The Shift

Red-Line: Mirrors

Red-Line: Trust Destiny

The Red-Line Trilogy Boxed Set

··········

Red-Line: The Fletcher Family Saga

Curse Breaker

High Child

Spark

Forged Lines

The Fletcher Family Saga Boxed Set

··········

The Family or Foe Saga with Detectives Daniels and Remalla

First Cut

Second Slice

Third Blow

Fourth Strike

The Family or Foe Saga Boxed Set

··········

Detectives Daniels and Remalla standalones and novellas

The Girl and the Gunshot (subscribers only)

A Hamburger Christmas

The Magic of Murder (subscribers only)

Murder Unveiled

....

Detectives Daniels and Remalla

Haunted River

Of Breath and Blood

Of Body and Bone

Of Mind and Madness

Of Power and Pain

Of Love and Loss

Dominion

Illusions

Vendetta

....

The Redstone Chronicles

Lost Souls

Lost Dreams

Lost Chances

Lost Hope

Lost Lives

Lost Time

Lost Love

Chapter One

"So now he's naked, and when he realizes he's not getting away, he stops, holds up his hands, and surrenders." Detective Gordon Daniels laughed. "And Rem stops and looks at me like 'what am I supposed to do with this guy?'"

His partner, Detective Aaron Remalla, smiled from across the dinner table and tucked a long tendril of dark hair behind his ear. "To be honest, I wished he'd kept running, although seeing him from that angle wasn't much better."

"Are you serious?" asked Marjorie, Daniels' wife. "He stripped down to nothing?"

"Nothing," said Daniels. "And Rem was left to handcuff him."

"You ever tried handcuffing someone without touching their ass? It's not as easy as it seems," said Rem. "I washed my hands for several happy birthday tunes after that." He pointed. "Your husband here had conveniently disappeared."

Daniels raised a hand. "I had to keep an eye out for other suspects."

"What other suspects?" asked Rem.

"That park has been known to have assaults," said Daniels.

Rem snorted. "It was the middle of the day. I don't think we were in any danger, unless you count me touching something that didn't need to be touched."

Marjorie rubbed Daniels' arm. "That's my brave husband."

"That's not the word I would use," said Rem. He pushed his plate back and wiped his fingers on a napkin. "Next time, you chase the weirdos."

Daniels nodded and tried not to chuckle. "You got it. I'm on weirdo duty, although I think we've met our quota this year."

Rem eyed his plate. "Boy, ain't that the truth?" He rubbed his face. "I don't think I can handle any more."

Marjorie squeezed Daniels' wrist, and he looked over at her, kissed her forehead, and stood. "I'll clean up," he glanced at Rem, "since you're still recovering from our naked friend. You can take a minute to talk to my lovely wife, who had her own crappy day."

Rem looked over at Marjorie. "You, too, huh?"

Marjorie took the last sip of her wine. "Yeah. I had a sixteen-year-old who hit his math teacher and was suspended, a seventeen-year-old so stressed out over her SAT's, that she's been stealing pills from her mother to stay awake at night to study, and a fourteen-year-old who hates school and wants to drop out and has parents that don't seem to care either way."

Rem's shoulders dropped. "Jeez. You did have a lousy day. I'll take naked guy over that."

"You think being a cop is hard, try being a high school counselor," said Daniels, collecting their plates. "We have some wacky stuff, but at least it's mostly adults."

"It's not always that bad," said Marjorie. "Most of the time it's just normal teenagers stressing over normal things, but every once in a while..."

"You get something crazy," said Rem, staring off. "I guess that happens with every job, doesn't it?"

"Unfortunately, yes," she said.

Rem stood and pushed his chair back. "Back in a sec."

"I got you some chocolate cake from Schultz's if you want it," said Marjorie.

"Chocolate cake?" Rem paused. "I can't say no to that. You got any milk?"

"What am I, a sadist?" asked Marjorie. "Of course, I have milk."

Rem smiled. "Sounds delicious."

"Coming right up." Marjorie stood.

Rem hesitated for a moment, looking as if he might say something else, but then stopped and left the room.

Daniels brought the plates to the sink, and Marjorie brought their wine glasses over. "How's he been this week? Any better?" she asked.

Daniels flipped on the faucet. "He's doing okay. I think today marks his second month back at work and three since the assault. Lozano's been giving us the lighter cases, but we're back in a routine. He has his moments, though."

"I can imagine. He seems...I don't know, quiet tonight."

"That may have something to do with our naked perp." Daniels rinsed a plate and put it in the dishwasher.

"No, it's not that. He only ate half his food. Did you notice?"

"Yeah. I noticed." He ran a glass under the running water. "The appetite is taking a little longer to come back."

"I'm glad I bought that cake then. I know he'll eat it."

Daniels smiled. "No question."

"Is he still hanging out with Mikey Redstone?"

"Yes. They're thick as thieves." He added the glass to the dishwasher.

"You think it's more than that?" she asked.

"I don't think so. It's staying friendly. It's what he needs right now."

Marjorie reached for the cake on the counter and opened the container. "Well, she's dealing with her own issues, especially after what happened with her and Mason on that last case." She pulled a plate from the cabinet.

"I know. That was a close call. She and Rem have both been through a few tough years."

"That's why they're good for each other. Like Mason said, shared pain helps ease a heavy burden." She put the piece of cake on the plate. "And he's right. I wish my kids at school would feel more comfortable talking to me."

"It's not easy, no matter who you are. Talking about your issues is difficult." Daniels picked up another plate and rinsed it. "Going to the department shrink after what happened to me was almost as scary as the incident itself."

"Once you did it, though, you felt better. It helped."

"It did. I'm glad I went."

"Is Rem still going?"

"Every Friday."

Marjorie nodded. "That's good."

Rem's voice returned from behind them. "I hear there's an excellent piece of cake waiting for me."

Daniels glanced back as Rem sat at the table. "I think Marjorie takes better care of you than me."

"I think it's my charm and good looks. It's a hit with all the ladies," said Rem.

Marjorie poured some milk in a glass and brought the cake and milk over to Rem. "Eat up, handsome." She handed him a fork.

"Thanks." Rem took it and sipped his milk. Daniels added the rinsed items to the dishwasher, closed it and flipped it on. He grabbed a dishrag and dried his hands.

Rem stabbed his fork into the cake and hesitated, and eyed Marjorie, who'd sat across from him. "You know," he said. "You don't have to worry about me. I'm doing fine."

Daniels came around from the kitchen and leaned a hip against the counter. He watched Marjorie, waiting to see how she'd answer.

She tipped her head. "I know, but I'm going to worry, anyway. It's my nature."

"Is that why you bought the cake? To make sure I'd eat?" asked Rem.

"He's got you on that one, babe," said Daniels.

"Guilty as charged," said Marjorie, raising her hand.

"Smart lady," said Rem, who took a bite and sighed. "It's delicious."

"Sorry if I hover," said Marjorie. "But I do like to check in every once in a while."

"Is that what you were discussing when I went to the bathroom?" he asked between bites.

"You caught that?" asked Marjorie.

"I am a detective," said Rem.

Daniels chuckled and sat next to Marjorie. "Nothing much gets past him. I've learned that the hard way."

"I don't want to pry," said Marjorie, "so I occasionally drill Gordon for information, but he's not always reliable. I sense he keeps a lot of your confidences, which is fair."

Rem made eye contact with Daniels. "You can ask me whatever you want. If I don't want to answer, I'll let you know."

She put her elbows on the table. "Good. How are you sleeping?"

"Be careful what you ask for, partner," said Daniels.

Rem picked at his cake. "Fairly well."

"Nightmares?" she asked.

"A few." He took a small bite.

Daniels didn't respond, but knew his partner had experienced more than a few.

"You like the department shrink?" she asked. "Is he easy to talk to? If not, I could refer you to someone else."

Rem shrugged. "He is, as far as shrinks go, okay. No complaints."

"Is it helpful?" asked Marjorie. "Do you feel comfortable talking to him?"

Rem licked icing off his fork. "For the most part. He knows everything that happened, but he just loves to talk about my feelings." He rolled his eyes.

"That's kind of his job," said Marjorie. "That's what helps you move through it, and hopefully get past it."

"Get past it," said Rem, quietly. He put some cake on his fork. "If that's possible."

"It's possible. It just takes time," she said.

Rem nodded and ate his cake.

"Have you talked about the PTSD with him?" asked Marjorie. "That's likely causing your lack of sleep and nightmares. Do you have flashbacks?"

Rem stopped chewing, and Daniels recalled a recent incident where Rem had frozen in an alleyway outside of a restaurant that had been robbed earlier in the day. They'd gone out back to look for any clues the thieves may have left behind, and Rem had stopped. He'd grabbed an outside brick wall and couldn't catch his breath. His hands had shaken, and he'd broken out in a cold sweat. Looking around, Daniels had seen a concrete slab that had been placed alongside the back of the alley behind a garden store which had probably been used to hold planter boxes or even as a decorative piece, but Daniels immediately recalled the stone slab from inside the abandoned warehouse, and realized Rem had as well. It had taken him a good fifteen minutes to get Rem out of the alley and back to the car.

Daniels waited to see how Rem would answer. His partner resumed his chewing. "Occasionally," said Rem.

Daniels suspected Rem had more flashbacks than he'd admit to, but kept to himself.

"How bad are they?" she asked.

"Marjorie," said Daniels. "Maybe we should let him eat his cake."

"They're not fun," said Rem. He took a sip of his milk.

"I'm pressing too much, aren't I?" She sat back. "Okay. I'll stop." She paused and narrowed her eyes. "Except for one more question."

"God help me," said Rem.

Daniels smiled. "You should have known better."

"Obviously," said Rem. "Shoot. What's your last question?"

She tipped her head. "You planning on asking Mikey Redstone out on a date anytime soon?"

Daniels groaned.

"What?" she asked. "It's a valid question. And don't tell me you're not curious."

"We're just friends," said Rem.

"Have you thought about it?" asked Marjorie.

"Sorry. You're out of questions." Rem took another bite of cake with a small grin. "You'll have to wait until next time."

"When will that be?" she asked.

Rem chewed and drank some more milk. "That's another question."

Marjorie scoffed, and Daniels chuckled. "You did say just one more."

"I didn't think he'd take me literally," said Marjorie.

"Now you know what I deal with every day," said Daniels. He tapped at the table and pointed at Rem. "You good with picking me up again tomorrow? Car's still in the shop. They're waiting on that part to come in."

"Sure," said Rem. "No problem."

Marjorie sighed. "Fine. I'll stop badgering you. But I'll be ready next time we talk."

"I know you will be," said Rem. He scraped some icing off the plate. "But thanks for checking in. I know it's because you care, and I appreciate that."

A loud wail sounded from above, and Marjorie checked the time. "What is J.P. upset about? He should be sound asleep."

"I'll check him," said Daniels, starting to stand.

Marjorie put a hand on his shoulder. "No. You stay. I'll go see what's bugging him. You sit and talk to your partner since my time allotment is up. Be back in a second."

Daniels sat. "Okay. Thanks."

Marjorie stopped next to Rem. "And you finish that cake."

"Yes, ma'am," said Rem. "That's one thing that'll be easy to do."

Marjorie headed up the stairs.

"Thanks for talking to her," said Daniels. "She's been worried about you."

Rem put his fork down. "I can see that."

"You did a nice job of answering questions without really answering them."

"At least I've learned something from all the perps I've talked to over the years."

"It's an acquired skill."

"One I've had a lot of practice with," said Rem. "Lucky me." He wiped his face with a napkin.

Daniels sensed an underlying issue but couldn't put his finger on it. "You don't have to finish the cake if you don't want to."

Rem took another bite. "I'm afraid of what might happen if I don't."

"I've taught her a few skills, so that's a legitimate concern." Daniels watched Rem poke at the remains of his cake. "You're sure you're okay? You do seem a little quiet tonight."

Rem put his fork on the plate. "It's nothing. Just one of those days." He pushed the plate away. "That's it for me. You better chuck it before I get in trouble."

Daniels nodded, but studied his partner. Some of the weight he'd lost had returned, but his cheeks still held a hollow look, and his couple of days' worth of stubble was likely designed to hide it. He couldn't deny that his partner had shown remarkable improvement in a brief period, especially after being taken and nearly sacrificed by a cult leader and his followers, and he'd attributed it to Mikey and her ability to snap Rem out of it when he needed it. But after Mikey's recent setbacks, Rem had been helping her instead of vice versa, and it had taken its toll, although Daniels doubted Rem would ever admit to it.

He stood and took the plate to the sink, where he dumped the remains and added the dish to the dishwasher. "No more evidence."

"Thanks." Rem fiddled with his napkin. "Listen, um…there is something—"

Footsteps on the stairs traveled and Marjorie returned, holding J.P., his red eyes shining with tears, and his cheeks rosy red. "It's his teeth. I think he's feverish. I'm going to give him something." She handed J.P. to Daniels.

"Hey, buddy," said Daniels, bouncing his one-year-old. "Are you teething? Hurts, doesn't it?" He wiped away a tear. "You thirsty?" He filled a sippy cup from his water bottle and handed it to J.P., who took the cup and sucked on it.

"I should head out," said Rem, standing. "Let you guys take care of teeth, diapers, and all that fun stuff."

"You want to change his diaper?" asked Marjorie. "Because you're more than welcome." She unscrewed a small bottle with a dropper and measured out a dose of medicine. "Here you go, sweetie." She popped it in his mouth and squeezed. "All better."

Daniels let J.P. drink some more water when J.P. balked at the medicine. "What were you saying?" he asked Rem.

"Nothing. It's no big deal." Rem took the last gulp of his milk. "Thanks for dinner. As usual, Marjorie, you outdid yourself." He put the glass on the counter. "And I appreciate the offer to change a diaper, but I'll pass." He eyed Daniels. "And I'll pick you up tomorrow morning."

Daniels watched his partner, knowing he'd missed something, but J.P. smacked his face, and he grabbed for the sippy cup that almost fell.

"Wait. Before you go," said Marjorie. "I forgot. I need a picture."

"Picture?" asked Daniels. "Of what?"

"Of us. All of us," said Marjorie. "They're doing a project at school where we bring in a picture of family, and that's us. We don't have anything recent, so let's take one now." She pulled out her cell.

"Now?" asked Rem. He swiped at his shirt.

J.P. screeched, and Daniels bounced him. "You sure about that?"

"Yes," she said. "Family's not about being perfect. Let's sit at the table and take a quick pic. It'll be fine."

Daniels gave in and sat with J.P. on his knee. "Whatever you say. Have a seat, Rem."

Rem hesitated and then shrugged. "It's your picture." He sat next to Daniels. Marjorie squatted in front and held out the camera to get them all in the photo. "Smile."

Daniels smiled and tried to distract J.P. long enough to get him to look toward the camera. Marjorie snapped a photo and then took a couple more.

"That should do it." She stood and flipped through the pictures. "I like this one. I'll text you both a copy." She punched some buttons on her phone.

"I can imagine J.P. looks great with his wild hair and snotty nose," said Daniels.

"He's fine. We all look good. We should take pictures more often. J.P. won't be little forever." She put her phone away and took J.P. "Come on, little dude. Time to go back to bed."

Daniels handed J.P. to her, and J.P. laid his head on her shoulder.

"I'm headed out," said Rem. "Thanks again, Marj."

"You're welcome. And don't think I haven't tabled my questions for later, and you know you can always call and talk if this guy," she nodded at Daniels, "is unavailable."

Rem smiled and ruffled J.P.'s hair. "I'll keep that in mind. Thanks."

"Good night," she said, and headed up the stairs.

"Night," said Rem. He walked toward the door. "See you tomorrow." He said to Daniels.

Daniels debated whether to press Rem about whatever was bugging him, but decided to wait for now. "Okay." He paused. "You call if you need anything."

"Now she's got you all worried, too." Rem sighed. "Relax. I'm all right. It's not all unicorns and rainbows, but at least I get the occasional glimpse of a horse and a partly sunny day."

"It's a decent place to start."

Rem opened the door and walked out. "I suppose." He paused. "I guess I just wish I could get past this phase without getting knocked back into it." He put his hands on his hips. "It gets hard, you know, with people looking at you like you're about to fall apart."

Daniels frowned. "Do I do that?"

"Sometimes, but it's usually when I'm about to fall apart." He shook his head.

"Catch twenty-two, isn't it?"

"Yeah. I suppose it is." He scratched his head. "I'll uh...see you in the morning."

"Yeah. See ya tomorrow." Daniels watched as Rem got into his car and drove away.

Chapter Two

THE NEXT MORNING, DANIELS waved as Rem pulled up to the curb in front of Daniels' home and stopped. Daniels opened the door and slid in, admiring the sunny day and cool temperatures. "Morning."

"Morning," said Rem.

Daniels closed the door, and Rem pulled away. "Thanks for being on time," said Daniels. "That's two days in a row. I should have you pick me up more often."

"Yeah, well. You're lucky. I was up."

Daniels took a closer look and noted Rem's droopy eyes. "Didn't sleep?"

"Maybe a few hours." He stopped at an intersection.

"I thought it was getting better."

"Depends on the week...plus...other things." Rem hit the gas and continued down the street.

"What other things? Something I should know?" Daniels recalled Rem's comment from the previous night. "Is it about what you were going to mention last night before we got interrupted? What were you going to say?"

Rem didn't answer and turned onto another, busier street.

"Rem?"

"It's nothing. I shouldn't have said anything."

"Well, it's obviously something."

"You mind if we stop and get some coffee? I need gas, too."

"That's fine. There's a place right up here on the corner."

Rem nodded. "Perfect."

Daniels waited. "Well?"

Rem sighed. "Fine. I'll tell you, but you're going to get upset and before I deal with that, I need some caffeine in my veins. I can handle you better when I'm awake."

Daniels shifted in his seat. "What the hell is going on?"

"Just wait, okay? Don't freak out, at least not yet anyway. No one is in immediate danger and it's not life-threatening, and no, I'm not quitting." He flipped on his signal, turned into the parking lot, and pulled up next to a gas pump. "You go get the coffee, and I'll get the gas. We can talk about it after I have a few gulps." He reached for his wallet. "I'll get some cash."

"Keep it," said Daniels. "I'll get it. I'm going to need some coffee, too, to brace myself." He popped the door open. "Be right back."

"Okay." Rem turned off the ignition and popped the gas cap.

Daniels closed his door and jogged into the convenience store, wondering what Rem was going to say. His mind whirled with possibilities, but he told himself to relax; his imagination was probably far worse than the actual issue.

Entering the store, he saw the attendant up front. "Morning," he said.

The attendant nodded and waved, and Daniels headed toward the coffee section in the back. Rows of coffee dispensers filled with everything from breakfast blends to dark brews sat atop a counter along with various creams and sugars. Daniels grabbed two cups, one large and another small, and filled Rem's with a medium roast Columbian variety.

Out of the corner of his eye, beside the coffee aisle, and near a rear exit, Daniels noticed a young boy, probably a preteen, standing by himself. Looking over, Daniels noted the boy's unkempt appearance; his jeans were ripped, his shirt was dirty, and his brown hair was uncombed and unwashed. His freckled, pale face had a flat expression, as if he wasn't sure where he was or what to do.

Daniels' radar blipped on, and he watched the boy as he filled Rem's cup, and then filled his own. After a few seconds, he added cream and sugar to Rem's and then placed lids on each cup. The boy remained quiet and didn't move. Eyeing the store, Daniels saw a man in one of the aisles wearing a baseball cap. The man walked toward a refrigerated section, turned, and headed toward them. Nearing the boy, the man came into full view, and Daniels saw him holding two bags of chips and a six-pack of soda. He was in his mid-forties, tall, thin, wearing his own unkempt clothes, and Daniels could see close-cut brown hair beneath the baseball cap.

He handed the chips to the boy. "Here, kid," he said. "Hold these."

The boy took the chips and turned his head. Cold crawled up Daniels' back when he saw the child had a swollen cheek and eye. Thinking of J.P., something shifted in Daniels, and he recognized that something was off. Watching the man and the boy, he realized the boy was scared. Years of experience had taught him not to ignore those messages, and he couldn't start now.

Holding his coffees, he approached the man. "Hi there," he said, keeping his tone friendly.

The man stiffened and turned toward him, his face tense. The boy looked up at Daniels.

"I know you?" asked the man. He lowered his arm and put his hand on the boy's shoulder.

"No." Daniels saw a small tattoo on the man's forearm and debated his next words. "I just noticed you two standing over here. Your boy here looked a little lost. You two need anything?" He eyed the child, whose gaze darted between Daniels and the man.

"We're good. Thanks," said the man. "Let's go, kid." He pushed on the child's shoulder.

Daniels had no reason to stop them, but his unease grew, and he couldn't let them walk away. "You sure everything's okay? I just noticed his bruised face." He gestured toward the boy.

The man stopped. "He's fine." His posture straightened, and his eyes narrowed. "Not that it's any of your business."

Daniels narrowed his own eyes. "It might be, actually. I'm a detective. And I'd just like to make sure he's all right."

The man hesitated, but then sneered. "Detective, huh?" He chuckled. "Well, ring-a-ding-ding. What do you think of that, junior? A real live detective."

Daniels glanced down at the child, who looked like he wanted to cry. He spoke to him. "You okay, son?"

The man took a step closer. "He ain't your son."

Daniels held his ground. "Maybe not, but if he's been abused, then that makes him my responsibility."

"Responsibility?" The man chuckled. "You hear that, kid? You're his responsibility now. I bet your momma would be happy to hear that." He squinted. "Boy's my nephew. He fell off his bike." He took another step toward Daniels. "You're relieved of duty, *Detective*."

That cold sliver became a spike, and Daniels gripped the coffee cups. "Is that true?" He looked down at the boy. "You fall off your bike?"

The boy didn't say a word, and Daniels wanted to grab his hand and pull him out of the store.

"Tell the detective." The man didn't take his gaze from Daniels.

The boy looked between them. "I...I...um..." He spoke so softly that Daniels barely heard him. "I don't know."

Daniels noticed the man's grip tighten on the boy's shoulder. "That doesn't sound like a boy who fell off his bike," said Daniels. "Maybe we should go to the station and talk about it."

"Station?" The man glowered. "I'm not going anywhere with you. We're leaving. And if you know what's good for you, you'll head in the opposite direction."

Daniels' skin tingled, and the hair on his arms raised. He wondered how far he should take this. He set his jaw. "Nobody's going anywhere until I know the boy's okay." The air electrified, and Daniels heard a buzz around him as if a swarm of bees was approaching.

The man took another step and encroached to within a foot of Daniels. Raising his hand off the boy's shoulder, he grinned. "Is that so?" He pointed a bony finger with a grimy nail. "We'll just see who's going where." The buzzing vibration grew louder as the man brought his finger closer and Daniels got a better look at the tattoo. He could read the word *Sam*. Anticipating the contact against his chest, he held still. If this guy touched him, he'd have grounds for an assault charge, and reason to bring him in. He waited, wondering what Rem would think when he walked out with this loser in handcuffs.

The boy suddenly spoke. "He...he's right. I...I fell off my bike. It's no big deal." He reached up, grabbed the man's arm, and pulled it down and away from Daniels. "I'm okay." His breathing came in quick gasps, and his face paled more. "He...he's my uncle. We just stopped to get some snacks."

The man's grin grew, and he dropped his hand back on the boy's shoulder and patted it. "See? He's just fine."

Daniels' mental war raged. The boy had backed up the man's story, but Daniels didn't believe him and he couldn't leave it alone. Something was up, and he sensed the boy was in danger.

"What's your uncle's name? He got one?" asked Daniels, holding the man's stare.

The boy didn't respond, and Daniels didn't blink. The man glared and opened his mouth to answer when Daniels heard a yell from the front of the store.

"Daniels. Where are you?" It was Rem's voice.

Daniels hesitated, and then glanced back. "Here."

Rem spotted him. "We got a call from Lozano. We got a ten fifty-four. We got to go."

Daniels cursed and eyed the drinks. He still needed to purchase them and figure out what to do about the boy. "Be right there."

"You get the coffees?" yelled Rem.

"Yes...and no." He turned back.

"What are you doing back there?"

Daniels stopped cold. The exit door was open, and the man and child were gone.

••••••••••

Rem pulled up in front of the house where an officer was rolling out crime scene tape around the perimeter. Police cars, their lights swirling, were parked out front. Rem opened the door and got out along with Daniels, who was still agitated. "Don't worry about it," said Rem. "It was probably nothing."

"You didn't see him," said Daniels. "That kid was scared." He stepped onto the curb and headed toward the house. "If you'd been in there with me, your gut would have been flaring just like mine." He grimaced. "Damn it. I should have brought them in."

Rem approached the tape and ducked beneath it, flashing his badge to an officer standing on the lawn. "Yeah, well, that would have been difficult, considering we got called here. You think they would have minded sitting in the car and waiting?"

"I could have called a patrol car. I could have gone to the station with them, and you could have handled this."

"Could haves and should haves are potholes, partner. Best not to step in them. I've stepped in a ton, and I'm still stuck in a few."

Daniels sighed. "I just hope he's okay." He jogged up the steps of the small one-story house, and Rem followed.

An officer stepped out of the front door. He was a few years younger than Rem, with thinning hair and a sharp nose. "Hey, Peterman," said Rem. "What's the story?"

"Hey, Rem. Daniels. Thanks for getting here so fast."

"We weren't that far away," said Daniels. "Where's the body?"

Peterman gestured. "Inside. Crime scene is on the way."

"You touch anything?" asked Rem, following Daniels and Peterman inside.

"Nope. Not a thing. We checked the house. There's no one else here."

Rem passed a small living and dining area and walked into the kitchen. There were plates in the sink and a bowl of soggy cereal on the counter. To the right near a breakfast table was a man's body, lying face-up, wearing jeans and a sweater. One chair was knocked over, but beyond that, nothing seemed disturbed.

"The housekeeper found him this morning. She called us. She comes in once-a-week to clean. She's out back, talking to Phelps. Her name's Lucy."

Daniels kneeled next to the body. "This guy's been dead for a while. He's cold and stiff." He looked up. "Any sign of foul play? Any blood?"

"Not that we've found. Guy may have just dropped dead from a heart attack for all we know. He's got a strange round mark on his sweater. It may be just a stain, though."

Rem leaned over and eyed the mark. "No idea what it is."

"And there's another thing."

"What's that?" asked Rem, straightening.

Peterman pointed toward the back of the house. "There's two bedrooms. One obviously belongs to our dead guy. The other one has an unmade bed, and kid's clothes in it, but no kid."

Rem shrugged. "Maybe he's in school."

"What did he do?" asked Peterman. "Walk around the body this morning?"

Daniels straightened. "An unmade bed doesn't mean much. Maybe he's got a kid who was here recently, or maybe not. Maybe our vic here just isn't big on making beds."

"His bed is made, though," said Peterman.

Rem eyed Daniels. "Well, if there is a kid, and this is Dad, then where's mom?" He walked around the kitchen counter when he heard a woman yelling from outside. An officer poked his head into the kitchen. "The mom's here. A neighbor called her. She's upset and wants to come inside."

"We'll talk to her," said Daniels.

"Thanks, Peterman," said Rem. "You studying for that Detective exam yet?" He smiled.

Peterman smiled back. "I'm getting there."

"Good. Keep your eye on the prize. We could use you." Rem followed Daniels back outside and saw a woman around the age of thirty with long, straight, black hair talking to a young officer, who was trying to prevent her from entering the house.

"Ma'am?" asked Daniels, approaching her and holding out his badge.

The woman stopped arguing with the officer and faced them. "What's going on? Why can't I go inside?"

Daniels introduced himself and Rem. "What's your name?" he asked.

"Victoria. Victoria Lambert." She wrung her hands. "Where's Ben? Where's Josh?"

Daniels made eye contact with Rem. "Who are Ben and Josh?" asked Daniels.

Her face fell. "Ben is my ex. Josh is my son. What is going on?"

"Maybe you'd like to sit down, Mrs. Lambert," said Rem.

"I don't want to sit down," she yelled. "What is happening?"

Another woman ran down the lawn, her long dark hair up in a messy knot. An officer followed behind her. "Mrs. Lambert?" she yelled.

Victoria spotted her. "Lucy."

The women embraced, and Lucy began to cry.

"Lucy. What is it?" Victoria pulled away, her face pale. "Where's Ben?"

Lucy sniffed and wiped her nose. "Ben's dead. He's dead." She burst into more tears, and Daniels waved at the officer.

"What?" asked Victoria. "Ben's dead? That can't be."

"Ma'am, come with us," said Rem. He gently took Victoria's arm. Daniels asked the officer to take care of Lucy, and the officer took her elbow and led her away.

"Oh, my God. Ben," said Victoria, hugging herself. "Oh, my God."

"We're very sorry for your loss, Mrs. Lambert," said Daniels.

Her face tightened. "Where's Josh? Where's my son?"

Rem's heart picked up its pace. "Josh is your son? Was he here?"

She bobbed her head up and down. "Yes. This was Ben's week to have him. Is he at school?" She held her face. "God. I have to call the school. I have to go get him."

Rem glanced at Daniels, knowing they were both thinking the same thing. Ben's body had been there too long to get Josh to school. "When's the last time you saw Ben and Josh, Mrs. Lambert?" he asked.

Victoria grabbed her phone. "I...uh...I dropped Josh off Monday. I talked to...to Ben briefly. Oh, God." She dialed a number and put the phone to her ear, her hands shaking. "What the hell is happening?"

Rem waited with Daniels to see what the school would say and prayed the boy was there.

"How old is Josh?" asked Daniels.

"Eleven," said Victoria. "He's...he's eleven." Victoria spoke and relayed the situation to whoever had answered. She told them she needed to pick up Josh immediately.

Rem and Daniels listened and Rem's heart thumped harder when Victoria's face went white, and the phone slid from her fingers.

Daniels picked it up and Rem tried to talk to Victoria. "What is it?" he asked. "Is it Josh?" Victoria had frozen, though, and couldn't seem to speak.

Daniels held the cell to his ear and spoke to the school. His own face went white, and he spoke to Rem. "Joshua Lambert has been absent for the last two days."

"Shit," said Rem. The case had just gone from a possible murder to kidnapping. "I'll get a hold of Lozano."

Daniels finished with the school and handed the phone back to Victoria, who remained in a shocked state. "Ma'am. Mrs. Lambert?"

"My son," she whispered. "Where's my son?"

Rem started to dial Lozano's number when he saw Peterman step out of the house. "Peterman," he yelled. "Any pictures in there? The guy's kid is missing. We need a picture."

Peterman nodded and returned to the house. Lozano answered and Rem gave him a quick run-down of the situation. With a child missing, it would be all hands on deck. Lozano told him to start the canvas and he'd notify the higher ups. Rem hung up and watched Daniels guide Victoria to a nearby police car.

He followed them over. "Lozano's on it. We need to start talking to the neighbors."

Daniels nodded and settled Victoria onto the seat of the patrol car. He squatted next to her. "Just sit here for a second. Try and relax. We'll find him. He's probably with a friend. Try not to worry."

She put her head in her hands. "Where is he? Where could he be?" She rocked back and forth.

"Does he hang out with anyone in the neighborhood?" asked Daniels. "What about other family? Does he have grandparents? Cousins?" He paused. "What about Ben's family? Anyone there that might have him?"

Victoria moaned. "I don't think so. He...Ben isn't...or wasn't...close to his brother, and his...his parents live on the east coast. My...my family would have told me." Tears sprang into her eyes. "Oh, God. Did somebody take him? Did someone take my baby?"

Rem saw Peterman emerge from the home, a gloved hand holding a picture. He ran over to Rem. "I saw this in his bedroom." He held it out.

Rem saw a picture of Ben and Victoria, with a young boy between them. He had had sandy brown hair, freckles and what looked like chocolate smeared on his face. "Is this Josh, Mrs. Lambert?" He pointed at the picture.

Victoria looked up, and Daniels straightened.

"Yes," she said, and her voice caught. "Yes. That's Josh."

Daniels cursed, his face pale and stricken.

"What's wrong?" asked Rem.

Daniels stared wide eyed. "That's him."

"That's who?" asked Rem.

"Damn it. I knew something was wrong." He waved at the photo. "That's the kid from the convenience store."

Chapter Three

REM SAT IN A chair in Lozano's office and watched his partner pace. Daniels' usually polished appearance was marred by his hair hanging in his face, his sleeves folded up to his elbows, and his rumpled shirt. "You need to relax. This isn't your fault," said Rem.

Daniels stopped and jabbed out a hand. "I was within arm's length of him, Rem."

"I know that, but you didn't know what was going on. How could you?"

"But that's just it. I did know. Maybe not the specifics, but I knew he was in trouble."

"Take it easy, Daniels." Lozano hit a button on his keyboard and sat back. "We all wish we could read people's minds and see out the back of our heads, but that's not the way it works. And you could look at this as good news. We know they're in the area."

"Literally twenty minutes from Josh's dad's house," said Rem. "The guy's either stupid or he's way more comfortable than he ought to be."

"He's not that stupid. He got away from me," said Daniels. "And the videos at the store? How do you explain that?"

Rem slunk in his seat and held the bridge of his nose. His lack of sleep and their insane day was catching up to him, despite his numerous cups of coffee. After ensuring several officers would canvas the neighborhood, Rem and Daniels had returned to the convenience store and asked to see the videos from that morning. The manager had taken them to the back office and pulled up the footage from the time of Daniels' arrival. They'd watched as Daniels entered the store and saw the top of Josh's head toward the back near the coffee counter. A tall advertisement placard obscured the area where Josh's captor shopped, and they waited for him to walk out from behind it. The moment he did, though, the footage had gone fuzzy and had remained fuzzy throughout the entire confrontation with Daniels, until Rem had arrived. Then the footage returned, clear as before.

Daniels had cursed and kicked a chair, while the manager tried to figure out what the problem was, but couldn't fix it. They'd returned to Ben's house afterward to assist with the canvas, and had talked with Victoria some more, but neither the canvas nor her answers had helped much with the search. Nobody had seen or heard a thing.

Lozano had contacted the media to put out Josh's picture and had arranged for a sketch artist to meet with Daniels the next day to get a picture of the man who'd taken Josh.

The coroner had received Ben Lambert's body, bumped it to a priority since it involved a missing child, and was doing the autopsy. The next step was to talk to family members. They'd stopped at the station, though, to update Lozano and get something to eat, although Daniels showed little interest in food.

"You got me," said Rem, thinking of the fuzzy footage. "But that's technology for you."

"How the hell does the video screw up while he's in it?" asked Daniels. "It makes no sense."

Rem took a deep breath. "I know it's frustrating, but we're getting the word out. The media is on it. Josh's picture is spreading far and wide, and soon, so will your sketch of this guy. We'll find him. Especially if he's sticking close to home. Somebody will spot them."

"After today, he could be anywhere. He's not going to hang around now," said Daniels, hanging his head. He held up his thumb and forefinger. "I was this close."

"You berating yourself gets us nowhere," said Lozano. "We work with what we've got." He checked his watch. "I know it's getting late, but start contacting the family. For all you know, the guy we're looking for *is* Josh's uncle."

Rem stood. "You heard the man. Let's go."

Daniels put his hand on his hips, looked between the two of them, and sighed. "Okay." He grabbed his jacket and headed out the door.

Rem followed. "We'll keep you posted, Cap." He grabbed the knob.

"Hey," said Lozano.

Rem hesitated. "What?"

"You keep an eye on your partner. I don't want him flying off the handle when we find this guy. I want this case to be open and shut."

"If we find Josh alive, he'll manage, but if we don't..."

Lozano paused, his face weary. "Then it's even more important. Let the courts handle it, not Daniels. You got that?"

Rem considered his response. "I'll do my best."

Lozano pointed. "You'll do your job. And so will your partner."

Rem nodded and closed the door.

• • • • • • • • • • •

Daniels sat at his desk and held his head, the look on Joshua Lambert's face flashing in his mind. *If I'd just listened to my gut.*

"Who do you want to talk to first?" Daniels looked up to see Rem standing beside his desk. "I say we talk to Ben Lambert's brother," said Rem. "Mrs. Lambert said they weren't close. But why? Could be something there."

"It's not Ben's brother."

"How do you know?"

Daniels stood. "Because I know."

Rem leaned against the desk. "Then who is it?"

Daniels paced again and tossed out a hand. "I don't know."

"You're not making any sense."

"You weren't there, Rem." He ran a hand through his messy hair. "This guy. He had a vibe. There was something about him. I...I don't know how to explain it."

"People who kidnap kids tend to have a vibe. That's not surprising."

"It's not just that. It was Josh, too. The look on his face." He groaned. "If the man who took him was his uncle, I'll eat my hair gel."

"You could. You got enough to make a meal out of it."

"This isn't funny." Daniels closed his eyes, seeing Josh's face again. "Josh didn't know the guy. He was scared."

"None of this is funny, but you standing there, threatening to eat beauty products, doesn't help. You know we have to investigate every clue, and that includes Lambert's brother. Maybe he is innocent, but he may also have information about Ben and the family that could be pertinent to the case. So, we go talk to him." He pushed off the desk. "You ready?"

Daniels opened his eyes and blew out a heavy breath. Seeing his partner, he noted his tired features and sunken cheeks, and for a moment, recalled their conversation in the car before all of this happened. "Yeah. I'm ready." He grabbed his jacket. "On the way, you can tell me what you've been keeping to yourself. We never got to it this morning."

"Never mind me. Let's deal with this first. My problems are minor compared to finding Josh."

"Still, you can tell me on the way. We won't solve this case while we're in the car." He headed toward the doors of the squad room.

"It can wait," said Rem.

"Rem—" The squad doors opened, and Daniels stopped. Victoria Lambert stood at the entrance, her purse hanging on her shoulder and her eyes red. "Mrs. Lambert?" he asked.

"I'm sorry. I couldn't just sit at home. They told me you were up here, and I just...just...I..." She gripped her elbows. "I'm so scared."

Daniels took her arm, and Rem came up beside her. "Have a seat." Rem gestured toward one of the chairs. "Can we get you some coffee?"

She walked toward Daniels' desk and sat in his chair. "I'm sorry. I know you're busy. I shouldn't be bothering you."

"It's no bother," said Daniels. "I'll get you some water." He walked to the jug of bottled water behind Rem's desk and filled a disposable cup. He brought it over. "Here you go."

"Thank you." She took it with shaky fingers and managed a sip. Rem took the cup from her and put it on Daniels' desk. "We're doing everything we can, Mrs. Lambert," said Rem. "We've got the whole force looking. We'll find him."

"I just don't understand. Who would do this?" She looked up. "Why did they kill Ben?" Her face crumpled and tears filled her eyes. "Are they going to kill Josh, too?"

Daniels' heart sunk, and he squatted beside her. "We don't know what happened to Ben. There weren't any signs of violence at the scene. We'll have to wait to see what the coroner finds." He patted her hand. "That's why it's important not to think the worst."

"Two days," she whispered. "My baby's been gone two days." She sniffed and wiped at her falling tears. "I can't imagine what he's going through."

Rem reached for a tissue from a nearby desk and handed it to her. "I know it's hard. But the good news is that we know Josh isn't far away. We saw him this morning. He's alive and in the area. Between that and my partner's description of the man who took him, we stand a great chance of finding him. Just hang in there. Our captain just told us that people are already calling the tip line. Someone's bound to have seen your son."

Victoria dabbed her cheek and wiped her nose. She reached over and pulled at Daniel's wrist. "Tell me what he looked like. You told me before, but I wasn't holding it together. Tell me again. Maybe something will spark. Please."

Daniels pulled an empty chair over and sat. "He's white and tall, maybe six feet, with short, dark brown hair, but he was wearing a baseball cap. He was thin, but he didn't strike me as weak. Probably in his early to mid-forties, with brown, narrow eyes."

She nodded and rubbed her temples.

"Don't forget the tattoo," said Rem.

"Hell. Sorry," said Daniels. "He had a tattoo. On his left forearm. It said 'Sam.'"

Her posture straightened, and her eyes widened. "A tattoo? On his forearm?" She held the tissue against her mouth.

"Does that ring any bells?" asked Rem.

"Oh, my God," said Victoria. She held her stomach.

"What is it?" asked Daniels. "Do you know him?"

"It said 'Sam?'" she asked.

"Yes." Daniels rolled closer to her. "Who is it?"

She shook her head. "It can't be. It's been so long. I...I mean...I...I was so young."

Daniels frowned and looked at Rem, who grabbed his own chair and swung it around. "Tell us what you know, Victoria." He sat in front of her.

She gripped the tissue. "It's not possible."

"Whatever it is, we need to hear it," said Daniels, trying not to sound impatient. "Who is this man?"

Victoria squinted her eyes shut. "I never thought I'd see him again. I...I was stupid. Ben and I, we were...were...going through a rough patch. We'd separated briefly and I...I...went out one night." She opened her eyes and more tears fell. "I got drunk and met this guy. He said he was from Fresno and in town on business." She moaned. "He had a tattoo on his arm. It said 'Sam.'"

Rem and Daniels made eye contact. "What happened, Mrs. Lambert?" asked Daniels.

Biting her lip, she opened her eyes and let go of a sob. "I slept with him." She held the tissue against her eyes. "And...and..."

"And what?" asked Daniels.

"I never told Ben..." she said, tears streaming down her face, "...but I...Oh, God." She sucked in some air. "It's possible the man who took Josh could be his father." Her shoulders shaking, she sobbed harder.

Chapter Four

Rubbing his eyes, Rem heard the elevator ding. The elevator stopped, and he watched the door open.

"How you doin'?" asked Daniels.

"Just peachy." Rem stepped off the elevator and turned toward the coroner's office. "How are you?"

"About the same."

"Great. We should start a comedy act."

"I doubt we'd sell any tickets."

"Well, at least we wouldn't be looking for a missing kid."

"Is that good or bad?" asked Daniels.

"I don't know. I'm too tired to think about it." Rem rounded the corner and opened the door to the lab.

After Victoria had calmed down long enough to think, they'd managed to get her to remember the name of the man she'd slept with twelve years earlier. She'd recalled it was Felix Randall, but it had been a long time since she'd thought of him. After her fling, she'd felt so guilty that she'd recommitted to her marriage, and she and Ben had sought counseling. Not long after, she'd realized she was pregnant, but had never told Ben about her one-night-stand. Victoria had believed that Josh was Ben's son and had never questioned it since.

After getting the name, they'd informed Lozano, who'd initiated a search on Felix Randall. Once Victoria stopped crying, she'd left with her sister, who'd come to pick her up. Rem and Daniels had contacted the coroner, telling her of the situation and asking her to test Ben to see if he was Josh's biological father. Victoria had provided them with Josh's pediatrician's name and number, and also agreed to provide some hair from Josh's hairbrush in case the coroner required it.

While on the phone, the coroner had asked Rem and Daniels to stop by the lab. She'd found something interesting on Lambert and wanted to show him and Daniels.

Once downstairs, they entered a large sterile area, with wide stainless-steel tables and bright lights. One table was occupied with a body covered by a white sheet. "Hey, doc?" yelled Rem. "You in here?"

A door off the back of the lab opened, and a woman wearing a white lab coat emerged. Petite, with short blonde hair, and large glasses that made her eyes look huge, she waved a folder in her hand. "Hey, Remalla. Daniels."

"Doctor Adams," said Daniels. "How are you?"

"Not bad for a lady that lives in a basement and cuts people open for a living. How about you?"

Rem pursed his lips. "Not bad for two guys that arrest naked people and hunt murderers and kidnappers."

"We've got quite the life," said the doctor, approaching the body on the table.

"Don't we ever," said Daniels. "What'd you find?"

She flipped the file open. "I know this much. He's male. Age thirty-six. Twenty pounds overweight with early signs of cardiovascular disease. Other than that, he was in good general health. No major trauma, and healthy organs, except for his heart."

Daniels walked up to the table. "Are you referring to his cardiovascular issues?"

"No, I'm not, which is why it's strange." She put the folder down on the empty table behind her and pulled the sheet down to reveal Ben's upper chest, exposing his colorless face and the scars from his autopsy. "Look at that."

Rem took a second to catch his breath. Seeing Ben Lambert lying on a slab with marks on his chest from the exam caused a flash of recall, and he saw himself lying flat on his own back, with a knife glinting above him. He stepped back from the table but could still see Ben's body.

"This bruise, right above his heart." She pointed. "He was hit in the sternum with something round. His heart is damaged as well. It's like an electrical current shocked it and it just stopped. I've never seen anything like it. Plus, the skin on his chest is burned."

"Burned? Like he was hit with something hot?" asked Daniels.

"Maybe. But the mark matches nothing I've seen before. It's not a cattle prod or a taser."

"And this isn't caused by any medical condition?" asked Daniels.

"None that I can think of. At least nothing that he suffers from." She covered the body. "Initially, when I first saw him, my guess was he died from natural causes, but after the exam, now I don't think so."

Sweat popped out on Rem's skin, and he took a slow, steady breath. Inhale and exhale, the shrink had advised him. One second at a time. *You're not there, you're here.* He put a hand on the empty table behind him to balance himself and recited the mantra in his head, not wanting to lose it in the coroner's lab.

"You're saying he was murdered," said Daniels. He glanced back at Rem, stared for a second, and looked back.

"Yes. I can find no other reason for his heart to have simply stopped and for this damage to occur, other than some external force. Whatever hit him caused the trauma. Now you guys get to figure what exactly that was." She removed her glasses. "Whatever it is, though, it packs a punch, so be careful."

"Thanks, doc. We appreciate the advice. You're checking whether our vic here is Josh Lambert's father?"

She nodded. "I've got a call in to the pediatrician, but I'll need a DNA sample to confirm."

"We're working on it. We'll get it to you as soon as we have it," said Daniels.

Sliding her glasses back on, she leaned to look around Daniels. "You okay, Detective? You look a little pale."

Rem forced out a slow breath. "It's my stomach. Something I ate."

"Then this is hardly the place for you," she said. "Something about the smell. There's a bathroom around the corner if you need it."

Rem nodded, but didn't answer, seeing the flash of steel, and feeling it slice down his chest. "Thanks, Doc."

"You guys have questions, you know where to find me. You'll have my report in the morning." She turned, grabbed her folder, and headed back toward her office.

Daniels turned and took Rem's arm. "Come on. Let's get you out of here."

Rem let Daniels slowly guide him out of the lab and back out into the hall. He stopped outside the elevators and leaned against the wall.

"You look like you're about to puke," said Daniels. "You need the bathroom?"

"Just give me a second." Rem drew in a deep, shaky breath, and then exhaled. "I'll be okay." Seeing his fingers tremble, he shook them out.

"Hold on," said Daniels. He disappeared back into the office and returned carrying a folding chair. He opened it and put it on the floor. "Sit."

Rem didn't argue and fell into the seat. He leaned over and put his head in his hands. "Thanks."

"Was it the body?"

"Yeah." *Inhale, exhale.*

"Take your time."

Rem nodded. "At least I didn't collapse in front of the doctor. That would have been a treat." He tried to smile, but couldn't pull it off.

"You going to make it through the rest of the day? We should still talk to the family."

"I'll make it." He rubbed his temples, feeling the start of a headache. "I just need to get out of here. Get some fresh air."

"Probably smart. This place does not induce unicorns and rainbows."

After sitting for a few minutes, Rem pushed on the wall, and Daniels helped him up. "Definitely no unicorns and rainbows." Feeling steadier, he supported himself while Daniels returned the chair. His breathing evening out, he walked to the elevator and hit the button, but a wave of dizziness hit, and he wobbled.

Daniels caught his arm and held him up. "Whoa. What's your hurry?" asked Daniels.

"It's okay. I'm okay. I just need to get up to higher ground."

The elevator arrived, and Daniels helped Rem on and hit the button. As they ascended, the spinning eased, and Rem stood straighter but kept a hand on the wall. "It's better now."

"You sure?"

"Yeah. Thanks."

The elevator slowed and came to a stop. The doors opened and, taking a full, deep lungful of air, Rem shook off the flashback, stepped out, and almost ran into Lozano.

"There you two are," said the captain. "I was coming to find you. We ran Felix Randall from Fresno's name." He waved a paper. "Only four results–two men in their twenties, a Black man in his seventies, and one who died in his eighties thirteen years ago."

Daniels cursed. "Shit. He used a fake name."

"Or he's not from Fresno," said Lozano. "Which means we need to check every Felix Randall we can find who fits the profile."

"Wonderful." Rem groaned. "This day just keeps getting better and better."

Chapter Five

THE NEXT MORNING, DANIELS walked down the corridor and into the squad room. Rem had picked him up again but had dropped him at the repair shop to get his car, then Daniels had stopped to meet with the sketch artist to work on a picture of Josh's kidnapper.

Entering the squad room, he saw Rem sitting at his desk, eyeing his laptop and a yellow pad full of notes. "Hey." He slid off his jacket and threw it over the back of his chair.

"How'd the sketch go?"

"Fine." Daniels sat. "It should hit the news channels soon. Lozano's at the press conference with the chief now."

Rem sighed. "Great. Then we'll have ten thousand more tips to investigate." He ruffled through his notes.

"Is that what you're working on?"

"Yeah. Apparently, lots of people have seen a kid Josh's age. Unfortunately, none of them are Josh." He held up a separate piece of paper. "But I'm compiling a list of the tips we should follow that might have promise, or at least the ones that don't involve Josh being abducted by aliens. Lozano's got a task force going through the tips, too. It'll keep us busy."

"What about Felix Randall?"

"Research is working on it. I'm sure that'll be another long list."

"There can't be that many Felix Randall's that fit the profile and have a tattoo on their arm."

"Let's hope." Rem picked up a cup of coffee and sipped from it. Daniels had noticed earlier that Rem had looked better that morning. His eyes were brighter, and he had more spring in his step than the day before, although Rem had still not told him about whatever had been plaguing him, and someone else besides Daniels was worried.

"I should tell you," said Daniels. "Mikey called me on the way over."

Rem held his coffee, and his face furrowed. "Mikey? Why'd she call you?"

"She's concerned. You canceled on her last night."

"Uh, I think we both know about our day yesterday."

"She realizes we're on this case, but apparently, it's the second time in a row. You canceled last week, too. She tried to call you this morning, but you didn't answer."

Rem waved the paper. "I'm a little busy."

"She understands, but you know her. She'll be the bull knocking over all the damn china until she figures out what's going on. She knows the reason you're ditching her is because you know she's going to ask about what's bugging you, and you're avoiding it."

Rem sighed and went back to his notes. "She thinks too much. Like you. Can we get back to work now? I've got a lovely list to give you, so I hope you ate your Wheaties this morning."

"You still haven't told me either. We can never seem to get to it without being interrupted, or just being too damn tired to talk."

"I'm better today. I actually slept well. It doesn't seem like such a big deal now."

Daniels chuckled. "Nice try, partner." He sat up. "But you started this conversation, and if you think I'm just going to let it die, you're mistaken."

"We've got things to do."

"You can take five minutes."

"We don't have five minutes." He set the paper aside. "Besides, it'll be a distraction."

"Why, if it's not that big of a deal?"

"I don't think it is, but you, on the other hand…"

Daniels bit back his impatience. "Just tell me."

Rem groaned and shoved back his notes. "Fine." Putting his elbows on the table, he paused, as if collecting his thoughts. "Two weeks ago—"

Daniels' desk phone rang.

"You got to be kidding," said Daniels, eyeing the phone.

"Saved by the bell," said Rem with a slight smile.

"I'll ignore it."

"No, you won't. It might be important. Answer it. It might have to do with Josh."

Daniels put his hand on the phone and pointed. "We're not done."

"Of course not." Rem went back to his notes.

Daniels answered. "Detective Daniels."

A male voice replied. "Well, ring-a-ding-ding. Detective Daniels. We speak again."

Daniels' belly curdled, his chest tightened, and he straightened in his seat. Rem immediately looked up, and Daniels gestured at his phone and spoke. "Is this Josh's uncle? From the convenience store?" he asked. Rem's eyes widened, and he grabbed for his own desk phone and dialed, likely to find out who was calling Daniels. Daniels took a breath and tried to think. "How's Josh? Is he okay?"

"It's Sam, detective. And he's doing just fine. Boy's in good hands."

Daniels' mind raced with how to engage. "To what do I owe the pleasure? Did our encounter in the store spook you a little?"

"On the contrary, Detective, I found it thrilling. Very few have the guts to confront me, and not many live if they do. Plus, your name is familiar."

Daniels recalled Rem shouting his name when he'd entered the shop. "My reputation precedes me."

"That it does, Detective. That it does."

"Since you know me, it's only fair I know you."

The man chuckled. "I bet you'd like that." He paused. "You can call me Rudy."

"Rudy, huh? Got a last name, Rudy?"

Rem spoke to someone on the phone, and Daniels saw Lozano enter the squad room. Rem spoke to him quietly, and Lozano stopped.

"You'll learn it soon enough, I'm sure. But by then, I'll be long gone."

Daniels set his jaw. "Where's Josh, Rudy? If you don't mind, I'll call him by his real name."

"Call him whatever you want, but he's Sam to me. I told you. He's fine. I just need to teach him a few things. Then I'll move on."

"Teach him what?" He gripped the phone, and his stomach twisted. "Don't touch him, Rudy."

"You've been working too long in your crappy job, Detective," said Rudy. "It's not sexual. I wouldn't do that to a child. But the boy needs to know who he is."

Daniels thought of Victoria Lambert. "You know Victoria Lambert?"

"You could say that." He paused. "It was a memorable night."

Rem gestured to keep Daniels talking, and Lozano stood anxiously beside Daniels' desk. "She's worried sick," said Daniels. "You need to let Josh go."

"In due time, Detective. She's been a good mother to him, but he needs his father, too. Boy needs to learn some things. Things her husband couldn't teach him."

"And what's that Rudy? What are you going to teach him that Ben couldn't?"

"He's a special boy. He's like his dad." Rudy paused. "Do you have a son, Detective?"

Daniels' heart thumped. "That's not your concern."

Rudy laughed. "I'll take that as a yes. So you know about that bond, between a man and his child. It's sacred. And Sam needs to know who he is, and what he can do. He's old enough now."

"What is it that he can do?"

"Like you said. That's not your concern. That's between him and me. Just like..." he hesitated. "Never mind."

Daniels wondered what he'd been about to say. "Just let him go. He's scared, Rudy. He misses his mom."

"He's a strong boy. He'll be fine. You'll find him soon enough, but until then, maybe you should be careful."

Daniels eyed Rem from across his desk. "What do you mean?"

"You saw my face. I realize what that means. I suspect the sketch will be out soon, if it isn't already. It'll make my job harder, but not impossible."

"You're a kidnapper, Rudy. The entire force is looking for you and Josh. You step outside to catch some air, and they'll know it."

"I'm not worried about that. I can handle myself. Have done so for a while now." He paused. "I'd be more concerned about yourself."

Daniels held his breath. "Are you threatening me?"

"Let's say I've taken an interest. You're a brave man, but also a foolish one."

"How exactly do you know me?"

"You arrested someone I know, but you won't capture me."

"We'll see about that."

Rudy's tone turned harsh. "The closer you get, the more dangerous it becomes. Remember that when you learn the hard way what I'm capable of."

"This isn't about me and you, Rudy. Maybe I bruised your ego, and I'm sad if I did, but my concern is Josh."

Rem wrote furiously on a pad.

"I have to go now, Detective, but it's been fun talking to you. I'll think about calling again, but that all depends on you."

"Rudy, listen..."

"Goodbye, Detective."

Daniels heard the click, and the line went dead. "Damn it." Daniels hung up the phone.

"Got something," said Rem. He thanked the person on the line and also hung up. "Guess where? He's in Fresno."

"You get an address?" asked Lozano.

"Yes." Rem ripped off a paper.

"Let me have it," said Lozano. "I talked to Fresno's chief last night. I'll get them on it ASAP. Maybe we'll get lucky."

"Guy's not stupid," said Daniels. "He'll be long gone. He's leading us on a goose chase."

"One way to find out." Lozano took the paper from Rem and headed toward his office. He turned back. "Oh, and the sketch is out with the media. Get ready for some more tips to track down."

"Wonderful," said Rem. He sat back. "What'd Rudy have to say?"

Daniels sighed and told Rem about the conversation.

Rem nodded. "At least we know the Fresno tip is a good one."

"Yeah, except Felix Randall is not his name."

"You think Rudy is?"

Daniels shrugged. "I don't know." He rubbed his temples. "He called Josh 'Sam,' which is the same name as the tattoo on his wrist. That obviously means something. You think he may have lost someone close? Maybe a child named Sam?"

"Possibly. Makes sense."

"So he grabs Josh because he knows Josh is his child, or at least he thinks he is, and then wants to impart some wisdom to him, because he lost his own kid?

"It's definitely a theory," said Rem. "But why's he calling you?"

"I arrested someone he knows."

"You've arrested a lot of people."

"Yeah. That's a tiny needle in a big haystack." He tapped his pen on his desk. "I'm guessing it's also because I got in his face, and he didn't like it. Or maybe he did, and he's enamored with me."

"You do have a certain charm. Especially when you're angry."

"So I've heard."

Rem pushed back and stuck a sneakered foot on the edge of the desk. "You think you should be careful?"

"The guy's holding a kidnapped child. I doubt he's going to have time to come after me." He shook his head. "No. I think he's blowing off steam. I can ID him, and now so can everyone else. Maybe he hopes by contacting me, it'll make me back off."

"He seemed to suggest that the further you go, the madder he'll get."

"Too bad for him. It's called being a detective."

Rem dropped his foot and picked up his coffee cup. "You should still be cautious." He stood and refilled his mug from a pot on the counter behind him. "You think we can find the person he knows that you arrested? We could go through old cases. See if the name Rudy pops out. Or Felix Randall. Or Sam." Rem put the pot back and added cream and sugar.

"On top of everything else we need to do?"

Rem stirred. "It does seem a little daunting, doesn't it? We can give it to Research. They can throw it into a computer and see if it spits out something of interest."

"I suppose it's worth a shot."

"Daniels."

Daniels spotted Lozano sticking his head out of his office. "Yeah, Cap?"

"I've got the Fresno Chief on the line. He's sending officers to the location, but he wants to talk to you. Find out what was said on the call."

Daniels stood. "Okay." He pointed at Rem. "You want to handle Research?"

"Sure. I'll give 'em a call." He sipped his coffee. "Let me know if Fresno P.D. cracks the case."

Daniels half-smiled. “You’ll be the first.” He headed into Lozano’s office.

Chapter Six

After giving the Fresno Chief and Lozano his update, Daniels waited to hear that the Fresno police had pulled up to an abandoned farmhouse on the south side of the city. They'd found no sign of Rudy or Josh, and it hadn't appeared as if anyone had been there recently. It confirmed for Daniels that Rudy was leading them around by the nose, and that he and Josh could be anywhere.

Frustrated, he left Lozano's office, ready to give Rem the update. His partner wasn't at his desk, although his filled coffee cup remained beside his pad of notes. He eyed another detective sitting two desks down from Rem, who appeared to be going through his own list of leads. "Hey, Silvers."

Silvers looked up.

"You see Rem?"

He bobbed his head. "Yeah. He was here a second ago, but then he got up and shot out of here. Looked like he was in a hurry."

Daniels frowned. "Did he say anything about where he was going?"

He made a tick mark on his pad. "He neglected to give me his itinerary. Sorry."

Daniels returned to his seat, wondering where Rem might have gone in a rush, and looked more closely at Rem's messy desk. Along with his notes and list, another paper had been added to the pile. He stood and walked over, seeing it was a piece of stationary. An envelope sat beside it, and Daniels saw it was addressed to Rem. Eyeing the bold writing on the paper, he picked it up and read it.

You may be free now, but your freedom comes at a cost. The light will never escape the dark. The light can pretend, and ignore and defend, but the dark remains, and will return to claim its prize.

However, all is not lost. The light is never alone, and the light will leave behind another light far greater and more powerful than can be imagined.

Hold fast to this and know that even as you join the dark, you will live on forever.

I look forward to that and to you, once again, joining me.

It is where you belong.

Chill bumps breaking out on his skin, Daniels dropped the note back onto Rem's desk. Holding his rolling stomach, he knew immediately where Rem had gone. He turned and headed out into the hall outside the squad room. At the end of the corridor, he entered the men's bathroom. "Rem?"

The stalls were empty except for one. A toilet flushed, and Daniels peered beneath the door, seeing Rem's legs moving into a standing position. The stall door opened, and Rem emerged, a pallid tint to his skin.

"You okay?"

He walked to the sink, flipped on the faucet, splashed his face, and rinsed his mouth. "Just peachy." He wet a paper towel and turned off the water.

"I saw the note."

Rem held the wet towel to his ashen face, leaned against the back wall, and slid down it until his butt hit the floor. "Lucky you."

"Have you—"

The door opened. Daniels turned and stuck his foot out, stopping the entry, and saw Silvers' face through the crack. "It's occupied, Silvers."

"What are you talking about?" asked Silvers. "Come on, I got to use the john."

"Use the one downstairs."

"What for?"

Daniels paused. "I had chili and beans for breakfast with a side of tacos and hot sauce. Believe me, you don't want to come in here."

Silvers narrowed his eyes. "You don't eat that stuff."

"Which is why I'm warning you off. Go downstairs." Daniels pushed on the door. "Trust me."

Silvers pushed once more and groaned. "Fine."

He left, and Daniels closed and locked the door.

"Chili and tacos, huh?" asked Rem from the floor, his head back and face still covered.

"I stole it from you." Daniels walked over and sat on the floor beside Rem.

"What do you think I just barfed up?"

Daniels grimaced. "Gross."

"Just kidding, except for the tacos part, which is a damn shame. They were good."

"I'll get you some for lunch."

"Not unless you want to stay in this bathroom all day." He lowered his head and pressed his palms against his eyes with the wet towel.

Daniels leaned back against the wall. "Any idea who sent the letter?"

"I don't know. Some crazy groupie? A lost follower? My neighbor? Mary Poppins?"

"What about Allison?"

Rem pulled the towel from his face. "She's in jail, awaiting trial. Last I checked, it's hard to send a letter without it being postmarked and logged. That envelope had no return address."

"Doesn't mean she's not responsible." He looked over. "It sounds like something she'd do just to mess with your head."

Rem hesitated. "There's something else to consider."

"What's that?"

Rem fiddled with the paper towel. "It's what I didn't want to mention, but now that I'm getting letters, maybe I should have."

Daniels sat up. "Did something else happen?"

"Phone calls." Rem looked over with haggard eyes. "One a few days ago and one last week."

"Phone calls? What phone calls?"

"See? This is why I didn't want to mention it. You're getting all worked up."

Daniels worked to keep his voice calm. "Who called you?"

"I don't know. The first one was a voicemail from a female on my house phone. The second was on my cell. I answered, and a male voice said, 'The light will join the dark.' And that's it. He hung up. Same on the voicemail. I tried tracking the numbers, but they're not registered."

"Why didn't you tell me this?"

Rem raised his hand. "What are you going to do? What can I do? Should I spend the rest of my days trying to track down every kook and nut who followed Victor D'Mato and Allison who got away that day? It's impossible." He laid his head back. "They're just trying to scare and intimidate me. I figured if I just ignored it, they'd get bored and go away." He sighed. "But now I get that letter, so maybe my plan is backfiring."

Daniels shifted to face Rem. "And the letter said a lot more."

"Yeah. I noticed."

"Whoever is doing this, what do you think they want? You think they'd come after you? Finish what Victor couldn't?"

"Your guess is as good as mine."

"Then I'm not the only one who should be cautious. You think we need someone to watch your house?"

Rem raised his knees and rested his arms on them. "No. I can't live like that. I can't be looking over my shoulder every time someone says 'boo.'"

"This is a lot more than 'boo.' These people are dangerous."

"I know that," said Rem, his voice raising. "Hell. They could pester me for years. And if Allison is still pulling the strings, there's no telling what she could do. You saw how those people were. They have this blind devotion to her." He pointed. "And don't forget about that loon, Margaret Redstone. She's just as crazy as Allison.

Daniels leaned a shoulder on the tile. "We need to keep track of everything, then. The phone calls. The letter. Get it fingerprinted."

Rem scoffed. "Last time I checked, it's not illegal to send a letter."

"It's not the letter, it's what's written in it."

"Just a bunch of mumbo jumbo to a lay person."

"Rem, if we can tie that letter back to Allison, it can be used against her at trial."

Rem rolled his eyes.

"At the very least," said Daniels, "we need to talk to the warden. Find out who she's talking to, and who's visiting her. Maybe we can figure out what the hell she's up to."

"I'll tell what she's up to. Driving me crazy." He clutched his head. "At this rate, I'm going to have to move to India and take up meditation and chanting." He spoke softly. "Maybe she can't get to me there."

Daniels' heart fell, but at the same time, he got angry. "Well. I'll be damned if she's going to win. If we have to, we'll have her thrown in solitary confinement."

Rem scoffed. "I don't think it works that way."

"We'll see about that." He eyed his partner, who looked as energetic as a sick puppy. "You plan on sitting on the floor for the rest of the day?"

"It's tempting."

"Yeah, well. I doubt I can fend off Silvers a second time. He's stronger than he looks."

Rem didn't respond, but stared at the ceiling. "I need to ask you something. My shrink wanted me to bring it up to you earlier, but I didn't have the nerve. But now I think I better."

Daniels sat cross-legged beside Rem. "Okay. What is it?"

Rem swallowed and ripped at the towel. "A lot has happened, you know, with me."

Daniels nodded, wondering where this was going.

"The last three years have been rough."

Daniels waited.

"I guess...I guess...I was wondering if you still wanted to be partners...you know...with me."

Daniels narrowed his eyes, not sure he heard right. "What the hell kind of question is that?"

"It's a fair one." Rem poked at a hole in his jeans. "I haven't exactly been at a hundred percent recently, and by the looks of it, I may not be there for a while. You deserve to have someone you can rely on."

"Are you serious?" Daniels tried not to laugh. "Rem, you could be at fifty percent, tied up over a pyre of flame, and if I, or Marjorie, or J.P. or even Mikey, were in trouble, you'd cut through the rope with your fingernails, piss out the fire, and come to our rescue. There's nobody I'd rely on more. You should know that." He chuckled then. "Hell. I'd take you at twenty-five percent over any other cop out there at a hundred percent."

Rem set his jaw. "Daniels, I almost fainted behind a gardening store, came close to puking on the coroner, and I'm sitting here on the fucking bathroom floor after barfing up my breakfast tacos because I got a mean letter. I think that lends itself to a small crisis of confidence."

"Rem, cut yourself some slack. It's barely been three months since you were drugged and assaulted, kidnapped, mentally tortured, thrown on a slab, assaulted again, and almost sacrificed by having your neck sliced open. That you're even here is a freaking miracle. I'd give it a little more time before you think you're all washed up. And now you have to deal with some asshole making phone calls and sending letters. It's a lot, but the fat lady hasn't sung. Not if I have anything to say about it." He reached over and squeezed Rem's shoulder. "Hang in there, okay? We'll figure out what's going on. And don't worry about me. I'm not going anywhere."

Some of the weight seemed to lift from Rem's shoulders. "The offer stands, you know, in case you change your mind. No hard feelings." He rumpled the wet towel into his fist.

"I won't change my mind, but thank you for the kind consideration." He eyed the bathroom. "You ready? Or you want to stare at the toilet a little longer?"

Rem raised his head. "I could go for some different scenery."

"Good." Daniels got to his knees and stood. "Then come on, partner." He held out a hand. "We've got work to do."

Rem sighed, offered his hand, and let Daniels help him up.

....

Rem sat at his desk, doing his best to focus on the notes he'd taken, and trying not to think about the letter he'd received. Closing his eyes, he took a long, slow breath. *Inhale. Exhale.* Opening his eyes, he studied the leads, trying to determine which to investigate first.

"Good news."

Rem looked to see Daniels leave Lozano's office. "Please tell me I've been promoted and they're transferring me to Hawaii, where I can sit on a sunny beach and sip out of coconut shells for the rest of my days."

"You can do that here."

Rem shrugged. "Somehow, it doesn't seem quite the same."

Daniels returned to his desk. "Lozano's taking the letter. He's pissed and wants to find out what's going on with Allison. He'll get it fingerprinted and make some inquiries. If she's meeting or talking with people she shouldn't be, we'll know it soon enough."

"You think that will change anything?"

"Of course. If we can stop her from communicating, or at least control who she talks to, it might cut that cord she has with the people who follow her."

"You're way more optimistic than I am."

"That's my job. And I take it seriously." He rifled through some papers on his desk. "If I'm going to ask you to hang in there and fight through this, then I'm going to help you do it, and if that means I'm irritatingly positive, then so be it. I'm not going to let these weirdos win."

"I'm going to remind you of that when we start digging through these leads, and we get to number one thousand and ten, and we're no closer than we were with number one."

"I was talking about you and your case. Not Josh's. I reserve the right to be not so positive about that."

"That's too bad," said Rem. "Because I think we're going to need it."

Rem's phone rang, and for a moment, he thought of the two calls he'd received with the creepy messages, but then forced himself to push past it, and answered. If Daniels could be positive, then so could he. "Detective Remalla."

He listened and sat up. "Sure. Put him through." He held the phone to his shoulder and spoke to Daniels. "I got the tip line. Somebody called. Says he knows the guy in the sketch, but only wants to talk to a detective."

Daniels' mouth dropped. "Shit."

Rem stared up at the ceiling and whispered. "Please be legit." Then he put the phone back to his ear and heard a soft 'hello?' It sounded like a young male.

He introduced himself, and listened, taking notes along the way while Daniels waited. Nodding and his hopes rising, he thanked the man for his help and hung up.

"Well?" asked Daniels, his eyes wide.

Rem stood. "Get your jacket, Mr. Positivity. We got a lead. And it's a good one."

Daniels jumped out of his seat. "They know Rudy?"

Rem headed for the doors. "Even better. He says Rudy took him, too, and he wants to talk." He waved a paper. "We're going to meet him. Right now."

"Holy..." Daniels grabbed his jacket. "Chalk one up to the power of positivity." He followed Rem out the squad doors.

Chapter Seven

Rem drove down the dusty road and eyed the surrounding hills. “We close?”

Daniels pointed, eyeing his phone. “Yeah. Should be just up here. There. Take a right. This should be it.”

Rem slowed as he neared another dirt road with a banged-up mailbox on the corner. Barbed wire fencing ran along the side of a long drive, and he turned, moving through dust kicked up by his tires.

“Boy,” said Daniels. “I hope this kid is the real deal, or we’ve just wasted an hour driving out here.”

“And the hour back.” Rem drove until he saw a small, one-story white house that looked to be about a hundred years old. There was an old brown pickup truck in the driveway, and as Rem approached and parked, he saw a nearby barn, a chicken coop, and a pen of goats. “This must be it.” He killed the engine.

Daniels opened his door and stepped out.

Hearing the goats bleat and the cluck of the chickens, Rem left the car and looked around. Except for the animals, the area was quiet, even peaceful, and he envied it. “Not a bad place to be if you’re looking to get away from it all.”

Daniels came around to the driver’s side. “You’d last one day out here before you started bitching for the city. There are no taco stands within a sixty-mile radius.”

Rem shut his door. "Yeah, well, right now, getting away from it all is looking pretty tempting."

Daniels nodded. "I suppose it probably is."

They walked toward the front door, and Rem was about to knock when he heard a voice yell from behind them. "I'm out here." He turned to see a young man sticking his head outside the barn and waving. They turned and walked toward him, passing the chickens and goats, and approached the barn.

"You Henry?" asked Rem. He perused the man in front of them, who wore worn coveralls and a sweaty long-sleeved t-shirt. Thin and tall, he couldn't have been over twenty years old. His hair hung in his face, and he shoved it back.

"Yeah. That's me. You the detectives?"

Daniels and Rem showed him their badges and introduced themselves. Henry studied the badges for a second before he waved them into the barn.

Rem and Daniels followed, and Henry grabbed a pitchfork. There were six stalls inside, and two of them were occupied, each with a horse. "This is Knickers and Bonita." He rubbed Bonita's nose. "I call her Bonnie, though." He patted her neck.

Daniels walked over to Knickers and ran a hand down the horse's smooth hair. "You told my partner you know the man who took Joshua Lambert?"

Henry stabbed the pitchfork into some straw. "Yeah. I do." He tossed some straw into an empty stall.

"You want to tell us about that?" asked Rem.

Henry stabbed some more straw and held it. "He took me, too." He tossed the straw into the pile.

Rem stepped closer and rubbed the side of Bonnie's face. The horse nickered and bobbed its head. "Can you tell us what happened?"

Henry held still and then stuck the edge of the pitchfork into the dirt. "I was eleven. Like Josh."

"It was the same man?" asked Daniels.

"Yeah. I'm sure of it. I walked into the house earlier, and the TV was on. I don't watch it much, but my grandfather does. He owns the house, and I live with him. Help him do chores and take care of the animals."

"Where is he?" asked Rem.

"At the post office. He works there three days a week," said Henry. He gripped the end of the pitchfork. "Anyway, I saw the press conference, and when they held up that sketch, I froze." His face lost a little color, and he went quiet.

"You know his name?" asked Daniels.

Henry shook off his reverie. "It's Rudy. At least that's what he called himself."

"You get a last name?" asked Rem.

"No," said Henry. "At least not that I can remember."

Rem made eye contact with Daniels. "Why don't you tell us what happened?" asked Daniels.

Henry hooked a thumb in a pocket and stared at the straw. "I was eleven. A lot of it is a blur, but I remember being at school, and this man picked me up. Said he was my uncle, and my mom told him to come get me. I went with him, but we didn't go home."

"Where'd you go?" asked Daniels.

"I don't remember exactly. It seems we went to a lot of places. We never stayed in the same location long. He said we had to be careful and lie low."

"Did he say why he took you?" asked Rem.

Henry looked up. "Said I was his kid. That he needed to teach me things. Said he was special, and I was, too. I had gifts that no one else had, and it was his job to explain and help me, and once he did, then he'd let me go."

Rem rubbed Bonnie's nose. "Was it true? Were…are you his kid?"

Henry sighed. "I don't know. Maybe. Probably. My mom…she's an alcoholic. My granddad, he's told me what she was like when she was young. There were a lot of men." He picked up the pitchfork and stabbed some more straw. "We don't get along that well. When I came home, even though she knew I'd been taken, she questioned my story. I didn't talk much after they found me. Doctors said I was traumatized. She thought maybe I was making it up and had been hiding at a friend's place. Once I graduated from high school, I left home. Been out here ever since." He tossed more straw in a pile.

"It's quiet out here," said Rem.

"It's a good place to be, especially when you're trying to forget." Henry paused. "Even nine years later."

Rem dropped his hand from Bonnie's nose, thinking of his own situation. "That's good to know."

"You ever talk to anybody besides us about what happened?" asked Daniels, glancing sideways at Rem. "It helps."

"I'm not much for talking. Prefer to stay busy." Henry put the pitchfork against a wall and wiped his forehead with a towel that hung from a nail on the wall.

Rem thought again of the letter. "What was so special about Rudy? What was he trying to teach you?"

Henry rubbed his neck with the towel. "That much I remember, and mainly why my mom thought I was lying. The cops, too, I think, had their doubts."

"What do you mean?" asked Daniels.

Henry returned the towel to the nail. "Rudy...he...wasn't ordinary. He could do crazy things."

"What things?" asked Rem.

"It's...It's hard to explain." Henry picked up the pitchfork again. "It was an electricity thing. He could harness it and manipulate it. And use it against others." He stabbed some more straw and tossed it. "And he could protect himself."

Rem frowned. "What do you mean?"

"I saw him use his...abilities...whatever you want to call it, on someone." He stopped shoveling. "He touched them with his finger." Henry closed his eyes. "I'm pretty sure he killed some homeless guy. Said he was teaching me what was possible, and when I could do it too, he'd be done with my lessons."

"With his finger?" asked Daniels.

Henry opened his eyes. "Yeah." He held the tip of the pitchfork with a white knuckled grip. "He would do this thing, where he'd get focused. And then there'd be this weird hum in the air, like it was vibrating or something. Then he'd reach out and touch you in the chest, and there would be this pulse, and whoever he was touching would convulse and collapse. He did it to a pig, and then later, to the homeless guy in the park."

Rem took a second to absorb Henry's story.

"You said the air would vibrate, like a hum?" asked Daniels. "Almost like static electricity?"

Henry nodded. "Yeah. It was weird."

Daniels looked over at Rem. "That's what it felt like at the convenience store. When Rudy raised a finger at me, but Josh stopped him."

"Be glad he didn't touch you, because if he had, you'd be dead," said Henry.

Daniels narrowed his eyes. "Let me ask you something. Would that leave a circular mark on the chest where the victim was touched, almost like a burn?"

"Hell, yes," said Henry. "I saw it on the pig. It was a round circle."

Rem thought of the mark on Ben Lambert's sternum. "Are you saying he's delivering some sort of electric charge and stopping the person's heart?"

Henry raised his hand. "I can only tell you what I saw. I'll leave the rest to the fancy doctors."

"And he was teaching you this?" asked Daniels. "He said you could do the same?"

"That's where things get a little fuzzy," said Henry. "But yes. He said I had the same abilities, and I was old enough to learn them."

"And did you?" Rem crossed his arms. "Learn them?"

Henry dropped his head and went quiet. "I think so," he finally said. "I remember I could feel tingling and vibrations under my skin, but I don't remember much more, and then one day it ended."

"Ended?" asked Daniels.

"Yeah," said Henry. "I was just standing on the street. By myself. Somebody found me and called the cops. I got asked a bunch of questions, most of which I wouldn't, or couldn't, answer, and I went home. They never caught Rudy, though, and I haven't seen him since."

"Do you recall ever using those abilities, like Rudy did?" asked Rem.

"I don't know. I'm not sure I want to." He stared off. "There was one time, though...a couple years ago, where something happened."

Daniels patted Knickers' neck. "What was that?"

"I'd just moved out here, and I was taking care of the goats. One of them was pregnant and gave birth, but something was wrong. It took a lot longer than it should have, and when the baby was born, it was dead. Granddad said it happened sometimes. You could tell he was sad about it, and he'd left." Henry paused. "I recall staring at it, and the tingles ran up my arms. The air got thick, and hummed, like you said." He nodded at Daniels. "I started shaking and then I felt this energy run through me, and I lifted my hand and touched the baby goat. Something shot through me, and I fell backwards. It almost knocked me flat. But then I got up, and I couldn't believe it."

"What?" asked Rem.

"That damn goat was alive. Its eyes were open, and it bleated. Within an hour, it was up and walking around. My granddad was thrilled. Said it was a miracle." He rested his weight on the pitchfork. "I still don't believe it."

Rem wasn't sure what to believe, either. "You mentioned something else. That he could protect himself. What did you mean?"

Henry shook his head. "That's even harder to explain."

"Try," said Daniels.

"Guy couldn't get injured," said Henry. "Said he could prevent it. He'd somehow mastered control over his body's responses." He laid the pitchfork handle against the barn wall and leaned a hand beside it. "He shot himself once, to show me. Through his hand. He didn't even react. There was nothing. The bullet seemed to go right through without so much as a blood drop."

Rem scratched his head. "You sure you're remembering correctly?"

"I know it sounds crazy, but it's one of the few things I'll never forget. He told me I could do it too, with training and practice, but it was a mastered skill. Said the only time he was vulnerable was during the ten seconds just before he zapped someone. Said that required him to become...I don't know...more solid, or more contracted. Dense. That's when he was at risk. But outside of that, he was impervious to injury."

"Huh," said Daniels. "And you saw this? Or do you think he was messing with you?"

"He wasn't messing around. I witnessed it," said Henry.

Uncertain, Rem scratched his jaw. "Did he ever hurt you?"

"Only once," said Henry. "After he first took me, he started calling me 'Sam.' I argued back. Told him I was Henry. He backhanded me. Said I was Sam, and I would stay Sam while I was with him. I didn't argue after that."

"How long were you with him?" asked Daniels.

"Eight days," said Henry, softly. "Longest eight days of my life."

"Did he say or do anything else unusual, or mention any family or friends?" asked Rem. "Did he tell you who Sam was? Do you remember any places he took you? Did you see anyone else?"

Henry chuckled. "Those days run together like a giant blur. I don't recall a lot of the day to day. I remember we were in an RV, so we could stay mobile. I think it was brown. I don't recall seeing anyone else, or him talking about anyone, other than mentioning Sam. He had a tattoo on his arm with Sam's name, so I knew it was someone important." He stuck his hand in a pocket. "For some reason, I remember a blue horse with starry eyes."

"A blue horse?" asked Rem. "Were you near a farm?"

"Not that I recall. I can't remember where I saw it. The only other thing I remember is that he took me to a cemetery."

"Cemetery?" asked Daniels. "What cemetery?"

"It was outside the city. We went there a couple of times. I think it was Peaceful Pines, or Peaceful Palms. Something like that. All I can remember about it was that there was a bird, with wings spread out like he was ready to take flight."

"A bird? Like a real bird?" asked Rem.

"No," said Henry. "Like a statue bird. It may have been on a tombstone. I can't be sure."

Daniels stepped away from Knickers' stall. "Anything else you can tell us that might help catch this guy?"

Henry exhaled. "Just be careful. He's dangerous. He can be all high and happy one second and turn mean and ugly the next."

"Sounds like my partner," said Rem.

"I was about to say the same thing," said Daniels.

"And don't get cocky," said Henry. "He doesn't like cocky."

"Then we're definitely not going to get along," said Rem.

"I hope you find him, and Josh, but it won't be easy to catch him," said Henry. "You sure as hell won't be able to shoot him."

"Let's hope it doesn't come to that," said Daniels.

Henry nodded. "Once he teaches Josh, then he should leave him somewhere where he can be found. Like he did with me. Hopefully, he won't hurt him."

"How do you know when the teaching's over? You pass a test?" asked Rem.

Henry's face paled, and Rem thought of his own reflection in the bathroom mirror from earlier. "I think so," said Henry.

"I'm guessing you passed it?" asked Daniels.

"Yeah," said Henry, his face somber. "I think I did, but I've blocked it."

"Any ideas what it was?" asked Rem. "If you were to take a guess?"

"A guess?" asked Henry. He reached for the pitchfork again. "I suppose I could take a guess." He stabbed at some straw and threw it into the stall. "I'm pretty sure I may have killed someone."

....

Rem drove down the road while Daniels navigated again. "You're telling me you believe him?" asked Rem. He stopped at a red light.

"I don't know what I believe," said Daniels. "But I know what he means by the hum of electricity. I felt it when Rudy raised his finger and was about to touch me, but Josh stopped him."

The light turned, and Rem crossed the intersection. "So, you think Rudy was about to zap you in the chest and stop your heart, and Josh knew it because he witnessed it with his dad?"

"The kid looked terrified. And he had a bruise on his face. And Rudy called Josh 'Sam.' It corroborates Henry's story."

"You think this guy can control electricity and somehow control his own body to prevent injury?"

"I'm not saying I understand it, but we've seen what the power of belief can do, and if put in the wrong hands, it can be dangerous."

Rem turned down another road. "I don't know if I'm buyin' it just yet."

"You saw the mark on Ben Lambert's chest. You heard what the doc said. His heart was damaged with no plausible explanation." He snapped his fingers. "And that may explain why the video at the convenience store went fuzzy. Maybe his erratic energy or electric…whatever…caused it."

Rem rested an elbow on his door and rubbed his forehead. "Let's think about this. Rudy loses someone named Sam, which we assume is a child, then he goes after another son that he had with a stranger, and tries to pass on his abilities, and when he succeeds, he lets the kid go. And then, years later, he grabs another offspring with another stranger, and he's doing the same thing. Does this make any sense to you?"

"It doesn't have to make sense to us. Only to Rudy."

"Who is this guy? And why is he so caught up with teaching his kids how to do weird things?"

"Maybe the same happened to him when he was a child. His dad showed him some skills and taught Rudy how to kill. He got a taste for it. Thinks he's pretty powerful. Rudy grows up and gets married. Has a son, and is prepared to do what his dad did, only tragedy strikes, and his child dies. Now he's transferring that need to his illegitimate offspring."

"That's a hell of a leap. And how is he tracking these kids? It sounds like he had a lot of fun in his youth, but how does he know he's the father of Henry and Josh?"

"I don't know. Maybe he isn't."

Rem glanced over. "Something tells me that DNA test the coroner is doing is going to show that he is."

"I think you're probably right." Daniels eyed his phone. "Hell. If the man can manipulate energy, maybe he can sense the location of his own children."

"Like some sort of drug-sniffing dog?"

Daniels' shoulders raised. "I don't know."

"I sense a visit to Redstone in our future. If anybody can understand and explain this stuff, it'll be Mason."

"If we're visiting Mason, then be prepared to talk to Mikey."

"Yeah. I know. I can't avoid her much longer, anyway."

Daniels shifted in his seat. "Do you not want to tell her what's going on?"

"It's not that. She already knows about all the other stuff. We've been pretty open about our histories with D'Mato and his cronies."

"Then what's holding you back?"

Rem rubbed his jaw. "She's been through a lot recently. I just didn't want to give her something else to worry about."

"Last I checked, she's pretty tough. I think she can handle it."

"She's tough, but vulnerable, too. As much as she tries to hide it."

Daniels raised a brow. "Sounds like someone I know."

Rem frowned. "Smart ass."

"The truth hurts." He pointed. "It's up here. See the gate?"

"Yeah. I see it."

After leaving Henry, Daniels had called Lozano and updated him, and told them to check RVs as a possible location for Rudy and Josh. He also asked Lozano to pull Henry's case file and to check for any unsolved deaths of vagrants or the homeless from nine years earlier, near where Henry had been released. Daniels had refrained from telling Lozano about Rudy's electrical skills, choosing to wait until they got more information. While Daniels talked to Lozano, Rem had done a quick search on his phone for any cemeteries with a name similar to Peaceful Palms or Pines. He'd found a Peaceful Pines about thirty minutes closer to the city and accessed the directions.

Arriving at the cemetery, Rem pulled in and drove under a wrought-iron gate. Large-trunked trees with heavy foliage surrounded a thick, green lawn dotted with tombstones. He parked under one of the trees.

"It doesn't look too big," said Daniels. "Hopefully, our bird will be easy to locate."

"Let's go find out." Rem got out of the car and Daniels followed. "You want to take the right side, and I'll take the left?" asked Rem.

"Sounds good. I'll meet you at the other end."

Rem nodded and headed down the rows of tombstones on his left, looking for a bird with its wings spread. He walked briskly, seeing mostly old stones, some falling apart, and most worn and sun-bleached. But as he moved along the aisles, the stones became newer, and less weathered. He made it down another row and kept going. Glancing over, he saw Daniels doing the same, but from the opposite end of the cemetery.

Rounding another aisle, he noted the dates were more recent and saw fresh flowers left beside various stones. Quickly eyeing each grave marker, he stopped when he caught sight of a tombstone in an aisle ahead. It was large, and a small stone bird stood at the base, its wings wide as if ready to fly.

"Daniels," he yelled. "Over here." He jogged over to the stone, and once in front of it, he read the inscription.

Daniels ran up next to him. "Is this it?"

"Looks like it." He pointed and read from the marker. "Samuel Halpern. Aged eleven years old. Gone too soon, but forever in our hearts."

"Son-of-a-bitch," said Daniels. "Rudy's last name is Halpern."

Chapter Eight

Mikey Redstone entered her brother Mason's office at SCOPE and sat at his desk. She tossed her small purse over the back of the chair and stared off, thinking about her morning and trying to make sense of it.

After sitting a few minutes, she heard the door to the front office open. She swiveled toward the computer monitor and punched a button on the keyboard. The monitors came to life, and she saw Mason on the screen. Seconds later, the inner door opened, and Mason walked in.

"There you are," he said, wearing a collared blue shirt and jeans with boots. "I tried to reach you this morning. Your phone went straight to voicemail."

Mikey reached for her cell. "Yeah. I'd turned it off." She flipped it back on.

Mason took off his cowboy hat and threw it and his keys on the desk. "Since when do you turn off your surgically attached phone?"

"Since this morning."

Mason paused, and she could feel his stare. "You okay?" he asked.

"I'm great." Her cell flickered to life. "How was your meeting with Mrs. Crabstone? Anything interesting?"

He took a second to answer and smoothed his handlebar mustache. "It went okay. I did a reading for her. She wanted to talk to her father. He'd been abusive, and she needed closure."

Mikey fiddled with her phone.

"And she's missing six million dollars. I told her where to find it and she's splitting it with me," he added.

"That's great."

"Mikey?"

She looked up. "Three million will do a lot for the agency. Maybe you could take a vacation, too."

He smirked at her. "What's going on with you?"

"Nothing."

Mason walked over to the couch that sat against the wall across from the desk. "Did you talk to Remalla?"

"I called Daniels this morning. Rem didn't answer the phone."

"No. I meant recently. They're on their way here. They want to ask me a few questions about their current case. Should be here any minute."

"They're coming now?" She shook off her thoughts about her morning and tried to focus. "Why didn't Rem call me?"

"Maybe because your phone was off?" asked Mason. "Based on my law enforcement experience, I'd say that's a likely reason."

"Smart ass."

He tipped his head at her. "Where were you that you had to turn your phone off?"

Mikey hesitated, uncertain how to answer, when a bell chimed, signaling someone was up at the door. She turned toward the monitors and saw Daniels and Rem. Hitting a button, she spoke. "Come on in." A buzz sounded, and she watched them enter. "They're here."

The door to the inner office opened, and Daniels and Remalla walked in. "Hey, Mason," said Daniels. "Thanks for seeing us on short notice." He eyed Mikey. "Mikey."

"Hey, Daniels," said Mikey. "Hey, Rem."

"Hi," said Rem. "And before you get on my ass, I know you talked to Daniels."

"Only because you were avoiding me," she said.

"I wasn't really avoiding you." He stopped beside the desk, and Daniels went to the couch. "I just needed to think a few things through."

She put an elbow on the desk. "Yeah, well, then just tell me. Don't ignore me. It gets on my nerves."

"I get it," he said. "I'm happy to go through it with you, but right now, we need to talk to Mason."

Mason sat on the couch. "Have a seat." He gestured. "What's on your mind?"

Daniels sat in an overstuffed chair beside the couch, and Rem sat next to Mason.

"You heard about the kidnapping?" asked Daniels. "Of Joshua Lambert? We found his dad dead in his home and Josh's been missing for three days."

"It's all over the news," said Mason. "What about it?"

Mikey stood. "Anybody want any coffee?"

"You know my answer," said Rem.

Mason and Daniels declined.

"We talked to a young man this morning who told us he'd been taken as well," said Rem. "By the same guy. Nine years ago, when he was the same age as Josh."

"His name's Henry," said Daniels. "He told us Rudy, the man who took Josh and Henry, has strange abilities."

Mikey turned on the coffee machine and grabbed the pot.

"Abilities?" asked Mason. "What kind of abilities?"

Rem and Daniels glanced at each other. "Henry said Rudy can manipulate energy, more specifically electricity," said Daniels. "He can summon it and use it against others. When the M.E. did her exam on Ben Lambert's body, she found that Josh's dad had a circular mark on his chest and his heart had been damaged. The M.E. couldn't explain it, but now it makes sense. Henry told us Rudy could zap people, and was teaching him to do the same, and is probably doing the same with Josh."

Listening, Mikey added grounds to the filter.

"Electricity?" asked Mason. "He can harness it?"

"And he's learned how to protect himself," added Rem. "He can somehow prevent injury."

"You ever hear of anything like that?" asked Daniels. "In your line of work, you're more likely to encounter it than us."

Mason clasped his hands together. "I have, although I've never experienced it. It's called electrokinesis. It's the ability to control an electric charge or current with your mind, and it is usually directed through the hands. The person who masters it is called an electromancer."

Rem sat up. "Are you serious?"

Mikey clasped the empty coffeepot but stopped behind the couch.

"There's actually a name for this?" asked Daniels.

"Yes," said Mason. "And you said he can prevent injury?"

Rem nodded. "According to Henry, Rudy shot himself through his hand, and had no ill effects from it."

"That probably has to do with him somehow manipulating his own magnetic field," said Mason. "If he can alter it at the molecular level, which would be astonishing, then I suppose it's possible he could prevent injury."

"Could it cause a camera to blur?" asked Daniels.

"Absolutely," said Mason. "He could wreak havoc on any number of video, audio, or other devices. If he can avoid damage from a bullet, he can certainly mess with electronics."

"Is it genetic?" asked Rem. "Could he pass it on to his offspring?"

"I'd say it's more than likely," said Mason. "He probably inherited it himself."

"I'll be damned," said Daniels, sitting back.

Rem rubbed his jaw. "Henry said something else. He said Rudy would be vulnerable for a few seconds—"

"Ten," said Daniels.

"Yeah," said Rem. "Ten seconds before he zapped someone. Said he had to focus, or concentrate his energy, and during that time, he could be susceptible to injury."

"Probably because he's ramping up the energy," replied Mason. "The molecules condense in order to solidify and direct the energy. He can't redirect it at that point, so he's at risk. But once he discharges it, then it frees him up, so to speak. And then he's safe again."

Rem shook his head. "Well, hell. This case just took a turn. Assuming this is true, how do you stop a guy like this?"

"Very carefully," said Mason. "He could electrocute you if you got close. It wouldn't be easy putting handcuffs on him." He held out a hand. "And obviously, shooting him doesn't work."

"I guess it depends on when you shoot him," said Daniels.

Mikey dropped the coffeepot. It hit the wood floor and shattered.

Mason jumped up, along with Daniels and Rem. "Mikey?" asked Mason. He came around the back of the couch, avoiding the shards of glass. "What's wrong?" He took her hand. "You're shaking."

Rem put a knee on the couch and leaned over the back of it. "You're as pale as all the ghosts Mason talks to. What's wrong?"

Mikey blinked and held her head, realizing Mason was right. Her hands were trembling. Her mind whirled, and her memories flashed.

"Sit down." Mason guided her to the couch, where she sat beside Rem. Mason squatted beside her. "What the matter?"

"I…I…I don't know." She took a deep shuddered breath. "I just suddenly got hot, and I…it's hard to breathe."

Rem took her wrist and squeezed it. "Just take it slow. Inhale and exhale."

"I'll get you some water," said Daniels. He walked to a small refrigerator they kept in a back closet and pulled out a bottled water.

Mikey dropped her head.

"Does this have something to do with where you went this morning?" asked Mason.

Mikey tried to think, but her mind wouldn't still. "I...I don't know."

"Where did you go?" asked Rem. He looked at Mason. "Where did she go?"

Daniels cracked open the water bottle. "Here. Take a sip."

Mason took the water from Daniels and handed it to her. Mikey grasped it, took a tentative sip, and gave it back. "I don't know where she went," said Mason. "She didn't tell me."

Mikey's heart rate slowed, and the spots that had formed in her vision faded, but then a clear picture popped in her head, and she sucked in a breath, and closed her eyes.

"Mikey? What is it?" asked Mason.

"I think she's remembering something. Give her a second," said Rem. Mikey felt him take her hand and she squeezed it. "Slow breaths," he said.

"Remembering what?" asked Daniels. "We were just sitting here, talking about Rudy."

Mikey squeezed Rem's hand harder. "Oh, shit," she said, her memories swirling fast. She opened her eyes and tried to do as Rem said–take slow steady breaths.

"Mikey, you're scaring me," said Mason.

"Focus on my voice, Mikey," said Rem. "You're not there. You're here. You're right here. Safe and sound."

Mikey honed in on his words and took a deep breath. Then took another.

"There you go," said Rem. "That's it. Just go slow."

Her mind began to quiet and Mikey focused on her body, sitting on the couch and her fingers clenching Rem's. "That man," she said, softly.

"What man?" asked Daniels.

"The...the...electric one. He...he..." She had trouble forming the words. Another memory reared up, and she bit her lip.

"Rudy?" asked Rem. "Do you know him?"

She shook her head. "I...I don't know. But...but...something about him..."

Daniels pulled out his phone. "We have a sketch. Do you want to see it? See what he looks like?"

"How could she possibly know Rudy?" asked Mason.

"Maybe he reminds her of someone," said Rem.

Daniels held out the phone. "You want to see it?"

Mikey hesitated and then nodded her head, and he showed it to her. A white-hot flare shot through her stomach, and she gasped, her memories returning. Holding her stomach, she fought the urge to be sick.

"You know him?" asked Mason.

"I've seen him," said Mikey.

"Where?" asked Daniels. "Recently?"

"No," said Mikey, forcing herself to calm down. "He...he...he was a friend of Victor's."

Rem's hand stilled on her back. "What?" he asked.

"Are you sure?" asked Daniels.

She thought back. "Yes. I saw him. When...when..." Another blob of spots distorted her vision, and she closed her eyes again.

"Mikey?" asked Mason, his voice low and deep. "Did he hurt you?"

She opened her eyes. "No. But I think he may have wanted to." Sniffing, she felt a tear run down her cheek.

Mason grabbed a tissue from a box on an end table beside the couch. "Here."

"What happened?" asked Rem. "What do you remember?"

She took the tissue and wiped her face. Now that the memory had surfaced, she started to feel more composed, and the spots faded. "Back...back when I was with Victor, and I...well...there was a time when he...he preferred me..." She paused and exhaled.

Rem rubbed her back. "Go slow."

"I…uh…remember he had a visitor. Out at that bungalow. At the beach." She dabbed at her eyes. "There was a group of us, and this guy showed. I hadn't seen him before, but Victor and he seemed close." She blinked, thinking back. "We were out by the water, sitting in front of a bonfire, drinking and smoking weed, and Victor came out with this guy." She tipped her head. "It was him. The guy in the sketch."

Daniels put his phone away. "What happened?"

"He…he hung out at the party for a while. I didn't like him. He had a weird vibe, and he kept staring at me. I stuck close to my friends and to Victor, but I saw him pull Victor aside, and they spoke. It got heated, and there was this strange hum in the air. One man in the group approached them. He was high and stupid, and Victor's friend touched him on the chest. The guy flew backwards and curled up in the fetal position, shaking and crying." She gripped Rem's hand. "And I saw the friend look at me, and my stomach turned. Victor spoke in his ear, and then that man looked at another woman in the group." She paused. "He…Rudy…left Victor and walked over to the woman, and he spoke to her and took her hand. She…she went still and looked at Victor and he nodded at her." Mikey bit back a sob, feeling the same dread that she'd felt at the party years ago.

"It's okay," said Rem. "You're not there."

"She went with him, back to the bungalow, and Victor came back to me, and we stayed on the beach, but hours later, I saw her when we returned after the bonfire. The man was gone, but the look in her eyes told me everything, and I knew he'd hurt her." She lowered her head and held her temples. "And I realized then that Victor's friend had wanted me first, and Victor had told him no, and it should have been me sitting there, looking terrified, lost and confused." She pressed the tissue to her mouth. "And I let her go, because I was thankful it wasn't me. I let Victor feed her to the wolves." Fresh tears surfaced, and they ran down her face.

"That is not your fault," said Rem. "There was nothing you could have done to stop it." He put his hand on her shoulder and squeezed it.

"I can still see the look on her face," said Mikey.

"You did the best you could, Mikey," said Mason. "Victor's the one to blame here. Not you."

Mikey sniffed, wiped her face, and sat up. "That was him, though. The man in the sketch. This Rudy person? That was Victor's friend. I'd swear it on Mom's grave."

Daniels shot a look at Rem. "That makes this case a hell of a lot more interesting."

"It sure as hell does," said Rem. "Rudy was friends with Victor." He looked back at Mikey. "Was he a follower? Was he at any other functions with Victor's groupies?"

"No," said Mikey. "He wasn't a follower. I sensed he was more of an equal. He'd stopped by that one time, and Victor offered one of his ladies for a good time. I don't recall seeing him again." She shook her head and wiped her eyes, feeling more stable.

"Have some more water," said Mason, handing her the bottle.

Mikey took it and drank some. "I'm better. Thanks."

Daniels sat back in his chair, his face serious. "It begs the question, though. You think Rudy knew Allison?" He tensed. "Is she the one I arrested that Rudy knows?"

Mikey felt Rem squeeze her fingers.

Rem rubbed his face with his free hand. "My mind's racing here. I have to think."

"What would it matter if he knew Allison?" asked Mason. "He wasn't around, that we know of, when Victor died and Allison took over."

"Exactly," said Daniels. "That we know of. I just find it highly coincidental that the man we're chasing has ties to Victor, and around the same time, you start getting voicemails and love notes." He nodded at Rem.

"Except for the note, I got the voicemails before we were ever onto Rudy," said Rem.

Mikey frowned. "What notes? What voicemails?"

Rem groaned, and Daniels filled her in on what had been happening with Rem.

“Why didn’t you tell me?” she asked.

“He didn’t want us to worry,” said Daniels.

She nudged Rem in the shoulder. “We made an agreement to talk about these things.”

“We agreed to talk about our past experiences, not current,” said Rem.

“Don’t split hairs with me,” said Mikey.

Mason grunted, stood and sat in the empty chair across from Mikey. “You two can argue semantics later, but Daniels poses an important question. Are Allison and Rudy in touch?”

Mikey thought about her morning with concern. “It could be more than just Allison we need to worry about.”

“Why do you say that?” Mason frowned. “Does this have something to do with where you were earlier?”

“Yes. It does.” Mikey paused. “I...I may have done something stupid.”

“What are we adding to the list?” asked Mason.

“Don’t get mad,” said Mikey.

“Too late,” said Mason. “I don’t even know what it is, but I’m preparing.”

“What’d you do?” asked Rem.

Mikey steeled herself. “I went and saw Margaret.”

Mason’s eyes rounded. “You what?” He scowled. “At the psychiatric hospital?”

“Yes,” said Mikey. “I wanted to talk to her.”

“I can’t believe this.” Mason stood and stomped around beside the desk. “What for? She’s unstable. I told you that.”

“She’s my sister, Mason. I feel responsible.”

“She’s insane,” said Mason.

“She has a mental illness.”

"A mental illness that would take your life the moment she had the opportunity," yelled Mason. "She almost killed you once. You want her to try again?"

"Of course not." Mikey yelled back. "I just wanted to see her."

Mason stopped pacing and gripped the back of his chair.

"What happened when you went?" asked Daniels. "What did she say?"

"This ought to be good," said Rem. He let go of Mikey's hand and sat back on the couch.

"It was just gibberish," said Mikey. "Nothing that made sense." She glanced at Rem. "I doubt it meant anything."

"Humor us," said Daniels.

Mikey swallowed. "Don't freak out, okay?" She said to Rem. "She mumbled about the light returning to the dark. That I should be careful around the light. The dark would return to claim its prize. And something about a new light surfacing. She was all over the place."

Rem's pallor deteriorated, and Daniels straightened. "Sounds a lot like your note," said Daniels.

"Sure does," said Rem.

"You think Rudy has some connection to Margaret, too?" asked Mason.

"Your sister was a rather devoted disciple of Victor's and Allison's," said Daniels. "It's certainly possible."

Rem pushed up on the couch. "This is just getting more and more confusing. I don't know what to think."

Daniels' cell rang, and he pulled it out. "Hold that lack of thought. It's Lozano." He answered and spoke to his captain, his eyes widening. "Yeah," he said, standing. "We're on our way. Send the address." He hung up and smacked Rem's knee. "We've got a possible sighting of Rudy and Josh. Lozano's texting the location. Let's go, partner."

Chapter Nine

Rem stood at the register of the convenience store while the attendant helped a customer. Daniels stood outside, speaking to a uniformed officer.

The attendant finished ringing up the patron and sighed at Rem. “I already talked to the other cops. You guys are scaring away business.”

“This won’t take long,” said Rem. “I just need to know what you saw.”

The attendant put his hands on the counter. “Fine. I came on my shift about an hour ago. I was doing my thing, helping customers, and minding my business. I had the TV on up front, and they kept showing that news conference from this morning and flashing that guy’s face, along with the kid’s. I checked out a customer and then they walked in.”

“Who walked in?” asked Rem.

The attendant rolled his eyes. “That guy and the boy. The man was wearing a baseball cap and sunglasses, and so was the kid. I stared for a second, because I wasn’t sure if I was seeing right. He wandered down an aisle, picked up a six-pack of soda and some chips. He brought them to the counter, and I checked them out.”

“How were they acting?”

“The kid didn’t say a word. The guy didn’t look at me. He kept his face down, but when he pulled out cash and handed it to me, he knew I recognized him.”

“What’d he do?”

“He just smiled at me. Like he thought it was funny. He lowered his sunglasses and told me to wait to call the cops until he left and got down the street, or he'd return later, and I'd end up at the morgue." He raised a brow. "The look in his eyes, man. I didn't argue. He left, holding the kid's hand. I waited one minute and then called you guys."

"Which way did he go?"

"He turned left outside the store and crossed the street. Then he disappeared."

"What was he wearing?"

The attendant gave Rem a description of Rudy and Josh's clothing, and Rem thanked the attendant, left him his card in case he remembered anything else, and stepped outside.

"Anything?" he asked Daniels. He squinted in the sunshine.

"Not much," said Daniels. "They're canvassing the neighborhood, looking for anything or anyone that looks like an RV, or Rudy and Josh."

Rem kicked at a rock on the pavement. "How much do you want to bet they're long gone?"

"Maybe. Maybe not." Daniels looked around the area. "I mean, why are they here anyway? The whole city is looking for them, and Rudy just walks in here without a care in the world. It doesn't make sense."

"Well, we know he likes junk food."

"You can get junk food outside the city. You should know."

"That's true."

"Why would he stick around?"

Rem eyed the store and surrounding shops. "Maybe there's something here he likes or wants to be around. Is there an RV park around? Maybe that's where they were staying, and they grabbed some snacks before hitting the road."

Daniels paused and knitted his brow. "Wait a minute." He stared at a street sign, and then walked to the intersection and looked down the street.

"What is it?"

Daniels returned. "You may have said the magic word."

"You thinking junk food? Because I sure am." Rem rubbed his stomach. "I could go for a candy bar."

"No," said Daniels. "Park." He pointed. "You remember what Henry said? About Rudy teaching him?"

"What about it?"

"He said Rudy killed a homeless man in the park." He gestured down the street. "There's a big park, with trails and a playground not far from here. Before J.P. was born, Marjorie and I went there to see some sort of 'Shakespeare in the Park' thing. They were doing *Taming of the Shrew*."

"You think Rudy likes Shakespeare?"

Daniels rolled his eyes. "No. I don't think Rudy is into the Bard of Avon."

"Who?"

Daniels sighed. "I think we should check out the park. Maybe Rudy's been scoping it out, planning on doing the same with Josh like he did with Henry, and if he is..."

"We might have a dead homeless guy on our hands."

"If not already soon. I think it's worth a look." He gestured. "It's a block away. We can walk it." He turned and headed toward the intersection, and Rem gave a last look at the convenience store, thinking about the candy bar.

"We'll stop on the way back," said Daniels. "Let's go."

••••••••••

Josh Lambert walked beside Rudy, fighting back tears because he knew Rudy didn't like it when he cried. Rudy held his hand, and they walked along a path with other people, some on roller skates and skateboards. Josh passed another kid in a field flying a kite with his dad and Josh thought of his own dad and wanted to cry harder, but Rudy yanked on him and told him to keep up, and Josh stopped looking at the people because they made him sad.

"Up here, Sam. Near the trees. What do you see?"

Josh looked up to see a row of tents and various people sitting outside of them, most with dirty hair and wearing old clothes. The roller skaters and skateboarders headed toward the other side of the park where there were more people. "I don't know," he whispered.

Rudy yanked on his arm. "Don't play dumb. You're smarter than that. What do you see?"

"People in tents. I think they're homeless."

"They are." Rudy walked closer. "This is where I want you to practice."

"I don't want to."

"I don't care. You can't learn without practicing. My dad taught me, and I'm going to teach you."

"But you're not my dad."

Rudy stopped and glared down at him. "Don't talk to me like that. I know you don't know me, but you'll respect me. You understand? Your mother told you one thing, but I'm telling you another. The dad you had taught you certain things, but it's my turn now. If you want to be the man you should be, then it's my job to teach you. You're not just some kid who likes to play baseball and get A's in school. That's worthless compared to what you're capable of. You got it?"

Josh's chin quivered, and he bit his lip but nodded.

"Good." Rudy pulled Josh's baseball cap down lower and straightened. "Follow me."

Unable to do anything but comply, Josh walked beside him. They passed a few tents, and Josh saw a few men and women lying down and sleeping and others sitting up, asking for money when Rudy strode by. Rudy ignored them until he got to the end of the row. Passing a red tent with a hole in it, Rudy guided Josh up a small ridge. A man slept just beyond it on a blanket, and when he saw Rudy and Josh, he lifted his head.

"What do you want?" he asked.

Rudy squatted beside him. "My name's Rudy and this is my son, Sam. We need a favor and we're willing to pay for your help."

The man slowly lumbered into a sitting position. "What is it?"

"Just sit there and watch," said Rudy.

"Watch what?"

Rudy looked at Josh. "I want you to try."

"No. I don't want to," said Josh.

"You won't hurt him, but you need to understand how it feels. Raise your hand and focus, like I showed you."

Josh swallowed. "I'm scared."

"Everybody's scared, kid. It's time you learned how to deal with fear if you ever want to be strong."

"What's goin' on?" asked the man by the tent.

"I want the boy to touch your arm," said Rudy.

"My arm? What for?"

"You want your money?" asked Rudy, his face turning mean. "Then stop your squawking. He's not going to hurt you."

The homeless man frowned. "Then get on with it. I ain't got all day."

"C'mon, Sam. Practice. This vagrant doesn't have all day." Rudy grabbed Josh's arm and lifted it. "Like I showed you."

"Please. I don't want to do it." Josh held his arm out and fought the weird feeling that began to bubble up in his body. He didn't feel comfortable when his skin would turn bumpy.

"I want you to try." Rudy's voice turned cold, and Josh could tell he was getting angry. "Cause if you don't..."

Josh bit back a sob and reluctantly held his arm out. His finger trembled and tiny bumps popped up on his skin.

"That's right. There you go," said Rudy. "Now touch his arm."

"This better be good," said the homeless man. "How much you payin' me?"

"Enough to make it worth your while," said Rudy.

Josh's ears rang, he heard humming, and he touched the man on the arm.

The man jumped. "Ouch." He pulled back and rubbed his elbow. "What was that? Did he just shock me?"

Rudy smiled. "He did. Not bad, huh?" He patted Josh on the shoulder. "That's my boy."

Josh prayed that was all he would have to do.

"You two are crazy," said the man. "Give me money and get out of here."

Rudy's face changed, and Josh scooted back. He wanted to run and find a person in the park to help him, but knew he couldn't. He had to be brave.

"Don't call my son crazy," said Rudy.

"I'll call him whatever I damn want," yelled the man. "You know what? Screw your money. Just get lost." He resumed his position on the ground and mumbled. "And people think I'm nuts."

"Apologize to my son," said Rudy.

"It's okay," said Josh. "Let's go."

The man looked up. "You should apologize to me. You're the one taking up my space. Leave me alone."

"I said..." replied Rudy. "...apologize."

Josh heard the hum return. He shivered and grabbed Rudy's arm. "Let's go." The humming throbbed in Josh's ears.

The man raised up on an elbow and yelled at Rudy. "You and your kid can go—"

Rudy raised a finger and touched the man on the chest. The man gasped, jolted, went rigid, and collapsed backward, his head hitting the ground with a thunk.

Josh stared in horror and wanted to scream, but Rudy stood, looked around and grabbed Josh by the hand. "That's what people get for not being nice. Come on, Sam. Let's get out of here."

•••••••••••

Daniels stopped at the edge of the park, eyeing the crowd. A small carnival had been erected in a large, open area. A few rides were swirling while the riders screamed, parents played with their kids in a nearby play area, and a group of teenagers threw a frisbee in an adjacent field. Food trucks lined the street, and a young girl walked by with a mound of cotton candy.

Rem watched her go by. "We're definitely stopping here."

"We're looking for Rudy and Josh, not sweets."

"I get it, but if it doesn't pan out, when in Rome..."

Daniels shook his head. "How do you want to do this?"

"It's pretty big. If he's here, he won't be easy to find. Maybe we should approach it from the other end."

"How so?"

"Look for the homeless. If that's what he's after, then let's start there."

Daniels stuck out a finger. "That's a good idea, Watson."

"I have my moments, Sherlock, although they're getting a little scarce lately."

"Give it time. They'll come around."

"The positive attitude strikes again."

"Told you to get used to it."

Rem looked around. "You want to start down by the water?" He nodded toward a large pond that sat in the middle of the festivities. "It seems a little quieter there. Plus, there're more trees to sit under."

"Sounds good."

Daniels headed down a walkway that led to the water's edge. Rem followed and as they neared a section where customers could access paddle boats, Daniels spotted a section of trees where a few people slept, and a row of tents was erected. "Looks like that's our destination."

"I'm right behind you."

Daniels walked down the path toward a tree where a man with dirty, unkempt hair and wearing ragged clothes held an old newspaper and appeared to be reading it.

"Excuse me, sir?" asked Daniels.

The man looked up and frowned. His teeth were brown and his fingernails grimy. "What do you want?"

"Sorry to bother you, but we're looking for a man." He held out his phone with the sketch of Rudy. "Have you seen him, with an eleven-year-old boy?"

"You're asking the wrong guy, sport. I don't see so good." He went back to his newspaper.

"You know anyone else who sees better than you?" asked Rem. "Someone who's familiar with the park? Spends a lot of time here?"

The man lowered his paper. "Talk to Scout."

"Scout?" asked Daniels. "Who's Scout?"

The man nodded. "He's got the tent on the end. Wears red sneakers he found at the thrift shop. They're his favorite. If anyone knows who's hanging around, he does." He pointed at his eyes. "And he's got eyes like a hawk. He can spot tossed food faster than anyone." He smiled with crusty lips. "Some kid dropped his cookie on the trail the other day and started bawlin'. His parents took him off, and Scout picked up the cookie and brought it over to me. He's a good guy."

"Sounds like it. Thanks," said Daniels.

"Sure." He returned to his paper.

Rem turned toward Scout's tent, and Daniels followed. "He sees pretty good for someone reading the paper," said Daniels.

"That paper was two years old, and he was reading it upside down."

"That's even more impressive."

Rem chuckled. "Hey. Would you bring me a cookie if someone dropped it?"

"Do you want me to bring you a cookie if someone dropped it?"

"Sure. Why not?"

"Because it was dropped on the ground, probably by a kid with a snotty nose and fingers who likely sneezed on it."

Rem snorted. "What happened to Mr. Positive?"

"He's been replaced by Mr. Obvious."

"Figures." Rem approached the tent at the end. It was red with dirt smeared on the side and a ripped hole in the top. "What do we do? Knock?"

Daniels leaned over and noticed the front flap was open. "Scout? Hello? You in there?" He didn't see anyone inside. "I think he's currently out and about, looking for kids with slippery fingers.

"Hey." Rem smacked him on the arm. "Look. Up by the tree."

Daniels followed Rem's sight line, and saw a figure, wearing red worn sneakers with holes in the soles, lying flat on his back, beneath a large Ficus. He walked over, and approaching the man, noted the man's gray pallor. "Scout?"

"Scout?" Rem kneeled beside him and paused. "He's not looking too good." He shook the man's shoulder and took the man's pulse. His face fell. "Scout's dead."

"Are you kidding?"

Rem stood. "Well, if he isn't, he's damn shy. He's still warm, too. We need to call—" He froze. "Daniels."

Daniels noted his partner's tone, and turned, looking in the same direction. In the distance, walking down the trail beside the water, was a man in sunglasses and a baseball cap on his head, walking with a kid, who also wore a baseball cap and sunglasses.

Daniels' heart raced. "Is that…?"

"I think it might be," said Rem.

The man turned, as if sensing eyes on him. He lowered his glasses, made eye contact with them, and grinned. Then he grabbed the boy's hand and broke into a run.

••••••••••

Daniels took off in a sprint, and Rem followed, staying right behind him. They flew by the homeless man with the paper, and back to the trail they'd just left. Rem tried to keep his eyes on Rudy and Josh, but the farther and deeper they went into the park, the busier it became, and the harder it was to track them.

They ran past the kids playing frisbee and the play area, and Rem thought he saw a man with a baseball cap take a sharp left and then disappear into the midway section of the carnival. Daniels had shortened the distance between them, but dodging parkgoers, pets, and children made it more difficult.

Reaching the section where Rudy had veered into the crowded carnival, Daniels stopped, breathless, and Rem stopped behind him, looking frantically through the crowd. "Anything? You see him?"

Holding his side, Daniels turned, looking. "Everybody around here is wearing a damn baseball cap and sunglasses."

"I know." Rem grabbed his cell. "I'm going to call it in. We need more manpower." He dialed a number.

"I'm going farther in. Check out the rides."

Rem nodded. "I'll check out the games section. Meet you at the end."

Daniels nodded and disappeared into the crowd. Rem made his call, requesting reinforcements, and headed into the busy and noisy games area, where people tried to shoot at balloons and toss rings over bottles, while carnies barked out how lucky they could be, and the prizes they could win.

Rem kept an eye out, but didn't see Rudy or Josh. He made it back to a food court and what looked to be a small art fair, with tents erected and artists displaying their wares. Seeing Daniels beside a tent full of pottery, he jogged up to him. "Any luck?" he asked.

"Nothing." Daniels blew out a puff of air. "Shit. We had him. We were close."

Rem eyed the edge of the park and a quiet street that ran behind it, where several trucks and cars were parked, which probably belonged to the vendors who'd set up their tents in the art section. "Let's go look back there."

He jogged over and stepped beyond a chain-link fence that marked the boundary of the park. Daniels followed, and they walked between the vehicles, looking for anything or anyone suspicious. Getting to the end, Rem cursed. "Nothing."

Daniels started to turn, then stopped. "Rem. Look."

Rem stepped beyond a truck and eyed where Daniels pointed. Parked beneath a canopy of trees, which provided plenty of cover, but blended in with the rest of the parked vehicles, was an RV. He held his breath, and they walked closer.

"It's not brown," said Rem, as they neared it.

"It's been nine years," said Daniels, quietly. "He could have bought a new one."

Approaching the quiet vehicle, Rem pulled his weapon. Daniels did the same as they came up alongside the door. Rem looked closely at the side paneling. "Hey," he whispered and pointed. "Check it out."

Daniels leaned to look, and Rem scratched at the blue paint, which flecked off, revealing a brown color beneath.

Daniels' eyes widened, and he stood to the side of the door. Rem stood along the opposite side and nodded.

Using the butt of his gun, Daniels banged on the door. "Police. Open up."

There was no response. His heart thudding, Rem banged on it next. "Police. We need to talk to you. Come out with your hands up."

Nothing.

Daniels reached up and took the knob. "It's unlocked," he whispered. He pulled the door open wide, took the two stairs up and swiveled, his gun up and aiming toward the right. Rem ran in behind him, aiming toward the left.

The RV was empty. They stood in a small living area with a couch and table. Fast food wrappers and disposable cups littered the floor and a pillow and blanket lay on the couch. Beyond Rem was a tiny hall, with a bathroom and bedroom. It was silent, except for their breathing, and Rem took steps toward the back. He checked the bathroom, seeing a bar of soap, shaving cream, and some kid's toothpaste. Moving slowly, he checked the bedroom, finding a rumpled bed, and spotting what looked like a child's sock on the floor and a small, wrinkled t-shirt next to the sock. "It's clear back here."

"Clear up here," said Daniels.

Rem turned, passed the messy living area, and headed into a kitchen, where Daniels stood. Dirty plastic plates and bowls were stacked up in the trash, and the countertop was dotted with crumbs and spilled liquid.

"Looks like they took off in a hurry," said Rem.

"Looks like," said Daniels. "But they left something behind."

"What's that?"

Daniels tapped at the refrigerator door with a knuckle and Rem saw the picture attached with a magnet. It was of a young Rudy, probably in his early twenties, smiling and holding a young child who appeared to be around the age of five. They were sitting in a kitchen and the child was on Rudy's lap.

"Now we've got his picture," said Daniels. "And I'm guessing Sam's, too."

"I doubt he wanted to leave that behind."

"I doubt it, too," said Daniels. He holstered his gun. "I'll call Lozano."

Chapter Ten

THE NEXT MORNING, DANIELS sat at his desk and yawned. After their crazy day yesterday, he and Rem had remained at the park, helping to canvas the area and show Rudy and Josh's pictures around, but with no luck. Rudy and Josh had disappeared.

By the time they'd left, they were both exhausted and had gone home, planning to be back early the next morning and start again. Rem had been too tired even for cotton candy.

Eyeing the time, Daniels was about to call his partner when the squad doors opened, and Rem walked in, looking every bit as weary as Daniels felt.

"Mornin'," he said.

"Morning," said Daniels. He swirled his bottled green juice, hoping it would help him wake up. "How'd you sleep?"

"Not great. You?" Rem went to the coffee machine.

"Not great. Dreamed of chasing Rudy and then getting zapped by him."

Rem scooped up some grounds. "I dreamed of Rudy slicing a knife down my chest."

Daniels grimaced. "You always have to one-up me, don't you?"

"Sorry about that." He added grounds to the filter and grabbed the pot.

"Any more voicemails or letters?" asked Daniels.

"Nope. Nothing."

"Good."

Rem added water to the pot from the large bottle behind him. "How do you want to start today?"

"That's a good question." He thought about it, trying to sort out all that had happened. "The coroner should do Scout's autopsy this morning. And we should get a preliminary forensic report of what they found at the RV. That might give us something. Plus, whatever turns up on Rudy Halpern. Maybe Lozano heard something yesterday."

"Let's hope." Rem poured the water from the pot into the machine, returned the pot to its holder and flipped on the coffeemaker. "Go, baby, go. I need you today." The coffee percolated, and he patted the top of it.

"There're also a ton of leads to follow up on from yesterday," said Daniels.

"And now that we have his actual picture," said Rem, sitting at his desk, "We'll have a ton more."

"It was on the news last night. Did you see it?"

"The only thing I saw last night was my pillow." Rem sighed and rubbed his eyes.

"I don't blame you."

They talked for a few minutes about what leads and tips to follow and Rem got his coffee and sipped it, groaning in relief.

Daniels took another swig of his green drink when Lozano walked into the squad room, looking as weary as Rem.

"Mornin', Cap," said Rem.

"Cap," said Daniels.

"Good morning." Lozano walked past their desks. "I need to see you both in my office." He barely broke stride.

Daniels grabbed his juice. "That can't be good."

Rem picked up his coffee mug. "Can it get any worse?"

"You really want me to answer that?" Daniels stood along with Rem.

"No," said Rem. "Let me live in my world of unicorns and rainbows."

"You got it."

They walked into Lozano's office, and Rem took one chair and Daniels the other.

"We need to talk," said Lozano. He loosened his tie and slid it off, along with his jacket. He threw them over the back of his chair and sat.

"What is it?" asked Daniels.

"Sounds serious," said Rem.

Lozano turned on his computer monitor, and his screen lit up. "While you two were out yesterday, I got some information for you. Let's start with Rudolph Halpern."

"Here we go," said Daniels, sitting up.

Lozano shook, clicked his mouse, and stared at the screen. "Age forty-two. Parents deceased. No siblings. Married young, at nineteen, to a Beth Hoggart, age eighteen. They had a son. Samuel Halpern, when Beth was nineteen. Two years later, Beth disappeared. Her family, not Rudy, reported her missing. Rudy said she up and left. The family said otherwise. Beth was never found and although suspicious, the cops never filed charges."

"You think he killed her?" asked Rem.

"Never found a body, but I think the writing's on the wall," said Lozano.

"Sounds like it," said Daniels.

"It goes quiet then," said Lozano, "until Samuel's death, at age eleven. It was an accident. Samuel rode his bike into the street and got hit by a car. No helmet. He was DOA."

Daniels closed his eyes. "God."

"Yeah," said Lozano. "The man who hit him stayed at the scene. Reports say he was apologetic and horrified. Charges weren't filed."

"Because Sam was in the wrong place at the wrong time?" asked Rem.

"Maybe," said Lozano. "But more likely because the man was dead. He was found in his bed a week after the accident. Doctor determined it was a heart attack."

Daniels shot a look at Rem. "Heart attack?"

"Somehow, I'm guessing it wasn't," said Rem.

"Me, too," said Daniels.

"Me, three," said Lozano, "based on what the M.E. said about Ben Lambert."

Rem took a healthy sip of his coffee. "So, we think Rudy killed his wife, lost Sam, and then killed the man responsible. What happens after that?"

"A year after Sam's death, Henry LaCosta, age eleven, goes missing. The whole force is out looking, but no luck, until he turns up on a city street eight days later. Cops found him and brought him in but couldn't get much out of him. They never found his kidnapper."

Daniels sighed. "Did you learn about any dead homeless people found in the area after they found Henry?"

"I didn't find any official reports, but I talked to one detective who worked Henry's case. He retired last year, but he still vividly recalls Henry. After they found him, they initiated a canvas of the area, trying to determine if anyone saw anything. During the canvas, they found a dead panhandler in a nearby alley. Hadn't been dead long. They never associated him with Henry's kidnaping though. Guy was a John Doe and never identified."

"That corroborates Henry's story," said Daniels.

"You think Rudy makes these kids kill someone before he lets them go?" asked Lozano. "Or is he doing the killing and telling the kids they're doing it?"

"That's a great question, Cap," said Rem. "But we don't know."

Daniels fidgeted in his seat. They had not yet told Lozano about the theory of Rudy's electrokinesis. "If we ever find Rudy, maybe we can ask him."

"And find out how he's killing them," said Lozano.

"Yeah," said Rem, eyeing Daniels. "What happens after Henry?"

Lozano returned his attention to the screen. "Nothing for a while, until Rudy gets arrested a few years later for drunk and disorderly. He punched a cop, too. Got a year but served eight months."

"He got arrested?" asked Rem, raising a brow at Daniels. "That's interesting."

Daniels tapped at his drink. "It sure is."

"What's even more interesting is who's in prison with him," said Lozano. "He was briefly a cellmate of Victor D'Mato. Victor was doing a short stint for narcotics possession before his cult activity picked up."

Rem's eyes widened. "Shit. Mikey was right."

"Mikey?" asked Lozano. "Mikey Redstone?"

Daniels filled Lozano in on Mikey's memories of Victor and Rudy.

Lozano leaned back and rubbed his chin, lost in thought.

"You look like you know something," said Daniels.

Lozano sat back up. "Maybe. Let's finish with Halpern." He went back to the monitor. "Once he gets released, he disappears again. Then Josh Lambert goes missing."

Rem put his coffee on Lozano's desk. "I'm guessing in between that time, Victor gets out, starts attracting followers, and he and Rudy hook up again."

"Which is when Mikey sees him," says Daniels.

"And we all know what happens after that." Rem rubbed his chest.

"Rudy's not a follower, though," said Daniels.

"Doesn't mean he's not hanging around," said Rem. "Maybe he's just not into weird ceremonies or living forever."

"He can't have gone too far," said Lozano.

Daniels frowned. "Why do you say that?"

"I did some digging on that note of yours," said Lozano. "Unfortunately, there were no prints on it, but I contacted the warden of the jail Allison's in. He had some interesting information."

"What's that?" asked Rem.

"They've kept track of her visitors and phone calls. Her sister visited two months ago. Nothing big there."

"Her sister?" asked Daniels.

"Yeah." Lozano pulled out a notepad from the desk and checked his notes. "Annie Davidson. Apparently is the exact opposite of Allison. Is married with two kids, and lives in L.A. No red flags." He flipped to another page. "Allison's two phone calls were monitored and recorded. They were both to her sister, and her sister tried to steer her to repent and ask for forgiveness. Apparently, Annie is religious."

"Good luck to Annie," said Rem.

"Who else visited?" asked Daniels.

"Her attorney," said Lozano. "Which is another story. I'll get to him in a second. The person I want to talk about is her visitor last month. A..." he checked his notes, "Ronald Hardin."

"Who is Ronald Hardin?" asked Rem.

Lozano clicked on his mouse and swiveled the screen. "They got a shot of him entering the facility. See for yourself."

Daniels and Rem leaned forward, and Daniels dropped his jaw. "Hell. That's Rudy."

Rem paled. "Rudy visited Allison?"

Lozano turned the screen back. "He did."

Rem fell back in his seat. "Why?"

"What did they talk about?" asked Daniels.

"No idea," said Lozano, with a glare. "All the cameras and audio equipment went fuzzy after he arrived. This is the only shot they got of him. The warden couldn't explain it."

Rem swallowed. "So we have no idea why he was there?"

"Believe me," said Lozano, "I've made my disgust known. It's inexcusable."

"It wasn't long after that, you got your first phone call," said Daniels.

Rem squeezed his temples, trying to process the new information. "It doesn't make sense. Why would Rudy give a shit about me or Allison? He doesn't sound like the groupie type, and certainly not the type to take orders from a woman."

"There's no telling what she told him, or offered him," said Daniels. "Maybe Rudy's lonely, and he likes Allison. It seems he has an affinity for Victor's women."

"There's something else to consider," said Lozano.

Rem massaged his neck. "I knew I should have stayed in bed this morning." He sat up. "What is it?"

"Allison's attorney," said Lozano. "She got a new one last month. Kenneth Measy."

"Never heard of him," said Daniels.

"Be glad you haven't," said Lozano. "He's a slimeball. Hits below the belt and will easily land a sucker punch to win a case. Prosecutors call him Greasy Measy."

"Nice," said Rem.

Lozano aimed a pen at Rem. "This is the problem. You're the key witness in Allison's case. Your testimony will put her away for a long time, and you're the only one who can pin D'Mato's death on her. Measy knows that, and I wouldn't put it past him to try and make you look just as crazy as Allison. There's already the issue of you being drugged during the assault. If he can give a jury a reason to question the legitimacy of your testimony, he'll do it."

"You think Measy is responsible for the voicemail and notes?" asked Daniels.

"I can't prove anything," said Lozano. "But with Halpern showing up around the same time as Measy, I'd be stupid not to wonder." He aimed the pen at Daniels. "And you need to be aware, too. Your testimony is crucial, as well." He flicked his gaze back to Rem. "But without you, the case goes nowhere."

Rem slumped in his seat. "Wonderful."

"Let them try," said Daniels. "If we know what they're up to, we can counter it. Track every voicemail. Test every note. If we can trace just one of them back to Measy or Allison, then it all backfires."

"I concur. Don't let this crap get to you," said Lozano. "It's voicemails and letters. That's bearable."

"You're assuming that's where it will stop," said Rem. "We've got at least another six months before this goes in front of a jury." He picked up his coffee. "And we still don't know what Rudy's involvement is in all of this." He stilled and stared at his mug. "What if...?"

Daniels leaned closer. "What if what?"

"What if Rudy's insurance?" He sighed. "If Measy can't get to me, maybe Rudy will." His gaze fell on Daniels. "If I wake up dead one morning, and it looks like a heart attack, then you know where to look."

••••••••••

Two days later, Daniels sat at his desk and raked a hand through his hair, exhausted and frustrated. They'd spent the day tracking tips and talking to possible witnesses with no luck and had returned to the station to provide updates to the task force assigned to find Josh Lambert. He expelled a groan. "How in the hell could we have been so damn close to catching them two days ago and then everything goes dead? Where the hell are they?"

Rem looked up, his face fatigued. "It's not totally dead. That last person we talked to said she saw them eating in the diner across the street from her apartment."

"That was the restaurant owner and his son."

"Still." He picked up a piece of notepaper. "And Mrs. Winters swore they were living in her sister's house."

Daniels snorted. "The only people in her sister's house were her sister and her husband. It was the housekeeper who brought her kid to work that Mrs. Winters suspected."

"That you know of. Maybe Rudy stayed there. Maybe we should put eyes on it. You never know."

"Now I know you're tired, because you're making no sense."

Rem stifled a yawn. "If you can be Mr. Positive, figured I'd give it a shot, too. How am I doing?" He held his head and closed his eyes.

"You're a regular Mr. Rogers."

"Thanks."

Daniels eyed the time. It was after seven. "Why don't you go home? Get some shuteye. We'll start fresh tomorrow."

Rem cracked an eye open. "Don't tease me."

"I'm not. You're exhausted. So am I."

"You realize we're six days into this. We're getting close to Josh taking his final test."

"Yeah. I know." Daniels rubbed his face. "Shit."

Rem sat up. "The RV revealed nothing, other than Rudy's a slob and likes fast food, and that picture, of course. And since Scout died the same way as Ben, we have to assume that was Rudy showing off to Josh. If Henry's timetable is accurate, and it seems it is..."

"I know. I know."

"Then maybe we should plan on what to do when we find Josh. Cause at this point, finding Rudy seems unlikely."

"You mean start looking for dead people the minute he turns up?"

Rem nodded. "And let's hope Josh is more verbal than Henry was."

"I hate to tell you this, partner, but none of that is going to help us find Rudy. Once he leaves Josh behind, he's gone."

Rem rifled through some papers. "You forget his connection to Allison. He may not disappear into the sunset. Like Lozano said, he may stick around."

"You really think he could come after us?"

"He's already called you once."

"Just once though, and you haven't received any more voicemails and letters, so maybe he's decided Allison is just as cuckoo as we all know she is. If he's smart, he'll move on."

"That's the question." Rem put his elbows on his desk. "Is he smart?"

The squad doors opened and Shorty, the tall and lanky officer who manned the front desk, entered and approached them. "Hey, Rem. Daniels. How's it goin'? Any solid leads?"

"I wish," said Daniels. "How are you? Still getting calls up front?"

"They've slowed, but they're still coming in. Let's hope one of them pans out," said Shorty.

"Let's hope," said Rem. "You here to see Lozano?"

"Yeah," said Shorty. "He and I talked last week about getting a drink tonight, but I'm guessing with everything going on, it will be a raincheck."

Daniels eyed Lozano in his office. The shades were open, and he was on the phone. After a few seconds, Lozano hung up.

"I'll go reschedule," said Shorty and headed toward the office.

"Maybe next week," said Rem, "we'll all go get a drink."

"Maybe," said Shorty, walking away. "Let's hope."

Daniels watched Shorty stick his head into Lozano's office. "The offer still stands," he said to Rem. "You should go home. I doubt we'll crack this case tonight."

"What about you? You're just as tired."

"I'll finish up our report, and I'll be right behind you." He rubbed his shoulder. "I'm sure Marjorie wouldn't mind seeing her husband for a few minutes this week." He looked up. "And maybe I'll even get to see J.P. before he goes to bed."

"Then you go. I'll finish the report. Go hug your wife and kid," said Rem.

Daniels eyed his weary friend. Rem had showed a remarkable determination since receiving the letter and learning Rudy and Allison had connected, but he suspected his partner was diving into work to distract himself from thinking about it. Daniels had seen it before, after Rem had returned to work after Jennie's death. He'd pushed himself almost to death, to the point where Daniels had said something, and even then, it was hard to get Rem to slow down.

"You need to get some sleep, and some downtime," said Daniels.

"And you don't?" asked Rem. "You think me going home means I'll sleep? Unlikely."

Daniels started to answer when Shorty stopped on his way out. "We postponed until next week. But if you catch this guy, you two can join us."

"Sounds great," said Rem. "I hope to hell we can."

"Hey, I almost forgot." Shorty reached into his pocket. "This was delivered earlier, and I meant to bring it up, but got busy." He pulled out a letter and dropped it on Rem's desk. "You guys have a good night."

Rem stared at the letter. So did Daniels. "Uh, yeah," said Daniels. "You, too, Shorty. Good night."

Shorty left and Daniels stood. "You think…?"

Rem had gone quiet. "Looks the same as the other one."

Daniels walked closer, and Rem grabbed a pencil and used the eraser to slide the letter closer. "The handwriting looks the same," he said. Anxious, he grabbed a tissue from a box on the desk. "Here goes nothing." Holding the bottom tip and securing the envelope with the tissue, he slid a pen beneath the flap and ripped it open. "Don't know why I'm doing this," said Rem. "The last one didn't have prints."

"You never know. Better to be safe," said Daniels. He stood over Rem's shoulder, watching as Rem carefully slid the letter out. It looked like the same stationery and Rem opened it.

Hello, Detective.

I'm not one for metaphors, so I'll save the dark and the light crap for those who care, and cut to the chase.

You know the truth. You got in too deep. You fell for a woman who hurt you and you retaliated by spreading lies. You wanted her, you got her, and when she rejected you, you used your powers as an officer to abuse her. I get it. We've all been there. But it's time to fess up and be a man. Tell the truth. Don't send a woman victimized by two men of power to a life of imprisonment.

Things like that can weigh on a mind. Weigh it down like a body tied to cement blocks. If you can't bring yourself to do what's right, perhaps consider another option.

Your life can't possibly matter that much. Maybe you should put a gun to your head and pull the trigger. I hear it does wonders for the soul.

Just a suggestion.

Take care, Detective.

Rem's hand shook, and Daniels grabbed the tissue and took the letter from him. He took a slow breath. "I'm going to have fun finding this guy and wrapping my hands around his neck."

"I get to go first." Rem squeezed his fingers into fists and blew out his own deep breath. "That's definitely not from a D'Mato follower."

"If it is, then it's not a typical one," said Daniels. He reread it and cursed to himself. "I'll take it to Lozano." He folded it.

"What for? There won't be anything on it."

"You know I have to. We might find DNA on the flap." Daniels walked to his desk and found a plastic bag. He slipped the letter inside and picked up the envelope and added it. "If this came from Measy or Rudy—"

"How are we possibly going to prove that?" Rem looked up with haunted eyes. "Lozano's right. They're messing with my head. Trying to get me to back off, or look bad to a jury."

"I know." Daniels zipped the bag closed. "The light and dark stuff isn't working, so they're pushing harder."

Rem nodded. "Yeah." He sighed, closed and opened his eyes. "You know what? I'm going to take you up on that offer and get out of here." He stood. "I need to clear my head. You mind?"

"Of course not." He frowned. "You okay?"

Rem grabbed his jacket. "Don't worry. I'm not going to take the letter's suggestion. I might take a few shots of Jack Daniels, though."

Daniels couldn't blame him. The letter had shaken him, as well. "I get it. Call me when you get home. I'll take this to Lozano and head out soon."

"Okay. Thanks." He dumped his empty disposable coffee cup in the trash, slid on his jacket, and left.

His heart thudding and worried about Rem, Daniels took the letter to Lozano. Lozano read it and was just as horrified. Lozano said he would take care of it, and Daniels returned to his desk, planning to finish up a few things and get the hell out of there, but still thinking about Rem.

His phone rang and groaning, he debated ignoring it but picked it up, anyway. "Daniels."

"Well, ring-a-ding-ding, Detective. How are you tonight?"

Everything froze up in his gut, and Daniels went still. "Rudy?"

"You got it. I enjoyed our chase the other day. You and your partner are quick on your feet."

Daniels eyed his captain in his office, who was on the phone. "We got close."

"Close means squat, Detective. I'm here and you're there. I think we know who's winning this game."

Daniels' heart pounded harder. "How's Josh? Is he okay?"

"Sam is just fine. He's better in my hands than his mother's. He's learning a lot."

"You need to let him go. Don't do to him what you did to Henry."

Rudy paused. "You talked to Henry?"

"We did. He's not as happy about your parenting skills as you may think."

"He's a good kid. Talented. If he'd pursued his calling, I think he could have been better than me."

Daniels tried to think. "Where are you? You need to let Josh go. Henry was traumatized—"

"I didn't call to talk about them, Detective. I called to talk about you. You have something I want."

Daniels bounced his knee and thought of the photo. "What's that?"

"I left something important behind, and I want it back."

"Anything you left behind is evidence, Rudy. I can't just pull it off the shelf and give it to you."

"I think you can. In fact, I know you can, if given the right encouragement."

Daniels gripped the phone. "You turn yourself in and bring Josh, then you can have whatever you want."

Rudy chuckled. "I made this call out of consideration to you. I know you have a job to do, but so do I. You make this difficult..."

"I'm not the one who's making this difficult. You are." Daniels told himself to stay calm. "You tell me where you are, turn over Josh, and I'll make sure you get the picture back."

There was a silence, and he heard Rudy breathing over the phone. "You're about to find out exactly where I am, Detective."

"Where?" Daniels waited, and then he heard a click and the line went dead.

Chapter Eleven

MARJORIE DANIELS DRIED HER hands on a dish towel and flipped on the dishwasher. She eyed her cell, thinking about calling Gordon, but knew he was busy trying to find Josh Lambert. Hearing a squeal, she turned and saw J.P. walking toward her, carrying a small plastic ball. Drool covered his chin, and he was chewing on the toy.

"Hey, cutie pie." She picked him up. "How about we go get a bath and get ready for bed? Then we'll call Daddy. How's that sound?"

J.P. squirmed and used his favorite new word. "No." He pushed on her and she let him back down.

"Ten minutes, little guy. But that's it."

J.P. ran back into the other room with a screech. Shaking her head, Marjorie eyed the full trash can and walked over to pull out the bag when her cell rang.

She returned to the counter and picked it up, but didn't recognize the number. She answered. "Hello?"

"Mrs. Daniels?"

"Yes. Who's calling?"

"Well, ring-a-ding-ding. How nice to speak with you."

Marjorie frowned. "Who is this?"

"I'm a friend of your husband's."

"Gordon?"

"Yes. The delightful Detective Daniels."

Something about his tone made Marjorie tense up. "What's your name?"

"You can call me Rudy."

Marjorie held her breath, remembering Gordon telling her about the man he was searching for in connection to Josh Lambert's kidnapping. His name was Rudy. "What do you want?"

"I want to talk to you."

"Gordon's not here." She cursed herself. "I mean, not yet. He's on his way."

"Oh, I know exactly where your husband is. And it's not with you."

Marjorie's hair rose, and she clenched the phone. "Why are you calling?"

"Like I said. I thought we should talk."

Her heart rate zoomed, and taking a shaky breath, she attempted to sound calm. "I have to go."

"You have a lovely house, Mrs. Daniels. Reminds me of the one I used to have. I especially like the rug in the living room. The blues go well with the paint." A shock of cold shot through Marjorie, and her belly flipped. "You might want to check your son, though. He's pulling on the lamp cord. You don't want him to get hurt."

Panic coursed through her, and she ran into the living area, seeing J.P. beside the end table, pulling on a cord.

"Best you stay inside tonight, Mrs. Daniels. I wouldn't want anything to happen to you and that sweet boy of yours."

Shaking, Marjorie ran toward J.P. and, just before picking him up, she eyed the window that faced the backyard. A man was standing outside, his body silhouetted in the light, and she screamed and grabbed J.P. Still holding the phone, she ran to the front closet, flung the door open, and with trembling fingers, accessed the gun safe. She grabbed Gordon's personal weapon and raced into the downstairs guest bathroom, where she closed the door, locked it, and huddled in the corner.

•••••••••••

Lozano hung up his phone with a curse. “No luck on the trace.”

“What do you mean?” asked Daniels. “Why not?”

“They got some sort of interference. Couldn’t get a final location.”

Daniels hung his head. “Figures.” He looked up. “Probably doesn’t matter, anyway. He’d be gone before we got to wherever he is.”

“He wants that picture? Think we can use it to draw him out?”

Daniels sat back in his seat. “I don’t know. Maybe next time he calls, I can ask him.”

Lozano raised the plastic bag with the letter in it. “You think this is from Rudy?”

“It’s possible,” said Daniels. “If Allison fed him some sort of sob story when he visited her, then maybe she’s got him convinced that she’s the victim, and not Rem.”

“He didn’t strike me as being that stupid.”

“Or maybe he’s just doing exactly what we expect. Trying to make Rem think twice about testifying or give a jury a reason to question his testimony. I doubt Rudy cares either way who the guilty party is.”

“We also have to consider Measy. It wouldn’t be hard for him to write a letter like this.”

“Yeah. I know.” Daniels eyed the ceiling. “Damn. This whole thing is a mess.”

“I don’t like it. He’s calling you and threatening Remalla. You think Remalla can hold up under this pressure?”

“It’ll be tough, but I’ll help him through it. Just so long as Allison goes to prison for a long time. If she doesn’t—” His phone rang, and he pulled it from his pocket. “It’s Marjorie, probably wondering where I am.” He answered. “Hey, babe.”

Marjorie shrieked into the phone, her voice shaking. "He's here, Gordon. That man. He's outside."

Daniels stood. "What? What man?"

"The...the man. Rudy. He called himself Rudy. He...he called me."

"Where are you?"

Lozano stood and listened.

"I'm...I'm in the bathroom. I got your gun, and...and I locked myself in with J.P." Daniels heard J.P. wail into the phone. "Gordon...he's...he's outside." Her voice fell to a terrified whisper. "I saw him."

Chills ran up his legs, and terror slammed into his chest. Daniels forced himself to project calm. "Stay where you are. I'm on my way, and I'll send a patrol. Don't move."

Lozano got on the phone, and Daniels knew he was calling it in.

"Gordon. I'm scared."

Daniels thought of Rem and where he would be on his way home. "I know you are. I'm coming." He ran out of Lozano's office, grabbed his keys, and ran out the door. "I love you. Stay—"

The line disconnected, and she was gone.

....

Rem drove down the street and stopped at a light, his mind still on the letter. The words echoed in his head. *Your life can't possibly matter that much. Put a gun to your head and pull the trigger.*

Rem squeezed the steering wheel and tried to think of something else, but the ugly thoughts wouldn't fade. Was this his fault? Had he screwed it all up? A honk from behind him made him jump, and he realized the light was green. He hit the accelerator. *Shut up,* he told himself. *Don't let it get to you. It's just words on a page. Move on. Don't let Allison win.*

His phone rang, and he picked it up from the seat, and saw it was Daniels. He sighed, knowing his partner was worrying about him. “Hey,” he said after answering.

“Rem,” said Daniels, breathing hard. “Where are you? Are you near my house?”

Rem sat straight. “Not far. I’m about to pass your neighborhood. What’s wrong?” He heard a car door slam.

“Rudy just called Marjorie. He’s there, at my house. Marjorie’s hiding in the bathroom with J.P. and my gun.”

Icy fear fluttered through Rem’s stomach, and he hit the gas. “I’m two minutes away.”

“Lozano’s sending reinforcements, but you can get there faster. I’m right behind you.”

“I’ll get to her. Don’t worry.” He came up to a stop sign and blew through it.

“If he’s hurt her—” His voice shook.

“Stay cool. I’ll get there.” Rem hit the gas and heard Daniels’ tires squealing through the phone.

“I’m pulling out of the station now. You be careful and take care of my wife and son.”

“I will. See you soon.” Rem hung up and screeched around a corner, turning into Daniels’ neighborhood. He raced down a street, grateful it was later in the day, and the road was empty. He took two more turns and flew down the road. Approaching Daniels’ house, he hit the brakes, and the car came to a screeching halt in front of the home. The car still rocking, he jumped out and pulled his weapon.

Eyeing the area as he ran up to the house, he saw nothing and no one. All he heard was a dog barking in the distance. Breathing hard, he peered in the front window. The house was quiet. The kitchen and living room lights were on, but he didn’t see Marjorie or J.P. His back against the brick, he tried the front door, but it was locked.

Thinking, he debated checking the back, when a patrol car pulled up, the lights flickering, but the sirens off. Two officers jumped out, and Rem met them as they ran up the lawn. "Check the backyard and the alley. I'll take the house."

They nodded and ran down the driveway toward the rear. Rem dug into his pocket and pulled out a ring with a couple of keys on it. One of them was his house key, the other was Daniels'.

Not wanting to kick in Daniels' door, he inserted the key and opened the door. It opened with a soft squeak, and he pushed it wider. He dropped the keys back into his pocket and swiveled around the door, his gun pointed down. The house was silent, and he stepped inside. "Marjorie?" He moved farther in, seeing the quiet kitchen.

Hearing a child's squeal, he stepped behind the stairs and saw the closed bathroom door. Light emanated from the bottom, and he walked closer. "Marjorie? It's Rem. You in there?" He didn't want to scare her, but he also didn't want her to shoot him.

He heard a noise, another squeal, and then the door opened. Marjorie stood with J.P., her face white, and holding Daniels' gun with a tight grip. J.P. squirmed and began to cry. "Rem?" she said, her voice quiet.

Rem didn't waste time and grabbed her by the arm. "Come with me."

"He's here. I saw him in the backyard."

He took the weapon from her and tucked it into his jeans. "How well do you know your neighbors?"

She stammered. "I...I...don't know."

Rem guided her out the door and stayed close, keeping an eye out. He pulled her to the right.

"Where are we going?" She held J.P. close.

"To make some new friends."

Keeping her close, they walked up to the house next door and Rem knocked.

"They just moved in last month," said Marjorie, her voice a little steadier.

"Then consider this a great way to break the ice." He knocked again.

The door opened, and Rem saw a middle-aged man with thinning hair, a mustache and round glasses. Seeing them, his eyes narrowed, and he lowered his glasses.

Rem held out his badge. "Excuse me, sir. I'm Detective Remalla, and this is your neighbor, Marjorie Daniels and her son J.P. I need you to take her in while we check her house. She may have an intruder."

His jaw dropped, and he stood silent before he opened the door wider. "Of course. Come in."

"Thank you," said Marjorie, who walked in and looked back. "Rem..."

"Stay here," said Rem. "Don't come out of this house unless I or Daniels come to get you." He eyed the homeowner. "Sir. Lock your doors and windows. Don't answer the door to anyone but me or her husband."

The man nodded quickly. "Yes. Okay."

"I'll be back as soon as it's safe."

The man closed the door, and Rem heard the locks engage. He ran back across the lawn and returned to the front door, just as he heard a car approach, tires squeal and Daniels' car pulled up behind his.

Daniels jumped out, his gun in his hand, and Rem met him on the front porch. "Where's Marjorie? Where's J.P.?" He was breathless and scanned the house.

"They're safe," said Rem. "I got them over at your neighbors."

Daniels eyed the house next door. "You're sure?"

"We need to check inside. Two officers are checking the back." He tugged on Daniels' arm. "They're okay. I promise. We need to clear your house. See what's going on."

Daniels blinked, finally looked at Rem, and nodded. "Okay."

They approached the front door, and Daniels went inside first. Rem followed. "I'll check the kitchen," Daniels whispered.

Rem went into the living area. The lamp was on, but there was nothing out of place. He went back out toward the stairwell and double checked the bathroom where Marjorie had been hiding.

Daniels came out from the kitchen, his face a scowl. "Kitchen's clear, but the back door is open."

They looked upstairs. Daniels raised his weapon and went first. Rem stayed behind him to watch his partner's back. Their footfalls were silent on the wood, and when they reached the top, Daniels headed toward his and Marjorie's bedroom. Rem headed toward the nursery and guest bedroom. Checking both and finding nothing out of place, he went back out into the hall. Daniels left his bedroom and shook his head. "Nothing."

"Nothing down here, either."

With purposeful strides, Daniels ran down the stairs. After reaching the bottom, he turned. "I'm going next—" He kicked something on the floor, and it skittered across the wood and banged against the opposite wall.

Rem walked over and picked it up. It was a small picture frame, but the glass was broken and the picture was missing.

Daniels stepped close and took it from Rem, his expression darkening. "Marjorie framed the picture of the four of us in the kitchen, the one that she took when you were here last."

Rem set his jaw. "It was in this frame?"

"It was," said Daniels, setting the broken frame on the front table. "And now that bastard has it."

"Why the hell would he take that?"

"I think I have an idea." Daniels stood for a second, his expression unreadable, and he met Rem's stare. "I'm going to ask you the same question you asked me."

"What's that?" asked Rem.

"You still want to be my partner?"

"Why wouldn't I?"

Daniels narrowed his eyes and glared. "Because when I find Rudy, I'm going to kill him."

Holstering his weapon, he walked out the door.

Chapter Twelve

REM PULLED UP INTO his driveway and stopped. Eyeing the time, he saw it was almost ten o'clock. After returning to Daniels' neighbor's house and ensuring Marjorie and J.P.'s safety, Daniels had grabbed a few things from their home and had taken them to a hotel while Rem stayed behind to handle the investigation. They'd double-checked the area with no sign of Rudy, although they'd found footprints in the backyard. A canvas of the neighborhood had turned up nothing and forensics had dusted the house, but their initial results only seemed to show the fingerprints of Daniels and his family.

Daniels had stayed with Marjorie and J.P., and Rem had finally left, but remained in contact with his partner, keeping him up to speed with the progress.

Sitting in his driveway, he groaned with fatigue and popped the door open. Lozano had blessedly told him to sleep in the next morning, and he didn't have to be at work until noon. He slid out, closed the car door behind him, and headed to the front door. Stepping up on the porch, he jumped when a shadowed figure stood and faced him.

"Rem?"

He froze and held his chest. "Mikey?"

She walked closer and into the light. "Yeah. It's me."

"You scared the hell out of me. I almost went for my gun."

"Didn't you see my car?" She gestured toward the street.

He looked and saw her car parked right in front of his home, and then he slumped. Obviously, he was tired. “No.”

“Some detective you are.”

“I’m not at my best right now.” He headed toward his door and unlocked it. “Why are you here? Is something wrong?”

Her face fell. “I called you. Did you get my message? I heard about Daniels. I wanted to be sure you guys were okay.”

Walking in, he sighed. “Sorry. Haven’t checked my voicemails.” He held the door. “Come on in.” He tossed his keys on the front table. “How’d you hear?”

“I saw it on the news. They didn’t say the name of the family, but I had a funny feeling, so I called Lozano.”

“Your funny feelings are usually accurate.”

“Is Daniels okay? How are Marjorie and J.P.?”

“Everybody’s fine, thank God.” He slid off his jacket and tossed it on a kitchen chair.

“How are you?”

Rem could only imagine how he looked. “I’m running on empty.” He pulled open the fridge door. “You want a beer?”

“I wasn’t planning on hanging out. I know you’re tired.”

He pulled out two beers. “I am, but I can’t just hit the hay. I need to unwind a bit, then I’ll crash, and say a small prayer that I sleep.”

Mikey took the beer from him. “You’re sure?”

“You know that if I wanted you to leave, I’d tell you.” He closed the fridge. “Don’t be surprised if I conk out on you, though. I’m not going to be very good company.”

She shrugged. “It’s fine. I doubt I’ll be good company, either.”

“Good. We’ll sit in silence together.” He twisted off his beer cap and took a long pull. “I just want to find something mindless to watch and not think.”

"That shouldn't be hard." Twisting off her own cap, she followed him into the living room, and he flipped on the TV. He found an old movie and tossed the remote onto the table. He kicked off his shoes and sat back against the cushions.

"You think it was him...Rudy, tonight, at Daniels'?" she asked after sitting beside him.

"Pretty sure. Rudy called Marjorie and told her it was him. He was in their backyard."

"Shit. Are you kidding?"

"I wish I was."

"Why is he targeting Daniels?"

"It's a great question." Rem laid his head back. "I don't think Rudy likes him. Maybe it's because Daniels has the family Rudy lost, or maybe Daniels just gets under his skin. He tends to do that with certain people."

"What about Rudy's connection to Victor? Does this have something to do with all of this?" She picked at her label.

He glanced at her. Mikey didn't know yet that Rudy had visited Allison in jail, and he debated whether to tell her. "Hard to say."

She didn't respond.

"What's on your mind?"

"Nothing. Just wondering." She sipped her beer while the movie quietly played.

Rem chuckled. "Since when do you beat around the bush? What's bothering you?" He realized her concern for Daniels was obvious, but for her to show up on his doorstep at ten o'clock at night was unusual.

She picked at a couch cushion. "I just...I just remembered something else. You know...from that night when I saw Rudy at Victor's."

Rem studied her, noting her own weary features. "What's that?"

"I remember Victor liked the woman he'd pointed out to Rudy, too. He'd said she was pretty." She rubbed her head and fidgeted. "And it made me jealous. I didn't like her because of that, and when Victor suggested her to Rudy, I felt relief. He chose me over her because he liked me more, and it makes me ill to think about it." She stared off. "Who the hell was I back then?"

"You were a messed-up kid trying to figure it out, manipulated by a man who took advantage and hooked you up on drugs, which made it hard enough for you to stand straight, much less think straight. You shouldn't be so hard on yourself."

"I wish I could remember her name." She paused. "I've been dreaming about her."

"Is that why you look tired?"

She raised a brow at him. "Obviously, it shows."

"You can't possibly look any worse than me."

"You do look pretty bad."

He smiled. "I appreciate the honesty."

She stopped messing with the cushion. "Sorry. I came to check in on you and I'm talking all about me."

"It's okay. I'm used to it."

"I'm serious," she said, shoving him in the shoulder. "How are you? Any more letters or voicemails?"

Rem remembered the latest letter and hesitated. "Got one this afternoon."

"You did? What did it say?"

Rem considered how to answer. "It kindly suggested that everything that happened with Allison was my fault and I should do everyone a favor and shoot myself."

Her eyes rounded. "What? Who would send something like that?"

"There's a potential list of suspects. Rudy, Allison's attorney, or Allison herself, although that's unlikely. She probably directed one or the other to do it. Or it could be a crazy follower who's taking directions from one of the above."

"Like Margaret?"

Rem thought of Mikey's sister. "I guess that's possible, but she's locked up, so it makes it harder for her to send threatening mail." He sipped his beer, wishing he could forget the letter. "The theory is they're trying to scare me off from testifying against Allison, or make me look unstable enough to question my testimony. I'd been drugged when they had me, which is what her defense will use against me, so if they can push a few buttons and hope I go over the edge, that will help their case."

"They would go that far?"

"Allison's facing life in prison. That kind of goes against her mantra of living life to the fullest. If her or her attorney can discredit me, and maybe use Rudy to help, then it's a win-win for them."

"Rem. That's terrifying."

"Now you see why I don't sleep well, and why I didn't want to worry you." He thought back on his time with Victor's goons. "You, of all people, know what they're capable of."

"Rem, they almost killed you once. Don't you think they could try it again?"

He eyed the ceiling. "I can't stay in hiding, Mikey. I have a life to live and a job to do. Without it, I'd go stark raving mad."

"Have you ever considered selling insurance?"

He smiled softly. "It's crossed my mind once or twice, but I have to think of Daniels. He wouldn't survive two days without me."

Mikey reached over and took his wrist. "This scares the shit out of me. I don't want something to happen to you."

Rem sighed and considered the risks. "Listen. You need to be careful, too. I hadn't thought of this before, but as a former follower and friend of mine, they could use you against me." He patted her hand. "Maybe you and I should keep our distance for a while until things settle down."

She dropped her jaw. "I will not. I'm not going to let those crazies intimidate me."

"Now you know how I feel."

Mikey smirked, and he knew he'd successfully made his point. "It's tricky, isn't it?" he asked.

She put her beer on the coffee table. "How far do you go to protect yourself and the ones around you before you lose yourself in the process?"

"You let me know when you have the answer." He set his beer down next to hers and rested his head back against the couch.

"You're a tough nut, Remalla," she said.

He closed his eyes. "And you're a regular nutcracker." A punch hit him in the gut, and he groaned.

"You better be nice, or I'll eat all your popcorn while you sleep on the couch."

Feeling his fatigue get the best of him, he yawned. "My popcorn is your popcorn."

She stood and flipped off the TV. "It's late. You need to go take a hot shower and hit the bed. I need to go."

Rem cracked an eye open and saw her holding out a hand.

"Come on, sport," she said. "Or you'll fall asleep out here and regret it in the morning."

Not having the strength to argue, he took her hand, and she pulled him up. Getting his tired legs beneath him, he stared down at her. "You okay?" he asked.

"Are you?" she asked back.

He stared into her dark eyes, and the tiny diamond piercing in her nostril reflected in the lamplight. For a moment, he wanted to run his thumb down her cheek, but all the baggage he carried reared up and he allowed the moment to pass. "I'm doing the best I can." Her gaze held his, and he wondered what she was thinking.

"Me, too, Remalla. Me, too." She took his fingers and squeezed them. "Let's hope it's enough."

Chapter Thirteen

REM ENTERED THE SQUAD room the next morning, holding a cup of coffee he'd bought on the way in to work. Grateful he'd managed a decent night's sleep after the previous day's events and Mikey's visit, he eyed Daniels' empty desk. He put his cup down, slid off his jacket, and wondered where to start the day. Rudy was now wanted for criminal trespassing along with kidnapping, and Rem felt the urgency when he realized the next day would be day eight for Josh.

Groaning, he was about to sit when Lozano emerged from his office, holding his own cup of coffee, and approached his desk. "Remalla."

Rem straightened. "Hey, Cap."

"You get some rest? You look a little less like death."

"Thank you. Thought I'd try a little mousse in my hair this morning," he joked and ran a hand through his long locks. "What do you think?"

"It's too long."

Rem sighed. "Guess you're not impressed."

"You heard from Daniels?"

"He's at the airport, putting Marjorie and J.P. on a plane with Marjorie's mom. He's getting them out of town until this mess with Rudy blows over."

Lozano grunted. "I don't blame him. Last night was frightening."

"I agree," said Rem. "He should be here in an hour or two."

Lozano nodded. "I wanted to let you know. Kenneth Measy is coming by tomorrow."

Rem's chest tightened. "Allison's attorney? Why?"

"He wants to talk to me. I want you to be scarce. Don't give him an opportunity to approach you. You got that?"

"Why does he want to talk to you?"

"I'm sure he wants to warn me off about the inquiries I've made into Allison at the jail and threaten me about her mistreatment. He can stuff it where the sun don't shine." He sipped his coffee. "But I'm also sure he'll let me know just how slippery the state's case is, and how he intends to destroy you and Daniels on the stand."

Rem's stomach fell. "That's comforting."

"It's an intimidation tactic. By showing up here and telling me, he knows it'll get to you, and as a bonus, if he runs into you, he can throw it in your face. Don't give him the satisfaction. You'll likely be out anyway, looking for Josh, but just in case."

"I'll stay clear."

"Good." He eyed Rem's messy desk. "You planning on following up on more leads today?"

"Yeah. There's more to check. It's our last option. Let's hope something pans out, or I'm afraid Josh will have to endure Rudy's final test."

"If nothing else, Rudy will hopefully leave him somewhere like he did with Henry. At least we'd get him back alive."

"True. But I hate for the kid to endure any more than he has to."

"I don't like it either, but I'll take what we can get."

"I want to catch Rudy, too. If he's got more offspring, or if he has some involvement with Allison, I doubt we've seen the last of him."

"We deal with what we can, when we can, Remalla." Lozano shifted his hold on his coffee cup. "Sometimes, it's a waiting game. You do your best, let the game play out, and hope you're still standing at the end."

"I've come a little close to the not standing part."

"Maybe, but you're here, aren't you?" He tipped his head. "You're a survivor, Rem. You don't go down without a fight. You stick it out long enough, then eventually, the other side makes a mistake, and you've won. The question is, how long can you hang in there?"

"Depends on what they keep dishing out."

"You've dealt with a lot worse than letters and voicemails, and if it gets worse, we'll reevaluate. But for now, don't give in to these bastards. You're smarter and braver, and in my experience, that's what sticks in the end."

"Thanks, Cap. I hope you're right."

He smiled. "I'm always right, Remalla. Haven't you figured that out yet?" He raised his coffee. "Now, if I can just get my wife to believe that."

"Good luck. I hear that's a rare occurrence."

"I think the search for the Grail is easier." Lozano headed toward his office. "Keep me updated on your progress, and on Daniels."

"I will." Rem sat as Lozano disappeared into his office.

Drinking his coffee, Rem tried to organize his desk and figure out where to start. Rudy's call to Daniels had not been traced, so that was a dead end. There were no other leads to follow other than tips from the public, and Rem dug through those from a spreadsheet on his computer, careful not to investigate the ones already taken by other members on the task force.

Making some notes, he began to make a plan.

"Remalla." Rem looked to see Lozano sticking his head out of his office. "Come in here for a sec."

Rem stood and grabbed his coffee. He walked into Lozano's office. "What is it?"

"There's a dead body. I want you to check it out." He scribbled on a notepad.

Remalla almost choked on his drink. "Dead body? Cap, I'm knee deep with Rudy and Josh."

"I know that, but it's your neighbor."

Rem frowned. "What are you talking about?"

Lozano read an address from the paper. "That's your neighborhood, isn't it?"

Rem ran through the house numbers on his street. "I think it's the house across from me. There's a dead body?"

He handed Rem the paper. "Go check it out. Maybe it's a simple fall from a ladder or the guy's been ill, but if not, then it's just a little too coincidental it's near your home. I want to be sure we're not dealing with something related to this case."

Rem realized Lozano was thinking of Rudy. "You think this has something to do with what happened to Daniels last night?"

"I don't know. Which is why I want you to go. Let me know what you learn. Hopefully, it's nothing, and you can get back to Josh."

Rem nodded. "Okay. I'll go check it out." Eyeing the paper and keeping his coffee, he left the squad room.

••••••••••

Rem approached the scene and parked, seeing two officers standing out in front of the home that was indeed across from his own. Rem didn't know his neighbor well. The man who owned the house rented it out, and if Rem recalled, this renter had only been in it for a month. He stepped out of his car and walked over.

"Charlie," he said, recognizing one of the officers. "What do we have?"

Charlie stuck out a thumb. "He's in the back. You can go around the side."

Rem leaned over and saw a side fence with an open gate. "Thanks." He took the small rock pathway across the lawn, walked past the gate and into the backyard. Another officer stood beside a covered body lying in the grass. "Hey, Withers."

Withers looked up from his phone and put it away. "Hey Remalla." He gestured toward the body. "I hear he's your neighbor."

"Yeah. I live across the street." He stepped close. "Anything interesting?"

"Possibly. I've called Crime Scene. They should be here soon."

"Crime Scene? You obviously know something."

Withers nodded. "Body's cold, so he's been out here a while. He's in his bathrobe, so I'm guessing he came outside before going to bed. Maybe he needed some air."

"What's weird about that? Maybe he just collapsed." He recalled the last time he'd seen his neighbor. "Guy was probably in his late sixties. Maybe his ticker gave out."

"That's just it. I know you're looking for the kidnapped kid, and I've been keeping up. I heard about the kid's dad."

"Ben Lambert? What about him?"

Withers kneeled and lifted the covering. "Check out his chest."

Rem squatted beside Withers. His neighbor was lying on his back, eyes open, face white, with no visible injuries. His robe was splayed open, and Rem's gaze fell on the round, dark circle above his heart.

Withers pointed. "Isn't that what happened to Ben Lambert?"

••••••••••••

Daniels pushed open the door to the squad room and entered. Seeing Rem sitting in Lozano's office, he tossed his jacket in his desk chair and walked over. Lozano saw him and waved him in.

"Hey," he said, sitting in a seat beside Rem.

"How're Marjorie and J.P.?" asked Lozano.

"Good. They're fine. On a flight out of here. They're going to stay with Marjorie's grandfather in Arizona." He looked between Rem and Lozano. "But that's just between the three of us."

"I hear you," said Lozano. "I'm glad they're okay."

Daniels nodded and eyed Rem. "You have any luck finding that asshole?"

"I wish." Rem's shoulders fell. "Although I think we have a new lead."

"What's that?" asked Daniels.

"My neighbor across the street is dead."

"Well, that's unfortunate," said Daniels. "But how is that related?"

Rem sat back with a huff. "Because he's got a nice round circle on his chest, right above his sternum. Coroner's got the body. I asked her to rush the exam, but I suspect she'll say it was his heart."

"Just like Ben Lambert," added Lozano.

Daniels pursed his lips. "So, Rudy's running around my place yesterday, and then he kills your neighbor? Why?"

Rem shrugged. "My guess? The neighbor was an accident. He went outside for some air, or maybe he heard something, and stumbled upon someone that he wasn't supposed to. And got killed because of it."

Daniels sat back. "That sounds way too careless for Rudy. Killing a neighbor draws more attention to him. And Rudy is a planner. He doesn't do anything without it being intentional."

"You sound like you've got a good read on this guy," said Lozano. "But Rudy is just as capable of making a mistake as anyone else."

"Why is he at your neighbor's, though?" Daniels asked Rem.

"I've been thinking about that," said Rem. "The owner of that house rents it out. It's only been occupied for a month. What if Rudy thought it was empty?"

"A simple look through the window should verify it wasn't," said Daniels.

"Or Rudy was in the yard." Rem shifted in his seat, "and watching my place, but the neighbor interrupted."

"You think he's watching your house after walking through mine? He's a busy guy," said Daniels.

"You got any better ideas?" asked Lozano. "Who else would it be that could leave a mark like that?"

Daniels leaned over and rubbed his face. The terror of the previous night had relented a little, but he could still hear Marjorie's frightened voice on the phone. The fear he'd felt on the frenzied drive to his home still curdled his stomach, and he'd barely slept in the hotel room. Every noise had made him jump, and the thought of how close he'd come to losing his family made his fury grow. He clenched his fingers together at the memory. "Sorry, Cap. I don't know. I'm still not thinking straight."

"You need the rest of the day?" asked Rem.

Restless, Daniels stood. "No. I don't need the rest of the day. I want to catch this guy." He curled his hands into fists. "And when I do..."

Lozano pointed at him. "Daniels, if you can't handle this case without being a vigilante, you're officially off of it." He glared. "You go off half-cocked with revenge on your mind, then no good defense attorney worth his salt won't use that against us. You got that?" He sat back. "We've got enough to handle with Measy. Let's not add more to the pile."

Daniels put his hands on his hips. "Cap, that man went after my family—"

"And your partner here knows all about that. You're not the only one who's felt the sick and gut-wrenching fear of loss. Be thankful you got to them safely, but remember, you're a cop first."

Daniels kicked at his chair, but knew Lozano was right. He'd only scratched the surface of what his partner had endured. He had to pull it together.

"Just because I've been through hell doesn't make yours any easier," said Rem. "Let's not compare stories. What you went through is terrifying. Don't discount it just because you think I've been through worse. None of this is easy."

Daniels huffed and sat. “No. Cap’s right. But I just can’t stop thinking that they could have…” He hung his head, unable to finish the sentence. “I’ll get it together.”

“Good,” said Lozano. “And when you do, go out there and find this guy. But on this side of the law, not the other.” His phone rang. “I’ve got to take this. You let me know your plan when you have one.”

Daniels almost chuckled, and Rem raised a brow.

“Go on. Get moving. None of us, including Rudy, is getting any younger,” said Lozano, and he answered the phone.

Chapter Fourteen

Rem refilled his coffee cup from the pot behind his desk. "You got any ideas on where to start with this plan of ours?"

Daniels sat and tapped some papers on his desk. "If we're right about your neighbor, then Rudy's been hanging around your place. Why?"

"Probably for the same reason he's hanging around yours. To spook me." Rem returned the pot and sat.

"If he hadn't killed the neighbor, you wouldn't have known he was there. How does that spook you?" He raised a hand. "And where's Josh in all of this? Who's watching him while Rudy's running through my backyard, and your neighbor's?"

Rem straightened. "You think he has help?"

Daniels leaned in. "Maybe." He stared off. "If that's true, then maybe someone's watching Josh while Rudy runs his errands. Or Rudy sends this helper off to do whatever dirty work he needs done."

"Like keeping an eye on me?"

"It's possible. If your neighbor died during the night, that's plenty of time for Rudy, or whoever, to get from my place to yours, assuming it was the same person."

"Marjorie said it was Rudy."

"And maybe it was, or maybe it was someone who looked like him. Hard to tell in the dark."

Rem thought through the events of the previous evening. "If it wasn't Rudy at my place, then there's somebody else out there who has this weird electrokinesis."

Daniels' face fell. "You think Rudy's got another kid mixed up in this?"

"Maybe one who didn't get out, and Rudy took in and trained."

"Holy hell." Daniels held his head.

Rem thought of Mikey, and knew he'd have to tell her to be careful and stay aware. He wondered if whoever had killed his neighbor had seen her on his porch. Thankfully, it had been dark, and his porch light had been off. "We may be wrong. It could have been Rudy."

"Or we may be right." Daniels furrowed his brow. "What does your gut tell you?"

Rem put his coffee down, feeling slightly nauseated. "My gut and I haven't exactly been friends lately. I tend to puke when I'm anxious, and I'm tired of wasting food." He wiggled his mouse, and his screen brightened on his computer. He flipped to his email, seeing an unread one. "Not that it matters either way. We still don't have a direction to go in, accomplice or not."

"What about looking for missing kids that never turned up?"

"From where and what age? Male or female?" asked Rem. "I don't know about you, but I don't intend to still be on this case ten years from now."

Daniels blew out a deep breath. "Yeah. I know."

Rem opened his unread email and froze. "Daniels."

"It can't hurt to check, though. At least in this area. They'd be an adult now, so we could go back maybe ten years. Maybe something will turn up."

"No. Look." Rem's heart raced, and he swiveled his monitor around.

Daniels frowned and leaned in. His eyes widened, and he read the email aloud. "The Light will be extinguished by the dark. Be prepared to face the evil you created. The light will only live until the dark chooses. Your only hope is for you to decide whether to extinguish the light first." He sat back. "Shit. Now it's coming by email."

Rem swiveled the monitor back. "That's good news."

"Why is that good?"

"Because there's a return address."

Daniels stood and walked over. "Where?"

Rem pointed. "It's from Golden State Psychiatric Hospital."

Daniels' jaw dropped. "Margaret Redstone."

"Yeah," said Rem. "Margaret Redstone."

....

"I don't like this." Daniels pulled into the parking spot outside the psychiatric hospital. "You should stay in the car. I'll go talk to her."

"I'm not sitting in the car," said Rem. "I need to be there."

"No. You don't." Daniels shut off the engine. "You know what she'll say. She's unstable. One look at you and she'll go off."

"Maybe that's exactly what we need. For her to go off. If she's been talking to someone, she may let it slip."

"We can't exactly get in her face. This will be recorded. It could be used against you at trial."

"What do you think I'm going to do? Strangle her? Although it's tempting, I doubt they'll let us close enough."

Daniels gripped the steering wheel. "Have you stopped to think that maybe this is exactly what Measy wants? To get you here, and have you talk to her?"

"We're investigating a case. We're doing our jobs. How can he use that against me? If Margaret Redstone has been in touch with Rudy, and you know it's possible she has, then we need to talk to her. She may very well know where Josh is."

"Now you're getting a little too far from shore. You know anything she says, we have to take with a grain of salt."

"And so will any jury I face. She's in here for a reason."

Daniels shook his head. "You heard what Mikey said about when she visited."

"And I read the email. I've got the general idea about what to expect."

"It's one thing to read or listen to it. It's another to talk about and confront it, especially with someone who was there when you were taken. Next to Allison, this is as close as you can get to facing what happened to you."

Rem shifted in his seat to face him. "What do you think I'm gonna have to do when Allison goes to trial, huh? I'm going to have to stare her in the face and talk about it to a room full of people. I might as well yank off the training wheels and see how I do."

"Rem...there will be preparation for that. You have no prep for this. You're walking in there cold turkey."

Rem sighed and rested an elbow on the door. "I can't sit here and do nothing. I have to deal with this, and you know my presence is the key. We need her to get emotional. What's the point if you're the only one who goes in and nothing happens?"

"She knows my connection to you. She'll use that. And this woman is never quiet. I'll doubt she'll stop talking now."

Rem slumped against the seat. "I know you're trying to protect me, and I appreciate that, but maybe the time for protection has passed." He looked over. "I've been haunted by this for months, and if I don't do this, I think that only continues. Maybe it's time to face the boogeyman instead of running from it."

Daniels closed his eyes and opened them. "Rem, you have nightmares almost every night. You have PTSD and flashbacks. The mere mention of Allison's name makes you ill, and I know you're still sleeping with the lights on." He raised a hand. "And now you want to confront Margaret

Redstone, who, for all you know, could be in on all of this. I think you can understand why I think this visit might make things worse."

Rem held his stare. "Or maybe it could make things better." He hesitated. "But I won't know until I walk in there and find out."

Frustrated, Daniels debated what to do, but knew when his partner had made up his mind. "You do this, and you can't show the slightest weakness. One wince, sigh, or worried look, and she'll sense blood in the water. This lady doesn't play games."

"I can play it tough." He bounced his knee. "Besides, you can tell when I'm clinging to the end of the rope. You'll get me out of there."

"Not necessarily. This is going to require you and me both to play it tough. If she senses my concern for you, she'll exploit that. One sideways glance, and she'll go in for the kill. You know these Redstones and their funny gifts. If you're right, and she made those creepy statues that got to me and Georgios, God knows what else she can do." He tapped a finger on his knee and thought about it. "We need a safe word."

Rem knitted his brow. "A what?"

"You know. A word you can say that tells me you're done. And then we'll get out. Any ideas?"

"You're serious?"

"Do I look like I'm kidding?" He waved a finger. "C'mon. Use that wacky brain of yours to think of something."

Rem stared for a second and then exhaled. "Okay. Okay. A safe word. Let me think." He closed his eyes. "Um...I don't know...how about a Lone Ranger reference?"

Daniels raised a brow. "The Lone Ranger?"

"What's wrong with that?"

"I just figured you go for John Wayne instead, or maybe zombies."

"Would you prefer John Wayne or zombies?"

"No. The Masked Man will do." Daniels popped the door open. "C'mon, Tonto."

•••••••••••

Rem showed his ID and signed in along with Daniels. They relinquished their weapons, and a woman behind the desk took them. "You can pick them up on the way out." She locked them in a drawer beside her. "Barry will take you back to the visitor's room. Please be aware that your meeting will be recorded and supervised. Do not make physical contact with the patient and be aware that she will be handcuffed. Her history of violence requires it. You'll have up to one hour with her."

Rem swallowed, wondering how he'd handle ten minutes. A buzzing sound made him jump, and the door beside them opened, and a man appeared with a big smile. "I'm Barry." He widened the door. "C'mon back."

Daniels gave Rem a look. "You're sure about this? You can still back out."

Rem patted his partner's arm, straightened, and threw on a steely persona. "I'm ready. Let's do this."

Daniels nodded. "Okay."

They followed Barry down a long white hall with a tiled white floor. The muffled sounds of yelling echoed down the corridor, and Rem couldn't help but think of the insane asylums from the movies. Crazed patients with wild hair and spittle flying from their lips made him shrivel, and he mumbled at himself to stay focused. If his nerves got the better of him, this interview would be over before it started.

They passed a small room where an old TV played a grainy black and white movie. A man sat on a couch and stared off, his eyes dull and glassy. A woman sat in a chair beside him, looking as if she was knitting something, but when Rem looked closer, he could see her knitting needles were straws and her yarn was a piece of string.

His heart thudded, but he kept going, until Barry stopped outside a door.

"Just wait in here," he said. "Someone will bring her in. You sit on one side of the table, and she'll be on the other. The person who brings her will remain in the room. Cameras will be watching, and no contact with the patient."

"No problem there," said Rem.

Daniels offered him one last glance and Rem sucked in a breath and followed him in.

The room was the same white tile as the hallway, with a rectangular metal table in the middle. One chair sat on one side of the table and two chairs were on the other. There was nothing else in the room.

The door closed behind them and everything went quiet, until they heard a clang and a buzz, and then another door across from them opened, and a large man with a bald head and arms the size of a bodybuilder's walked in, guiding a small woman with long, black, straight hair, wearing a blue jumpsuit, and her hands cuffed in front of her. Her eyes widened when she saw them, and their icy blue color instantly transported Rem back to that night on the slab, the torches blazing, with Allison hovering over him, a knife gleaming in her hand, and Margaret grabbing his hair.

The memory almost caused him to falter, and he realized Daniels may have been right. This might be too much, too soon. He thought about the Lone Ranger, but then he told himself to stay calm. She was just a woman in handcuffs, sitting at a table. She couldn't hurt him.

He stayed where he was and leaned against the far wall. Daniels didn't look at him, and Rem knew why. They had to play this with no hint of emotion.

Once Margaret was in her seat, Daniels walked over, pulled out the chair, and sat across from her. The large man who'd brought Margaret returned to the door and stood beside it.

"Margaret Redstone?" asked Daniels. Margaret didn't even look at him. Her gaze remained on Rem. "I'd make the introductions, but I think you know who we are. We'd like to ask you a few questions."

Rem stayed against the wall and met her look. His heart was thumping, chill bumps broke out on his skin, and he made a significant effort to act unaffected.

Daniels raised a hand and waved it in front of her. "Hello? Margaret? You there?"

She made no response.

"We want to talk to you about Rudy Halpern. You know him?"

Her gaze remained on Rem.

"You emailed my partner." He gestured toward Rem. "You care to tell us why? Did someone ask you to do that?"

No response.

"Have you had any communication with Allison Albright? Or any of Victor's followers?"

She blinked and finally spoke. "I don't want to talk to you. I want to talk to him."

Hearing her gravely, deep voice, Rem remembered it, and how in his drugged state, he'd thought it had sounded like a low growl. It had scared the hell out of him. All he wanted to do was head for the door, but he walked forward and took the seat beside Daniels instead. "You want to talk to me?"

Her eyes narrowed, and she smiled. Her bright teeth glimmered in the fluorescent light of the room. "I dreamed of you. I knew you'd come."

Rem slapped a flat stare on his face. "Your dreams are way better than mine."

"You are the light."

"I'm not as light as you may think. Especially nowadays." He sat straight. "Did you send me the email?"

"The dark is near. Do you know that? You must feel it."

"Who is the dark?" asked Daniels.

She looked at Daniels for the first time. "You cannot save him. No one can." She looked back at Rem. "You'll have to save yourself, if you have the courage."

"I'm doing just fine," said Rem. "I won't be taking your, Allison's, or any other kook's advice. I plan on hanging around for a while."

Margaret stared, barely blinking, which unnerved Rem. "And that is why you are the light." She leaned in, and Rem had to force himself not to pull back. "But you are not as strong as you think. I know your weakness." Her voice lowered. "I sense it."

"That's not hard, lady," said Daniels. "Everybody knows he eats like a goat and dresses like one, too." His tone sharpened. "And just because you're sitting there with your crazy eyes and spooky voice doesn't provide you with any more knowledge about him or anyone else." He put a hand on the table. "So stop the insanity performance, because we're not the judge and jury. I think you know something. Who is Rudy Halpern?"

Leaning back, she smiled. "You know Rudy?" Her laughter bounced off the walls. "Rudy is a lost man. Driven by pain and hammered by remorse. He is as dark as Victor was, and his soul cannot be reclaimed." She closed her hands into fists and her handcuffs clinked together. "I was his once. I know his demons, and I know his fury." Her eyes darted between Rem and Daniels. "If he has targeted you, then you will die." She met Rem's look. "Unless Allison tells him otherwise. And if she has, then you will only suffer instead."

"I don't buy for one second that Rudy takes his direction from anyone," said Daniels. "He does whatever the hell he wants."

"Rudy is a man," she said with a sneer. "He can be manipulated just as any man can."

"Rudy has taken a boy," said Daniels. "His name is Josh, and he's eleven years old. If you know where Rudy is keeping him, you need to tell us."

She moaned and closed her eyes. "The boy is not the first and likely not the last. I know of Rudy's desires. He longs to pass his gifts to another. Victor helped him do that. But now Victor is gone." She opened her eyes. "Rudy will not be found. Until he wants to be."

"How did Victor help Rudy?" asked Daniels. Margaret didn't answer, and Daniels tried again. "Where would Rudy take Josh?"

Ignoring Daniels, she tipped her head and widened her eyes at Rem. "Have you spoken to Mikey?"

Rem did his best to not show any discomfort. "Yes. I know you spoke to her, too."

"She thinks she can save you, but she cannot." She cackled loudly, and Rem's heart raced. "She likes you. Do you like her?"

"I didn't come here to talk about Mikey," said Rem, and then regretted his words.

Margaret grinned. "You want her, don't you? You want to feel her body beneath yours. I know how that feels. I dream of you, beneath me." She let go of a long, slow breath. "It is most pleasurable."

Rem almost yelled *Hi-yo Silver*, but scowled instead. "Listen up, Margaret." He gripped the edge of the table to keep his hands from shaking. "You can sit there and try to freak me out with all your psychobabble and convince everyone around you, including your family, that you're too demented to have a conversation, much less stand trial, but you forget. I was there. I saw you with Allison. You weren't crazy. You were pissed. She had the power and Victor's ear. Victor listened to her, not you. You made the crazy statues to impress him, and you knew exactly what you were doing. You may have a few screws loose, and you apparently can't seem to find your way without having some powerful, pathetic man to guide you, but you're not clinically insane. You're ambitious." He glowered at her. "You think Rudy's manipulated? Well, maybe you ought to look in the mirror. You're just spewing what Allison's shoveling, but I suspect when Allison goes to prison that you'll want to pick up any debris Allison leaves behind, whether it's me, Rudy, Mikey, or anyone else. Good luck with that, though, because your ass isn't going anywhere either. So direct that freaky gaze of yours somewhere else, because I'm not impressed."

Daniels sat quietly and crossed his arms, and Margaret's gaze never wavered from Rem's. He steeled himself for her response.

Her piercing gaze bore through him, and she put her arms up on the table, her handcuffs clanging on the metal. "You forget as well, Detective. I was there, too. I was first in line, ready to partake of your offering. I saw you lying on that stone, your body tied, your breathing labored, and begging for release. I saw her slice the knife down your skin, and the tears run from your eyes." She rested her chin in her hands. "The fear pulsing from you was electric. My body hummed in response. I wanted you, and would have taken you right there, in front of everyone." She sighed and smiled. "What do you think I dream of, every night, when I'm alone in my bed?"

Rem swallowed and tried not to react.

"You may be right," she said. "Maybe I'm not insane. But you better hope they never let me out of here, because if they do, I look forward to finding you. Your fear turns me on, Detective. It's turning me on right now." She slid her hands across the metal, her fingers wide, and offered an evil grin. "I'll be imagining you tonight, on this table, your hands bound, and your chest bloody, begging for mercy, and I'll scream your name, over and over." She chuckled softly, and it slowly became an ugly laugh. "Will you dream of me, too, Detective? Will you tell me you want me, like you did Allison?"

Rem's stomach lurched, and Daniels stood. "You heard enough, Tonto?"

Rem found it difficult to move. "Yeah, Kemosabe. I've heard enough."

"Good. Then let's go." Daniels took Rem's arm, and Rem pushed up, trying not to grab the table for balance.

"Tell Mikey and Mason I said hello." Margaret sat back, her grin still wide. "I haven't forgotten about them either." She eyed Daniels. "And good luck in your search for Rudy. If you have any chance of stopping him, you'll have to find him before he finds you." She stretched in her seat. "Preparation is key, don't you think?" Her gaze fell on Rem. "Sweet dreams."

Daniels guided Rem out of the room. Barry appeared and shut the door behind them. "I'll show you out," he said. "I hope your visit was productive."

"That's one way of putting it," said Daniels.

Rem wondered if he was as pale as Daniels. Focusing on putting one foot in front of the other, he made it back to the front desk. Signing out, his vision swirled, and everything began to close in on him. Eyeing the exit door, he mumbled to the woman who'd signed them in. "Just give my gun to him." He looked at Daniels. "I'll be outside." He ran down the hall, slammed the door open, and rushed out into the fresh air. Breathing deeply, he laid a hand on the wall and hung his head, hearing Margaret's cackle in his ears. He spotted a nearby bench and went to sit on it. Dropping his head between his knees, he closed his eyes and took more deep breaths. His vision stopped swirling and holding his head, he felt someone sit beside him.

"How you doing?"

Rem opened his eyes to see Daniels sitting on the bench. "You gonna tell me I told you so?"

"It's tempting." He exhaled his own deep breath. "But I hate to kick a man when he's down."

"I appreciate that." Seeing his fingers shake, he curled his fingers into fists. "Guess I'm not as strong as I think."

"You're the strongest person I know. Most would have never done what you just did." Daniels held out Rem's weapon.

Rem took it and holstered it. "Yeah, well. It didn't go as I'd hoped. She won."

"For now. But she's got the upper hand. She's insane, or at least pretending to be, and you're not."

Rem rubbed his eyes. "How the hell am I going to get through a trial? That Measy is going to make mincemeat out of me."

"You'll be ready. Consider this practice. Hell, if you can do this, you can do anything."

"I'm not too sure." He dropped his hand. "That guy just needs one screw up on my part, and Allison could go free."

"You're worrying too much. We've got Allison dead to rights. Between you, me and the couple of followers who are going to testify against her, she'll never see the outside of a cell. I don't care how dirty Measy gets. He can only go so far."

"Far is a long way."

"If any of his misconduct gets tracked back to him, then he'll be disbarred. I'll make sure of it."

"Something tells me he's good at covering his tracks." Feeling more centered, Rem sat back against the bench.

"He keeps going, and it's bound to catch up to him. This case is big, and the media is all over it. He wants to win because of the attention it will bring him. But it could be his downfall. His ambition, like Margaret's, will ultimately ruin him."

"I can see Mr. Positivity is back in business."

"You know it."

Rem looked over. "How are you feeling? You were looking a little green in there yourself."

"She's quite the lovely lady. I wanted to puke on her jumpsuit."

Rem's memories flashed. "Her eyes and that voice. It took me right back to that night. I almost didn't make it." He rubbed his stomach.

"But you did." He leaned over and rested his elbows on his knees. "What did you make of her comments about Rudy?"

Rem tried to remember what Margaret had said. "It's obvious she knows him. She said she was his. I'm guessing that was during her time with Victor."

"Maybe Victor handed her off to Rudy just like that woman at the bonfire."

"It sounds like they spent more than one night together. She said Rudy is eager to pass off his gifts to someone else, which sounds to me like Henry and Josh aren't the only ones he's victimized."

"Our theory may be accurate. Someone's helping Rudy."

"Who though? Could it be another child he raised, or did he find someone to take under his wing?"

"I don't know, but it's another threat we'll have to be conscious of." Daniels paused. "What she said at the end was curious."

"Yeah. It was a little cryptic. We'll have to find him before he finds us."

"And to prepare. But prepare for what?" Daniels sat back. "I can't figure it out. Is Rudy working for Allison, Measy, or for himself? Is he a threat to us, or does he just want to scare us off?"

"Maybe he sees it as killing two birds with one stone. Allison calls him in, tells him to mess with me, and maybe you too, hoping to intimidate us and prevent or damage our testimony in order to protect Allison, but that doesn't stop him from taking Josh, and imagine his surprise when we're the ones assigned to the case."

"Works out well for him," said Daniels. "By messing with us, it also hinders us from finding Josh."

"Except he screws up, gets overconfident, and loses his picture of him and Sam. He gets pissed at you for taking it, goes after Marjorie and takes a family photo from you. An eye for an eye."

"Meanwhile, his associate, whoever he or she is, helps with Josh, and maybe keeps tabs on you in the meantime, so Rudy is always in the loop."

Rem nodded. "Makes a pretty picture, doesn't it?"

"The question is, how does it end? What's his plan?"

Feeling stronger, Rem stood, shook out his hands, and stretched his neck. "You think he still wants his picture back?"

"I'm sure he does." Daniels stood as well.

"Then my guess? He does whatever the hell he wants. Maybe he pretends to appease Allison because it serves him in case she goes free. But when it comes down to it, Allison's in jail and he's not, and what Rudy wants, Rudy gets."

"Which means he's not going anywhere."

"It's just a matter of when he strikes again."

Daniels eyed the ground, his face serious. "Then maybe we need to talk."

Rem raised a brow. "About what?"

"Doing exactly what Margaret said." He looked up, his face somber. "Preparing."

Chapter Fifteen

CAPTAIN FRANK LOZANO SAT in his office and hung up the phone. Tired and hungry, he opened his drawer and pulled out a granola bar. He tore off the wrapper, leaned back in his chair, and took a bite. He thought of the last solid meal he'd eaten. It had been chicken and roasted vegetables, which his wife Sheila had left in the fridge for him two nights ago. Since then, it had been sandwiches or salads from the cafeteria, or nothing at all. He was running on empty, much like his detectives.

Chewing the bar, he eyed the squad room through his glass window and saw Daniels and Remalla sitting at their desks. Remalla was on the phone, taking notes while Daniels did the same. They'd recently returned from visiting Margaret Redstone at the state's psychiatric unit, and Lozano wondered for the millionth time whether that had been wise. While he understood the need to track down every lead that could help them locate Josh Lambert, he also realized the stress his detectives were under.

Acutely aware of the trauma Daniels and Remalla had experienced at D'Mato's hands, and considering Rudy's involvement with Allison, Lozano wondered how much more his two men could endure. But he also reminded himself that they were smart and courageous and, despite the peril to themselves, they'd continued to pursue Rudy. It's what made them good cops. He had to respect their decision, but also ensure their personal feelings remained on the sidelines. It was a thin line when it came to chasing a bad guy and protecting your loved ones, and when one threatened another, the line became that much thinner.

Because of that, he kept a close eye on them, determined to protect them from their own demons, no matter how hard that might be, even if it meant taking them off the case. When it came down to it, he was responsible for their well-being and he'd choose protecting his men over any perp or victim, as hard as that might be, and even if his detectives disagreed.

Taking the last bite of his bar, Lozano sat up and tossed the wrapper in the trash. Needing to stretch his legs, he stood and left his office, looking for an update.

He approached Remalla's desk, who was still on the phone, and spoke to Daniels. "How's it going? Anything new since you saw Margaret Redstone?"

"Well, there's not much to report on Josh," said Daniels. "There were a couple of leads, but they fell through. Titus and Georgios are out following up on another possible, so we'll see. The tip line is slowing, and we're hacking away at the ones remaining. Maybe we'll get lucky. Beyond that, we're basically waiting and hoping Rudy releases Josh."

Rem hung up and waved a paper. "Guess what I found on Margaret."

Daniels sighed. "That she and Rudy are still in touch, and you tracked her history back to an address where you found Rudy and Josh hiding out?"

"Well, that would be nice, but no." He put the paper down. "Margaret's had a few visitors during her stay. Mikey, Mason, and their big brother Max have gone to see her."

"We expected that," said Daniels.

"But there's also a fourth visitor. A woman."

"You get an ID?" asked Lozano.

Rem eyed his notes. "A Wendy Wilson. ID appears to be false. But whoever this lady is, she visited with Margaret last month for forty-five minutes."

"Where's the video of her visit?" asked Daniels.

"That's the problem. There isn't one. System crashed that day. Nothing was recorded. They don't even have a picture."

"That's the same thing that happened with Rudy at the jail," said Lozano.

"What are the odds of that?" asked Daniels.

Rem picked up his coffee. "Our theory is looking more like fact. Rudy has a friend."

"A friend who visited Margaret Redstone," said Lozano. He eyed the water dispenser and walked over to it. "That's troubling," he said, helping himself to some water.

"Damn. I wish we'd known that sooner," said Daniels. "We could have asked Margaret about it."

Rem shrugged. "You honestly think she would have told us anything useful?"

"Probably not, but it would have been interesting to see her reaction."

Rem shrugged. "I don't think she's fazed by anything. She probably would have just laughed at us."

Lozano sipped his water and returned to Rem's desk. "What about a description? Anybody remember what this woman looked like?"

"They're working on it," replied Rem. "It's been a month, and they need to get in touch with the people that were on duty that day. Said they'd let me know."

"What about the email you received?" asked Lozano. "Did they mention how Margaret was able to contact you?"

Rem snorted. "Apparently, patients have access to a computer for up to an hour a day. But internet usage is highly restricted and monitored. They're not sure how Margaret was able to access the facility's email account, but they'll do some digging and see what they can find out."

Daniels scowled. "Translation. You'll never hear from them again. They don't want to admit they screwed up."

"That's my guess," said Rem. "Unless I keep pushing. Or get another email."

"Figures," said Daniels.

"Give me the info," said Lozano. "I'll see if I can do a little of my own digging and get some answers."

Rem handed his paper to Lozano. "It's all yours, Cap. Good luck." He tossed his other notes into a pile. "So, for now, we're back to square one. We need to get out there and keep looking for Josh."

Daniels added his own notes into a folder and closed it. "Yeah. I know, but it's been a long ass day, especially for you. Are you up for it?"

"If Josh is still out there, then we need to keep on it. You're beat, too, after your day yesterday."

"It sucks, but you two will just have to hold each other up," said Lozano. "Let's pray Josh is released soon."

"Okay." Daniels, standing. "I've got some places to start. Let's go."

"I'll make some phone calls on this," said Lozano, holding up the paper. "I'll let you know if I can move things along."

"Thanks, Cap." Remalla stood and reached for his jacket when his phone rang. He hesitated, but tossed his jacket back in his seat. "Let's hope this is good news, because I'm tired of bad."

"Let's hope," said Daniels.

Lozano took his water and the paper and headed back to his office.

••••••••••

Rem answered. "Remalla."

He heard a chuckle and some breathing. "Ring-a-ding-ding, Detective. I heard you visited a friend of mine today."

Rem clenched the phone and snapped his fingers at Daniels. Daniels' eyes widened, and he grabbed for his own phone. Rem took a steady breath. "Rudy?"

"You win the magic money. Too bad I can't give it to you."

"Do you have any money?"

"More than you'd think."

His mind racing, Rem closed his eyes. Opening them, he saw Lozano return and stand beside Daniels' desk. "To what do I owe the pleasure?" asked Rem.

Rudy chuckled. "Your partner is irritatingly uncooperative. I thought I'd try you next."

"He tends to be that way when you threaten his family."

"If he'd have worked with me, it never would have happened. I'm a reasonable man, Detective. If I'd wanted them dead, they'd be dead. Your partner needed to learn a lesson."

"And what's that?" asked Rem.

"That he needs to grease the wheels."

"He did. He made you an offer. You want the picture. We want Josh. That still stands." Rem heard a buzz travel through the line and almost held the phone away from his ear. "You still there?"

The buzz softened, and Rudy returned. "You understand loss, Detective. You can empathize. Your partner can't." He paused. "Plus, I have some knowledge of where you stand right now, where you've been, and where you're going. I find myself in a unique position to help...or to hurt."

Rem went still. Was Rudy referring to his meeting with Allison? "We've done a little checking ourselves. We know your connection to Victor D'Mato."

"And I know yours. It appears we have a little in common."

"I wouldn't go that far."

"You know Allison, don't you? In the biblical sense? Seems we have that much to reminisce on."

Rem gritted his teeth. "Let's just cut to the chase. What do you want?"

"A couple of things. I want my picture. You want Sam. We're getting to the end of our journey here, and Sam is well on his way in his studies. He's an apt pupil. But before I walk away into the sunset, I need to finish a few things."

"You have to release Josh unharmed."

"That's always been my plan. I wouldn't harm Sam."

"No dead people, either, Rudy. He can't hurt anyone."

"That I can't promise. But I have one ace up my sleeve. You return the photo by the end of today, and I'll walk away."

Rem eyed Daniels, who hung up and dialed another number. "How does that help us?"

"You'll get Sam. Tomorrow, if all unfolds properly. I'll consider my debts to Allison paid and fade into the sunset. But, if you want to play hardball, I'll hang out for a while...and help out an old friend."

Rem's head pounded with tension. "What are you trying to tell me?"

"I'm telling you, there is a very simple solution to all of this. I'll go away once I have the photo. If I stick around, I might as well keep busy. Allison made a few requests. Let's just say she has ample reason to avoid a prison term."

"That's why you're calling, then? To threaten me?"

"To assist you. Daniels didn't listen. Maybe you will."

"I'm a cop, Rudy," said Rem. "I don't make deals with the Devil."

"Being a cop got you into this mess. Maybe you should consider another line of work."

"We want Josh alive and well, and no dead bodies along the way. You do that, and I'll get you the picture."

Rudy paused, and that strange buzzing returned. Rem's skin prickled.

"I'd hoped you'd be smarter, but I get it. You show strength to ensure your colleagues don't question your competence. It's the curse of those affected by trauma." Rem heard a crackle and a pop. "That's your choice, but I'll pass along a message," said Rudy, his voice distant. "You have an out when you're ready."

Rem held the bridge of his nose. "What are you talking about?" He knew Daniels had the location and had dispatched officers, but Rudy seemed in no hurry to get off the phone.

"She wants to see you."

Rem's chest tightened. "Who?" he whispered.

"Allison."

He almost laughed. "The hell that's going to happen."

"Since I'm hanging around, you may want to reconsider." He paused. "She's planning on it."

Rem hung his head, tired of the mind games. "Listen, you son-of-a-bitch. I don't care what she thinks she's planning, but whatever it is, it's going to fail. I'm going to be at that trial, ready to testify, and I look forward to looking her in the eye and saying adios as they take her away for a long, long time. The stupid intimidation games aren't going to work. It's only pissing me off."

"That's too bad. Just remember. I gave you a choice."

"You can take your choices and shove 'em. And you'll be lucky if you get that picture back. You had *your* shot. Maybe Daniels and I will roast marshmallows, and we'll stick that picture in between a piece of chocolate and a damn graham cracker."

Lozano's brow furrowed.

"Careful, Detective," said Rudy.

Rem's outrage erupted. "No. I'm tired of being careful. You better release Josh safe and sound, and free from harm, because if you don't, that picture burns and there won't be any safe place for you to hide. And I'll make sure your pretty face gets slapped in front of every media camera from sea to shining sea."

There was a brief silence. "I'll be in touch, Detective. You have a pleasant night."

Rem's anger bubbled over. "And you can go fuck yourself." He heard a click, and he slammed down the phone.

Lozano's face remained flat, but his eyes spoke volumes. He spoke to Daniels. "Anything?"

Daniels held the phone to his ear. "The trace leads to an old grocery store. Closed for business. It's an empty parking lot, but they're checking the scene."

Rem stood and paced. "Shocking."

They waited until Daniels spoke into the phone again and hung up. "Place is empty. Nothing. But they'll keep looking."

Lozano looked between the two of them. "Both of you. In my office."

Rem groaned as Lozano walked away. Daniels walked up beside him. "Sorry," said Rem. "I lost my cool."

"Don't be sorry about that. Be sorry you did it in front of Lozano."

"Yeah. Me and my timing."

They walked into Lozano's office, and Daniels closed the door. Rem paced along the far wall and Daniels stood beside Lozano's desk.

"You want to tell me exactly what that was?" asked Lozano, sitting in his chair.

Rem massaged his neck. "Sorry, Cap. I lost it."

Lozano narrowed his eyes. "You had a suspect on the line who's holding a kidnapped child, and the one thing we've got to keep him going, you threaten to destroy, and then you tell him to fuck off?"

Rem huffed and leaned against the wall. "It seemed like a good idea at the time."

"In his defense, Cap, Rudy's a button pusher," said Daniels.

"And you're both cops. You're supposed to be above that," answered Lozano. "You're supposed to be better than him."

"That man threatened Daniels' family, and now he's threatening me." Rem pushed off the wall. "Said if I didn't agree to return the picture, that basically he'd hang around and I'd be sorry. Then he said when I've had enough, my only option was to visit Allison."

"What? He wants you to visit Allison?" asked Daniels.

"No. *She* wants me to visit. She wants to see me." Rem crossed his arms. "That's when I told him what he could do with his picture."

"I don't blame you," said Daniels. "I'd have told him the same."

Lozano glared. "Then you force me to reconsider whether to keep you on this case."

Rem dropped his jaw. "What?"

Lozano sat back in his seat. "I don't think you can be objective. I questioned whether it was too soon to bring you back. I gave you the lighter cases, but when Josh disappeared, it was all hands on deck. But now, with Rudy and his connection to Allison, you talking to Margaret Redstone and flying off the handle with Rudy, I'd be stupid not to realize that this may be too much."

Rem stomped up to Lozano's desk. "You can't take me off of this."

"Yes, I can," said Lozano. "When's the last time you spoke with Dr. Meadows?"

Rem fought the urge to curse. "I've been seeing him regularly."

"When's the last time?" repeated Lozano.

"A couple of weeks. Not that long."

"Cap," said Daniels. "Cut him some slack. We're going on little sleep, and it's been a long week. We're both emotionally and physically exhausted."

"And that's the other thing, Daniels," said Lozano. "You're personally affected, too. You had to fly your family out of town to keep them safe. Don't tell me you don't harbor a grudge against this man. I don't need either of you going off half-cocked and blowing this investigation. I don't care how much this man baits you, you cannot afford to lose it." He tossed out a hand. "Hell, Remalla, any good attorney could take what you just did out there and make it look like you're irrational and overly emotional.

A stunt like that could jeopardize this entire case. That's the last thing you need when it comes to Allison and her trial."

Frustrated, Rem eyed the floor. "I hear you."

Daniels sat in a chair across from the captain. "Listen, if Rudy sticks to his timetable, he may give up Josh tomorrow. There's no telling when or where it could happen. I hate to tell you this, but I think you're going to need us. The more bodies on this, the better."

Rem looked up, and Lozano raised a brow. "And what happens if you two are the ones to catch Rudy?"

Daniels glanced at Rem. "We bring him in," said Daniels, "like we're supposed to, unless he chooses not to play nice, then we defend ourselves, but by the book."

"It's unlikely we'll find him, though," said Rem. "He'll probably drop Josh off on some street corner and disappear. The odds of us finding Rudy tomorrow are slim to none."

"Then what happens after that?" asked Lozano. "I don't need you two running around like a couple of vigilantes. If he really wants that picture, he'll be back. What are you going to do then?"

"That depends," said Daniels. "If Rudy does what he's threatening, we reserve the right to defend ourselves."

"And like it or not," said Rem, "even if you take us off this case, it doesn't mean Rudy does. If he continues to call or threaten us, I can't exactly hand the phone off to Titus and tell him to handle it."

Lozano pointed a pen at Rem. "If I say you're off the case, then you're off. Let the man call, and you can damn well give it to someone else."

Rem went quiet. "Are you saying you've lost faith in me?"

"I'm saying you've been to hell and back," said Lozano. "Maybe you need some time to cope and work through it."

"By sitting in my house, or chasing shoplifters, or naked guys dealing drugs?" Rem closed his eyes. "I can't do that."

"Cap," said Daniels, "he's going to have to face a jury and confront Allison. He's already confronted Margaret Redstone and managed. You take him off this, and you're basically advertising that he's not equipped to do the job. Measy will take that and run with it."

Lozano leaned back and rocked in his seat. "My worry is you, Remalla. This is getting to you. What happens if Rudy backs up his threats, and it becomes more than a voicemail or a letter?"

"Hell. I've come this far. Don't count me out just yet." Rem paused. "I swear. I'll pull it together. I won't give an attorney a reason to give Rudy a free ride."

"I want you to see that doctor. Soon," said Lozano.

"I'll make an appointment," said Rem.

Lozano studied them. "You two make any more turns in the wrong direction, or I even get the slightest whiff that you can't handle this case with professionalism, I won't hesitate to assign you to the latest shoplifting case. You got it?"

Daniels nodded. "We got it."

"And don't get me wrong," said Lozano. "I want Rudy, but I also want you two in one piece. The more caught up in this you get, the more personal it becomes. That may be Rudy's intention, but you can't let that sway you. You've both been through a lot, and if that's going to make it difficult to remain on the up-and-up, then step aside now."

"We can handle it," said Rem.

"You better." Lozano looked between the two of them, as if gauging their truthfulness. "Go on. Get out of here."

Remalla sighed in relief.

"And Remalla. Remember to stay clear around here tomorrow. I don't want you running into Measy," said Lozano.

"Got it," said Rem.

"Measy?" asked Daniels.

Lozano filled Daniels in on Measy's planned visit the next day.

"Don't worry," said Daniels, raising a brow. "I'll make sure Rem stays clear."

Lozano's phone rang, and he answered. "Lozano." He paused. "Hey, Shorty."

Rem walked to the door, and Daniels followed. "Well, that was close," said Rem.

Daniels opened the door. "Don't take it personally. He's looking out for us, and this case."

"Still, I screwed up. I let Rudy get to me."

Daniels patted Rem's arm. "I would have done the same."

Lozano waved a finger at them, and they stopped and waited. Lozano finished the phone call and hung up. "We may have something." He wrote something on a piece of paper.

"What is it?" asked Daniels.

"Somebody called the main line and talked to Shorty. A woman who knows Rudy. An old girlfriend. Name's Donna Kentwood. Wants to talk. Says she can meet tomorrow morning first thing." Lozano raised a brow at them. "You want it?" He held out the paper, and Daniels reached for it.

"Hell, yes," said Rem. "We'll talk to her." He eyed Daniels. "An old girlfriend? Can't wait to hear what she has to say."

"Let's hope she can tell us something," said Daniels, studying the paper. "Tomorrow should be interesting."

"By the book, right?" asked Lozano.

"By the book, Cap," said Daniels.

"Consider me a librarian," answered Rem, and he followed Daniels out.

Chapter Sixteen

Torches burned, and their flames heated the air. Rem began to sweat. Terrified, he tried to exit the white-tiled room, but the door wouldn't open. He pulled on the knob and banged on the door, yelling for Daniels or anybody to come help him, but no one answered. It remained eerily quiet until the door across the room opened and Rem whirled, seeing the bald man with the huge arms enter. Frantic, Rem pushed back against the wall as the man encroached. Rem flailed at him, but he had no strength, and the man picked him up like he weighed no more than one of the fold-out chairs in the room, and he lifted and slammed Rem on his back onto the metal table.

The breath rushed from his lungs in a gush, and Rem fought, but the man secured his hands and feet. Unable to move and desperate, Rem pleaded for help, but the man just stood and stared, his face impassive.

Rem's hands turned numb, and his panic bloomed when Margaret Redstone entered. No longer handcuffed, she approached him and smiled. Her icy blue eyes gleamed in the light, and she ran a hand through his hair, gripped it, and pulled his head back. She loomed over him. "The light will be mine tonight." She ran a finger down his cheek. "I've dreamed of this."

Rem struggled against his bindings, but with no effect. He whimpered as Margaret climbed up on the table and straddled him. "The light will merge with the dark, and we will become one." Leaning over him, she cackled. "Tell me you want me."

Rem tried to scream, but his throat locked up, and when she brought her lips to his, tears sprang to his eyes. Feeling the warmth of her mouth against his own, he made one last lunge, pulling at his wrists and ankles, and jolted awake.

Blinking and breathing fast, Rem tried to get his bearings. Sweat dampened his clothes and the unvoiced scream stuck in his throat. His heart thudded, and he gripped at the cushions beneath him, realizing he was lying on his couch. His body trembling, he sat up. The lamp light softly lit the room, and his television flickered while a commercial played.

He swung his legs over, rested his head in his hands, and forced a deep breath. The dream had been bad. One of the worst, in fact, and he had to admit that maybe his visit to Margaret Redstone had been harder on him than he'd care to admit.

Still seeing her on top of him, and hearing her cackle, he cursed and rubbed his face. He had no idea what time it was, but he remembered coming home, flipping on the TV, throwing a cold pizza in the microwave, and sitting on the couch to decompress before going to bed.

Checking his watch, he saw it was only eleven o'clock. He'd probably been asleep for maybe an hour.

"Shit," he said to himself, clenching his trembling fingers. He made a mental note to make that appointment with Dr. Meadows the next day. After that nightmare, Rem had to wonder if Lozano had been right. Was he getting in too deep? Could he handle whatever might come as a result of this case? He exhaled slowly. *Hold it together. It's just a dream.* He stood on wobbly legs, trying to forget Margaret's icy blue eyes. His stomach rumbled, and he thought of his pizza still in the microwave. He'd fallen asleep before he could eat it. "One foot in front of the other," he spoke aloud, but the panic from the dream bubbled up. "You're okay," he whispered. "Breathe in. Breathe out." Taking some steps and feeling more grounded, he was about to walk out of the room when he heard a loud buzz; his lamp and TV flickered, and the lights went out.

Plunged into darkness, the terror rushed back. Rem froze and reached for the wall. Finding the edge, he gripped it when the torches flashed again in his head, and he followed his fingers to the wall, turned, and leaned back against it. His eyes had not adjusted and in the murky dark and silence, he flashed back to the small room, with the musty old mattress, the bucket, and the unrelenting fear. He moved along the wall and into the corner, where he slid to the floor and gripped his knees.

His hands trembling, he closed his eyes. Hearing the faint squeak of the mice, or maybe rats, in the room with him, he whimpered and pulled his legs up.

Breathe. Just breathe. He tried, but it became difficult to get air in his lungs. Everything became smaller and closer, and his vision spun. *Shit. Shit. Shit.* Unable to stop the downward spiral, he bit his lip, seeing himself back in that horrific, enclosed space, all alone, with no light, waiting and wondering when he would die. All the tricks the doctor had suggested to pull himself out of a tailspin failed, and he fought back panic. He had to get out of there. They were coming for him. And once they found him, they would take him back to that slab, where they would tie him up, and Allison would be waiting with her ugly sneer and gleaming knife.

Fighting tears, Rem hung his head and shivered.

A noise shattered the silence, and he jumped. His mind whirled. *They're coming. They're coming.* His breathing coming in rapid gasps, he tried to calm down. The noise came again, and in some small hazy part of his still logical mind, he realized it was a phone. His phone was ringing.

Desperate, he patted at his shirt. Where was his phone? Then he remembered it was in his pants pocket, and he dug it out, almost dropping it when it rang louder and he jumped again. Forcing himself to focus, he eyed the display, and saw it was Daniels. He tried to pull it together, but his brain wouldn't relent, and he had the thought that maybe it wasn't Daniels. Maybe it was Margaret, and she'd found a way to mimic Daniels. Should he answer?

Answer the phone. Answer it. He tentatively hit the green button and got the phone to his ear. He breathed heavily into it, but could only mumble.

Daniels' voice traveled over the line. "Hey. Did I wake you? Sorry. I'll be quick. I just called to see if you wanted me to pick you up tomorrow, and we'll head to the interview instead of meeting at the station. You might get thirty minutes more sleep out of it. What do you think?"

Rem could barely function a sentence. His throat was so dry it felt like he'd swallowed dirt.

"Rem?"

Then he heard another squeak, and he swore he felt something run over his foot. He sucked in a breath.

"What's wrong?"

Rem tried to formulate a word. Anything to tell Daniels he was back in that room, but all he could muster was a meek, "It's dark."

"What's dark?"

"The...the room." His mind tried to correct him. "Hou...house."

"Your house is dark?"

Rem shut his eyes. They'd adjusted enough that he could see ambient light from the street, but that just scared him more. Were the torches encroaching? Were they coming for him? He didn't know what was worse. The vision of them arriving or remaining in blind ignorance. He thought he heard a footstep and bit back a sob. "They're here," he whispered. "I see...torches."

"Stay right where you are. I'm on my way. Keep talking to me."

Rem heard another squeak and gripped his phone so tight, he dropped it, and lost his connection to Daniels.

••••••••••

Daniels leapt to his feet, finding his car keys, grabbing his weapon from the safe, and ran out of the house. Thankfully, he'd still been in his clothes and didn't need to change. He heard a shuffling and a thunk over the line. "Rem?" No answer. "Rem?" He ran to his car and got in. "Rem? Answer me."

He heard another shuffle, a muffled breath, and a whisper. "Daniels?"

"I'm here. I'm in my car. Give me fifteen minutes." He had to keep Rem talking. "Where are you? In your bedroom?" He knew Rem still struggled with the dark. Had there been a power outage?

He heard a shuddered breath. "I hear them."

"No one is coming for you. I promise." But Daniels just as quickly thought of Rudy. Was he responsible for this? He backed out and gunned the engine. Flying down the street, he tried to keep Rem tethered to the here and now. "Listen to my voice. Just hang in there. Deep breaths."

"I'm scared." Rem spoke so softly, Daniels could barely hear him.

"I know you are. But stay calm. Keep breathing. No one is after you. We'll get the lights back on, and it will be fine."

Rem went quiet, but Daniels could still hear him breathing, and he kept talking while he drove down the roads, flying through lights and stop signs, until he made it to Rem's street. Stomping the gas, he flew down it until he arrived at Rem's house and pulled into the driveway behind Rem's car. The house sat in darkness, but Daniels noted the lights were on at the neighbor's homes. Only Rem seemed to be affected by the outage.

Daniels assumed then that this was no accident. He got out of the car and ran up the drive. Nearing Rem's door, the air hummed, and the lights illuminated. The porch light flickered on and looking through a window, Daniels could see an interior light on as well. He knocked. "Rem? You there? I'm right outside the door."

He tried the knob, but it was locked. In his mind, he had to assume foul play and check the exterior of the house.

Rem exhaled sharply through the phone. "I can see."

"I'm going around to the back. Wait there. Don't move. And don't shoot me when I come in."

"O...Okay."

Daniels jogged around to the back along the driveway. Seeing nothing, he made it to the garage which Rem never parked in because it was too full of old furniture and boxes that belonged to his Aunt Audrey, who'd owned the home previously and was now in assisted living. The garage door had never fully closed properly, and it stood partially raised about two feet off the ground.

Daniels squatted and peered in, but he didn't have a flashlight, and couldn't see anything. He stood and did a quick check of the backyard, but it was quiet. Running back around to the front, he spoke to Rem through the phone. "I'm at the door. I'm going to use my key. Okay?"

He heard a quiet, "Yeah."

Daniels pulled out his keys and unlocked Rem's door. He stepped inside and closed the door behind him, but eyed the house, remembering checking his own home twenty-four hours earlier. "Rem?" He walked into the living room, not seeing Rem at first, and then turned and saw his partner huddled in the corner, pale as ice, the phone to his ear and clutching it like a lifeline.

Daniels hung up and squatted in front of Rem. "Hey. I'm here."

Rem didn't seem to recognize his presence until Daniels touched his knee and he jumped. Then his eyes widened, his shoulders dropped, and he groaned. "Hey."

"It's me." He reached for the phone and took it from Rem's trembling fingers. "You're okay."

"The rats. Did...did you see them?"

Daniels realized Rem's memories hadn't fully faded. "You're home. In your living room. There are no rats, and nobody's coming for you."

"The torches...they were burning."

"Take it easy." He put a hand on Rem's arm. "What happened?"

"I...I...heard them coming. I was sure..." He darted his eyes around the room.

Daniels had to consider someone could be in the house. "Stay put. I'm going to look around." He put Rem's phone on the coffee table, stood, and, holding his gun, walked into the kitchen. Nothing was out of place. Thinking of the garage, he passed the small laundry room off the kitchen and went to the back door, which was locked, and opened it. He flipped on the light, but saw no one, just the furniture and boxes. Seeing the open garage door, he approached it and bent low, looking under it, and spotted a loose thread hanging from a ragged edge, as if someone had rolled beneath the door and caught their jacket or shirt on the wood. He made a mental note to return and bag the thread. Before leaving, he spotted the breaker box on the wall. It sat beside a refrigerator where Rem kept extra drinks. The door to the box was open, and he stepped closer to it. Catching a whiff of what smelled like burning rubber, he checked the breakers. They strangely felt warm to the touch even though it was a cool night. Beyond that, it looked undisturbed, except for the odd smell.

With one last look around the garage, he returned to the kitchen, closed and locked the door. He checked the upstairs and Rem's bedroom, but found nothing suspicious.

He returned to the living room and saw Rem still on the floor with his elbows on his knees and his head lowered. "Hey," he squatted again. "You back with me?"

Rem looked up with haunted eyes. "I think." His hands shook, and he clasped them together.

"It's just us in the house." He sat in front of Rem. "Can you tell me what happened?"

Rem hesitated. "I...uh...had a nightmare." He cleared his throat. "About Margaret."

"Were you in your room?"

"No. Out here. I...I fell asleep on the couch." He rested his head back against the wall. "When I woke, I was pretty shaken, but I got up to go to the kitchen, and that's when everything went dark." He clenched his eyes shut. "And I...I lost it."

Daniels studied his partner, confident he was past the worst of it. "Let me ask you something. Your breaker box in the garage. You keep it open?"

Rem opened his eyes. "The breaker box?" He raised his head. "You think this was deliberate?"

"Buddy, when I drove up, your house was the only one in the dark. So you either didn't pay the bill, or something's up. The minute I hit the porch, everything came back on. That garage door of yours is partially raised, and your breaker box is open. Do you remember if you left it like that?"

Rem blinked, as if trying to gather his thoughts. "Um..no. It stays closed. Otherwise, the fridge door bangs into it."

Daniels nodded. "Then I think somebody messed with you tonight. Either Rudy or his accomplice."

Rem squeezed his temples. "Well, they did a damn good job." He sighed. "I was back in that room, and any light I saw was the torches. I thought they were coming to get me." He lowered his arms and hugged himself.

"The doctor gave you something, didn't he? For anti-anxiety? You want it?"

"I hate those pills."

"I know, but they do occasionally serve a purpose."

Rem's pale face began to show some color. "Has it come to that? I can't get through a dark house without a flashback and medication?" He shook his head. "Maybe Lozano's right. I bit off more than I can chew. Maybe I'm not ready."

"Rem, this was an orchestrated attack on your psyche. Combine that with having just woken from a nightmare, and after the day you had, you're lucky you're doing as well as you are. Anybody else would be sharing a cell with Margaret Redstone."

Rem tensed. "I can't even handle hearing her name."

"You think you can handle getting up? I bet the couch is more comfortable."

Rem eyed the sofa. "I think so."

Daniels stood and offered a hand while Rem used the wall and Daniels' support to balance himself and get to his feet. He wobbled a second, but then made his way to the couch and sat.

Daniels went into the kitchen and got some water and a shot of vodka, and brought it back to the living room. "Here." He offered the vodka. "If you don't want the pills, take this. It'll help settle your nerves." He set the water on the coffee table and sat. "I'd call this in, but that means a couple more hours of wake time, with likely no results. Unless you think otherwise. They might pull prints from the breakers."

"And I might go sing a show tune on the street, but that's about as likely as finding prints. We'll just let Lozano know tomorrow."

"I found a thread hanging from the garage door. I'll bag it and bring it in."

"Okay."

"And don't worry. I'll hang here tonight. I still have a change of clothes upstairs from the last time I stayed, so I'll be good in the morning."

Rem drank the vodka, grimaced, and set the glass down. "I thought you wanted to stay at your place in case Rudy came back." He picked up the water and sipped it.

"Obviously, Rudy had other ideas."

Rem paused. "I wish I could tell you I was brave and to go home, but I'm not feeling too courageous right now." He gripped the glass. "If you hadn't called..."

Daniels hated to think Rem could still be huddled in that corner in a dark home. "Yeah, well, I did. And it's okay to be scared. The good news is you can still get some decent sleep tonight. Did you get dinner?"

"It's still in the microwave, although I'm not too sure I can eat it now."

"I'll check it." He stood.

"Hey..."

Daniels stopped. "What?"

"Thanks for coming over."

"Thanks for answering the phone."

Rem held his gaze. "You'd tell me, right? If you didn't think I could handle this?"

Daniels didn't hesitate. "I'd tell you."

Rem stared, as if waiting to see if Daniels would waver. "Okay."

"Try and relax. I'll go check the food." He watched Rem lean back against the couch, and thankful he'd called when he did, Daniels headed into the kitchen.

Chapter Seventeen

The next morning, Daniels pulled up in front of the small, one-story home with a leafy tree in the yard and surrounded by a white picket fence. He parked. "Looks pretty idyllic. Nice neighborhood."

Rem undid his seatbelt. "She must do well for herself." He took another slug of his coffee and set the cup in the coffee holder between the seats. Surprisingly, after his power outage, subsequent mental breakdown, and getting a few bites of pizza, he'd gone to bed and slept most of the night with no nightmares. Rem had to attribute it to knowing Daniels was upstairs, the power remaining on, and his physical exhaustion. "What's her name again?"

"Donna Kentwood." Daniels popped the door open. "Let's go find out what she has to say."

Rem left the car along with Daniels, and they walked to the front door and knocked. After a few seconds, the door opened and a pretty woman with shoulder-length brown hair and glasses stood in front of them.

"Mrs. Kentwood?" Daniels held out his badge along with Rem and introduced both of them. "We understand you have some information about Rudy Halpern?"

She wrung her hands and looked between the two of them, then stepped back. "Come in."

"Thank you," said Rem.

They walked into a home with white-paneled walls, rug-covered floors, and a quaint warmth to it.

"Let's go in the kitchen," said Donna, and Rem followed her into a white kitchen with blue cabinets. A small breakfast table sat in the corner with a vase of flowers, and Rem smelled cookies.

"Please," she said. "Have a seat. I made some coffee. Would you like some?"

"You spoke the magic words," said Rem. "I'd love some."

"That would be great," said Daniels. "Just black for me. Thanks."

Rem wondered how well Daniels had slept since he rarely drank coffee. "You can add his cream and sugar to mine," he said.

She smiled. "I will." She moved through the kitchen while Rem and Daniels sat at the small table. Rem noted the messy countertops. "Don't mind me," she said, grabbing some mugs. "I bake when I'm nervous. I've got cookies in the oven."

"Doesn't sound like a bad way to deal with nerves," said Rem. "I should try it myself."

"You're a terrible baker," said Daniels.

Rem dropped his jaw. "What do you mean? I made cookies for our last poker game. Everybody loved them."

"I almost broke a tooth on those suckers. We had to dunk them in milk to eat them."

"What's wrong with that?" asked Rem. "Nobody else was complaining."

"That's because we were drinking, which was required to get those puppies down."

Rem huffed. "See if I bake you anything again."

"I'd appreciate it if you didn't."

"Here you go," said Donna, bringing over the filled mugs. She set them down in front of Rem and Daniels.

They thanked her, and she sat across from them and set her own mug down. "I guess you want to hear about Rudy."

"What's your history with him, Mrs. Kentwood?" asked Daniels.

"Please. Call me Donna. And it's Miss. At least for the next month." She twirled a ring on her left hand. "I'm getting married."

"Congratulations," said Rem.

She nodded. "Thanks. I'm very lucky. I met a good guy, which is kind of a miracle, considering where I've been...and what I've done."

Daniels glanced at Rem. "Are you referring to Rudy?" asked Daniels.

She sat back. "Yes, and no. I...uh...had the proverbial troubled youth. I was a messed-up teenager, had parents who didn't know what to do with me, left home at eighteen, and got caught up in the wrong crowd..." She paused. "You name it and I think I've done it."

"How does that tie in with Rudy?" asked Rem. He sipped his coffee and almost sighed. It was the perfect combination of cream and sugar.

She fiddled with her fingers. "I...um...was a wanderer. Always trying to find my tribe. I experimented a lot with drugs, and...other things. I never really fit in anywhere for a variety of reasons until I met a man named Victor D'Mato." She shifted in her seat. "You heard of him? I heard he was murdered recently, which doesn't surprise me in the least."

Rem eyed his mug.

"We're familiar," said Daniels.

"He...offered me something I'd never found before. A place with people such as myself, where I felt accepted and welcomed. I didn't realize the price I was paying for that luxury until it was almost too late. It took a lot of doing to get me out from under his grasp."

Rem thought of Mikey. "Is that where you met Rudy?"

"It is." She played with the handle of her mug. "Victor introduced me to him. At some party at Victor's townhome. I was flattered at the time because Victor sought me out. Told me to take good care of him. Victor didn't do that with everyone." She stared at the table.

"What happened after that?" asked Daniels.

"I'm embarrassed to say that I liked Rudy. We started to hang out. He had a charisma about him. Plus, he was teaching me things, or at least trying to. I don't think I was a good pupil, though. Eventually, he got frustrated and found someone else."

"How long were you together?" asked Rem.

"Six months," she said.

"What was he teaching you?" asked Daniels.

She stilled. "This is the part, Detectives, where I hesitate to comment, and why I almost didn't call you."

"Don't worry about us," said Rem. "We've heard it all."

"And seen a good part of it, too," added Daniels. "Trust me."

Donna leaned up and put her elbows on the table. "If you're familiar with Victor, then you know about the people he sought."

Rem took a second, but then understood. "You mean people with abilities?"

"And not the normal kind," said Daniels.

Her gaze held theirs. "Rudy could do things."

Rem considered something. "Could you do things, too?"

Her eyes widened.

"Is that why Rudy was attracted to you?" asked Daniels.

"You guys know him better than I thought," she said. "Victor, too."

Rem recalled huddling in the corner of his living room. "We have some experience."

A timer dinged, and she stood. "The cookies are done." She walked into the kitchen, grabbed an oven mitt, and opened the oven.

Rem eyed the baked cookies. "They look delicious."

"You're welcome to some," she said, pulling out the baking sheet and setting it on the counter. "There's no way I can eat all this. I already have a plateful I made earlier." She closed the oven and dropped the mitt in a drawer.

Daniels swiveled in his seat to face Donna. "What is it you do?"

"Other than make a great cup of coffee and bake cookies, apparently a lot better than me," said Rem, frowning at Daniels.

Her face fell. She leaned a hip on the counter and spoke softly. "I...I can see things."

"What can you see?" asked Rem, thinking of Jill Jacobs, a woman he'd dated and her psychic abilities. "Can you get inside a person's head?"

"No. Not like that." She paused. "I can see the future. Or at least bits and pieces of it."

Daniels hesitated, and Rem nodded. "Like big things? World events?" asked Rem.

"No. Not usually." She crossed her arms. "I usually see the short term, little stuff. Like maybe twenty-four to forty-eight hours in advance." Her face furrowed. "And before you call me a psychic, please don't. I hate that term. People expect me to be wearing robes and big rings. I don't tell many people about this, unless I trust them."

"You've always had this?" asked Daniels.

"As long as I can remember," she said. "I think it's why I struggled so much as a teenager. I was seeing things I couldn't explain, and when I tried to tell people, they laughed at me. My parents thought I was a liar. But when things I mentioned actually happened, they started looking at me like I was some sort of freak. So I shut up about it. That's hard enough to do when you can see the fight your mom and dad are about to have, or the broken finger your friend is going to experience when she's about to slam her hand in a door, but it's different when you can see an attempted suicide or a terrible accident." She hung her head. "I didn't know how to handle it."

"You can do this with everybody?" asked Rem.

"No. Not everyone," she said. "It would come and go. Some days, I'd see nothing. Others, it was non-stop. I couldn't go to the drugstore without seeing how the cashier was about to lose her job, or the woman standing next to me was about to get hit by her boyfriend." She shook her head. "That was another problem. I would always see the bad things. Don't know why I couldn't see a surprise birthday party, or a wedding proposal. That would have helped."

"Rudy knew about this?" asked Daniels.

"Yes. I think that's what he liked about me. I didn't realize it, but he was using me. He'd take me places to see what I could pick up on. Introduce me to people to find out what would happen to them. I think he thought I could offer him valuable information and provide some sort of protection."

"Protection from what?" asked Rem.

She hugged herself. "Rudy has his own demons...and abilities."

"The electrokinesis thing?" asked Daniels.

Her eyes rounded. "You know about that?"

"We do. He's killed two people that we know of," said Daniels.

Donna dropped her head and sighed. "He's killed more than that."

Rem sat up. "What do you mean?"

She turned and went back into the kitchen. "I told you he was teaching me things?" Donna pulled the parchment paper from the baking sheet and slid the cookies onto the counter. She put the cookie sheet in the sink. "I wasn't the only one. He took in a young kid. A boy named Lucas. He was fourteen years old and a runaway."

Daniels pulled a pad from his jacket pocket. "You know his last name?"

"He told me once," said Donna. "I think it was Morrow? Merrick?"

Daniels scribbled. "What happened with Lucas?"

"Rudy wanted to teach him, like me. He wanted us to be like him." She waved her hands. "Rudy could do crazy things with electricity. He boiled water with his finger, cooked eggs in their shells, warmed your socks, but he could also be destructive. He blew the power to an office building once, when he was angry about a bill, and he took out the power to people's homes if he didn't like them."

Rem met Daniels' gaze. "Sounds familiar," said Rem.

"But he could also do worse. In his zeal to train us, he used people, too. People who wouldn't be missed." She gripped the edge of the counter. "I saw him touch someone once, and they would go rigid, like they were in an electric chair. Some survived." She paused. "Others didn't." She checked the cookies, then she grabbed a bowl and a spoon and stirred something.

"You mention Lucas," said Rem. "Did Rudy ever try to train anybody else?"

"Not while I was there, but he mentioned others. Lucas and I weren't the first. He told me once that he took a boy named Henry. That was another issue. He'd always call the kids he trained Sam. You might get their actual name from Rudy once, but after that, it was always Sam." She stirred harder.

"Henry?" asked Daniels, raising his brow. "He was more than a runaway. Rudy kidnapped him. Did he tell you what happened to him?"

"Rudy said he'd been properly trained, and once he'd passed his test, Rudy had sent him home. That's all I know."

Rem eyed the bowl and wondered what was in it. "Did you pass the test?"

She stopped stirring.

"I'm assuming you took one," said Rem.

She resumed mixing whatever was in the bowl. "No. I didn't pass it."

"Why not?" asked Daniels.

"Because I refused." She paused. "I couldn't do it."

"What about Lucas?" asked Daniels.

"I don't know. Rudy sent me back to Victor before I could find out." She stopped stirring, went to the kitchen sink, flipped on the faucet, and started scrubbing the cookie sheet.

"Donna," said Rem. He could sense the trauma she'd endured and identified with it. "None of this is your fault. You did the best you could, considering what you were dealing with."

She stilled. "I was so stupid. I did stupid things. I should have known better. I left a fourteen-year-old kid behind because I was scared, and I'd...I'd seen what Rudy was doing." She closed her eyes. "I knew Rudy was teaching him terrible things, and expecting him to pass the test. I knew what would happen, and I didn't do anything."

"You were pretty messed up yourself," said Daniels. "And you were dealing with a madman. Try not to be so hard on yourself."

"Hindsight sucks, doesn't it?" asked Rem.

Donna opened her eyes and rinsed off the pan. "I still dream about it. It's like a broken record in my mind." She flipped the faucet off.

"You were a victim. I hear it takes time, but it's supposed to get better," said Rem.

She looked over at him. "You sound like someone who knows what I'm talking about."

Rem heard the squeak of the mice in his head. "Well, I can't see the future, and I haven't befriended Rudy, but I've been to a few places I wish I hadn't."

She studied him and then Daniels. "That damned Victor D'Mato. God knows the number of people he's hurt." Her brow furrowed, and she turned, rubbing her forehead.

Rem sensed there was more, and apparently, so did Daniels. "Something wrong?" asked Daniels.

Donna took a breath, shook her head, and grabbed a towel to dry the cookie sheet. "Just be careful. Rudy's a dangerous man."

Rem narrowed his eyes, not sure if he believed her. "What happened after you left Rudy? Did you ever see him again?"

"No," she said, putting the dried cookie sheet on the counter. "Never." She pulled out a piece of parchment paper and laid it on the sheet, then grabbed some spoons from a drawer and started digging into the bowl.

"While you were with him," said Daniels, "do you recall any places he would go? Where did you stay? Is there anything you remember that might help us figure out where he is, or where he might have taken Josh Lambert?"

Donna scooped out more cookie dough and doled it out on the parchment paper. "Check amusement parks."

Daniels scribbled in his notepad. "Amusement parks?"

Rem thought of the carnival where they'd chased Rudy. "Why?"

"He likes them. He likes to sit and watch the people walk by." Donna scooped out another spoonful of dough. Rem figured at the rate she was going, she'd be able to serve cookies to the whole neighborhood.

"Any place in particular?" asked Daniels.

She stopped and wiped her hands on a towel. "Actually, yes. It was called Glenville Park. They had rides and games. We went there more than once. Rudy put Lucas on some rides, and we did a few rollercoasters. The park's closed now, but it was his favorite place to go."

Rem smiled softly, thinking back. "I went there once."

"You did?" asked Daniels.

"Yeah. With Jennie." He looked over. "I think you were out of town with Marjorie."

"It closed down last year," said Donna. "But it's still there. I think there's a plan to renovate it."

Daniels nodded. "Why did Rudy go there? Do you know?"

Donna grabbed a plate and added a few of the cookies from the oven to it. She brought the plate over and set it on the table. "Help yourself, because if you don't, I may have to open a bakeshop."

Rem grabbed one and bit into it. He moaned in pleasure and swallowed. "Well, if you do, let me know. I'll be first in line."

"Maybe she can give you a few tips," said Daniels. When Rem glowered at him, he returned his attention to Donna. "Why that park?"

"Rudy is very much a creature of habit." She grabbed the spoons and scooped out more dough. "He tends to hang out in the same places and do the same things. He likes routine. Which is why I think he's still in the city."

Daniels straightened. "Why's that?"

"He told me once that he doesn't like authority. He'd very much be offended if anyone thought he could be pushed around just because the police were looking for him. When he had Henry, he told me he'd stayed in the city. Never left. Said he'd found a pretty lady, and they'd walk around with Henry, and they looked like any other family on the street. Nobody was looking for a family. They were looking for a scared kid alone with a scary man. He said the best disguise was to hide in plain sight." She added another scoop of dough to the parchment paper on the sheet. "If you ask me, he's still visiting amusement parks, and if I were to guess, he's still going to Glenville Park."

Daniels stood and neared the counter. "Why? If it's shut down?"

Rem had finished one cookie and grabbed another. He stood and joined Daniels at the counter. "It was a nice park, but not that nice."

"It's not about the park. It's about the memories." She scraped the side of the bowl. "I think it's where he used to take his son."

Rem stopped chewing. "Sam?" he asked through a mouthful.

"Yeah. Sam." She held the spoons. "I saw a picture of him once, with Rudy. Rudy kept it with him all the time. I think whatever happened to him is what tipped Rudy over the edge."

"A picture, huh?" Daniels lowered his notepad. "Was it of Sam sitting on Rudy's knee?"

She knitted her brow. "I think so."

"Wonderful," said Rem. "What would he do if he lost the picture, or if someone took it?"

Donna chuckled. "I wouldn't even want to think about it." She hesitated, and her face dropped. "You don't have it, do you?"

"Rudy left it behind in an RV when we were closing in," said Daniels. "And he's not too happy about it."

She stared at them, her face a mask of concern.

"Is there anything else you can think of about where he might be?" asked Daniels. "Other than the amusement park?"

Donna continued to stare, but then shook her head. "None that I can think of."

Rem popped the last of the cookie in his mouth and accessed his wallet. "Here's my card. If you think of anything, call. The more we know, the better, especially for Josh's sake."

Donna wiped her hands again and took it. "I will." She opened a drawer and pulled out a plastic bag. "Let me get you some cookies for the road."

"You don't have to do that," said Daniels.

"Hey, sport," said Rem. "Don't forget who you're partnered with." He eyed the cookies. "I'd love some."

Daniels rolled his eyes. "By all means, then. Let's feed the bear."

She held out the bag to Rem. "Take as many as you like." She gestured toward the cookies on the counter.

Rem grinned and took the bag.

"You have no idea how happy you've made him," said Daniels.

"Listen," said Donna. "I...uh..." She rubbed her head again. "...My abilities."

Rem grabbed some cookies.

"What about them?" asked Daniels.

"I've learned over the years how to handle it. I can close it off usually if needed, and my fiancé, he's learned to accept and adapt. But sometimes...sometimes things come through, and I can't stop it."

Rem had almost filled the bag and zipped it closed.

"Are you trying to tell us something?" asked Daniels.

Rem came up beside Daniels. "I don't think you need to tell us Rudy's up to no good. Believe me. We know."

She held her elbows. "What I see is not always accurate. Things change. If you walk out that door and decide to fly to Florida, I have no idea if that could affect the outcome, or if the trouble will follow you there."

"What are you saying, Donna?" asked Daniels.

She looked between the two of them. "There's something you two need to know."

Chapter Eighteen

DANIELS DROVE UP TO the locked gate of Glenville Park. Beyond the chain link, he could see a Ferris wheel, roller coasters, and various other rides. Empty booths lined the walkways that led to the midway, and large, ragged flags advertising the amusement park blew in the wind. He parked and got out.

Rem did the same, and they stopped at the locked gate. "It's hard to visit if it's closed," said Rem. He jiggled the padlock.

Daniels eyed the gate and surrounding area. "You honestly think that would stop Rudy?" He strode along the gate. "Let's check around."

He walked onto the grass along the perimeter of the park. Rem followed. "This is a blast from the past," said Rem. "Coming here with Jennie seems like a lifetime ago."

Daniels continued past a grove of trees. "It kind of was a lifetime ago."

"Yeah. I guess. I don't even know who I was back then."

Daniels looked back. "Same guy, just more experienced."

"That's one way to look at it."

"There. Look." Daniels pointed at a ragged piece of fence that had been pulled from the ground. "Does that look like an entry point to you?"

Rem squatted in front of it. "One way to find out." He pulled on the fence. "After you."

Daniels got on all fours and squeezed through. Rem pushed the fence back and did the same.

They stood, and Daniels looked around. "You want to take one side, and I'll take the other? We'll stay in touch by phone."

Rem nodded. "Sure."

They went in opposite directions–Rem toward the rides and Daniels toward what looked like a game and food area. Daniels passed several empty booths and faded tables and chairs attached to the ground, along with deserted kitchens. Trash littered the area, and the worn flags whipped in the wind, but he didn't see anything that indicated Rudy's presence. Turning a corner, he stopped when he saw a few tents of homeless erected along a walkway outside the chain-link fence. Approaching that section, he walked along it, thinking it would be a prime location for Rudy to target, but from what he could see, no one seemed harmed. He tried to talk to a few people through the fence, but none seemed interested in having a conversation about the park or Rudy.

Giving up on that angle, he jogged back up toward the rides and found Rem standing outside a large yellow rollercoaster with peeling paint. "Anything?" he asked.

"Not really. No," said Rem. "Although I passed a bench by the Ferris wheel with discarded candy wrappers on the ground. I think that's odd for an abandoned park."

"You think Rudy brought Josh here, and they sat outside the Ferris wheel?"

"Maybe."

Daniels gestured. "There are a few homeless tents back along the fence line. Could have been one of them."

"Or even just random kids hanging out. I saw some graffiti back there, so you know they're around."

Daniels put his hands on his hips. "I don't know if it even matters. If Rudy holds to a schedule, he might turn Josh over today, and if he does, it doesn't look like it will be here."

"We're assuming he'll turn him over today, but we don't know for sure. Just because he did it with Henry on day eight doesn't mean he'll do it with Josh. Guy might like routine, but he also likes his head games, and messing with the police is right up his alley."

"Then maybe we should bag some of the candy wrappers. See if we find anything on them."

"It's a long shot, but it can't hurt." Rem turned in circles and looked around the desolate area. His gaze stopped on something and he swatted Daniels on the arm. "Hey. Look."

Daniels followed his gaze and saw the carousel. "What is it?"

Rem walked over and stopped. "You see that?"

Daniels eyed the round structure with the colorful horses and benches, and remembered riding a merry-go-round when he was a child. He could hear the music in his head and his sister squealing while she rode a horse beside him. He was about to ask what Rem was talking about when he spotted a blue horse with stars in its eyes. "Is that…?"

"A blue horse with starry eyes, like Henry said? It sure the hell is." He turned and looked back. "It's not far from the bench with the wrappers." He paused. "I say we get eyes on this place."

Daniels nodded. "The sooner, the better."

• • • • • • • • • • •

Rem took the bag from the cashier, grabbed his drink and Daniels' bottled water, and returned to the car.

Daniels was on the phone and hung up as Rem slid in and closed the door. "I got the food," said Rem. "You want to eat in the car?"

"Sure," said Daniels. "Lozano's going to request a patrol to watch the park. I told him about the wrappers, too, and about what happened at your place last night."

Rem handed Daniels his sandwich and water. "What'd he say?"

"He thinks we should have called it in."

Rem unwrapped his burger. "Maybe we should have, but I was in no condition for it."

"We have the thread from the garage door. We'll bring that to the lab."

"Yeah. I guess that's something." He took a bite of his burger.

"I also mentioned Lucas Morrow or Merrick. He's going to pass it along to Titus and Georgios. Have them check into it."

"Another long shot, especially if the kid was a runaway."

"Probably, but we might get lucky." He opened his water bottle. "You want to talk about Donna and her story?"

Rem chewed and swallowed. "She sounds credible. I think she's telling the truth. Plus, that amusement park tip panned out."

"She also backs up our theory that Rudy gets others to help him."

"That seems pretty solid at this point."

"There was no indication of anyone else living in the RV, though," said Daniels, opening his sandwich.

"Doesn't mean he or she isn't around. Maybe Rudy didn't call them in for help until after we found the RV. He'd need a place to stay at that point, plus transportation."

"Good point." Daniels bit into his sandwich and sipped his water. "You want to talk about what else she mentioned?"

Rem settled back in his seat. "You think it's worth worrying over? She even said things can change. Her accuracy isn't a hundred percent."

"Doesn't mean we shouldn't prepare. Like Margaret said, preparation is key." He reached over and stole one of Rem's fries. "Unless you'd rather move to Florida."

"Believe me. It's damn tempting, except I'd be way too close to Mom. I love her, but she'd try me almost as much as Rudy."

"At least she couldn't zap you."

"You don't know my mom very well."

Daniels chuckled. "That's something else to consider. What do we do with Rudy once we catch him? Or better said, how do we put a guy like that in handcuffs?"

"It happened once before," said Rem, eating a fry. "He assaulted a police officer."

"I've been wondering about that," said Daniels. "Rudy had been drinking. I wonder if that's what stopped, or prevented him, from electrocuting the cop."

"It's an interesting thought, but something tells me we can't wait for him to get drunk before we take him in."

"Plus, the whole injury thing. We can't shoot him either, unless he's about to zap someone."

"The ten second window," said Rem. "That gives us something to consider."

Daniels held his sandwich. "I suppose it does." They shared a glance, speaking volumes while saying nothing. "If it comes to that."

"Let's hope not." Rem took another bite of his burger.

Daniels' cell buzzed as he bit into his sandwich. He picked it up and hit a button. "Oh, no," he said.

Rem frowned. "What?" He ate a fry.

"It's a text from Titus. They're at the station. There's been a catastrophe."

Rem stopped in mid-chew. "What's wrong?"

"I'm sorry, buddy." He glanced over. "The coffeemaker's dead."

Rem's heart sank. "Are you serious? The coffee machine? Are they sure? Did they jiggle the plug?"

"I'm sure they know all the tricks. They drink almost as much coffee as you. They wanted you to know, before you came in unprepared."

Rem lowered his burger. "Shit. That sucks."

"We could give it a memorial. Would that help? Maybe bury it outside the station?"

Rem sighed. "It needs a headstone. Here lies the coffee maker. Saver of souls. Gone, but forever remembered."

"You could bring it flowers."

"I just might. I think daisies were its favorite."

"No need to panic. We'll get another one. You can stop at the cafeteria on the way in and get a cup."

"I thought we were avoiding the station since Measy's meeting with Lozano."

Daniels ticked up a brow. "You are. I'm not."

Rem narrowed his eyes. "We're supposed to be playing it safe and by the book, remember?"

"Who says I'm not playing it safe? I just want to see the guy. Get a feel for him and find out what we're dealing with."

"What if he gets in your face? You know he'll probably try."

"Let him. I can stay cool."

"What world are you living in? He punches a few buttons, and that book will go out the window."

"I'll stick to the squad room. Anything he says will be heard loud and clear by anybody in the area."

"Is that your game? To trip him up instead?"

"It works both ways, partner."

Rem sighed. "Just be careful. If he's conspiring with Allison, there's no telling what he's capable of."

"Then maybe it's better we find out now, instead of later."

"I hope you know what you're doing." He took another bite of his burger.

"Trust me." Daniels smiled. "This guy thinks he's holding all the cards, but maybe we need to show him we've got a few, too."

Rem chewed and sipped his drink. "What cards are those?"

"The ones that may bend, but don't break, and might even convince him to think twice about playing dirty."

"You plan on doing magic tricks, too?"

"If necessary. I can pull a quarter out of his ear."

"Maybe try the stick out of his ass."

Daniels smiled. "Magic. Not miracles."

Chapter Nineteen

AFTER WALKING INTO THE downstairs cafeteria, Rem grabbed a cup and a donut and walked to the register. "Hey, Tony. How are you today?"

Tony rang up his items. "I can't complain, Detective. I've got food, water, shelter and the bills are paid."

Rem handed him his credit card. "You're living the high life."

"That I am." He rang up the purchase and returned Rem's card. "Enjoy your donut."

"I will. Thanks, Tony."

"You're welcome."

Rem grabbed his cup and donut and headed to the coffee dispensers. After he and Daniels had finished lunch, they'd returned to the station. Rem had headed to the cafeteria and Daniels to the squad room, telling Rem he'd text when the coast was clear. Rem was silently pleased to have a bit of quiet time. After the harrowing experience at his home the previous night, he'd had little opportunity to catch his breath. Now, at least for a few minutes, he could sit by himself and enjoy a coffee.

Filling his cup, he looked around but didn't see the usual cream and sugars near the dispensers. He spotted a woman wiping a table beside him. She had short red hair, a mole on her cheek that made him think of Marilyn Monroe, and her nametag read Sally.

"Excuse me. Sally?"

She looked over and smiled. "Yes?"

Rem waved. “I’m trying not to panic here because I don’t see the cream and sugar.”

Her eyes widened, and she looked behind him. “Oh, I’m sorry. That area was a mess. Police officers drink a lot of coffee. I was cleaning and moved them over to that table.” She pointed.

Rem relaxed. “Oh, thank God. Thanks.” He set his cup and donut down and headed over to the table, where he grabbed some cream containers and sugar packets and a few extra for the road. He returned, picked up his stuff, and found a quiet table. After he doctored his coffee, he found a paper left behind by someone, and read through it, enjoying his drink and donut, feeling more relaxed than he would have expected, considering everything. Some part of him felt guilty that he wasn’t trying to find Josh or Rudy, but another part felt relief that he could have a few minutes to himself.

Thinking of his partner, he wondered what was happening upstairs. Daniels had texted when Rem had entered the cafeteria and had told him that Measy was in Lozano’s office and to hang tight, which is what Rem planned to do.

Checking his watch, he wondered how long the meeting would go. He didn’t expect it to last long because Rem doubted Lozano would have much patience with Measy. His bigger worry was Daniels. The last thing either of them needed was for Daniels to confront Allison’s attorney, but Rem had to trust that his partner knew what he was doing.

Sipping his coffee, Rem flipped to the funny pages, and blinked when the text briefly went out of focus, but then returned to normal. When it happened again, he shook his head. He stared at the paper, and frowned when the letters began to run together, like liquid ink. “What in the hell?” he whispered. He touched the paper, but it seemed solid enough. His hand, though, did not. Rem raised it and moved his fingers, and stared in surprise when his skin began to slide off, like it was melting. It flowed down his wrist, and he chuckled, because it was so weird. Touching his palm with his other hand, which also started to melt, he tried to figure out what was happening. Why was his skin coming off?

Curious, and strangely undisturbed by the phenomena, he continued to move his fingers. He looked around the cafeteria, and saw other people melt, too. Their bodies took on strange shapes, and their faces drooped and dripped onto the floor. He couldn't figure it out. Did they know they were melting, because they didn't seem bothered by it.

He leaned over and spoke to a man who sat at the table beside him. "Excuse me," he said. The man's face dripped pockets of skin onto his plate. "Do you know your face is falling off?" he asked.

The man offered him a dull look. "My face is what?" he asked.

Rem gestured at him. "You. Your face. It's coming off." He smiled. "It's very weird, but I thought you should know." He scanned the room. "All these people should know. They're melting, too."

The man studied him, picked up his plate, and walked away to another table.

Rem shook his head. "Jeez. You try and help somebody." A chuckle bubbled up, but he couldn't determine what was funny. A melting body couldn't be good, especially if it was happening to him, too.

He stood, holding his coffee, and swayed. His donut finished, he tossed his plate, and wondered what he should do. This was obviously a dangerous situation. He walked over to Tony and leaned close. "Hey, Tony," he whispered.

"Yes, Detective? You need something?" asked Tony.

Rem stepped back when a piece of Tony's ear fell to the floor. "I...uh...did you see that?"

"See what?"

"Your ear." He eyed the ground and blinked.

Tony touched his ear with dripping fingers. "What about it?" He narrowed his eyes. "You okay? You don't look right."

Rem straightened, and it occurred to him that maybe he shouldn't be telling people they were disintegrating. He patted his stomach and almost spilled his coffee. "I'm great. Just great. You have a nice day." The words sounded slurred in his head, but he couldn't be sure.

"You want me to call your partner?" asked Tony.

Rem thought of Daniels. Daniels could help him figure out what was going on. "No. That's fine. I'll go find him. Thanks."

Tony watched him with a runny eye. "You sure?"

Rem projected as much confidence as he could muster. "I'm just peachy." He turned and headed out of the cafeteria, determined to find Daniels.

....

Daniels watched Lozano and Measy talk in Lozano's office. When Daniels had entered the squad room, he'd seen the two men in conversation. The blinds were open, and Daniels got a good look at the man who would be grilling Rem on the stand. He was of average stature, with graying hair, including a beard and mustache, and a generous belly. By the looks of him, he didn't appear too intimidating, but Daniels knew not to be fooled by appearances.

Titus and Georgios sat at their desks, farther down in the squad room.

"Hey, Titus. Georgios," said Daniels.

The two men looked over. Georgios himself had only recently returned to work after also being victimized by Victor D'Mato. "Yeah?" asked Georgios.

Daniels' and Rem's relationship with the two detectives had been strained prior to the D'Mato case, but now that they'd all suffered from and survived it, they'd developed a begrudging respect for each other. "How long have they been in there?" asked Daniels, nodding toward Lozano's office.

Georgios eyed the office. "Not long. Maybe fifteen minutes before you got back."

Titus closed a file on his desk. "You know that guy? Measy?"

"Not really, no," said Daniels. "I hear he's Allison Albright's counsel."

Georgios snorted. "Good luck, then. Guy earns his nickname. He's as slick as an oiled pig." He swiveled in his seat. "We had a drug dealer dead to rights. He was selling X to grade schoolers. Greasy Measy got him off on a technicality."

"And that's one of the better stories I've heard," said Titus. "Tell Rem to stay clear of that guy and to be ready at trial."

"You, too," said Georgios. "Measy plays dirty."

Daniels thought of Rem down in the cafeteria and wondered how to handle this. Was the man in Lozano's office partially responsible for what had happened last night at Rem's? There was no way to know.

Daniels stood, his gaze still on the two men in the office, and walked to the water bottle behind Rem's desk. He leaned over to refill his cup and got a faint whiff of burned rubber. After filling his cup, he set it on Rem's desk and sniffed, following the smell, which was eerily familiar to the smell around Rem's breaker box. He stopped at the dead coffee maker, where he leaned close, and realized the odor originated from the machine.

Concerned, he straightened. "Hey, Titus. Was this machine dead this morning?"

"Yeah. It was," said Titus. "Georgios tried everything. I think it finally hit the hundred-thousand-mile mark. Poor thing."

"It lived a good life, though," said Georgios. "Phyliss bought me a nice fancy one at home. I'll bring the old one in tomorrow. That'll keep us going a little while longer."

Daniels nodded, but his mind was elsewhere. Why did the coffee machine smell like Rem's breaker box?

He grabbed his water and stepped back to his desk, keeping an eye on Lozano and Measy, whose conversation appeared to become more animated, when the squad doors opened, and Rem walked in. He held a cup of coffee and stopped just inside the doors.

Daniels glared and put his water down. What was his partner doing? He walked over, glancing back toward Lozano's office. "What are you doing here? You're supposed to wait for my text. Measy's still here."

Rem stared at him, his eyes narrowed. "It's happening to you, too." He reached up and poked him in the cheek, then stared at his finger.

"What are you doing?" asked Daniels. "You need to go back downstairs." He looked again at Lozano's office, but Measy had not yet noticed Rem's arrival.

Rem kept staring, and then he looked around. "Huh."

"What's the problem?"

Rem swayed and leaned close. "I have to tell you something."

Daniels felt the first stirrings of concern. "What?"

Rem pointed. "Your face is melting." He raised his coffee cup. "So are Titus' and Georgios', but don't tell them. I don't want them to worry."

Daniels' heart thudded, and he studied Rem, who looked fine but obviously wasn't. "Rem? You okay?"

Rem blinked. "You know. I feel great. Better than I have in a long time, but I'm worried about my face. It's dripping onto the floor, and I don't think that's good for me." He patted his jaw. "I have appearances to…to…" He stared off. "…I don't know. Something. I lost my train of thought."

"You're seeing your face drip to the floor?" He held his breath.

Rem slid his foot along the tile. "Oops. I just kicked my eyeball." He looked down the room. "I should go get it."

Daniels took his arm. "Whoa. Hold up there." He studied Rem and realized Rem had to be on something. He glanced again behind him, monitoring Measy. "Our faces are melting?"

"I need to get my eyeball."

"I'll get it. Don't worry. Tell me about the faces." While Rem was distracted by his lost eye, Daniels reached for Rem's gun and slid it out from its holster. He slid it into the back of his pants. Rem didn't even notice.

Rem nodded and pursed his lips. "They are all sliding off. I tried to tell them in the cafeteria, but they wouldn't listen."

Daniels' mind raced, and he eyed Rem's coffee cup. "Is that your coffee?"

Rem raised it. "Yup." He giggled.

Shit, thought Daniels. Someone had spiked his partner's coffee, and he thought of the dead coffee maker and Measy's meeting with Lozano. The pieces clicked into place.

"Can I see that, partner?" he asked Rem, reaching for the cup.

Rem held the cup. "What are you going to do with it?"

"I'm just curious. I want to know if it's melting, too."

Rem's face reflected obvious confusion, and he studied the cup. "It is." His face fell. "That's a shame. I wanted more coffee."

"Let me take it. I'll get you some more," said Daniels.

Rem sighed. "Thank you." He gave the cup to Daniels. "That's why you're such a good partner. You're not scared about my face." He squinted. "But you might worry about yours. You're not looking too good."

Daniels set Rem's cup on his desk, determined to keep Rem from drinking anything else, and his stomach knotted when he eyed Lozano's office and saw Measy staring through the glass, right at Rem. The man's eyes were dark and round, like a shark sensing its prey.

Daniels went over to Rem and took his shoulder. "Come on. Let's go."

Rem stayed put. "But we can't. We have a problem. These people are melting. They should know. And I need to get my eye."

Daniels realized he didn't have time to convince Rem to get out of the squad room on his own. "Titus. Georgios." The detectives looked over. "I need your help."

The men stood and walked over. Rem swayed and Daniels held onto his arm. "What's up?" asked Titus. He eyed Rem. "You better hang out somewhere else. That asshole is here."

Rem furrowed his brow. "Asshole?" He whispered at Daniels. "God. What if that's melting, too? I didn't think about that."

Georgios narrowed his eyes at Rem. "Did he take something?"

Daniels cursed. "Listen. I've got to get him out of here." He glanced back and saw Lozano's office door opening. "Measy sees him like this, it'll be like leading Rem to the gallows. I think somebody spiked his coffee. Georgios, can you handle Measy while Titus and I get Rem out of here?"

Georgios looked toward Lozano's office, where Measy was stepping out. "With pleasure." He walked away.

Daniels said a silent thank you. "We've got to get him down to my car." He took Rem's arm and Titus took the other.

"Where are we going?" asked Rem. "What about my eye?"

"It's fine. I'll have Georgios get it. Let's go downstairs," said Daniels. He heard someone yell "Detective" from behind him and turned to see Georgios standing in front of an angry Measy.

"Hey, Counselor," said Georgios, standing with his arms crossed. "Just thought I'd check in and see if you'd set any other drug dealers free lately. Especially ones that deal to kids? You keeping busy with that?"

Daniels turned back, ignoring Measy's yell, and guided Rem out of the room. With Titus' help, they got him down the stairs and outside into the parking lot.

Rem managed to walk, although his legs wobbled, and he seemed increasingly delusional. "I think the sky is melting, too," he said, when they got him to the lot. "Isn't that what that little bird said? The sky is melting?" He chuckled and stared up.

Daniels maneuvered him into the passenger side of his car. "Close enough." He buckled Rem in. "Stay put."

Rem grabbed his arm and pulled him down. "You know the seat belt is worthless. It's melting, too. Just like your car." He patted the dash. "You sure you want to drive it?"

"I'll take my chances." Daniels patted Rem's arm, pulled away, and got the door closed.

"What the hell did they give him?" asked Titus. "And why?"

Daniels watched Rem through the window, who continued to pat the dash as if surprised it was there. "They're trying to discredit him. Before he testifies. I knew they were low, but I didn't expect this."

"Where are you going to take him?"

Daniels tried to think. "That's a great question."

"Be careful. If they're smart, they'll be watching your house and his. They'll want witnesses and maybe photos. That's what I'd do at least."

Daniels couldn't help but wonder if they were being watched now. Anyone could snap a few photos of an inebriated Rem leaving the station with Daniels' help, and God knows where or when they could turn up. He had to get Rem some place quiet and safe. "I think I have an idea. Thanks for your help, Titus. Georgios, too."

"You bet. Just get him out of here till that crap wears off. We need Allison Albright to enjoy prison for a long, long time."

"Don't I know it." He walked to the driver's side and stopped. "Hey. Can you get Rem's coffee? I put it on my desk. Get it tested. That will work to our benefit if it comes back positive."

Titus nodded. "You got it."

"And tell Lozano I'll be in touch as soon as I've got Rem situated. And if something breaks with Rudy and Josh, let me know."

"Will do." Titus turned and jogged back to the station, and Daniels got in the car with Rem and drove off.

• • • • • • • • • • •

Mikey studied her phone while Mason screwed together a chair from the floor of his office.

"You have the Stanton's tomorrow at noon. Mrs. Stanton is the one who wants to talk to her brother, who passed last year from an overdose. And then there's Marvin Bingham. Says there's a poltergeist in his house, plus his wife left him, and he's wondering if you can help locate her."

"Sounds like a case for Trick."

"You want me to schedule Bingham for next week, then?"

"Yeah, probably. Try to keep next week light, though. With Trick moving into the office and getting started, he and I are going to need some adjustment time." The screwdriver jerked, and Mason cursed. "Why the hell can't Trick bring his own damn furniture?"

"You honestly want a nicked and battered desk and office chair? That would drive you nuts."

Mason sighed. "I'm scared to think what else he's bringing with him."

"Probably his collection of shot glasses."

Mason's face fell. "Don't even say that."

"You've got plenty of shelf space." She gestured at the walls. "I'm sure he'd be happy to use it."

"Don't you have something else to do?" asked Mason. He swiveled the chair and groaned when the arm rest fell off. "Why am I doing this, anyway? I should make Trick do it next week."

"Because he'll end up sitting on the couch and leaving chair parts all over the floor."

He held his head. "What have I gotten myself into?"

Mikey smiled, and Mason's phone rang. "Thank God," he said. "Maybe it will be a case I can help with, and I can get off this floor." He pulled out his phone. "It's Daniels."

"Daniels?" asked Mikey.

Mason answered and barely got the word "hello" out before he went quiet. Mikey waited and knew something was wrong.

"I'll meet you out back." Mason hung up and stood. "I should be careful what I ask for." He headed toward the exit door at the rear of the office.

"What's wrong?" asked Mikey.

"It's Remalla. Daniels says he's been drugged. He's bringing him here to ride it out."

Mikey stood in shock. "What? Drugged? How did he get drugged?"

"I don't have all the details, but he's almost here." He pushed the exit door open. "Wait here and hold the door so it doesn't lock on me. I'll be right back."

Mikey tried not to think the worst. What had happened? She stood at the door, waiting, as Mason ran down the stairs to the first floor. The exit below backed up to an alley, and it made sense that Daniels would park there instead of out front, if he wanted to keep Rem's condition private.

After a few minutes, she heard grunting and footsteps on the stairs. Mason and Daniels appeared, helping Rem as they climbed up toward the office. Rem appeared to be okay, but a little off balance, until they brought him closer.

Holding the door, she watched Rem. "Is he okay?" she asked.

Rem looked up as they carried him closer. He stared at her, and recognition lit his eyes. "Hey, Mikey." His face fell. "Your face is melting, too. Did Daniels tell you?" His gaze fell to the ground. "Oh. Your lips just fell off." He giggled as Mason and Daniels brought him into the office. "You better pick them up. Daniels left my eye at the station."

Daniels and Mason sat him on the couch, and Rem laid back, his gaze on the ceiling. "Pretty," he said, slightly slurred. "So many colors." He raised his hand and pointed. Mikey looked up, but just saw the beige plaster.

She let the back door close and walked over. "What's wrong with him?"

Daniels stepped back, his face a mask of worry. "I think somebody spiked his coffee."

"Why?" asked Mason.

Rem giggled and touched the couch cushion. "It's like soup. I wonder if I can swim in it." He looked at Mason. "Do you have a bathing suit?"

"Somebody's trying to make him look incompetent." Daniels set his jaw. "Allison's attorney was at the station today. If he'd talked to Rem like this, I know he would have used it to jeopardize our case against Allison." He groaned. "And I'm not even considering anyone else who saw him. It could go to his credibility as a witness. He was drugged when Allison took him. If they can use this to show that he's a drug user, then they might make a jury think twice."

Rem struggled with his jacket. "Well, if you don't have a swimsuit, I'll go commando."

All three of them yelled "No," at once, and Daniels sat next to Rem. "Hey partner. Why don't you lie down? Just sleep it off. Maybe you'll feel better after a nap."

Rem smiled. "I feel great." He tried to stand. "Let's go catch some bad guys."

Daniels took his arm. "Later. Let the bad guys take a day."

Rem sat back. "You think that's a good idea? Should they do that?"

"Sure," said Daniels. "Why not? Everybody needs a day off."

Rem paused and then shrugged. "Okay." He studied his feet. "Don't forget my eye. You left it at the...the..." He tried to snap his fingers, but only wiggled them. "I don't know...where did we leave it?"

Daniels leaned over and rubbed his face. "I'll take care of your eye. Don't worry."

"What do you think they gave him?" asked Mason.

Daniels looked over and patted Rem's knee when Rem clasped his hands together, his animated face suddenly looking lost, and he began rocking back and forth. "He did this in the car. Just stares for a second like he knows something is wrong, but can't figure out how to get back."

Mikey sat on the other side of Rem. "It's like some sort of acid trip. Maybe LSD."

Daniels stood. "When I find out who did this..."

"Who could have done it?" asked Mason. "Was he at the station?"

Daniels' face paled. "He was in the cafeteria." He returned to Rem's side. "Hey, partner. You remember when you got coffee? In the cafeteria?"

Rem stared at his hands. "My hands are dripping."

"Who gave you the coffee?" asked Daniels.

Rem bobbed his head back and forth. "They were hiding the cream and sugar," said Rem. "I couldn't find it."

"Hiding it?" asked Daniels. "What do you mean?"

Rem blinked and smiled. "She had a mole."

"What?" asked Daniels. "Who had a mole?"

Rem widened his eyes. "I like sugar." He scratched his head. "I like cream, too. But I couldn't find it."

Mikey put a hand on his arm. "Hey, Rem. Do you remember if you were holding your coffee the whole time?"

He grinned at her. "I got a donut." Rem's gaze flicked over her face. "You're pretty." His face fell. "Except for your lips. They're still missing. You really should look for them. I'll help."

He tried again to stand, but Mikey stopped him. "Would you like some sugar now? I have some."

"You do?" Rem's eyes lit up.

"You bet." Mikey stood.

Daniels eyed Mason. "I've got to get back to the station. I need to find out who was working in the cafeteria. Plus, talk to Lozano."

"You want to leave him like this?" asked Mason.

"Hell, no." Daniels paused and spoke to Rem. "I'm just going to talk to Mason. I'll be right over there." He stood and pointed.

Rem nodded. "Don't forget my eye."

"I won't. I promise."

Mikey dug through a drawer, looking for the candy she'd bought a few months back for the child of a client who'd been in the office, but she kept an eye on Rem.

"This is the other thing," said Daniels, approaching Mason. "If I stay gone for the rest of the day while Rem gets better, then it gives Measy, Allison's attorney, more ammo to use against us. He'll ask why I disappeared in the middle of a kidnapping case for several hours, and oh, were you helping your partner detox?"

"It's a room of swords, isn't it?" asked Mason. "You don't know where to turn."

"Or who to trust," said Daniels. "Damn it. I never imagined they'd go this far."

"How could you?" asked Mason. "How could anyone?"

Mikey dug through another drawer. "He'll be okay if you need to go. I'll watch him."

Daniels paced, then stopped beside Mikey. "I won't be gone long. I just need to plug the leaks before we all start drowning."

"Don't worry," said Mikey. "He's in good hands. I'll call you if it gets worse, but hopefully he'll start coming out of it soon."

"I'll be here, too. I'll help watch him," said Mason.

Rem pushed up on to his feet. "If you're going, I'm going." He tripped on the coffee table and almost fell over.

Daniels walked over. "Take it easy, partner." He coaxed Rem to sit down again. "I need you to do me a big favor." He leaned over and got close.

"What's that?" asked Rem, his voice almost a whisper.

"Can you take care of Mikey and Mason for me? They could be in trouble."

Rem's eyes rounded. "I know. They're melting."

"Yeah," said Daniels. "That's why you should watch out for them, okay?" He put a hand on Rem's shoulder. "I need you to keep an eye out."

"But my eye is on the floor." Rem snorted like Daniels was an idiot. "I told you like a million times."

"You're right. And I'll go get it, but I need you to stay here. Can you do that?"

Rem hesitated, his face a mixture of confusion and worry. "You'll come back?"

"You know I will."

Rem glanced at Mikey and Mason. "You have candy?"

"There it is." Mikey yanked out a bag of peppermints. She held out the bag. "You like peppermints?"

Rem laughed like a child. "I love 'em."

"And look." Mikey pulled out a magazine. "You want to look at this?"

Rem studied it. "Not if it melts."

"Well, we'll give it a shot." Mikey brought the magazine and candy over and set them on the coffee table. "Here you go."

Rem grabbed the magazine and sighed deeply. "It's melting."

Mikey spoke to Daniels. "Go. He'll be okay. I'll stay with him."

Daniels watched Rem, and Mikey could see the indecision in his eyes.

"There's nothing you can do here anyway, except watch him like this," said Mikey. "Which I think is eating at your soul."

Rem grabbed for a candy and tried to unwrap it.

"You have no idea." Daniels closed his eyes and let go of a deep breath. "Okay. I'm going. You call me if you need anything or something changes." He headed for the back door. "I owe both of you for this. Big time."

"Don't worry about that," said Mason. "Just go save some sinking ships before yours goes down with the fleet."

"You better believe I will." Daniels eyed Rem once more before he opened the exit door and left.

Chapter Twenty

DANIELS KICKED AT A chair in Lozano's office. "What did Measy say?"

Lozano stood beside his desk. "He felt the need to inform me of how weak the state's case is and that if we think we can win based on Rem's testimony, we're mistaken. Then he told me if I continued to harass Allison with my constant inquiries, he'd file a complaint. I told him what he could do with his threats."

Daniels considered the events of the afternoon. "Did you know what time he would be here?"

"He called right before he showed up. Said he had a crazy schedule."

"So basically, the meeting was pointless," said Daniels. "He was just throwing his weight around and trying to intimidate us."

"Just like I thought." Lozano leaned against the wall, yanked off his tie and tossed it on his desk. "You're sure Rem was drugged, and this isn't a medical issue?"

Daniels glowered. "He thinks his eye is rolling around by my desk. He was perfectly fine this morning. It's when he came back from the cafeteria that he was out of it. Somebody got to him while he was down there."

"You think this was orchestrated?"

Daniels threw out a hand. "What are the odds, Cap? Rem gets drugged at the same time Measy is in your office for a worthless meeting, and the coffeemaker just happens to die this morning, forcing Rem to go downstairs to get coffee?"

"He would have done that anyway, with Measy up here."

"Then it was done as a backup. They knew Rem would go downstairs at some point."

"Whoever did this had no way of knowing when you'd be at the station. You could have stayed away all day."

Daniels shook his head. "They knew we'd be back, eventually. It wouldn't be hard to watch us, maybe even follow us. And when they realized we were returning, they call Measy, and he shows, and then whoever was tailing us waits for Rem to go to the cafeteria."

"That still seems like a longshot."

"Maybe. But they took the risk, and it paid off. And even if they'd missed Measy, you still have Rem walking around the station like some sort of zombie." He shoved the chair out of his way. "Hell, I already had someone ask me if Rem was okay when I walked back in."

"You don't think you should get him tested? Find out what they gave him?"

Daniels did his best not to show impatience. "And what happens when the test comes back positive? You going to just let it slide when one of your detectives is high as a kite while working a kidnapping case?"

"I can back up Remalla. But it's hard to go after someone for drugging your partner when you hide what happened. You choose to keep it quiet, then they get away with it. You can test that coffee all day, but if we don't come forward, then what's the point?"

"I can't take the risk that they'll drag Rem's name through the mud, accuse him of being a drug user, and try to ruin his reputation. I appreciate your willingness to back him up, but you know how people think. Unfortunately, in most people's minds, you're guilty before proven innocent."

"Remalla is a decorated officer, with high marks on his reviews and an even higher success rate with closed cases. You're forgetting that we have an effective state attorney. He can use that, along with Remalla's testimony, which would include how his coffee was spiked in our own damn cafeteria.

That could be very effective against Allison and Measy. Sometimes the truth is the best defense."

"It could also destroy a career," said Daniels. "You know what they'll say. That he's lying and using this case to hide his drug use. And it gives them reason to suggest Rem's drugging from Allison's assault and from when he was taken by Victor is because of his own personal use. Don't forget. We still have six months to go on this. That's plenty of time to sow doubt."

Lozano sighed and pulled out his chair and sat. "I still don't like it."

"I don't like it either, Cap. Believe me. I want to find who did this and make them pay for it, but it's not that simple." He grabbed the chair in front of Lozano's desk, pulled it close, and sat. "We have to realize the bigger picture here."

"And what's that?"

A knock on the door made Daniels stop. Titus poked his head in. "I got the security cam footage from downstairs. You want to see it?"

"Yes. Come in," said Lozano.

Titus entered. "Can I use your computer?"

Lozano stood, and Titus moved close and typed on the keys.

"What'd you find?" asked Daniels, stepping closer.

The screen flickered on, and Titus tapped on the screen. "This is from the camera in the cafeteria. It's not great, but it's something. I pinpointed the time that Remalla showed and found this." He hit a button and the video played. Daniels could see Rem enter the cafeteria, grab a donut and coffee cup, get in line, and pay. Eyeing the rest of the area, Daniels could see the cafeteria was about half-full.

"This is where it gets interesting," said Titus.

Daniels watched as Rem poured some coffee, but then looked around. He leaned over to speak with a woman wiping down a table with her back to the camera, and the video went fuzzy.

"What the hell?" asked Lozano. "What happened?"

"Hell if I know," said Titus. "Can't see a damn thing for another minute, until Rem takes a seat and grabs a paper." He paused and waited. "Right about now." The screen focused, and Daniels could see Rem sitting with a donut in front of him, drinking his coffee. A paper was on the table, and he appeared to be reading it. It didn't take long before he started to act strangely. He poked at the paper and then stared at his hands. After a few seconds, he talked to another person at a neighboring table, who left and found another place to sit. Then Rem stood with a wobble and spoke to Tony.

"Hell," said Daniels. "No wonder somebody asked me about him. I can't believe he made it up the stairs and back to the squad room."

The video ended, and Titus closed it. "That sucker gets to Measy, and he's gonna have a field day. And there might be video from between here and the cafeteria, too, which would show Rem returning. God knows what that looks like."

Daniels dropped his head. "We've got to keep this quiet."

"How quiet can you keep it when you know people are already asking about Rem?" asked Lozano. "If you hide it, it looks worse."

"And if you don't hide it, it could get worse," said Titus. "Georgios has been back a month after his episode, and he's still getting looks from other cops. You can see the doubt on their faces. The video doesn't show anyone tampering with Rem's drink and without definitive proof, coming forward is a crapshoot."

"What about a woman with a mole?" asked Lozano. "Didn't Remalla say something about that?"

"He did," said Daniels. "But hell. He could have been talking about somebody's nostrils for all I know. He thought everybody's faces were falling off."

"I asked around, but nobody seems to recall anyone with a mole," said Titus. "Unless it was the woman he spoke to before the footage blurred. What I don't get is why it blurred. Isn't that the same thing that happened with the video at the convenience store where you saw Rudy with Josh Lambert?"

Daniels nodded. "Yeah. It is." He made eye contact with Lozano. "I'm telling you. Allison and Rudy are working together."

"Whoa," said Titus. "Hold up. Rudy and Allison Albright?"

Daniels filled him in on Rudy's visit with Allison in jail and his and Rem's interview with Donna Kentwood that morning. He included Rudy's supposed electrokinesis.

Titus' eyes widened, and Lozano glowered. "Wait a minute," said Lozano. "You think Rudy is somehow controlling electricity?"

"It's a theory," said Daniels.

"You think he waltzed in here this morning and drugged Remalla, under all our noses?" asked Titus.

"No. I don't. We think he has an accomplice," said Daniels. "Which may be the woman in the video who might have a mole. My guess is she can do what Rudy does."

Lozano raised his hand. "I can understand that, as an associate of D'Mato, you think Rudy has some ability to manipulate energy. God knows D'Mato attracted those people, but he just as easily could have some sort of technology that he carries with him that affects video, and maybe even phone traces. If it's strong enough, it might even kill people. Have you considered that?"

Daniels didn't have the strength to argue. "Maybe. But whatever he's doing, it's working." He sat and stared at the ceiling, feeling the weight and worry creep into his bones. "Rudy told Rem that Allison wanted to see him, and also said Rem had a choice."

"What choice was that?" asked Titus.

"Basically, play along and go see her, or else," said Daniels. "I'm guessing what happened today is part of the what else."

"But what about Josh?" asked Titus. "How does he fit into all of this?"

Daniels massaged the back of his neck, feeling the start of a headache.

"Josh is a casualty of Rudy," said Lozano. "Allison is a separate piece of the puzzle, and unfortunately, the two have collided, making for one damn big mess."

Daniels tried to think it through. "Allison is using Rudy, whether it's because of his unique abilities, or some crazy technology, I don't know, but she knows Rudy can get to me and Rem." He considered something else. "And she must also realize Rudy's a loose cannon. Rudy may say one thing and do another. But Donna said he's also a man of routine."

"What do you mean?" asked Lozano.

"Once Rudy gives up Josh, which we assume he will…" said Daniels, "…then what happens?"

Titus eyed the clock. "So far, it's not looking like it will be today."

Daniels tapped at the armrest. "Maybe that's why they went after Rem now. Because once Rudy gives up Josh, he might disappear."

"But what about the picture?" asked Lozano. "That's what he wants. He's not leaving without that."

"No. I know," said Daniels, thinking. "He's got some sort of plan up his sleeve. Something that gives Allison what she wants, while also getting him what he wants."

Titus frowned. "Allison wants to see Rem, Measy wants Rem compromised, and Rudy wants his picture. Right now, Rudy and his assumed accomplice are using Josh as leverage. But once Josh is released, Rudy loses his bargaining chip. But if he still wants that picture, he'll hang around until he gets it, and maybe help Allison and Measy at the same time. It's a win-win for all of them, which means you and Rem are still in his crosshairs."

"Allison's plan is to use Rudy to convince Rem to see her?" asked Lozano. "With Rudy as unstable as he is, it's risky. It could backfire on her."

"It's also pretty damn smart." Titus crossed his arms. "Rudy's depraved enough to go where others won't. Drugging Rem and threatening to ruin his career could be enough to get to him. Add Daniels to the mix, and he just might take that leap."

Daniels didn't even want to think about that. "If we keep this incident quiet, their plan might not work."

"You might keep it under the radar for a while," said Titus, "but if Measy knows what happened, which is likely, then he'll be looking for evidence." He nodded toward the computer. "The video is probably not the crazy smoking gun he wanted, and you might get away with telling people Rem wasn't feeling well. But all of us in this room, including Georgios, know what happened today." He paused. "If Measy calls us to the stand, are we all going to lie?" He smirked. "Don't get me wrong. I'll back you up either way, but it's something to think about."

Daniels squeezed his temples.

"Allison knows Rem's allegiance to the people he loves, and she'll use it." Lozano aimed a pointed stare at Daniels. "And Rudy is her perfect messenger boy. He's already messed with you and your family, Daniels. He'll do whatever it takes to get what he wants. Which is why maybe we should call her bluff and come forward with what happened today."

Daniels had to consider another option. "What if we offer to give Rudy the picture back?"

"Absolutely not," said Lozano with a glare. "We don't negotiate with murderers and kidnappers. I think your partner would agree."

Daniels stood, frustrated. "My partner is currently seeing melting body parts and thinks his eyeball is lying on the squad room floor. He's been through enough to warrant the return of Rudy's picture." He paced. "If that's what it takes to get Rudy to back off, then maybe it's worth it."

"Listen to what you're saying," said Lozano. "Are you going to do this every time the going gets rough? You start now, then it becomes a dangerous precedent."

"Then what do you suggest we do?" asked Daniels. "Wait for Measy to do his damage and, assuming Rudy hangs around, prepare for whatever he has planned next?"

Lozano stood. "If we catch this guy, then most of our troubles go away, wouldn't you agree?"

Daniels hung his head.

"I know you're worried about Rem. Now that we know what they're capable of, we'll be careful. I'll add a patrol to Rem's house, and we'll watch him." Lozano paused. "I'll talk to the state's attorney and see what we can do about Measy. If we can link Measy to any witness tampering, it will end his career. But if you don't come forward with what happened to Rem, then that becomes more difficult. But I'll leave that decision to you. You already know what I think."

"Georgios brought the coffee sample to the lab. We should know something soon," said Titus. "But if we need those results to disappear, along with this video, we can make it happen."

"Titus," said Lozano. "I didn't hear that."

"It's Daniels' partner, Cap," said Titus. "You back up your partner, no matter what."

"Not when it comes to breaking the law, you don't." Lozano raised a brow. "You got that?"

Daniels eyed Titus. "Yeah, Cap," said Daniels.

Titus held Daniels' gaze. "Sure thing, Cap."

"I suggest you take this conversation somewhere else," said Lozano. "I think I've said my piece, and you know where I stand. Any other decisions, well..." He shuffled some papers on his desk. "...you're both seasoned detectives. I trust you to make a judgement call. Just be sure you're prepared for the consequences."

Daniels needed to call Mikey and check in. "I hear you."

"Me, too," said Titus.

"Then go on. Get out of here. Find Rudy and Josh. Bring them in and you may find a lot of your problems are solved."

Daniels headed for the door, along with Titus.

"And Daniels," said Lozano.

Daniels stopped. "Yeah, Cap?"

He aimed a steely gaze. "You choose to go public, I'll back you and Rem up a hundred percent. It's not just partners that look out for each other."

Daniels held the doorknob, knowing Rem's drugging was just the beginning of their problems, and that the likelihood of capturing Rudy was slim to none. He recalled what Donna Kentwood had told him and Rem, which he'd kept to himself, and nodded. "Thanks, Cap." He held the door for Titus and followed him out.

Chapter Twenty-One

A SOFT BREEZE BLEW Rem's hair, and he closed his eyes, feeling the warmth of the sun on his face. He sat on the bench in front of the wishing well, just down from the carousel, and remembered the last time he'd sat there. Smiling at the memories, he dug into his pocket, searching for a coin to throw into the well, when someone sat beside him. Smelling a familiar scent, he recognized Jennie's perfume, and looking over, he saw her. Her long, soft brown hair blew in the same breeze, and she smiled. "Hey, honey."

His heart thudded. "Jennie?"

"Yeah. It's me." She rested her arm on the back of the bench and shifted to face him. "How are you?"

Rem debated what to say. He couldn't recall how he'd arrived at the amusement park on his own, but had some recollection of being at the station earlier. There'd been a problem, and he'd left, but that's all he could remember. "I'm not sure. But I think I've been better."

She put a hand on his shoulder. "You're still as handsome as ever."

His confusion faded, and he took her hand. "And you're still as beautiful." His body warmed at her touch. "I've missed you."

She squeezed his fingers. "I've missed you, too. But I'm always close."

"Not quite close enough."

Jennie watched him, and her eyes gleamed when she caught sight of something behind him. "You want to have some fun?"

Rem raised a brow. "What did you have in mind?"

She stood and tugged on his hand. "C'mon."

Rem stood and let her lead him to the Ferris Wheel. A vague memory flickered of them riding it before and he'd held on for dear life when they'd reached the top and he could see how far up they were. "Are you serious?"

Jennie grinned. "It'll be fun."

"You remember I couldn't look down the last time we did this?"

"C'mon, honey. You only live once."

Eager to make her happy and savor his time with her, he couldn't say no and he followed her on to an open cart. Not seeing anyone else around, he wondered who was operating the ride, but the second they sat, the door closed, and the wheel began to turn. Rem's stomach churned, but he kept his eyes on Jennie and not on the view.

Jennie sat against the edge and looked out as their height increased. "Isn't it beautiful?"

Rem enjoyed her glee. "Certainly is."

She met his gaze and slid closer to him. "I like being here with you."

He put his arm around her and pulled her next to him, feeling her body against his. The wheel continued to turn and rise, but he barely noticed. "I wish you hadn't left."

She grabbed onto his hand. "I know." She paused. "But you know we signed up for this, don't you?"

He felt her thumb graze his skin. "What exactly did I sign up for? Because I think maybe I wasn't given the whole story."

"You were." She shifted closer. "We both were." Sighing, she eyed the view. "Don't you realize yet why you're here?" She looked back. "What your true purpose is?"

He couldn't stop staring at her. "What's that?" He raised a hand and ran a tendril of her hair through his fingers.

"You protect people. It's what you wanted."

"I did?"

She nodded. "And I signed up to protect you."

Rem frowned, not understanding.

A gust of wind blew, and Jennie reached up and took a strand of his own hair and pushed it back from his face. “Don’t you realize that if I hadn’t died, you would have?”

His stomach fell, but not because of the height. “What do you mean?”

“I protected you, just like you protect others. It wasn’t your time, but it was mine, and I left because I can do a better job of watching out for you from this side, and not the physical one.”

Rem dropped his jaw. “You left to protect me?”

“I had to.” She cupped his face. “As much as I love you and would have stayed with you until I was old and gray, we were never meant to be together forever, at least not in the physical realm. You were meant to stay, and I was meant to return.”

“I would have gone. I would have left first.” He went quiet, remembering the pain of losing her. “I wish I had.”

“No. You don’t mean that.” He opened his mouth to argue, but she kept talking. “Do you know the number of people you’ve helped?” she asked. “The people you’ve rescued? Those who would have suffered or died without you? And I’m including Daniels in that scenario, too. He needs you just as much as you need him.”

“But I needed you, too.”

She grazed his cheek with her thumb. “Sweetheart, you have me. You always have. And you always will. Everything’s connected, my love. Just because I’m not someone you can see, hear, and touch doesn’t mean I’m not there.” She paused. “But I know it’s been hard.”

Reaching its apex, the Ferris Wheel slowed and stopped, the cart gently rocking in the wind. Normally, Rem would be white-knuckling it, and focusing his gaze on the floor, but all he could see was Jennie. “I wasn’t very strong when you left. I’m still not sure how strong I am.”

She lowered her hand from his face and took his own. “You’re stronger than you think. And I know you’ve struggled, and I know there will be future challenges, but you can handle them. Know that there is a purpose and a reason for all of it." She offered him a sly smile. "And you will find love again. I've made sure of it. And when you're ready to see her, you will."

He gripped her fingers. "I don't want to fall in love again. It's too hard, and it scares me."

Jennie rested her forehead against his, and the wheel began to turn and descend. "You weren't meant to be alone. Your heart is too big to keep to yourself. Don't deny someone that."

He breathed in her scent and wished they could stay on the Ferris Wheel forever, but something told him their remaining time was short, and he sensed that when they reached the bottom, she would be gone. "You can't stay, can you?"

She raised her head. "I can, but you can't. You have things to do."

His heart fell. "What if I said no?"

She held his gaze. "If you truly wanted to stay, you would, but you know you can't. There are more people to help."

He closed his eyes, but just as quickly opened them, fearing she would be gone. "What if we just stay for a little while? Stop the wheel, and just sit and enjoy each other's company?" He let go of her hand and stroked her cheek. "I can leave later."

The wheel seemed to move faster, and she put her hand on his knee. "Time is short, my love. The longer you stay, the harder it will be to go, and people are worried about you. Plus, I need to tell you a few things before you return."

He did his best not to plead, knowing in his gut that he would have to leave, no matter how hard it would be. He forced himself to ask the obvious. "What do I need to know?" The wheel reached the three-quarter mark, and the ground loomed below.

She found his hand again and took it. "Everything will work out, no matter how bad it may seem. You will be okay." She placed her palm over his stomach. "Trust your gut because that's how I talk to you, okay?"

He put his hand over hers and held it against him. "Okay."

"Stick to the park, despite what others say, and tell Daniels to take the shot."

Rem shook his head. "Am I supposed to know what any of that means?"

"You will when the time comes."

The ground edged closer. "Anything else?" His throat constricted, knowing she would be gone soon.

"Just know that I love you."

His eyes welled. "I love you, too." He swallowed, holding back tears. "Always will."

"Say hi to Daniels for me. And thank him for watching out for you."

"I will. He'll be happy to hear from you."

"If he paid more attention, he'd hear from me more often."

He chuckled softly. "You should stand at the foot of his bed in the middle of the night. He'd love that."

Jennie grinned. "I'll consider it. Maybe when he needs a good kick in the pants."

Painfully aware of the slowing wheel as it neared the end of its revolution, he took her hands in both of his. "Thanks for visiting me."

"You needed it. And you were in a place to receive it." She squeezed his fingers. "You be well and stay strong. I love you. So much."

His breath caught, and he whispered. "I love you, too."

The wheel came to a stop, and the door opened. Rem took a shuddered breath and blinked. Taking every second with her he could, he focused on the feel of her skin against his, her scent in the air, and her essence surrounding his own, and then she faded. Trying to hold on, he saw the wheel fade as well, and feeling a warmth fill him, he began to float. Jennie and the park disappeared, and he clenched his eyes shut, distraught in his loss, but even that faded, and then he felt nothing at all.

His limbs suddenly heavy, Rem opened his eyes. Blinking, he didn't know where he was. His vision swam and cleared, and he saw two eyes staring down at him. Someone nudged his shoulder. "Rem?" It was a woman.

He blinked again, trying to clear his head, and saw another person staring down at him.

"Rem? You awake?" It sounded like Daniels.

His body felt like dead weight, and he wanted to shut out the world and find Jennie again. He closed his eyes and let his mind drift and tried to remember where he'd seen her. Had she told him something? Her smile echoed in his mind, but the prodding on his shoulder distracted him. Moaning, he felt a trickle of sweat run down his back when the warmth enveloping him turned to heat. Feeling something over him, he pushed at it, and realized it was a blanket. He was lying on something soft. Touching it, he guessed it was a couch.

"Rem?" Daniels spoke again. "Can you sit up?"

Rem hovered between one world and another, and couldn't decide which one to join, but quickly felt the pull of those poking at him, and realized he didn't have a choice. He opened an eye and recognized Mikey. He attempted to speak and managed a croak instead. "Where am I?"

Daniels' face came into view. "You're at Redstone's office. How do you feel?"

Rem tried to assess his physical condition, but his body didn't want to cooperate. "Did I get hit by a car?"

"That might have been preferred," said Mikey. "But no."

Rem tugged at the blanket, and Daniels studied him. "How many eyes do you have?"

Rem carefully moved an arm and rubbed his head, thinking Daniels had lost it. "Last I checked, two. Should I have more?"

Mikey backed away. "I'll get you some water."

Rem heard another voice. "Looks like he's coming out of it." It sounded like Mason.

Daniels sat beside him. "Can you sit?"

Rem's body ached, and his head throbbed. He moaned when he tried to move. Reaching out, he forced himself to reconnect to the world, and Jennie faded from his mind. Daniels took his hand, and Rem gripped onto it and tried to pull up. His muscles protested, but with Daniels' help, he got into a sitting position. His dry throat made his voice crack. "What happened?" For a moment, his vision spun, and he leaned over and rested his forehead in his hands. "How'd I get here?"

"You remember anything?" asked Daniels. "From the morning, or being at the station, or the cafeteria?"

Rem tried to think back. Everything swirled, and he couldn't even be sure what day it was, but then a memory flickered. "We talked to someone this morning."

"Yeah, we did," said Daniels. "You recall who?"

He groaned when he tried to sit back. "A woman." He remembered cookies, and a face came into focus. "Donna Kentwood."

"So far, so good," said Mason.

Mikey came over with a glass of water and handed it to him. "Here. Drink this." She sat on the other side of him.

Rem took it and sipped on it, but then his thirst engaged and he drained the glass. "Thanks."

Mikey took the glass back. "I'll get you some more."

"What happened after Donna Kentwood?" asked Daniels.

Rem grunted. "Let me think." He shut his eyes and recalled driving with Daniels. "We went to the amusement park." The Ferris Wheel popped in his head. "Did I ride the Ferris Wheel?"

"The park's closed, partner," said Daniels. "No such luck. We just walked around."

Rem could see the view from the top of the wheel in his mind's eye. "You sure?"

"I am. You remember what happened after the park?"

His memories slowly returned. "We got something to eat, and...uh, went back to the station." He turned his head to see Daniels. "Right?"

"You win the gold star," he said. "What happened then?"

Rem sighed, wondering why Daniels felt the need to quiz him. Mikey brought him more water, and he drank that, too. "I...I went to the cafeteria." His body tensed, and he recalled Measy. "I was avoiding the squad room."

"You were," said Daniels.

"I...uh...," said Rem. "I got some coffee and a donut."

"Now we're getting to the good part," said Mason, who leaned against his desk.

"You recall anything after that?" asked Daniels.

Rem blinked, his thoughts suddenly fuzzy. "I went to sit." He paused. "No. Wait. I couldn't find the cream and sugar." He shook his head. "I asked someone. A woman, where it was."

Daniels shifted on the sofa, his face serious. "You remember what she looked like?"

Confused, Rem rubbed his aching neck. "What the hell is going on here? Why am I at Mason's office?"

"Bear with me," said Daniels. "What did the woman look like?"

"Just go slow," said Mikey, sitting beside him again. "Think it through."

Rem took a deep breath. "Fine. She was average height, thin, with red hair, and she had a mole on her cheek. It made me think of Marilyn Monroe."

Daniels took out his notepad and scribbled on it. "Did you get a name?"

Rem didn't understand what was going on. "Um...her nametag said Sally." His mind traveled further. "I went to sit down." He recalled the paper. "I found something to read, ate my donut, and drank my coffee, and then I..." His stomach fluttered and he held his breath. "I...I..." He lifted a hand and stared at it. "I think my skin melted." He blinked, remembering the drips of people's faces and bodies hitting the floor. He held his stomach. "What happened to me?"

Daniels put his notepad away and hesitated. "You were dosed with some sort of hallucinogenic, probably in your coffee, and probably by this woman named Sally." He paused. "You made it to the squad room, and I got you out of there and brought you here to sleep it off."

Rem's stomach gurgled, and he felt the first stirrings of shock. "Some woman named Sally drugged me in the cafeteria?"

"She did," said Daniels.

"Her name's not Sally," Mikey said.

Rem looked over, and so did Daniels. Mikey stared at the floor, her face pale.

"What are you talking about?" asked Mason, pushing off the desk.

Mikey looked up. "I know her." She paused. "When you mentioned the mole and red hair..."

"How do you know her?" asked Daniels.

Mikey's mouth hung open. "Her name's Ginger. It's the woman from the bonfire who Rudy went off with instead of me."

Chapter Twenty-Two

The next morning, Daniels parked the car in front of the station. Rem sat in the passenger seat, staring off into the lot. After getting him home yesterday, Daniels had made him eat and drink something before Rem had collapsed into bed, mentally and physically spent. Not wanting to leave him alone and vulnerable, Daniels had stayed another night. That morning, though, Rem had woken up sullen and quiet, and all attempts Daniels had made to get him to engage had failed. Even buying him a large, loaded coffee at the nearby convenience store hadn't worked.

Daniels spoke to him before getting out of the car. "Listen. We should talk before we go inside."

Rem held his coffee and popped the door open. "There's nothing to discuss. Let's go." He slid out.

Daniels slid out, too, and eyed Rem across the hood. He couldn't force his partner to engage, but considering the events of the previous day, they needed to discuss a few things. "Rem. Wait."

Rem ignored him, though, and Daniels cursed and closed his door. He jogged to catch up with Rem, who entered the station.

Shorty stood at the front counter and greeted them as they entered. "Morning," he said.

"Hey, Shorty," said Rem.

"Hey, Rem," said Shorty, his eyes narrowing. "You doing better today?"

Rem slowed. "Yeah. I feel fine."

"Good. I was a little worried about you. You kept asking where my nose was yesterday."

Daniels almost audibly groaned. The number of people Rem had bumped into after leaving the cafeteria kept growing.

Rem hesitated. "I…sorry about that."

"It's this case, Shorty," said Daniels. "The hours take their toll."

"I hear you," said Shorty. "Glad you got some rest. Hopefully, something will break soon on Josh Lambert."

"I hope you're right," said Daniels.

Rem didn't say anything and headed up the stairs.

Daniels tried again. "Rem, maybe we should—"

Rem rounded the landing and almost ran into Titus.

Titus stopped. "Hey, Rem. You okay?"

Rem set his jaw. "Yeah. I'm fine."

"Good," said Titus. "After what happened, I can imagine you're pissed." He eyed Daniels. "The offer still stands if you want to lose the video. Georgios would be more than happy to stick it to Measy."

"Great. I appreciate it," said Daniels. He watched Rem, who'd gone still. "I'll let you know."

"I'm headed to the cafeter—" Titus stopped, eyeing Rem's coffee. "Sorry. I was going to ask if you wanted anything, but I'm guessing that's a no."

"We're good," said Daniels. "Thanks."

Titus nodded and headed down the stairs.

Rem stood rigid in the stairwell. "He knows?"

Daniels stepped up next to him. "He does."

Rem's face furrowed. "Who the hell doesn't know?"

"If you'd give me five minutes to talk to you, I would explain," said Daniels.

Rem's knuckles turned white on his coffee cup. "What am I? The damn laughingstock of the precinct?"

"No. You are not." An officer ran up the stairs and passed them, and Daniels lowered his voice. "Come with me." He pulled on the shoulder of Rem's jacket, made it to the second floor, and found an empty interrogation room. Rem followed, and Daniels closed the door behind them. After closing the blinds, he eyed his friend, who paced in the room. "I've been trying to talk to you all morning, but you haven't exactly been chatty."

Rem smacked his cup down on the table with a thunk. "What is there to say? I got dosed by some chick named Ginger in the damn cafeteria. I obviously made a complete fool of myself, which everyone seems to have witnessed, and I'm guessing was the whole point." He stopped and ran his hands through his hair. "I'm still trying to come to grips with what happened, and now I have to deal with everybody looking at me like I'm some sort of freak."

"Nobody's looking at you like you're a freak," said Daniels.

Rem threw out a hand. "How do Titus and Georgios know I was drugged? What the hell happened yesterday?"

Daniels kept his cool. "If you'd sit for one second and let me tell you what is going on, you'd understand."

Rem shook his head and shut his eyes. After taking a second, he opened his eyes, pulled out a chair, and sat. "Fine."

"Thank you." Daniels took a breath and recalled the events of the prior day and filled Rem in on what had happened. "That's why Titus and Georgios know. If it hadn't been for them, it could have been a lot worse. Thankfully, I got you out before Measy could get to you. The only safe place I could think to bring you was Redstone's."

Rem stared at the floor, his fingers clenched on the table's edge. "What about Lozano? Did he see me, too?"

"No, but I told him what happened. He wanted us to come forward. Get you tested."

Rem's grip tightened. "Did you? Get me tested?"

"No. Georgios took your coffee down to the lab, though, to find out what they gave you."

Rem stood abruptly and paced. "This whole thing was orchestrated to make me look like an unreliable cop and drug user, which will play beautifully into Measy's hands."

"Which is why I didn't want to get you tested." Daniels raised a hand. "Lozano thought we should call their bluff and use it against them. That's when Titus mentioned we could get rid of the cafeteria video if we wanted to prevent Measy from getting it."

"I hate to tell you this partner, but it may not matter." He stopped. "What are you going to do when they call you to the stand and ask about whether you've ever seen me on drugs at work? What are you going to say? And what are Lozano, Titus, Georgios, and God knows who else they'll call, going to say?"

"You know we'll back you up. We'll tell them you were drugged."

Rem whirled. "But we can't prove that. Just like we can't prove that Allison drugged me. They can make all of this look like it's on me."

"Not with our testimony."

"That depends on what the jury believes. And I can't ask you to lie. That's risking all our careers. Never mind mine."

Daniels straightened. "Measy won't get away with this."

Rem turned and walked to the window, his hands on his hips. His face stony, he smacked the wall, then turned and shoved a chair. With a curse, he grabbed the table and overturned it. His coffee spilled onto the floor and the table fell to its side with a bang as Rem kicked and knocked over the other chairs in the room.

Daniels let him vent, knowing how he'd feel if it had been him.

His fury fading, Rem paced, breathless.

"Feel better?" asked Daniels.

"Not really, no." He threw out his hand. "I feel so...so..."

"Used?"

He hung his head. "Worthless and stupid." He looked up with somber eyes. "When are these people going to stop?" His voice dropped to a whisper. "First Allison, and now Ginger. I can't catch a break. And now I could lose my career over this. Never mind the trial."

Daniels steeled himself, determined to be the voice of reason Rem needed right now. "You are not going to lose your career. Lozano and I will back you up a hundred percent."

"And you could both end up damaging yourselves in the process." He righted a chair and sat. "Hell. Maybe I should just resign."

"Rem, we cannot give in to this," said Daniels. "We do, and what's stopping any other criminal from doing the same thing to another cop down the line? We have to hang in there and face it head on. Measy is used to manipulation, and Allison is feeding him information on exactly what to do. Add to that Rudy as her personal assistant, and now Ginger, who's helping Rudy. I know it sucks, but we'll stop them, and resigning is not going to do that." He grabbed another chair and sat in front of Rem. "I don't care if you walked the halls offering to pick up everyone's body parts and asked Measy to play patty cake, we are not giving in. We may all go down with the ship, but not without a fight. You got that?"

Rem hesitated. "You got any ideas on how to do that, because right now, I'm feeling pretty defeated. All the cards seem to be in Measy's and Allison's favor." He sat back. "Unless..." He held Daniels' look.

Daniels scowled. "Oh, hell, no. You are not visiting Allison."

"Maybe if I do, this all goes away."

"Are you still affected by the drugs? Because you know you can't trust anything she says. She wants to mess with you. That's her plan."

"Maybe if I see her, I can figure out what she's up to."

"Rem." Daniels held up a finger. "Absolutely not. Anything you say to her can be used against you. Just going to see her could be damaging."

"You don't think the situation I'm in now is any less damaging? Shit." He stood. "I'm at the mercy of a bunch of nutcases who've sent me nasty messages, left me in the dark, and now drugged my coffee. Not to mention what they did to you and your family. I think we may be running out of options."

"That's exactly what she wants you to think." He stood as well. "Neither of us knows what will happen after Rudy releases Josh. He and Ginger could disappear, and we'll never see them again."

"You're living in Alice's Wonderland if you think that's going to happen."

"And you don't know what Measy has against you as far as yesterday. His reliance on eyewitness testimony is risky. You know how cops are. We're not going to throw you under the bus."

"Somehow, I think they were ready. They didn't plan on relying solely on testimony."

"Then we have to wait and see. Let's find Josh Lambert and go from there. Who knows? Maybe we'll catch Rudy and Ginger, and Allison's plan goes down the drain. And we can talk about how we want to handle the cafeteria video."

Rem sighed and studied the floor. "If Measy gets it, I'm toast. We can talk about how I was drugged by Allison and Ginger all day, but without proof, it's worthless."

"Maybe not. If he brings it up, you'll at least get the opportunity to explain what happened. Maybe we should actually trust a jury and the prosecutor to get to the truth." He leaned in. "Nobody in this building believes you're a user, Rem. You have to believe that."

"I don't know what I believe anymore."

Daniels put a hand on his shoulder. "Which is why I'm here. Let me help, but don't shut down on me. I can take the wheel for a bit until you get your bearings."

"My bearings are rolling all over the floor. Like my eye."

"Well, the good news is your eye was never actually rolling on the floor. Same goes for your bearings. The show tune is still playing, and the fat lady isn't singing. Let's not give her a reason to start."

Rem rested his back against the wall and stared off. "Okay. I'll try." His shoulders slumped and his eyes narrowed.

"What is it?"

He sighed and stretched his neck. "I think I'm supposed to tell you something, but I can't remember."

"Tell me something?"

Rem rubbed his eyes. "I had a dream when I was out of it. I remembered parts of it this morning. Jennie was in it. We were riding the Ferris Wheel."

"At the park?"

Rem nodded. "Yeah." He lowered his hand. "She talked to me, but it's a blur. I can't think of what she said."

"It'll come to you when you're ready. You've had a few other things to deal with."

"I guess."

Daniels eyed the spilled coffee. "We need to find a mop."

"Sorry. I wasted a perfectly good drink."

"It can be replaced." Daniels walked to the table, pulled it up, and set it back on all fours.

"Not by one from the cafeteria. Don't think I'll be going there anytime soon."

Stepping around the puddle of coffee, Daniels set the other chairs back up. "You might talk to Tony. He was at the register. He's a little worried about you."

Rem groaned. "Great. God knows what I said or who I talked to yesterday."

"Look at it this way, partner. It could have been worse. The drugs had you seeing missing body parts, but you're lucky you didn't act crazier than you did, and you didn't get mean. That would have been a totally different ball game."

"Chalk one up for the Remalla humor. At least it saved me this time, instead of getting me in more trouble."

Daniels headed for the door. "Let's go find a mop and get you some more coffee. Hopefully, Georgios brought his machine from home."

"Let's hope," said Rem. "Or it's going to be a long damn day."

Daniels nodded, pleased to see that Rem's mood had shifted from the edge of the precipice, and hoped the day would go better than the morning. Stepping out into the hall, he saw a commotion as a couple of officers ran past him, and then Titus and Georgios stepped out of the squad room, putting on their jackets. "What's the hurry?" he asked. Rem stepped out behind him.

"There you are," said Titus. "Cap was wondering. I barely made it to the cafeteria when we got a call that there'd been a sighting of Josh. He was spotted down by the pier. Cap wants everybody on it."

"This could be it," said Georgios. "Maybe that asshole finally let the kid go."

"Down by the pier?" asked Rem. "Why there?"

"God knows. Maybe he likes the water," said Titus.

They followed Titus and Georgios down the stairs and into the parking lot. "Send us the address," said Daniels.

"Will do," said Georgios.

Daniels ran to the car, and he and Rem got in. Daniels waited for the text as Rem slid on his seat belt. Buckling it, he stopped and picked up something from the seat. He held and stared at it.

Daniels noticed it was a candy wrapper from Redstone's office. Rem had carried a few out after leaving Mason and Mikey the previous day. "Something wrong?"

Rem crinkled the paper in his hand but seemed lost in thought. "Stick to the park," he whispered.

"What?" asked Daniels. His phone buzzed, and he accessed the text message, seeing the address. He started the engine.

"Wait," said Rem.

Daniels put it in reverse. "What's wrong?"

"Why would Rudy let go of Josh at the pier? He's never been near the pier before."

"Maybe he's starting something new."

"But he's a man of routine, remember?"

Daniels almost pulled out of the spot, but hesitated. "What are you thinking?"

Rem looked over. "Jennie said stick to the park."

Daniels wasn't sure how to interpret that. "That's great, but everyone's heading to the pier."

"I know," said Rem. He paused. "Which would make it damn easy to release Josh at the closed park instead. Don't you think?"

"You think the pier's a diversion?"

Rem raised a brow. "There's one way to find out."

Daniels considered that, but then he backed out, and trusting Rem's gut, headed toward the park.

Chapter Twenty-Three

THE PARK CAME INTO view, and Daniels turned into the lot while Rem spoke on the phone. He pulled up and stopped outside the chain-link fence where they'd accessed the grounds the day before.

Rem hung up and put his phone away. "Lozano's iffy on this, but he's willing to let us check it out. He's sending a car to back us up, but as soon as we realize it's a no-go, we head to the pier."

"He sounds optimistic."

"At least he was willing to hear me out." He studied the candy wrapper in his hand. "And to his credit, he didn't ask me how I was feeling."

Daniels killed the engine. "Lozano knows you're okay. You wouldn't be here if he didn't think you were up for it. He's not big on inquiring about feelings."

"Which I appreciate." Rem popped the door open and got out.

Daniels did the same and eyed the amusement park. The flags still flew, and the Ferris Wheel rose from the Midway. "You really think Rudy's here?"

Rem stared, his face serious. "I think there's a good chance. I clearly recall Jennie saying stick to the park."

"In your dream?"

"Yeah."

Daniels eyed the area and Rem. "Must have been quite a dream."

"It was." Rem scratched his head. "There was something else—"

"Car's here." Daniels pointed as a patrol car turned into the lot, drove up, and parked beside Daniels.

Two officers got out–a man and a woman. Daniels recognized the man. "Hey, Biggs."

"Hey Daniels. Rem," said Officer Biggs. He tossed out a thumb. "This is Benson. She's new. Still in training, but she's got lots of promise and a good head on her shoulders."

"That's good," said Rem. "Because we might need it."

Benson nodded. "What have we got?"

Rem explained his theory on Rudy releasing Josh in the amusement park. "We'll take the north side. You guys take the south. We'll meet in the middle. And check out the homeless on the far side. If Rudy sticks to the plan, one of them might be injured or dead."

Biggs went to his car and pulled out two walkie-talkies, and handed one to Rem. "We'll let you know if we find something," said Biggs.

"And be careful," said Daniels. "Josh is the priority. Get him out and let Rudy be. Rudy can be dangerous and I'd rather we all walk out of here alive with Josh than with Rudy in cuffs and one of us injured. Okay?"

"Sounds good to me," said Biggs. "You ready?" he asked Benson.

"I'm ready," she said. "How do we get in?"

Daniels and Rem walked to the fence and found the opening. They all climbed through and entered the grounds.

"Remember," said Rem. "No hero stuff. Find Josh and get out." He pulled his weapon and checked it, and hooked the walkie-talkie into his waistband.

"You got it," said Biggs. He eyed Benson. "Let's go."

•••••••••••

Rem followed the path he'd taken the day before, and Daniels walked behind him. Everything looked the same. They entered the rides section, and Rem passed a couple of rollercoasters and stopped at the Ferris Wheel. He looked up and around it, recalling it from his dream. He and Jennie had ridden to the top and stopped, and she'd told him to trust his gut, stick to the park, and...he squinted, trying to remember.

"Anything?" asked Daniels.

Rem turned from the wheel. "Nothing. It's quiet as a church." He pointed. "There's the bench where the candy wrappers were."

They walked over, but saw nothing. Daniels surveyed the area near the carousel. "Look."

Rem walked over and saw what Daniels did. "Is that a donut bag?"

Daniels straightened. "If anyone knows what a donut bag looks like, it's you."

"That wasn't there yesterday."

"No. It wasn't."

Rem looked around. "Let's go toward the carousel."

Daniels nodded, staying alert. They passed some empty booths, approached the merry-go-round, and stopped in front of it. The colorful, metallic horses stood silent in the stillness, and Rem wished they could talk and give them some tips on who'd been in the area. They walked around its circumference, but nothing stood out.

"Nothing from Biggs and Benson so far," said Daniels. "That's a good sign."

Rem stopped beside the wishing well and recalled sitting next to it with Jennie before her death, and also from his dream. He walked over and eyed the coins sparkling in the light at the bottom of the well. His gut churned, but nothing had roused serious suspicion. "I wonder if they've found anything at the pier?"

"Not from what we heard when we arrived," said Daniels. He leaned around Rem. "What's that?"

Rem turned to look, and Daniels stepped to the side of the wishing well. "Looks like somebody didn't like their breakfast."

Rem saw a partially eaten donut lying on the ground, with a row of ants already lined up to take it away. "Could be from a homeless person."

"Maybe, but why throw it away?" asked Daniels. "If you don't want it, give it to one of your friends. There are plenty of tents along the fence."

"Good point." Rem swiveled. "Let's check out the area around the bumper cars." He left the wishing well, passed the carousel, and entered a kiddie rides section with the bumper cars just beyond it. Passing a small train and little cars on their individual tracks, he stayed aware, checking down aisles and walkways. They made it to the bumper cars, and Rem stopped, beginning to feel they were wasting their time. "Nothing."

Daniels walked to the other side of the bumper cars and back around, shaking his head, when he paused just outside a large tent, which Rem recalled may have been a petting zoo. His face froze and his eyes widened. "Rem." And then he took off in a sprint.

Rem dashed after him, running toward Daniels and away from the cars, and rounding a corner, saw a boy standing beside the tent on a dusty and hay strewn path. A man lay on his side next to the boy, and another man was running from the scene as Daniels gave chase.

Rem recognized the boy as Josh Lambert and knew Rudy was the man running from Daniels.

"Stop. Police," yelled Daniels, in a full out sprint. He ran past Josh and the unconscious person and looked back at Rem.

"Go," said Rem, "I'll get him." He ran up to Josh, and Daniels kept going after Rudy. Breathless, Rem squatted beside Josh, acutely aware that Daniels was currently on his own. Josh stood in mute terror, his brown eyes as wide as the discarded donut by the wishing well. "Josh?" asked Rem. "I'm Detective Aaron Remalla. Are you okay?"

Josh didn't answer, but just stared at the man on the ground.

"Are you injured?"

Josh didn't answer.

Rem spoke on the walkie-talkie and got a hold of Biggs and Benson. Eying Josh, he conveyed to the officers what was happening and put down the walkie-talkie. "I'm going to check you out, okay?"

Josh made a small head bob, and Rem took Josh's shoulders and worked his hands down Josh's arms, torso and legs, but he did not appear to be hurt. "I'm going to check him next." He nodded toward the man laying against the tent. "More people are coming. Stay put. You're going to be all right."

Josh didn't move, and Rem moved over to the man lying on his side on the ground. He rolled him over and it was obvious from the tattered clothes, grimy hair and dirt-smeared skin that he was likely homeless. Rem leaned over him, his cheek to the man's face, and felt a small warm exhale, then checked his pulse. There wasn't one.

Rem pulled open the man's worn shirt and sucked in a breath when he saw the red circular mark on the man's chest.

"I couldn't do it," Josh whispered.

Rem looked over.

"I couldn't do it," Josh repeated. His pale face looked white in the sun.

"It's okay," said Rem. He turned back to the vagrant, just as Biggs and Benson rounded the corner. "Here," yelled Rem. "Over here."

Biggs and Benson ran over.

"Call it in and take care of Josh," said Rem. "And this man needs CPR. He's breathing but has no pulse and get an ambulance." He stood. "I'm going after Daniels. He's chasing Rudy."

"Go," said Biggs. "We got this. Be careful and don't get shot."

Rem nodded, but a memory flickered in his head. He saw Jennie on the Ferris Wheel. She took his hand, and her words reverberated in his mind. *Tell Daniels to take the shot.* "Shit," he whispered to himself. "Now I remember." And he took off in a full out run.

••••••••••

Daniels sprinted down the trail at full speed, trying to keep up, but Rudy was fast. "Rudy," he yelled. "Police. Stop."

Rudy didn't break stride though and kept going. They passed several small storage units which might have been used for vendors while the park was in operation. The trail turned rocky, and Rudy rounded a corner. Daniels almost slipped and fell, but made the turn. He slowed when he didn't see Rudy and pulled his weapon. He jogged farther down, but Rudy had disappeared. Breathing fast, he cursed himself. Where the hell had Rudy gone?

He continued down the rocky path, looking in between various sheds and empty bins and booths, angry that he'd lost him.

"Well, ring-a-ding-ding, Detective."

Daniels whirled and found Rudy behind him.

Breathing hard himself, Rudy grinned. "Looks like we meet again." A sheen of sweat made his forehead glimmer.

Trying to catch his breath, Daniels raised his gun. "Get down on your knees, Rudy. You're under arrest."

Rudy raised his hands. "You going to take me in?"

"That's the plan."

Rudy tipped his head. "You are a confident man."

"I'm also pissed. Get down on your knees. Now."

Rudy lowered his hands. "I don't think so, Detective. I think you know by now that I'm not your average suspect."

"You either get down and surrender, or I'm going to shoot you."

Rudy grinned bigger and took a step closer. "Really? You're going to shoot me?"

Daniels held his ground. "Don't mess around with me. I know what you're capable of. But you should know what I'm capable of."

"And what's that, Detective?" He took another step.

Daniels straightened his aim. "Killing you."

Rudy stopped. "I admire your courage. I think that's what I like about you. Few stand up to me." He crossed his arms. "I still want my picture."

Daniels narrowed his eyes. "And I want mine, but I'm not going to lose my life over it. You prepared to lose yours?"

Rudy pursed his lips. "Funny you should ask. Maybe I am." He took another step. "Unless I decide otherwise."

"I will shoot you," said Daniels, remembering the ten second rule, but having no idea when those ten seconds began.

"I know, and maybe that's for the best," said Rudy. "At least in Allison's eyes." He chuckled. "That woman really has it out for you, and especially for your partner. Despite what I've done for her, she'd probably wouldn't shed many tears over me."

Daniels fought to stay calm, but adrenaline coursed through him.

"Think it through, Detective. Maybe you shoot me, and assuming your timing is good, you kill me. But what happens when they find no weapon, and they believe you shot an unarmed man? There'll be an inquiry, and what are you going to tell them? That you feared I'd electrocute you with my bare hands?" He shook his head. "Good luck with that. Your career would be over, and it certainly wouldn't help your partner's case with Allison. Not many people trust the testimony of a dirty cop."

Daniels' anger grew, but he had to consider Rudy's argument.

"I got you thinking, don't I?" He chuckled. "We've already got the rumor mill going about your partner. Shouldn't take much more to push him over the edge and make his story about Allison less credible. All she needs is you out of the picture, and she's a free woman." He curled his fingers and shook them out, and Daniels detected a low hum in the air.

"Course, that means I'd be dead, which has its appeal in some ways, but not in others."

"None of that is going to happen," said Daniels.

"Isn't it?" asked Rudy, slowly encroaching. "Of course, the other option is I kill you. Have your partner find you curled up like a dead dog. That would effectively end your testimony and probably his too." He stared off. "He's already dealt with one soul-crushing loss. I think another is all it will take, and then he won't care what happens to Allison, and probably not even himself."

Daniels kept the gun on Rudy. "You don't know my partner very well."

"Maybe not, but I know gut-sucking loss. It can mess with your head."

"Everybody loses someone eventually, Rudy. You're not special."

Rudy's face fell. "I'm not talking about grief, Detective. I'm talking about soul-destroying, mind-bending despair. Losing a child or a soulmate is the only thing that compares. You don't understand that, but I think you got a glimpse of it the other night, when I visited your wife." He took another step. "Pretty lady."

Daniels gritted his teeth. "You need to watch yourself." The hum in the air became a buzz.

"And I think you need to decide how far you're willing to go. You shoot me dead, or I kill you, you risk your partner's sanity. You let me go, and you risk your own. You'll never again feel safe in your own home." He raised his hands. "What's it going to be?" He stepped to within a foot of Daniels' gun. "Maybe, instead," said Rudy, "the decision is mine. Just how do I want to play this?" He smirked. "Appease Allison, or amuse myself?" His gaze never wavered. "I really would love to put you in your place. I could kill that partner of yours, or maybe your child or wife. Then you'll know what pain is, Detective." His gaze focused into a laser glare. "You really should have returned the picture."

Daniels glared back and forced himself not to tackle and punch Rudy to death. "I'll do what I have to do, Rudy, and trust the pieces will fall into place. People like you dig their own holes until they're too deep to get out. I suspect yours is getting deeper by the second."

"I'm not the only one digging holes. You and your partner are going to need a ladder pretty soon if Allison and her bottom-feeding attorney have their way."

"Their methods won't work, Rudy. They'll get caught eventually, and Allison will never see the outside of a cell again."

Rudy took another step, and his chest almost bumped the tip of the gun. "Positivity sucks, Detective, and time's short. So, if you're going to shoot me, do it." He raised his hands. "I'm right here."

Daniels tightened his finger on the trigger, but knew Rudy was right. If Daniels shot him like this, he could never explain why. He would have to take Rudy in. "Get down on your knees. Now."

Rudy smirked. "Suit yourself. Let's see what happens." Slowly, he lowered himself until he was on his knees.

Daniels stepped around to the back of him. "Lie flat on the ground. Hands behind you."

Rudy did as asked and put his hands behind him.

Daniels hesitated, not knowing whether or not to touch him. Could he handcuff Rudy without getting injured? "Stay right there." He knew Rem would be there soon. Maybe he could wait until his partner arrived.

Rudy groaned. "I don't think so, Detective. Either you cuff me or I leave."

Daniels watched him but didn't move.

Rudy pushed up and began to stand.

"I said stay down. Don't move." Daniels stepped close, his gun aimed, when Rudy straightened, turned abruptly and reached out, his fingers grasping toward Daniels. The buzzing grew louder and pounded in Daniels' ears. Deciding he had to be within the ten second range, Daniels almost fired, but Rudy swiveled and shoved the gun down and away. He brought his hand up toward Daniels' sternum just as Daniels leaned away, and Rudy's fingers brushed Daniels' shoulder instead.

A powerful electric current flashed down Daniels' arm and into his chest. He gasped, lost his hold on the gun, and fell to his knees. The gun clattered to the ground. The current sizzled through his torso and down his legs, and curling up in bone-breaking pain, Daniels collapsed.

••••••••••

Rem raced down the rocky trail, looking down every off-shooting path he crossed, but didn't see Daniels or Rudy. He kept going, staying alert with his gun in hand. Acutely aware of the time, Rem understood what was at stake and that Rudy would not be taken easily. Worrying Daniels would be in over his head, he picked up his pace. Reaching almost the back of the park, he looked down another section, and his heart stopped.

Daniels was lying face down on the ground at the end, not moving.

"Oh, God. No." Rem flew down the section, past the empty sheds and booths and came up beside Daniels. "Daniels?"

His partner didn't move, and Rem got to his knees. Daniels' eyes were closed. Rem checked for a pulse, praying he would find one. Feeling faint heartbeats against his fingers, he said a desperate prayer of thanks, and rolled his partner onto his back. Rem cringed when he saw the burn mark on Daniels' shoulder. The fabric of his shirt had a jagged hole in it, and Rem could see Daniels' raw and red skin.

He jostled Daniels' arm and cursed that he'd left the walkie-talkie behind. "Daniels? Can you hear me?"

When Daniels didn't respond, he leaned over him and felt Daniels' breath against his cheek. Grateful his partner was breathing, he tried again. "Daniels," he said a little louder, and shook his shoulder.

Rem was about to try again when Daniels jolted awake. His eyes opened, and he sat up and shoved himself backward, away from Rem. He kept going until his back hit the wall of a storage bin, the metal denting when he hit it. He breathed in a deep gasp and held his chest.

Spotting Daniels' gun, Rem grabbed it and tucked it in his waistband. He approached Daniels and got in front of him just as Daniels grimaced and, clutching his arm, doubled over in pain.

Rem grabbed his shoulder to support him. "Easy. Take it easy."

Daniels wheezed into the dirt, breathing in shallow pants. His fingers found the ground, and he dug his nails into the rocks.

Rem wondered what to do. Should he get an ambulance? He leaned low to check his partner, hoping he would stay conscious. "Hey. Can you hear me? Are you okay?"

Daniels groaned and shut his eyes, but croaked out a few words. "Shit, that hurts." He rested his forehead on the ground.

"Take a few steady breaths," said Rem. "Just stay calm."

Daniels' grip eased, and his breathing gradually slowed. Eventually, he opened his eyes and attempted to sit up with Rem's help. "Where's Rudy?" he asked in a strained voice.

Rem watched Daniels to ensure he wasn't getting worse. "Never saw him." He tried to support Daniels when his partner coughed and clutched his injured shoulder. "What happened?"

Daniels blinked and blew out a breath. "I had him. I could have taken him in, but didn't know how to cuff him. Then he tried to get away, and he touched me." He grimaced again. "Damn. That packed a punch." His tension appearing to ease, but his face pale, Daniels leaned back against the bin.

"You need an ambulance?"

"No. Just give me a second."

"You sure? You're not looking too hot."

Daniels raised his knees and gripped his thighs. "I'll be okay. How's Josh?"

Rem kept an eye on his partner. "Scared and shaken, but he's alive."

"And the man on the ground?"

"Don't know. Not good. I told Biggs and Benson to call it in and get an ambulance."

Daniels rested his head back and stared at the sky, his breathing evening out and his skin regaining some color.

"Are you sure you're all right?" asked Rem.

Daniels rubbed his shoulder and winced. "My arm took a hit, but I think that's the worst of it. The pain's easing up."

Seeing Daniels improve, Rem let go of a relieved sigh and sat beside his partner. "Seeing you lying on the ground scared me to death." Rem wondered what he would have done if he'd rolled his partner over and seen the red circular mark on his chest. He closed his eyes, trying not to think about it.

"Sorry about that. I can imagine it didn't look good."

Rem thought of Jennie and opened his eyes. "Why didn't you shoot him?"

Daniels swiveled his head to look at Rem. "Wasn't as easy as you'd think."

Rem nodded. "It never is."

"Rudy casually mentioned that if I shot him, I'd have to explain why I killed an unarmed man. He had a point. Unless the M.E. can prove Rudy can flow electricity through his veins, it's not a good look." He rubbed his temples. "And it's even worse when I testify on your behalf and look like a vigilante cop."

Rem slid his gun into his holster and pulled Daniels' gun from his waist. "And I look like a recreational drug user who gets high while on the job." He handed Daniels his gun.

Daniels took it and returned it to its holster. "We got a problem, Rem. If we don't catch this guy, he's going to wreak havoc on us."

"He returned Josh, just like Henry. You think he's going to hang around?"

"I can almost guarantee it." He sighed. "It's not just about the picture, either. I think he's having fun."

"You mean messing with us gives him something to do in between kidnappings?"

"Something like that." He sat up with a groan and rubbed his injury. "I also think he likes running the show. He can choose what he wants to do and when. Allison's in jail and she relies on him, but he knows he can throw it back in her face whenever he wants. He's just biding his time, picking who he wants to torture and when."

Rem sat up next to Daniels. "Then maybe it's time we went on the offensive."

Daniels looked over. "You're thinking about what Donna Kentwood told us?"

"And Jennie."

Daniels frowned. "Jennie?"

"I remembered what she said. And I think it's time we listen." He stood and held out a hand. "This time I get to help you up."

Daniels looked up at Rem and took his hand. Rem pulled, and Daniels stood and groaned. "God. I hurt all over."

Rem patted his back. "C'mon, partner. Let's get you back, cleaned up and rested, and then we'll talk."

Chapter Twenty-Four

Rem entered the station the next morning, seeing Daniels at his desk. After finding Josh and getting Daniels back to the car in a sea of police vehicles and press, the day had turned into a whirlwind of reports, avoiding media, answering phones, talking to Lozano, and allowing Daniels time to rest and recuperate. Rem had convinced his partner to get a quick check up from Doc Martin, who'd helped them out on previous cases, and Daniels had reluctantly agreed. Martin had found no serious damage though and had directed Daniels to get some food and rest, and a day off, if possible.

Daniels had chuckled at that, but Rem had taken care of the food and sleep part, knowing that until Rudy was found, the days off would be few.

"Morning," he said. "How'd you sleep?" He walked to the new coffee maker Georgios had brought to the office and smiled at the full pot. He helped himself to a cup. "Feeling better after yesterday?"

Daniels sipped on an orange juice. "Pretty well. Arm's sore, but it's better."

"No visits from Rudy?" asked Rem.

"No. You?"

"None." Rem sipped his coffee. "For now."

Daniels nodded. "Yeah. For now."

They shared a look before Lozano poked his head out of his office. "I need to see you two."

Rem smirked. "Been here all of two minutes and we're getting called in."

Daniels stood. "It's that sparkling personality of yours. Cap must like it."

"Sparkling personality? Is that the new term for grumpy?" Rem headed toward Lozano's office.

"It certainly sounds better," said Daniels, holding his juice.

"I'll remind my shrink of that next time I see him."

They entered Lozano's office and sat. "How's it goin, Cap?" asked Rem. "You get some rest?"

"For the few hours I got, yes," said Lozano, sitting at his desk. "Finding Josh Lambert alive and well does wonders for the soul."

"It does," said Daniels.

"Now we just need to find Rudy," said Rem.

"Speaking of, that's why I called you in here," said Lozano. He picked up a file and waved it at Daniels. "You want to explain this report?"

"What's to explain, Cap?" asked Daniels. "Rudy got away."

"By punching you in the shoulder?" Lozano raised a brow.

"Guy's stronger than he looks," said Rem.

"You be quiet, Remalla. I'm talking to your partner," said Lozano.

Rem shrugged and drank from his mug.

"What do you want me to say, Cap?" asked Daniels. "That Rudy almost electrocuted me with his finger? I know you have your doubts about what Rudy can do. How do you suppose anybody else reading that report is going to feel about it?"

"How do you know he didn't have something in his pocket that he knocked you out with?" asked Lozano.

"Because I can see, that's why. The man touched me, and I went down like one of Rem's cups of coffee when he hasn't slept." He sat forward. "If I say what really happened in that report, you know the questions we'll get. As much as my ego hates to say Rudy got the upper hand because he punched me, I don't see what other choice I have."

Lozano stared at Daniels for a moment. “You pulled your weapon on him. Are you saying he disarmed you when you got punched?”

“I dropped it when he shocked me and it’s a good thing that’s the only thing I lost control of.”

Rem grimaced. “That would have been unpleasant.”

“If your life was in danger, why didn’t you shoot?” asked Lozano.

“And what happens when it looks like I shot an unarmed man?” asked Daniels. “That doesn’t look good to a chief of police, and certainly not to a captain.”

“It’s better than you being dead,” said Lozano. “And I refuse to believe we wouldn’t find whatever the hell Rudy’s using to kill people.”

Daniels sighed and rubbed his arm. “Yeah, well, it didn’t seem wise at the time.”

“He’s trying to protect me too, Cap,” said Rem. “He doesn’t want to give Measy anything to discredit our testimony on the stand.”

Lozano dropped the file on the desk. “Listen, you two. I realize that you’re under duress, and that with Allison’s trial looming, Rudy’s antics, and Measy’s transgressions, you’ve got a lot on your mind, but you can’t let all of that stop you from doing your job properly. You keep second-guessing and doubting the process, you’re both going to end up dead before we even get to a trial.”

“That may be exactly what Rudy wants,” said Daniels.

“Allison, too,” said Rem.

“Then don’t make it easy on them,” said Lozano. “If we need to, I’ll take you off the case. I can get Titus and Georgios to find Rudy.”

“Now that we’ve found Josh, we’d be all for it. But it’s not that simple,” said Daniels. “Rudy’s made it personal for both of us. Allison ensured that. You can put Titus and Georgios or anybody else on this if you want to, but if Rudy keeps harassing us, then it’s pointless.”

Lozano leaned back in his seat and crossed his arms. "It's obvious you two are in this up to your necks. Maybe I should have stuck to my guns and taken you off of this earlier."

"Too late now, Cap." Rem set his coffee cup on Lozano's desk. "At this point, we're just waiting for the other shoe to drop."

Lozano grunted and rubbed his face. "That's what worries me."

Rem glanced at Daniels, who swirled his juice.

After a second, Lozano grunted. "Fine. Here's what we're going to do. We'll go with what we've got. You'll stay on Rudy, but you have one inkling he's nearby, and I don't care if he's just tying his shoes, you call it in. No heroics, and you play it by the book. Stop worrying about your testimony and how it's going to look to someone six months down the line."

"It's not just Rudy, Cap," said Rem. "There's also Ginger to consider. All we've got on her is a first name and the fuzzy description I have of her from my delirious state. We have no idea who she is or what she's capable of. She's already drugged me in our own backyard."

"You deal with her just like Rudy," said Lozano. "If needed, I'll put a patrol on each of you until we get this sorted out."

"It's a waste of time," said Daniels. "And resources. If Rudy or Ginger want to get to us, no amount of patrols will stop them."

"It sure as hell won't hurt if you encounter Rudy or Ginger again," said Lozano. "At least you wouldn't be on your own."

"We're not convinced of that. More than likely, they'd just get injured, too," said Rem.

Lozano's brow furrowed, and he looked between the two of them. "What are you two telling me? That neither of them can be brought in alive without hurting or killing you, and if you shoot Rudy, you're under suspicion for wrongful death?"

"And both of those scenarios benefits Allison and Measy," said Daniels.

"Isn't that nice?" asked Rem, grabbing his coffee.

Lozano paused. "You two seem irritatingly calm, considering this whole situation."

Rem pursed his lips, and Daniels shrugged.

"What are you up to?" asked Lozano.

Rem sipped his brew and Daniels tossed an ankle over his knee. "What do you mean, Cap?" asked Daniels. He drank some juice.

"I mean, for a man who doesn't feel safe enough to bring his own family home and for another whose coffee was spiked in the downstairs cafeteria and who refuses to go back down there, you're acting pretty relaxed."

Rem blew on his coffee. "It helps that Josh Lambert was returned safe and sound. That's one for the good guys. And that homeless man we found with him is still hanging in there, last I heard."

"We're hoping, at least for now," said Daniels, "that maybe things will work themselves out."

Lozano studied them, his expression clouded. He grabbed a pen and tapped it on the table. "Whatever it is, you better know what the hell you're doing."

Rem wiped at a dribble of coffee that spilled on his shirt. "Don't worry, Cap. We'll be fine."

"Anything else?" asked Daniels.

His expression unchanged, Lozano put the pen down. "As a matter of fact, there is. Josh Lambert is coming into the station today with his mother to talk to us."

"That's great," said Rem. "Hopefully, he can tell us a few things about Rudy. Who's he talking to? One of the shrinks?"

"That's just it," said Lozano. "Josh told us he only wants to talk to the detectives who found him."

Rem sat up along with Daniels.

"Us?" asked Daniels. "He wants to talk to us?"

"Why us?" asked Rem.

"I don't know," said Lozano. "Maybe it's your sparkling personality."

Rem looked at Daniels, who raised a brow.

"I don't know anything about interrogating kids, Cap," said Rem.

Lozano glowered. "It can't be that hard, Remalla. Use smaller words." He leaned in. "And don't consider it an interrogation. Call it a conversation." He paused. "And don't curse."

"It's fine. We can do it," said Daniels. "What time is he coming in?"

"One hour," said Lozano. He waved. "Go on. Start prepping."

Feeling anxious, Rem stood.

"And Remalla," said Lozano. "You're uniquely suited to this. Just crack a few of your lame jokes. He's a kid. It'll help him relax."

"I don't know if I should be proud or insulted," said Rem.

"Pick either. I don't care," said Lozano.

Rem and Daniels headed for the door.

"And, hey," said Lozano.

They both turned before leaving.

Lozano eyed them. "You two keep your noses clean when it comes to Rudy, you got it? And if you don't, I don't want to know about it."

"I'm a stickler for a clean nose, Cap," said Rem.

"Since when? You never have a tissue," said Daniels.

"What for? You've always got one nearby," said Rem.

"Get out of here," said Lozano, shaking his head. "And let me know how it goes with Josh."

"Will do, Cap," said Daniels, and he closed the door behind him.

• • • • • • • • • • •

An hour later, they stood outside the interrogation room where Josh Lambert and his mother were waiting.

Daniels reached for the knob, but Rem grabbed his arm. "Hold up a sec."

Daniels eyed his partner. "What is it?" He noted Rem's worried look. "What are you so nervous about? You hang out with J.P. all the time."

"J.P. can barely speak. You can't compare the two."

"Rem, Josh is eleven. You've spoken to hardened criminals. This will be much easier."

"You don't know that. He's a kid. What if we scare him?"

"He's just been released by a kidnapper. I'd say his fear quota has been met. That's probably why he asked for me and you. I saw him at the convenience store and we both found him. He must feel more comfortable with us."

"Yeah, well. You take the lead. I'll hang back and jump in if needed."

"We're just going to ask him about Rudy. Hopefully, Josh will do most of the talking."

"That's just it. I don't want to traumatize him by reliving it. I have some idea what that feels like."

Daniels paused, finally understanding. "Which is why you're perfect for this. You can relate to what he's been through. If he gets upset, we'll slow it down. Believe me. You'll be better for him than any shrink." He waited until Rem relaxed. "Okay?"

Rem sighed and shook out his hands. "Okay."

Daniels took a couple more seconds until Rem nodded, and then he opened the door. They walked in and saw Josh sitting at the table, a soda in front of him, and his mother, Victoria Lambert, sitting beside him, holding a bottle of water.

Daniels went to the opposite side of the table, along with Rem, and they sat across from Victoria and Josh. Mrs. Lambert's eyes were red and fatigued, but she was less emotional than the last time they'd seen her.

Josh wore clean clothes, and his brown hair shone in the fluorescent light. His eyes were still wide, but not from fear. Daniels figured he was likely nervous. "Hi, Josh. Mrs. Lambert." He looked at Victoria. "If you recall, I'm Detective Daniels, and this is Detective Remalla."

Victoria nodded. "Yes. I remember." Her eyes welled, and she pulled a tissue from her pocket. "I heard you two found him."

"You can thank my partner here," said Daniels, pointing at Rem. "He had a feeling Josh wasn't at the pier."

She reached over and took Rem's hand. "Thank you so much." She sniffed and wiped at her eyes.

"We just did our jobs," said Rem. "I'm glad we got him home safe."

"How are you feeling, Josh?" asked Daniels. "You glad to be home?"

Josh eyed his mom and then fiddled with his fingers.

"You need to answer them, honey," said Victoria. "They're here to help." She reached over and took one of his hands. "You can trust them."

Josh nodded, and Daniels took his time. "I know this may be uncomfortable. You've had a tough week." He paused. "You think you can answer a few questions for us?"

Josh nodded.

"You're doing great," said Daniels. "There's no need to be scared. We'll take our time."

Josh eyed his fingers and nodded again.

Daniels felt for Josh, knowing it would be hard for anyone, much less an eleven-year-old, to talk about a kidnapping and the death of his father. But Rudy was still out there, and they had to hope Josh could help point them in the right direction. "Did you know the man who took you? Had you seen him before?"

Josh shook his head.

"Did he tell you his name?"

Josh looked up and stared at Rem.

"Josh, honey," said Victoria. "Can you answer his question?"

"His name was Rudy," said Josh softly, going back to studying his fingers.

Daniels watched him, noting Josh's anxiety. "You want some more time?" he asked. "You need a minute?"

Josh eyed Rem again. "How come he's not asking me questions?"

Daniels glanced at Rem, whose eyes widened. "Me?" asked Rem. "You want me to ask you questions?"

Josh hesitated, but then spoke. "Rudy told me you were scared once, too."

Daniels went still, and Rem's mouth fell open. "Uh…um…yeah," said Rem. "I was." He cleared his throat. "Still am sometimes."

"Me, too," said Josh, "Especially at night." He paused. "Rudy told me to be a man, and not cry," he whispered. "Did you cry?"

Rem clenched his hands together. "Uh…yeah. I did, as a matter of fact. Like a baby."

"Me, too," said Josh. "But it made him mad."

"I'm sorry about that," said Rem. "But there's no shame in crying. Sometimes, that's all you can do."

"Sometimes, it's the best thing you can do," said Daniels.

Victoria wiped her nose.

"I'm sorry about your dad," said Rem.

Josh stared at the floor. "Do we have to talk about him?"

"No. Not if you don't want to," said Rem.

"I don't," said Josh.

"Okay. No problem." Rem eyed Josh's soda. "You like that brand?" he asked, pointing. "I drink it all the time."

"He's not kidding," said Daniels. "He can eat chips and soda faster than a kitchen disposal."

"You like chips?" asked Josh.

Rem raised a brow. "I love 'em." He nodded at Daniels. "This guy here loves his veggies. But not me. I like pizza and brownies."

Josh smiled softly. "Chocolate chip cookies are my favorite."

Rem smiled, too. "You can't beat a warm cookie right out of the oven. I bet your mom makes a good cookie."

"She does," said Josh.

Victoria sniffed and blew her nose.

"Are you hungry?" asked Rem. "You want some chips?"

Josh eyed his soda and looked at his mom. "Can I?"

"Of course," she said.

"I'll go get you some," said Rem.

"No. You sit," said Daniels. "Talk to Josh. I'll get them." Daniels wasn't about to break the connection between Rem and Josh. "You like potato?"

Rem scoffed. "Who doesn't like potato? They're the best."

Josh widened his eyes at Rem. "I like potato chips, too."

Daniels smiled. "Potato chips it is. Be right back."

Victoria stood. "I'll go. You three sit and talk. I need to find the ladies' room and fix my face. I can't seem to stop crying."

"You sure?" asked Daniels. "I'm happy to go."

Victoria wiped a tear from her cheek. "I can see Josh is in good hands. I saw a vending machine on the way in. I'll be back soon." She rubbed Josh's shoulder. "You okay, honey, if I step out for a second?"

"It's okay, Mom," said Josh. "I'll tell them about Rudy."

More tears welled up, and Victoria kissed him on the head. "That's great. You'll be a big help." She tousled his hair. "You're a very brave boy."

"Thanks, Mom."

She straightened. "Be back in a minute."

"Thank you, Mrs. Lambert," said Rem, and she nodded and left.

Rem shifted in his seat and watched Josh. "You want to wait for your mom to come back?"

Josh shook his head. "No. I can talk."

"You are a brave kid, just like your mom said," said Daniels.

"Can you tell us what happened?" asked Rem. "On the day you were taken."

Josh's face fell and his voice softened. "I don't remember all of it."

"That's okay. What do you remember?" asked Rem.

Josh swallowed. "I was eating cereal. And I think there was a knock on the door. Dad...Dad went to answer...and...and...I heard a voice...and..." He bit his lip and gripped his fingers. "I don't know what happened next."

"That's okay. You don't have to say any more about that," said Rem. "What's the next thing you remember?"

Josh took a second. "I...I...think it was being in a car, only it was like a bus. It had furniture and stuff."

Daniels looked at Rem. "The RV"

"Yeah," said Rem. "Did he take you somewhere?"

"We mostly stayed in the car." He paused. "But sometimes we went to the park."

"The park with all the people in it, or the park with no people in it?" asked Daniels.

"Both," said Josh. "I think the park with no people reminded him of someone who died."

Daniels raised a brow. "Why do you say that?"

"He had a picture of a little boy. He told me he used to take him to the park." Josh paused. "And then he took me to a cemetery, and we sat at a grave." He looked up. "I read the stone, and it was a kid's grave."

Daniels and Rem shared a look. "Did it have a bird statue?" asked Daniels.

"Yeah," said Josh. "It did."

Daniels tapped his finger on the table and glanced at Rem. "Didn't Lozano put somebody on that graveyard to watch it?"

Rem nodded. "He did." He sighed. "Josh, do you remember what time of day you went to the cemetery?"

Josh pursed his lips. "Uh...it was late...like after dark. It scared me, but Rudy didn't care. I think we were sneaking in so Rudy wouldn't get in trouble."

"You're a pretty perceptive kid," said Daniels.

Rem let go of a long breath, leaned in and interlaced his fingers. "You're doing really well, but now I have a tough question, Josh, and I have to ask it. If you're uncomfortable, though, you let me know."

"Okay," said Josh.

Rem hesitated. "Did he hurt you?"

Josh kept his eyes down. "He hit me once, when he first took me, because I kept crying."

"He didn't do anything worse?"

Josh finally looked up. "We talked about this in school once, and my mom asked, too. It's when adults touch kids where they're not supposed to. Is that what you mean?"

Rem nodded. "Yeah. That's what I mean."

Josh shook his head again. "No, he never did that, but he would get angry and yell at me. And he'd hit the lady. That scared me."

Daniels sat forward. "Lady?" he asked. "What lady?"

"She was pretty, and she'd let me watch TV when Rudy wasn't there. And she'd give me chocolate."

"Did this lady have a name?" asked Rem.

"Rudy always called her baby, but she told me her name was Ginger."

"Ginger?" asked Rem.

"Mikey was right," said Daniels.

"Yup," said Rem.

"You ever watch old shows, like reruns?" asked Josh.

"Are you kidding?" asked Rem. "Rerun is my middle name."

"There's a channel my mom lets me watch. It's all reruns. I saw *Gilligan's Island* once. Do you know that show?"

"I love *Gilligan's Island*," said Rem. "The Skipper, Professor..."

"Don't forget Gilligan," said Daniels.

"The Howells," said Rem.

"And Ginger and Maryanne," said Josh. "She said her name was Ginger, because her mom told her she reminded her of Ginger from *Gilligan's Island* when she was born. She had red hair and a mole. I thought that was cool."

Daniels pulled out a notebook and pencil and started writing. "That's great Josh. You've got a good memory."

"You said Rudy hit Ginger?" asked Rem.

"Yeah. He'd yell at her a lot, and he hit her across the face once. He'd be mean to her."

"But he never hit you after the first time?" asked Rem.

"No," said Josh. "He'd get mad, but he never hurt me like Ginger. He always called me Sam, and then he'd look at me weird."

"He called you Sam?" asked Rem. "Did he ever say why?"

"No. I didn't ask because I was afraid he'd yell more."

"That was smart," said Rem. "Can I ask you something else?" He sighed. "Did Rudy try to teach you anything? Like something he could do that he wanted you to do, too?"

Josh went still, and his face paled.

"Take your time," said Rem. "I know it's scary to remember sometimes."

Josh touched his soda can and then gripped it. "He said I could do something special."

Daniels held his pencil. "What was it?"

"He tried to teach me, but I didn't like it," said Josh. "It made me feel strange."

"Strange how?" asked Rem.

Josh hesitated. "My body would shake, like when you're real mad, and you want to break something. I didn't want to learn it, but if I didn't try, he'd get angry. Told me I had to. He said someone named Henry could do it, and so could I."

"Do you remember what he was trying to teach you?" asked Rem.

Josh nodded. "He told me it was about electricity. Like the lights turning on and off and stuff. He said I could control it. But I didn't believe him. He still made me try, though."

"Did Rudy control electricity?" asked Daniels. "Did you see him do it?"

Josh went quiet, and then answered. "He boiled some water once, to show me, and...he killed a mouse."

"He what?" asked Rem.

"He touched it, and it froze, and I think it died." Josh bit his lip again. "I told him to stop. And I cried." His eyes rounded and shone with unshed tears. "That made him mad."

"Hey. It's okay," said Rem. "I would have hated that, too." He paused. "Why don't we take a second, okay? Catch our breath." He gestured. "Have some soda. Your mom should be back soon with those chips."

Josh sniffed and picked up his drink. "Okay." He took a sip.

Daniels looked between Josh and Rem. "Let me ask something different, Josh. Not about the electricity, but something else."

Josh put the can down. "What?"

Daniels tapped the pencil on the table. "Our Captain told us you wanted to talk to me and Rem." He tipped his head. "Why us?"

Josh darted his eyes between the two of them. "Because I saw your picture."

Rem leaned in, and Daniels straightened. "You saw our picture? Where?" asked Daniels.

"Ginger had them on her phone, and she showed Rudy." Josh wiped off a drip of condensation from the can. "Rudy showed me the pictures. He said you were looking for me. That's when he told me you'd been scared, too." He looked at Rem.

"Rudy had pictures of us?" asked Daniels.

Josh nodded. "I saw you with a lady and a kid, and one of you." He pointed at Rem. "Some by yourself and one with a girl in front of a dark house. Rudy told me you both took his picture, and he wanted it back."

Daniels' stomach curdled and recalled the break-in at his home. "Did you ever see a picture of me and him," he gestured at Rem, "with a lady and child? The child was on my knee."

Josh looked off. "Uh...yeah. I think so. Rudy put it up on the wall."

Daniels took a steady breath. "Wall? What wall? Were you staying somewhere? Or were you still in the car?"

"No," said Josh. "We left the car. Rudy said we couldn't stay there anymore. We went to an apartment." He furrowed his brow. "I think it was Ginger's because there was a lot of girl stuff."

Daniels scribbled in his notepad. "Any idea where this apartment is?"

"No," said Josh.

"Could you see anything outside the windows?" asked Rem. "Anything familiar? Any landmarks?"

"I could see the Ferris Wheel from the window," said Josh. "I think it was the Ferris Wheel Rudy liked to visit. We'd go there and sit on a bench. We'd eat candy."

Daniels wrote in his pad. "That's awesome, Josh. That's a big help."

The door opened, and Victoria Lambert returned, her eyes still red, but looking more composed. She held four bags of chips and brought them to the table. "Chips for everyone," she said, handing them out. "I figure we could all use them."

Rem took his and pulled it open. "That's great. Thanks, Mrs. Lambert."

She smiled. "You sound like one of Josh's friends. Please, you should both call me Vicky."

"Thanks, Vicky," said Daniels, opening his chips.

"Thanks, Mom." Josh sipped his soda and opened his bag of chips.

"How are you doing?" she asked him. "You okay?" She ran a hand over his hair.

"I'm okay," he said, eating a chip.

"He's a trooper," said Rem. "I'm impressed." He popped a chip into his mouth. "You must be very proud of him."

"I am," said Vicky. "He's always been a good kid. Takes good care of his mom."

Josh smiled, and Daniels let Josh take a break and eat a few chips before he asked the next question. "Can you tell us what happened yesterday when we found you? What happened to the man that was lying on the ground?"

Josh held a chip but didn't eat it.

"Do you remember?" asked Rem.

Josh nodded. "Yeah. But I wish I didn't."

Rem paused. "Yeah. I know. But if you can tell us, that would be a big help."

Josh dropped his chip in the bag. "The man was outside the fence. I think he lived there. Rudy talked to him, and he followed us into the park. I think Rudy offered him money." He went back to staring at his hands. "I was scared because of what happened to the other man who lived in the tent."

Daniels recalled Scout, and Rem stopped mid-chew. "Was that the man from the park with the people in it?"

"Yes."

"Did Rudy hurt him?" asked Daniels.

Josh gripped his bag. "He said he was showing me what to do. Said it was a lesson. I didn't like it. I wanted to run, but I didn't. Rudy...Rudy said if I tried to escape...he'd...he'd..." He nibbled his lip.

"He'd what?" asked Rem.

Josh eyed his mother. "He'd...hurt my mom."

Vicky found another tissue, and her tears returned. "Oh, Joshie. I'm so sorry he said that." She took his hand. "But I'm okay. He won't hurt me, or you, ever again."

Josh squeezed his mom's fingers. "I wanted to be brave."

"And you were. You protected your mom. You did exactly what you should have done," said Rem.

"What happened after he hurt the man in the tent?" asked Daniels.

"We went down to a path, and then we ran really fast. There were lots of people, and we got back to the car. Rudy grabbed things and put them in a bag, and we left. That's when we went to the apartment."

Vicky sniffed and wiped her eyes.

"You okay, Mom?" asked Josh.

Vicky smiled through her tears. "Sweetie. I'm fine. I'm worried about you."

"I don't want you to cry," said Josh.

Vicky smiled and ran her hand through his hair. "You're so sweet, but that's what moms do sometimes. But if you can be brave, so can I."

"Let's take a second and eat a chip," said Rem. "You hanging in there, Josh?"

Josh dug through the bag for a chip and ate it. "I think so."

"Great," said Rem.

They sat for a second and ate, and Josh sipped some soda.

After Josh seemed to relax, Rem asked the next question. "Let's go back to the park where we found you. What happened after the man followed Rudy?"

Josh swallowed and hesitated. "We walked around a little. Rudy had brought donuts, and he gave one to the man, but then the man got angry. He threw his donut away and said he wanted his money. He started to leave, but Rudy wouldn't let him. Then Rudy got mad and touched the man, and he fell."

"Oh, no," said Vicky, and she pulled out another tissue from her pocket.

"Is that when we showed up?" asked Rem.

"No. Not yet." Josh crinkled his chip bag. "The man didn't move, and Rudy...he...he...he wanted me to hurt him. To touch him with electricity." He looked up with big eyes. "I didn't want to."

"It's okay," said Rem.

"He...he told me to be a man. He wanted me to get angry, because he said it would make me strong, but I couldn't do it." His eyes welled up again. "I was scared, and Rudy yelled. A lot. Told me I couldn't be his kid." A tear escaped and trickled down his cheek. "I didn't understand because I...I have a dad." He looked down. "Or at least I did." His voice trembled, and he sniffed and wiped his face.

"Oh, honey. It's okay. Shhh." Vicky, her own tears falling, leaned over and hugged him and dabbed at his tears with her tissue. She looked at Daniels and Rem. "Are we almost done?"

Daniels nodded. "I think so." He looked at Rem. "You have anything else?"

Rem watched Josh, his expression a mixture of sadness and empathy. "You all right, Josh?"

Josh sniffed and nodded, and Vicky sat back but held his hand. "I think so," said Josh.

"Never mind what Rudy said. You're the strongest kid I know." Rem reached into his pocket and pulled out a couple of cards. He gave one to Vicky and one to Josh. "You ever need to talk, you call me. Doesn't matter if it's day or night. Your mom, too."

"Thank you," said Vicky, and she tucked the card into her purse.

Josh held the card and studied it. "Can I tell you something?"

"Anything," said Rem.

Josh bit his lip and Daniels half expected more tears to fall, but Josh held it together. "I was scared last night. I couldn't sleep." He paused and whispered. "I'm worried he'll come back."

Daniels' heart fell, and Rem leaned close, his expression somber. "Can I tell you a something, too?" asked Rem.

Josh nodded, his face pensive. "Yeah."

"It's a secret. I haven't told anybody," said Rem. "Except for him," he nodded at Daniels, "but he's my best friend, so it's okay."

Josh looked at Daniels. "What is it?"

Daniels waited to hear it, too.

Rem rested his elbows on the table. "I have to sleep with the lights on because I'm still scared."

"You do?" asked Josh.

"Yeah. But one day, I'll be better, and when I'm ready, I'll turn the lights off. But right now, I feel better when they're on."

Josh held Rem's gaze. "I slept with the lights on last night, too."

"I get it," said Rem. "It's fine. And don't worry about Rudy, He's not coming back. We'll have somebody watching just to be safe."

Josh kept staring at Rem. "My best friend's Tommy Gemsinger. You think I can tell him I'm scared of the dark...and...and he won't laugh?"

Daniels had to hold his own emotions in check. "If he's your best friend, he won't laugh."

"You can tell him anything you want," said Rem. "That's what best friends are for."

Josh nodded. "Okay."

Rem cleared his throat. "Remember. You think of something else to tell us, or just want to talk, you call me."

"I will," said Josh. He gripped Rem's card in his fingers.

Vicky dabbed her eyes with her tissue. "You ready, honey?" She picked up his soda, her purse, and water.

"Yes." Josh grabbed his chips.

"Thanks for talking to us Josh," said Daniels. "You were a big help."

Rem stood when Josh did. "Maybe one day, you, me, Daniels and Tommy can all get together for some catch. Would you like that?"

Josh nodded. "Tommy's terrible at baseball, though."

Rem smiled. "That's okay. We'll give him some pointers."

Vicky ushered Josh to the door. "Thank you both," said Vicky. "You handled this well."

"If you need anything, let us know," said Daniels. "And we'll be in touch if we have any other questions." He waved. "Bye, Josh."

"Bye, Josh," said Rem.

"Bye," said Josh, and he left with his mom.

Rem collapsed back into his seat and held his head. "God. That was hard." He moaned. "I almost lost it about a million times."

Daniels shifted in his seat to face Rem. "You did great, considering how you were going to hang back and watch from the sidelines. You made a real connection with him."

Rem raised his head. "He's a special kid."

"Takes one to know one."

Rem chuckled.

Daniels stood. "You know something?"

"What?" asked Rem, standing with Daniels.

"You're going to make a great dad someday."

Rem went still. "If that day ever comes."

"It will."

"But I appreciate the thought. Thanks."

Daniels shrugged. "What are best friends for?" He paused. "You know what? Today's your lucky day. How about I treat you to a large coffee from the cafeteria?

Rem made a face at him. "I thought you were my friend?"

"Got to jump back on that horse, eventually. What are you going to do, avoid the cafeteria forever?" He picked up his notebook. "If you do, Tony will take it personally."

"Yeah, well. Give me a few days. Then we'll see." Rem stepped around the table and went to the door.

"Well, I'm going down there to get a juice. How about I bring you some coffee back?" He raised three fingers. "Scout's honor. I'll keep my eye on it the whole time."

Rem hesitated. "I thought it was two fingers."

Daniels rolled his eyes. "It's three. You want the coffee or not?"

"You'll use a lid?"

"The tightest one I can find."

Rem left the room. "Fine. I'll risk it."

"Baby steps." Daniels handed Rem his notebook. "Be right back. And then we can update Lozano."

"And keep an eye on your juice, too," yelled Rem as Daniels headed down the stairs.

Chapter Twenty-Five

Daniels stood at the register while Tony scanned his items.

"Your partner, okay?" asked Tony. "I haven't seen him recently."

"He's great," said Daniels. "Just been a tough few days."

"I heard that kid was found. That's great news."

"No kidding." Daniels put his card away after Tony returned it.

"I figured that's why Rem was acting strange the last time he was here. Probably the stress."

Daniels paused, but then picked up his juice and Rem's coffee cup. "Uh, yeah. That'll do it to you. God knows we deal with enough of it."

"Ain't that the truth? You have a nice day."

"You, too. And see if you can get Rem to eat a veggie or two next time he's down here."

Tony chuckled. "I'm a cafeteria manager, not a miracle worker."

Daniels smiled. "Figured it was worth a shot." He stepped away and went to the coffee dispensers, his gaze automatically searching for a woman with red hair and a mole. Not seeing her, he filled Rem's coffee and doctored it, wanting to add less sugar, but already hearing Rem's complaining in his head. Stirring it, he set it and his juice bottle down to reach for some lids, and bumped elbows with someone. He looked over and saw Kenneth Measy.

• • • • • • • • • • •

Rem sat at his desk, thinking of Josh and trying to make notes from the interview, but his mind kept wandering. He thought of Donna Kentwood and what Lozano had said to him and Daniels. For the millionth time, the various scenarios played in his head, and he hoped they were on the right track. Based on Donna's information, though, they had to go on the offensive. He thought of Mikey then and remembered what Josh had said. He'd seen a picture of Rem and a woman in front of a dark house. That had to be from the night Mikey had waited for him on his porch. Worried Rudy or Ginger may have recognized her from the bonfire and her connection to D'Mato, he reached for his cell when it rang.

After eyeing the unfamiliar number, his stomach clenched. Based on his experience, unknown numbers didn't bode well, but he knew he had to answer.

Taking a breath, he hit the button, hoping it was a spam call. "Hello?"

"Detective Remalla?" It was a woman.

"That's me. Who's calling?"

"My name's Ginger."

Rem tightened his grip on his cell. "Ginger?" He glanced back toward Lozano's office and could see through the glass that his captain was on the phone.

"You know me?" she asked. "Did Josh tell you?"

Rem didn't like her mentioning Josh. "I believe you're a friend of Rudy's?"

"I am."

He thought of the woman in the cafeteria. "Were you the one who told me where to find the cream and sugar?"

She went quiet, but then answered. "You should drink it black."

His heart thumped. "I'll keep that in mind. Was that little stunt your idea?"

"I can't take all the credit. I may have suggested it, and Rudy helped me put it into action."

Rem's mind raced. He had to take his time and keep her talking. "Are you making his phone calls now, too?"

"For the moment. He thought it would be fun."

"You also his personal photographer?"

She chuckled. "You did talk to Josh, didn't you?"

"He's a smart kid."

"He is. I like him."

"I heard you gave him chocolate."

"I did. Candy, too."

Rem settled back in his seat, trying to look calm, and eyed Daniels' empty desk. "Why'd you take pictures of us?"

"Because Rudy asked me to."

"You always do what Rudy says?"

There was a pause. "Not always."

Rem thought of his neighbor. "Did you kill the man who lives across the street from me?"

Another pause. "You don't beat around the bush, do you?"

"Somehow I don't think you do either." He heard a gust of wind and determined she had to be outside.

"He surprised me," she said. "I thought the house was empty."

"You should work on your due diligence. Rudy must not have been happy."

"Never mind what Rudy thought. He got the pictures he wanted." She chuckled. "I got a few good ones, too."

"You should have told me. I would have smiled." Rem picked up a pen and clenched it.

She sighed into the phone. "Sorry about the lights. I hear you don't like the dark."

Rem stilled, his heart thumping harder. “Was that your handiwork, too?”

“You should fix that garage door. Work on that due diligence you mentioned.”

Rem held the tip of the pen against the table and forced himself to breathe. “That’s good advice. Whoever said it is pretty smart.”

“Not as smart as he thinks. Same goes for his partner. I hear he’s still too scared to bring his family home.”

“That happens when someone breaks into his house and threatens his wife and kid.” He set his jaw and closed his eyes.

“You two shouldn’t have taken Rudy’s picture.”

“Rudy shouldn’t have left it behind. Tell him to pack slower next time.”

“He still wants it back.”

“And I want to move to Hawaii and surf my days away, but that’s not going to happen.”

“Nothing’s impossible, Detective.”

“You and my partner would get along well. All that positivity might go a long way to solving our differences.”

“That ship has sailed, but Rudy wanted me to call and give you an option.”

Rem snorted. “He did, huh? Rudy got a busy schedule this afternoon?”

“He’s got stuff to do. Now that Josh is gone, he can focus on other things.”

Rem thought of Allison. “Like what?”

“You’ll find out soon enough.”

Rem watched the doors and hoped Daniels would be back soon. “I can’t wait.” He tried a new tactic. “I hear Rudy isn’t always very nice, especially to you. Is that true?”

She went quiet. “Rudy has a temper, but so do all men. He’s taken care of me. Taught me things. He’s made me strong.”

"You don't need abuse to make you strong, Ginger. Abuse by anyone is a sign of weakness. Strong men don't need to hurt anybody."

"You've never hurt anyone, Detective?"

"I've never abused anyone."

"From what I hear, you abused Allison. Took advantage of her, and now you're trying to make it look like everything that happened is her fault. You consider that being strong?"

Rem's stomach turned. "You heard wrong, Ginger. Your little buddy Allison is a sick lady, and she's going to prison."

"Maybe. We'll see."

Rem bounced his knee. "You want to tell me the purpose of this phone call, or did you just want to chat?"

"Partly to chat, and partly to send Rudy's message."

"I'm glad I can keep you entertained." He could hear more wind vibrate through the phone. "You must be outside. You enjoying the nice weather?"

"I am. It's a nice day, especially to watch someone."

Rem sat up, wondering if she could be in the parking lot. "You outside the station? You should have told us. Daniels and I would have come out and said hi."

"No. No such luck," she said. "I'm watching someone else right now. A friend of yours, and an old friend of mine. Her name's Mikey Redstone."

Rem froze.

••••••••••

Daniels stared at the shorter man with the fancy suit, graying goatee and paunchy belly. Measy smiled at him. "Hello, Detective."

Daniels narrowed his eyes, not trusting his tact, so he stayed quiet.

"I saw you walk in. I was sitting in the corner, and thought I'd say hello."

"You said it," answered Daniels, "now if you'll excuse me..."

"You getting some coffee?" He gestured and smiled. "Don't forget the cream and sugar."

Daniels clenched his jaw. "You and I should not be talking."

"Why not?" He grinned. "We're just having a casual conversation in a public place. Is that an issue?"

"You're Allison Albright's attorney, and I'm a witness for the prosecution." He turned to reach for the lid.

"And you think by us bumping into each other that I'll somehow sway your testimony?" He widened his eyes and held his chest. "I didn't know you held me in such high regard."

The sleaze coming off the man made Daniels feel nauseated. He grabbed a lid and didn't take the bait.

"No, Detective," said Measy. "That's not a concern of mine at all. Nor is your partner, for that matter. This case will be a walk in the park for me."

Daniels bit his tongue, wanting to tell this man exactly what he thought, but knew it was pointless. "I have to get back. Some of us actually have important work to do."

Measy scoffed. "Good to know. I have some important work of my own. You might want to convey to your partner that I know he is a liar. He set Allison up. He knows it, and I suspect you know it, too."

Daniels almost crumpled the lid in his hand. "Your client's going to prison, Counselor. Deal with it."

"Your partner's testimony has too many holes in it to count without Guinness getting involved. He better be sure he's ready."

"He's more than ready. And no matter how much intimidation or manipulation you try to use, it isn't going to work."

Measy chuckled. "Manipulation. Good choice of words. Because that's exactly what your partner is skilled at. Unless you know he's lying and you're backing him up. But that's what partners do, isn't it?"

Daniels pointed. "What I know is that Allison is as dirty as you are, and she's scared shitless. Tell her to get used to the view, because it isn't going to change."

"And you tell your partner that we know his tactics. He used Allison. He slept with her, did drugs with her at his instigation, and then told everyone he'd been assaulted. Funny, he didn't go to a hospital, get tested or make a report, but I guess we're just supposed to take his word for it. And then, according to witness testimony, he walked off on his own with D'Mato, and then tells everyone he was thrown in a dark room and held against his will. And imagine my shock that he's the only one who can testify to that, too."

"You really are telling yourself this nonsense?" asked Daniels. "I thought you were supposed to be good at this."

Measy barely paused. "And then, when he gets in too deep and bites off more than he can chew, he blames Allison for all of it. Tells everyone he'd been drugged and assaulted again, and yet, there's no hospital stay or drug test. Another convenience in a case full of them."

"They tied him to a slab and held a knife to his throat. She slit his chest open. You care to explain that?" He mentally chastised himself for letting Measy get to him. He had to get out of this conversation.

"But she didn't kill him, did she?" He shrugged. "They both got caught up in something stupid. Maybe they took it too far. I can admit my client could have been smarter, but she was caught up in lust. I suspect he was, too."

Daniels shook his head. "Lust? You're blaming this on lust?" He scowled. "You forget. I was there. I saw what I walked in on."

"You made assumptions about what you walked in on. Doesn't mean you were right."

"And the two followers who are testifying. They made assumptions, too?"

"They were completely caught up, just like your partner. Victor and his drugs messed with their heads."

Daniels told himself to leave, but his mouth didn't listen. "Your client killed Victor."

"Only your partner can testify to that, but there's no other evidence to connect her to his death. And the words of those two groupies mean nothing, especially when they're getting immunity for their testimony. Juries don't think too much of that."

Daniels stared, openmouthed. "You really are a piece of work, aren't you?"

"I'm just telling you what to expect. Your partner should be prepared."

Daniels loomed over Measy. "Then you better be prepared, too, because this little game you're playing won't work. If you really felt confident about this case, you'd sit back, delay and let the money roll in, but you're visiting my captain and casually bumping into me." He aimed a steely gaze at Measy. "You know we've got Allison dead to rights. She's evil, and she's terrified. Finding groupies in prison means something a little different than it does in the outside world. And you? You see the headlines with your name in them, and you're nervous you might actually lose this case." He tipped his head. "You're in too deep on this Measy, and you better be careful, because if we link any crap you're pulling to discredit me or my partner back to you, I'll have your credentials pulled so fast, you'll end up working in this cafeteria, instead of waiting for me to show up in it."

Measy stared back, his expression amused. "We'll see about that, Detective."

Daniels debated saying more, but stopped himself. "Maybe you should go now. I'm sure there's some other pond for you to slither into that needs your attention."

Measy nodded. "More than one, actually." He stepped back. "I look forward to my cross examination when you're on the stand."

"I can't wait," said Daniels.

"Let's hope it holds up."

"It will."

Measy blinked his eyes and Daniels saw the same look Measy had given Rem the day Rem had been drugged–like a shark eyeing its prey. "You be careful out there. Police work can be dangerous."

"Get out of here, Measy."

Measy blinked again. The look vanished, and he smiled. "Hope your partner enjoys his coffee." He waved a hand. "You have a nice day."

He turned and left, and Daniels stood in mute fury, hating everything about Measy, and knowing intuitively that the man would stop at nothing to win. Telling himself to calm down, he turned to put the lid on Rem's coffee when he realized that he'd left it unattended during his conversation. Anyone could have walked up behind him and added something to it while Daniels had been distracted.

Cursing at himself for letting Measy get to him, he picked up the coffee and dumped it and the lid into the trash and stomped out of the cafeteria.

••••••••••

Rem had to get a hold of Mikey, but also had to keep Ginger talking. He wondered where Daniels was. "Why are you watching Mikey?"

She laughed. "Because I can. It's like Rudy says, know your enemy's weaknesses. He's right. It's very effective. Besides, she and I go back a way. Maybe we should reconnect."

Rem held his breath and reached for his desk phone.

"You're freaking out, aren't you?" she asked. "Fine. You can relax. I lied. I'm not watching Mikey. I was earlier, but I left."

Rem debated whether to trust her. "Leave her alone, Ginger. She's not a part of this."

"That's completely up to you. Same with Daniels and his family. You want everybody safe, and Rudy wants his picture. Maybe once he has it, we can all walk off into the sunset and live happily ever after."

"It's not that simple. I know Rudy and Allison are working together."

"He's talked to her, but that doesn't mean he's working with her. Rudy makes his own decisions."

He detected an edge to her voice. "Unless he likes Allison. Men do stupid things for women. I doubt Rudy's the exception."

"He doesn't like her."

"You sure about that?"

"He's playing along with her because he knows it might benefit him. But he also knows she's weakened. He's smart playing both sides."

"You mean he's using her. Is he using you, too?"

She paused. "I'm not stupid, Detective. You would be wise not to underestimate me."

"And you shouldn't underestimate Rudy. He might say one thing and do another."

"I know Rudy better than anyone. He shouldn't underestimate me, either."

"Is that why you let him beat you?"

She chuckled. "Sometimes cowering is the best defense...until it isn't."

He detected a malice in her voice he hadn't heard before, and a chill ran through him. "Are we going to get to the point of this phone call?"

"Sure, although I've enjoyed talking to you." She paused. "Maybe in a different life, we could have been friends...or more."

Rem shivered, wishing he could tell this woman what he really thought of this whole situation. "Maybe. Guess we'll never know."

"Probably for the best." He heard what sounded like a car door open. "You messed up big time with Allison and got in over your head. I doubt it would have been any different with me." The car door closed. "But it might have been more fun."

Rem reluctantly recalled his time with Allison and made an assumption. "You sound jealous. Maybe you wanted what Allison had?" He remembered what Mikey had said about the bonfire. "Allison had Victor, and unfortunately, so did Mikey. Did you want Victor, but instead of noticing you, he ended up giving you to Rudy?"

"Nobody gave me to anybody, and Victor liked me just fine." The edge returned to her voice.

"You sure about that, because it doesn't sound like it to me." He told himself to slow down and not antagonize her. The last thing he needed was another enemy who wanted him dead.

The squad doors banged open, and Daniels strode inside, holding his bottled juice but no coffee. By the look on his face, he was irritated.

"I think it's time we get to the point of my call," she said.

"I'm all ears, Ginger," said Rem.

Daniels got to his desk and stopped, his eyes widening.

"Rudy has a proposition for you," she said.

"Give me one sec, Ginger. My captain is waving at me." Rem put the phone against his chest and whispered to Daniels. "Call Mikey. Ginger's been watching her. She needs to be some place safe." He returned to the call. "Sorry about that. You know how people in charge can be."

"Sadly, I do," she said. "You know, if you're tracing this call, it won't matter."

"I'm not tracing the call," said Rem. He watched Daniels pick up his phone and dial.

"Really? Why not?" she asked. "Isn't your captain hovering over you right now? Waiting to hear what I said?"

"No. He's back in his office. Has no idea I'm talking to you."

"Interesting. Then I guess I'll refrain from telling you this is between you and me, and Daniels, of course."

"No need. I won't say a word. I figured we'd get here eventually, and if it means keeping it private and working something out, then let's do it. What does Rudy want?"

Daniels eyed Rem and then started talking to whoever answered his call.

"Rudy wants Sam's picture, and you want to keep living life as best you can, which I'm guessing means without Rudy's interference. I can't promise Allison will go away, though. Unfortunately, there's not much I can do about her."

"You want me to believe Rudy will go away if I give him the picture?"

"That's the deal, yes."

"You honestly believe I should trust him?"

"I don't see that you have a choice." She paused. "The alternative is for him to hang around, and you really don't want that."

Rem exhaled a deep breath and dove in. "Okay. What's the plan?"

"I figured you might see it my way. Rudy wants the picture tonight. Put it in an envelope and leave it at Sam's grave. You have until midnight."

"You're not giving me a lot of wiggle room for time," said Rem.

"You're a Detective. Figure it out. I have a sense you'll find a way."

Rem held the bridge of his nose. "And if I don't comply?"

She sighed over the phone. "I think you will. I'd hate to involve Mikey in this mess, and Marjorie, too. Arizona really isn't that far away."

Rem gripped his pen harder. "You make a valid point."

"By midnight, Detective. I enjoyed speaking with you. Let's hope we don't have to speak again."

"Let's hope," said Rem. He heard a click, and the line went dead. He lowered the phone just as Daniels hung up.

"I spoke with Mason and told him about Ginger watching them," said Daniels. "He's taking Mikey to his place and will keep an eye on her. I told him to tell her you'd call and explain as soon as you could."

Rem held his temples.

"What happened?" asked Daniels.

Rem put his phone down. "You sure you want to know?"

"You know I do."

Rem thought about his options. "I could leave you out of this. We don't have to both risk our lives."

"That's not how it works, and you know it. And you know what Donna Kentwood told us. We're in this together, partner." Daniels' gaze looked toward Lozano's office. "Does he know Ginger called?"

"No."

Daniels nodded. "What'd she say?"

Rem sighed, knowing they'd committed and would have to see their plan through. "Care to make a trip to a cemetery?"

Chapter Twenty-Six

Crickets chirped, and the late-night breeze whispered through the branches of the trees. Rem tucked his hair back, climbed the fence of the cemetery, and jumped down to the other side. He heard a grunt and rustling, and Daniels landed beside him.

Daniels stood and wiped the dirt off his pants. "You know, Lozano stopped patrolling this place after we found Josh. We could have walked in the front gate."

Rem looked around, seeing the reflections of the tombstones in the moonlight. "Just seemed like the smart thing to do. The more careful we are in this mess, the better." An owl hooted, and he jumped.

"You okay?" asked Daniels.

"Just great," said Rem. "Visiting a cemetery at night is not exactly on my bucket list." He started walking, but continued to scan the area. "If something comes at us, all attempts at staying hidden are going out the window. I'm gonna scream like Marjorie did when she dropped you like a rock at the dunking booth at the precinct picnic."

Daniels walked beside him. "This is why you shouldn't watch those zombie movies."

"I'll try and remember that next time somebody wants me to leave a bribe at a tombstone at night."

"You have the envelope?"

Rem patted his jacket. "Of course. God knows I've had my issues recently, but I'm not that absentminded. Not yet, anyway."

They walked through the quiet landscape, the silent headstones the only witness to their presence.

"You sure about this?" asked Rem. "You can still back out."

"I could ask you the same thing," said Daniels. "You want to back out?"

"I'm not the one taking all the risk."

"You're taking as much of the risk as I am, if not more." He stopped and faced Rem. "We keep doubting our decision, then we might as well both back out. And we still can. I can call Lozano right now."

Rem stopped, too. "You know we can't."

"Exactly. But it can't be one or the other. It's both of us or none. Okay?"

"I'm just thinking of you and your family. You're a dad, and a husband. People need you."

"And you think people don't need you, too? You told me what you could remember from the dream about Jennie. Your life is no less important simply because you're single." He patted Rem's shoulder. "And if something happened to me, I know you'd take care of Marjorie and J.P."

"Don't say that," said Rem.

"Why not? It's true, isn't it?"

Rem sighed. "Of course it is, but you don't have to say it out loud."

Daniels nodded. "Sorry, I've been having some issues with my telepathy recently."

"You know what I mean."

Daniels resumed walking. "I know what you mean, but you and I going back and forth about the what ifs will only make this more difficult. Let's just stick to the plan and trust that what Donna told us, and our response, will take care of the threat. And leave it at that."

"After what Measy told you today, maybe it's better I go it alone. At least if I'm dead, I won't have to go through him grilling me on the stand and making me look like an idiot."

"Don't say that either," said Daniels. "Stop worrying about Measy. He's full of hot air and he's blowing it all over us. You can't let him get to you. He knows Allison's guilty, and he's desperate."

Rem followed Daniels, passing the tombstones, and hoped he was right. "I'll do my best, but if something happens with this plan and things go wrong..." He stopped and set his jaw, his heart thumping.

Daniels looked back and held his gaze. "I know, partner. Me, too."

Rem nodded. "Good." He turned back toward the headstones. "Let's get this over with."

They made their way through the cemetery and found Sam Halpern's grave. They approached it, and Rem saw the familiar bird with its wings spread. "Here we go." He glanced at Daniels. "Any last words before we do this?"

Daniels eyed the bird, the graveyard, and then Rem. "None that I can think of."

Rem pulled the envelope from his jacket and squatted. He set the envelope against the stone and stood.

They stared at it for a moment before Daniels looked over. "We good for tomorrow? After tonight, we should stick to our script. Better not to discuss anything after we leave here."

"I'll pick you up in the morning at the car repair shop as planned."

Daniels nodded. "I'll call you when I leave the house in the morning."

"Okay."

Rem eyed the envelope one last time.

"You ready?" asked Daniels.

Rem turned from the stone. "As I'll ever be. Let's get out of here before I hear a noise, break out into a full run and leave you in the dust."

Daniels smiled. "I may give you a run for your money."

Rem chuckled and started walking. "Let's hope twenty-four hours from now, I can take that bet." He glanced back at the stone, his mind wandering, and his stomach churning. "Let's get out of here."

••••••••••

The next day they stayed busy finishing reports, talking about the next steps to take after Josh's interview, and directing patrols to search for Ginger's apartment. If Josh had been accurate and the park's Ferris Wheel could be seen from a window, it provided an area to search, although the number of apartments in the area that would have the wheel in sight was numerous. It would take time to check them all and there was no guarantee Ginger would be found.

Daniels closed a file folder and eyed Rem, who sat at his desk. "You talk to Mikey?"

Rem sipped from his coffee he'd made from the machine behind him. "I did. I told her to keep an eye out." He glanced back at Lozano's office. The captain was busy talking to two other detectives. "I'm debating whether to request a patrol to watch her."

"You think that's necessary?"

"I don't know." Rem looked back. "Are they just threatening her to get to me? Or does Ginger or Rudy hold some sort of grudge because of her connection with Victor?"

"It's been years since that bonfire. That's a long grudge."

"Yeah, I know. But there's no telling what a psychopath might do. Ginger told me she knew our weaknesses. It makes we wonder if the people we love will ever be safe."

Daniels raised a brow. "Love?"

Rem smirked. "You know what I mean."

Daniels set his elbows on his desk. "I'm not sure I do. You and Mikey are close. You've shared your pasts with each other. I haven't pushed because

I know you need time, but have you thought about your relationship with her and where it's leading?"

"We're friends." Rem sipped his coffee. "Can we just leave it at that?"

Daniels wondered how much to say. "That's fine, if that's what you want."

"It's what I want."

"Okay," Daniels sat back. "For now."

Rem pushed some papers around on his desk. "Does it have to be more than that? What's wrong with being friends?"

"Nothing, but no man is an island. At some point, you'll want to get back in the game. And maybe she will, too. You going to be okay with just being friends when she's dating somebody else?"

Rem sighed. "Can we worry about getting through tonight before we discuss my love life? Let's just deal with one crisis at a time."

Daniels had to agree. "That's fair." Daniels picked up his cell phone. His own stomach churned at the thought of what lay ahead, and he had to hold the faith that he and Rem would survive the evening. But just in case, he needed to talk to his wife. "But as of tomorrow, when we're both alive and well, it may be time to think about the future, and what Mikey's place is in it." He stood and grabbed his phone. "I'm going to step out and call Marjorie."

Rem held a somber look. "Tell her...," he paused. "Well, tell her I look forward to seeing her and J.P. soon."

Daniels paused. "Yeah. I will."

Rem checked his watch. "When we leave here in a couple of hours..." A detective walked by their desks. "...I'll drop you at your place since your car's at the shop."

Daniels eyed the squad room, seeing Lozano talking in his office, and various detectives at their desks, working and speaking on the phone. Now that Josh had been found, the frantic pace had slowed, but with Rudy still on the loose and other cases to investigate, the energy of the room buzzed. "Sounds good."

They shared a knowing gaze before Daniels walked into the hall to call Marjorie.

Chapter Twenty-Seven

Rem stood at his kitchen counter, watching the time. Seeing it was close to ten o'clock, he picked up the large knife he'd been using to chop the carrots and began to slice the red pepper on the cutting board. He thought of his aunt in assisted living and remembered her vegetable soup. She'd made it occasionally for his uncle and she'd taught Rem the recipe when he was younger. Although it wasn't his favorite, he'd made it for her once when she'd first moved to the retirement community. He hadn't brought her any since and figured he should remedy that.

Thinking back on his youth, Rem recalled his mother threatening to take away his outdoor play time with the neighborhood kids unless he ate his veggies. Only then would he force himself to swallow whatever green thing was on his plate, and Aunt Audrey's soup was one of the few things he could manage. Cutting the pepper, he smiled at the memory.

Reaching for some celery, he listened to the silence. He'd turned the TV off and the only illumination came from the kitchen lights above him. Chopping quietly, he waited, expecting his visitor soon.

As time passed, his heart rate picked up its pace, and for a moment, he worried the plan had failed. Then he heard the faint turn of the knob behind him and the familiar squeak of his back door opening.

He swallowed, steeled himself, and, holding the knife, turned, seeing Rudy walk into his house and close the door behind him. Rem set the knife down and mentally prepared. The game had begun. Closing his eyes, he told himself to relax, and then opened them again. He leaned a hip against the counter. "I see you got my message."

Rudy entered the kitchen. "Well, ring-a-ding-ding, Detective. I have to admit. I was surprised to get an invitation to your home, but a little irritated I didn't see the picture in the envelope."

"We need to talk first, Rudy. You and me."

Rudy's eyes twinkled in the light, and he walked toward the sink. "Where's your partner? It's not like you to go it alone. I can't imagine he'd miss out on an opportunity like this."

"I told him I set the meeting for later. He doesn't know what time I mentioned in the envelope. And when he shows up and you don't, he won't be the wiser."

"You lied to him?" Rudy crossed his arms. "I find that hard to believe."

"He's got a wife and son he needs to be around for. You know how that is."

Rudy narrowed his eyes. "I have an idea."

"I had to leave him out of this, for his own sake. This is just between you and me."

"He won't like it when he finds out."

"Who says he's going to find out?"

Rudy studied Rem as if gauging his honesty, then picked up a slice of carrot that had fallen from the cutting board. "I didn't take you for a veggie man."

"I'm making my aunt's favorite soup."

"Kinda late for making soup."

Rem shrugged. "Kinda late for meeting with a killer, but you do what you gotta do."

Rudy chuckled and tossed the piece of carrot into the sink. "Fine, then. You got me here. You want to talk? Then let's talk. Where's my picture?"

Rem hesitated, but then pushed forward. "There are a few things to discuss first. Like, what's the situation with Allison? You going to keep playing her games?"

Rudy sauntered forward, his gaze on Rem, and leaned a hand against the fridge. "That's the deal you're trying to make with me? You give me the pic and I disappear, never to see Allison again?"

"Maybe. But I'd like to know what she and her loser attorney are up to."

"She told me a few things. And I did a few things to keep her happy. If she ever gets out, it's better to keep your enemies close."

"And if she stays behind bars?"

"Then no skin off my nose. She could still be a formidable enemy, though. Allison has friends who are loyal to her. No reason to rock the boat."

"Is Ginger one of her friends?"

Rudy smiled. "Women. Who can make heads or tails of them?"

"I'm guessing that's a no on the friendship."

"Ginger's a special lady with special talents. If Victor had spotted that sooner, he may not be six feet under, but that's water under the bridge. Ginger puts up with Allison because I put up with Allison."

"You sure? I get the impression Ginger's not too fond of her."

Rudy straightened. "I heard you two had a friendly conversation. I think she's fond of you."

"Women," said Rem, crossing his arms. "Who can make heads or tails of them?"

Rudy hooted. "They can be a pain in the ass."

Rem grabbed a kitchen towel and wiped his hands on it. "I've had my share of problems with them. I should know."

"So I've heard." He tipped his head. "You really should have thought things through with Allison. That woman is as slippery as a snail in water."

"That's why I wanted to talk. To find out what she's up to." Rem put a hand on the counter. "Was it her idea to drop something in my coffee?"

Rudy chuckled. "That was something else, wasn't it? I have to give credit to Ginger for that. Measy wanted something to use against you, and she made the suggestion. She's not someone you want on your bad side."

Rem's heart thumped so hard he wondered if Rudy could hear it. "You've been talking to Measy?"

"Just once. By phone."

"You plan to remain in touch?"

Rudy raised the side of his lip. "That all depends on what happens tonight."

"What about Daniels? You going to leave him and his family alone?"

Rudy went quiet and then spoke softly. "Whatever deal is made tonight is between you and me. I make no promises when it comes to Detective Daniels."

Rem shook his head. "It doesn't work that way, Rudy. You make a deal with me, then it extends to Daniels, too." He paused. "Or else there's no deal."

"I'll be the judge of whatever deals we make, Detective." He pushed off the fridge. "You're not calling the shots. I am."

"You sure about that?" Rem took a step forward. "Ginger seemed pretty confident on the phone. I think she's planning a takeover."

Rudy laughed. "You're funny, Detective. Almost as funny as that stupid partner of yours. You must think you can manipulate me like you did Allison, but you better pull your head out of your ass real quick." He took a step closer toward Rem. "I want my picture. You give it to me, and I'll walk away from Allison and Measy. That's the deal."

"Daniels, too. And Mikey."

Rudy grinned. "That's right. Little Miss Mikey. I'd almost forgotten about her. Until I saw Ginger's picture of you two from outside your door. Imagine my surprise when I remembered her from years ago." He moaned softly. "I liked her, and if it hadn't been for Victor, maybe she'd be in Ginger's place right now." His grin grew. "That's probably why Ginger doesn't care for her. Jealousy is her downfall, but her mean streak makes up for it."

Rem's heart slammed harder against his chest. "You leave Mikey and Daniels alone, or that picture will find its way to a match, which I'll personally light."

Rudy's grin fell. "I don't think you quite grasp the danger you're in right now, Detective."

Rem heard a low hum vibrate the air. "You're really ready to risk everything for a decades old picture of a child who died years ago?"

The hum grew. "That's a picture of my boy. I want it back."

"And I want you out of my life, and Daniels' and Mikey's too. And take Ginger with you. That's the deal."

Rudy sneered. "You don't get it. I did you a favor by coming here. I was willing to talk, man to man." He moved closer. "Give me what I want, or not only will I find Daniels and his pretty family, I'll find Josh, too. Maybe he needs to spend more time with his dad." He clenched his hands open and shut. "He could use the practice."

Rem set his jaw and glared. "Let me make one thing perfectly clear. I didn't ask you here to compromise, beg, or even inquire. I came here to make one thing straight. As of tonight, you're history, Rudy. Picture or no picture, you're done. You can take your attitude, your threats and whatever lightning flies from your finger, and shove 'em up your ass."

Rudy tensed, and the air electrified. Rem forced himself to stay put as Rudy encroached and the hum became a hard buzz.

"You are brave. I'll give you that," said Rudy. "But you should probably know what I'm going to do now."

"Please. Enlighten me. I can't wait to hear it." The buzzing pulsed, and Rem half expected to feel the counter vibrate.

"I'm going to do Allison a favor and kill you. Painfully." Rudy stepped within arm's length of Rem. "She won't like it because she wants to keep you alive, but she'll get over it, and Measy certainly won't mind." He curled his fingers into a fist. "Then I'm going to call Daniels myself and tell him what I did to you. Maybe I'll hang out and watch when he runs in and finds your burned body lying twisted on this floor, and then I'll tell him I want the picture, or his family will be next."

Rem swallowed and broke out in a sweat, but he didn't move.

"Then, when I'm bored, I'm going to find Mikey, and she and I will reconnect. I hear she made Victor very happy, and I look forward to finding out why. Maybe Ginger will join us."

It took everything Rem had not to lunge at Rudy and wrap his hands around his throat, but knew it would be a death sentence. His stomach twisting and his adrenaline surging, he took a last step toward Rudy. "One more thing before you kill me. I didn't quite give you all the information. I told Daniels if he didn't hear from me by now, to take the picture and destroy it. I made him promise." He eyed the clock. "I suspect right now he's enjoying a nice cabernet in front of a warm fire, while your picture crinkles in the heat."

Rudy's brows dropped together, and the pulsing air turned to pounding. He raised his hand and pointed a finger. "I'm going to have some fun tonight." He brought his finger to within inches of Rem's chest. "I hear Allison had some fun with you, too." The pounding roared in Rem's ears and the pulsing vibrated through his body. "But that's nothing compared to what you're about to experience."

Rem forced himself to stay still, and trembling, he prayed the timing was right. "Remember, Rudy. You had a choice." He took a step back and bumped against the counter, but Rudy followed. Rem started the countdown. "Ten...nine...eight..."

Rudy scrunched his eyes as the laundry doors opened, and Daniels emerged, his arm outstretched, his eyes menacing, and his gun trained on Rudy.

Rudy's look of superiority faltered, but then quickly returned.

"Seven...six...," said Rem, sweat dripping down his back.

Rudy shifted toward Daniels. "Well, hello, Detective. I should have known you weren't far away," he said, eyeing the gun.

Rem continued. "...five...four..."

"What are you going to do?" Rudy smiled. "Shoot me?"

"...three..."

Daniels straightened his aim. "Ring-a-ding-ding, asshole."

Rem whispered. "...two...one..."

Rudy sneered. "You don't have the guts." He shot his finger toward Rem and Daniels pulled the trigger.

Chapter Twenty-Eight

Lights blazed and flared from the tops of patrol cars lighting the dark street that buzzed with activity. Rem sat on his front steps and watched as an officer ran police tape in front of his property, trying to keep onlookers and press at bay. Daniels sat in a chair on the porch, looking worn and tired, but keeping his distance from Rem.

An officer ran past, and Rem scooted over, giving others access to go back and forth. The Coroner's wagon and Forensics team had arrived, and Rem knew they'd be taking the body from his house soon and examining the scene. Holding his head, he wondered if he'd ever get to go to bed, and where he would sleep, but then realized he wouldn't get much rest anyway, so what did it matter?

Lozano exited the house. He'd arrived not long ago and hadn't said a word to either Daniels or Rem, but had found the lead officer and had spoken to him before going into the house.

Rem massaged his temples, hoping it would help his pounding headache. He wished he could talk to Daniels, but they'd said all they could say before the police had arrived, and they'd been told to separate by the lead investigator at the scene. Daniels' weapon had been taken, which had been expected, and they'd been sitting there since, watching the activity escalate around them.

Footsteps traveled down the porch and stopped at the steps. Rem looked up to see Lozano staring down at him. The captain grabbed a chair that sat beside a small table where Daniels was sitting outside Rem's front window and dragged it over, away from Daniels. He sat next to Rem and interlaced his fingers. "You want to tell me what happened tonight?"

Rem took a deep breath and tried to think clearly. "Rudy's what happened, Cap. He came to my house and threatened me. Grabbed the knife from my counter and said he wanted the picture or else he'd go after Mikey and Daniels. I told him I couldn't get it for him, and I may have said a few choice things myself. He came at me and that's when Daniels showed with the gun and shot him."

Lozano stared for a second. "What was Daniels doing here?"

"I was going to take him home since he'd dropped his car off at the repair shop, but we figured instead of me going back and forth in the morning, it made more sense for him to stay upstairs. He went to bed early but must have heard me and Rudy arguing. He came down with his gun, went around the back of the stairs and came out through the rear of the kitchen, just as Rudy lunged at me with the knife, and he fired." Rem recalled his dream and Jennie telling Daniels to take the shot. "He saved my life, Cap."

Lozano watched him for a second and then stood. "Stay put," he said to Rem, and then he dragged the chair toward Daniels, where he sat again. Rem imagined he was asking Daniels the same questions.

He and Daniels briefly made eye contact, and Rem nodded as Daniels answered Lozano.

•••••••••••

The next day was a whirlwind of questions and reports. Rem sat at his desk, weary after a long, exhausting twenty-four hours. He'd eventually been able to leave the crime scene to stay the night at Mikey's since she was at Mason's, and had assumed Daniels had been allowed to go home. They couldn't talk until their statements had been taken, and they were cleared to communicate. Daniels would have to undergo the investigation required when an officer discharged his weapon in the act of deadly force. That was routine, though, and based on what Rem was hearing, there were no red flags. Daniels would likely be cleared after the investigation, and the prosecutor and the review board approved his return to duty.

Near the end of the day, Rem stifled a yawn and sipped on his umpteenth cup of coffee as officers continued to stop by and offer their support. He appreciated it, but all he could think of was Daniels and the questioning he must be going through. Knowing how long it had taken for him, Rem hoped Daniels was holding up. Although Rem had taken the risk of being killed by Rudy, Daniels had pulled the trigger, and that was never easy, no matter how evil someone was or what they were about to do.

An hour later, Rem was about to hunt down Lozano to find his partner when Daniels walked into the squad room, looking as exhausted as Rem felt.

Relieved, Rem stood. "You okay?"

Daniels collapsed into his chair. "Just peachy."

Rem sat again. "I'm guessing by your presence that we're allowed to speak?"

"Nobody's stopping me, so I guess so." He swiveled his head toward Rem. "You finish answering all their questions?"

"Yeah."

"Any issues?"

Rem shook his head. "None. You?"

"Seemed pretty clear cut. Nobody acted concerned, at least."

"Any ideas how long this might take before you can get back to work?"

"No idea." He sat up in his chair. "I guess it takes as long as it takes."

Rem nodded. "I'd offer to make you some coffee, but I think I'm too tired to get up."

"That's okay. I'm too tired to drink it."

The doors opened, and Lozano strode into the squad room, his face weary. Seeing Rem and Daniels, he stopped by their desks. "You two done with your questioning?"

"Seems that way, Cap," said Rem.

"Good," he said. "Get your butts in my office." He gestured with a file in his hand.

"I'm officially on leave, Cap," said Daniels. "Can't I go home?"

Lozano scowled. "You're not on leave from me." He stood waiting until Rem and Daniels slowly stood and trudged into his office. Once there, Lozano stood at the door. "Stay put. I need to deliver this file. I'll be right back." He closed the door behind him.

They sat in the silence, and Rem groaned in fatigue, too tired to worry about why Lozano wanted to speak with them.

"You okay?" asked Daniels. "You haven't said much."

"I could say the same," said Rem. "Probably because we haven't been allowed to talk."

Daniels rested his head back against the chair. "Sorry. My brain's a fog."

"Besides, I'm not sure what there is to say, other than it was a clean shoot. He would have killed me if it weren't for you."

"I wish we could tell them the truth. Knife or no knife."

"Yeah, I know." Rem paused. "I keep thinking about my provoking him. What if I hadn't? What if he'd gone for the deal?"

Daniels looked over. "You can't think like that. We talked about this, and you heard what Donna said. That man planned to kill us both. Picture or no picture. If he hadn't killed you last night, then he would have killed you later, and God knows who else." He sighed and paused. "Are you second-guessing what we did? Because if you are, tell me now."

Rem shook his head. "God, no. We did what we had to do. I won't say otherwise."

"Should I have not taken the shot?"

Rem faced his partner. "You did exactly what you were directed to do. Everything Donna said happened. Combine that with Jennie's dream, and we have to trust that we'd be dead otherwise. Maybe not last night, but eventually, and God knows what could have happened to Marjorie or Mikey." He sighed. "I'm not second-guessing anything, but it doesn't mean I might not feel a little guilty, but I can live with that. I'm more worried about you. What you did took guts."

"It was him or us. I didn't lie about that." Daniels eyed the ceiling. "But I understand about the guilt part. I wish there could have been a better way."

"I hear you, partner." Rem huffed and leaned back. "Damn. I forgot my coffee, but I don't have the energy to go get it."

"You drink any more coffee, and you won't sleep tonight." Daniels closed his eyes and opened them when the door opened, and Lozano entered.

"Watch me," said Rem. "Course, it'd be nice if I could sleep in my own bed."

Lozano shut the door, stepped to the other side of his desk, and sat. "You want some cheese with that whine, Remalla?"

"Sorry, Cap. It's been a long day," said Rem.

"Tell me about it," said Lozano. "Between the two of you, the Chief, and the press, it's been a circus."

Daniels fought back a yawn. "I can imagine."

"How you holding up?" Lozano asked Daniels.

"I'm hanging in there," said Daniels. "But Rem's right. It's been a long day."

Rem asked the question he'd been mulling over. "Is he going to be okay after all this? They going to give him a hard time over the shooting?"

Lozano grunted. "He shot the man who took Josh Lambert and killed Josh's father. You two brought down a kidnapper and every parent out there who's been keeping an extra set of eyes on their kids a little longer every day can now breathe a sigh of relief." He leaned back in his chair. "All signs show it was a clean shoot, but you know they have to jump through the hoops."

"It's fine, Cap," said Daniels. "I'm just happy I can bring Marjorie and J.P. home."

Rem nodded. "And Mikey can come out of hiding."

"There's just a few questions I have of my own," said Lozano, tapping his armrest.

Rem sat up. "What's that, Cap?"

Lozano looked between the two of them. "What I saw at the scene perked my interest. Since when do you slice vegetables, Remalla, much less eat them?"

"I was making my aunt's veggie soup." Rem picked at a nick in the chair. "I hadn't made it in a while."

"Funny you were making it the night Rudy showed," added Lozano. "And you were slicing them with that knife, which you'd left on the counter."

Rem swallowed, feeling the heat of Lozano's stare. "I guess it was one of those weird coincidences."

"Uh huh." Lozano rocked in his seat before he leaned up and put his elbows on his desk. "It's also interesting how Rudy threatened you with that knife when that's not his MO."

"He likely grabbed it to intimidate Rem," said Daniels, his back straightening. "Probably hoped Rem would cower to him."

"It didn't work, though. I just made him mad," said Rem. He glanced at Daniels and Daniels glanced back.

"Just seemed strange," said Lozano. "He didn't use a knife on Ben Lambert or the two homeless men."

"Maybe when he saw it sitting out," said Rem, "he decided to switch things up."

Lozano studied them. "Maybe." He paused. "There's another thing I'm curious about."

"What's that?" asked Daniels, whose weariness faded with Lozano's questions.

"That patrol I pulled off Sam Halpern's grave. There'd been a mix-up in communication, and they went out there the other night."

Rem tensed in his seat and didn't look at Daniels. "They did?"

Lozano tapped his index fingers together. "They figured out that they didn't need to be there, but before leaving, one officer thought he saw two men walking through the cemetery."

"Really?" asked Daniels. "Two men?" He rubbed his jaw.

Lozano narrowed his eyes. "The officer said it was dark, but neither of the men matched the description of Rudy, so he left it alone and didn't report it."

"Huh," said Rem. "He's probably right then. Probably just two kids checking out a graveyard at night. You know how teenagers can be."

Lozano's gaze never wavered from either Daniels or Rem. "Guess we'll never know."

"Guess not," said Daniels, shifting in his seat. "Anything else, Cap?"

Lozano shifted his attention to Daniels. "Just one thing. You said you brought your car to Benny, the mechanic, yesterday?"

"Yeah. I did," said Daniels. "Kept hearing that dinging sound."

"You know Benny's a friend of mine?" asked Lozano.

Daniels nodded. "That's how we found him."

"I called Benny this morning to ask about bringing my wife's car in for an oil change. He told me to tell you that your car is just fine. He couldn't find anything wrong with it."

Rem made an uncomfortable laugh. "Well, that's good news."

"It sure is," said Daniels, bouncing his knee. "Save me some money."

Lozano's expression didn't change. "It's a good thing you brought it in, though, or you wouldn't have been at Rem's last night to save his life." His gaze flickered back and forth between Rem and Daniels, and Rem stayed quiet. "It's also good your car wasn't in Rem's driveway, otherwise Rudy would have known you were there. He might have killed you both, or not shown at all."

"You're right, Cap," said Daniels. "It's a really good thing." He gripped his thigh but met Lozano's gaze, and Rem sensed the silent communication flying through the room.

Lozano looked back at Rem and Rem pursed his lips. "Thank God everything turned out the way it did," said Rem. "We were lucky."

Lozano's look suggested he was debating his next steps. "That's one word for it." He paused and slowly leaned back in his seat. "Before you go out to celebrate, don't forget that Rudy's cohort, Ginger, is still out there."

Rem relaxed, sensing Lozano had chosen not to press harder into the circumstances of Rudy's death. "We know."

"You think she's a threat?" asked Lozano.

Daniels sighed, looking more relaxed. "We hope not. Maybe with Rudy gone, she'll move on."

"We're not saying she's not dangerous," said Rem. "But she's not the one who kidnapped Josh, and she even helped Josh when Rudy had him. Rudy's messed with her for years. Maybe she'll realize her newfound freedom and take advantage of it. Not that we won't still look for her and have a warrant out, but hopefully her malice toward us will wane with Rudy's death."

"You sure about that?" asked Lozano. "She's wanted for killing your neighbor, and don't forget what she did to your coffee."

"We can't be sure about anything," said Daniels. "But we can't live in the shadows forever. We'll keep an eye out and our feelers up."

"You better," said Lozano. "She might not take kindly to you two killing the man who shaped her into who she is."

"Or maybe she'd thank us if she could," said Rem. "She doesn't have to do somebody's dirty work anymore and get roughed up in the process."

Lozano studied them. "Just be careful, okay?" He straightened. "I don't want another body on your floor with a knife in her hand. You hear me?"

Rem flicked his eyes toward Daniels. "Believe me. Neither do we," said Rem.

"Definitely not," said Daniels, rubbing a temple with his finger.

Lozano eyed them a moment longer before releasing a deep breath. "That's all I have. You two go home. Get some rest."

"I wish," said Rem.

"You can stay at my place till they release your house," said Daniels, standing.

"Thanks," said Rem.

"And stay away from the vegetable soup," said Lozano, opening his drawer and pulling out a pen.

"That won't be a problem for Rem," said Daniels, heading for the door.

"You have my word," said Rem, following Daniels out. "I doubt I'll make it again." He grabbed the knob but stopped. "And thanks, Cap."

Lozano raised his head, and they shared a look that expressed more than what could be said, before Lozano waved. "Go on. I'll see you tomorrow."

Rem nodded and left the office with Daniels.

Chapter Twenty-Nine

THREE DAYS LATER, REM stood in his kitchen after staying the night in his own bed. The crime scene unit and forensics had released his house the previous day and he, Daniels and Mikey had cleaned it, doing their best to remove all shades of Rudy's presence from that night. Mikey had even smudged all the rooms, burning sage Mason had given her and waving it throughout his home, intent on removing any remaining negative energy. Rem couldn't be sure how much it had helped, but he had to admit, his home felt lighter afterwards.

The coffee machine beeped, and Rem reached for a mug, wondering what lay ahead for the day. With Daniels still on administrative leave, Lozano had kept Rem at his desk, and while he enjoyed the lightened workload, he was getting bored. Not knowing how much longer his partner would be out though, Rem had to satisfy himself with keeping busy until Daniels returned.

His phone beeped, and after filling his mug, he reached for his cell, seeing a new text message. He opened it. *Check your email* was all it said. A shiver ran through him, and he thought of the previous creepy messages he'd received. Was this another one? Could it be from one of Allison's crazy followers, or Ginger, or even Measy? The return number was unknown, so he couldn't be sure.

Telling himself to stay cool, he flipped over to his personal email and saw a new entry in his inbox. The return address was not familiar to him and was mostly a mixture of letters and numbers. Clicking on it, he held his breath, expecting to see another threatening letter, but saw a link and the words *Open it.*

Debating what to do, he questioned whether to call Daniels, but Marjorie and J.P. had returned home the previous day, and he didn't want to bother his partner. Telling himself to get over it, he clicked the link, and a video popped up on his screen.

His face came into focus, and the camera drew back, and Rem saw himself at the station, walking down a hall. Only it was more like wobbling. He held onto door frames, stumbled, bumped into people, and stopped one person, a man in uniform who Rem spoke to. The officer frowned and walked away.

The hair on the back of Rem's neck rose as he watched himself, clearly under the influence, attempt to return to the squad room. Swallowing, he knew how bad it looked. A minute passed, and the video froze on his dazed face.

Rem's stomach flipped. Glad he hadn't eaten anything yet, he held his churning belly when another email appeared in his inbox from the same address.

Anxious, he opened and read it.

Not exactly sure how to headline that video, but I'm sure the press can help. I can imagine the public outcry when one of the Force's finest is found under the influence while at work.

And don't think Daniels will escape scrutiny. The scandal, and his zeal to protect you, will ruin his career, along with yours.

If you want it to go away, then I need to see you. Today.

A.

Rem choked back a gag and closed the email. Holding the counter, he doubled over, trying to figure out what to do. Allison wanted to see him and was threatening his career and Daniels' if he didn't comply.

He tried to think. What would the ramifications be if the press got the video? Could he explain what happened? Lozano had said he would back Rem up if needed. But Rem also knew that in the court of public opinion, there would be little he could do to prove his innocence. Measy knew that public perception would be all that mattered and would use that against Rem. The police in general would take a hit from this, and if that happened, Rem's career would matter little.

Rem shut his eyes, imagining the scrutiny–the investigation that would ensue, the looks from fellow officers, and even from the public if they recognized him from the footage. Daniels would fall on his sword trying to protect Rem, and Lozano would likely do the same. Opening his eyes, Rem realized he had no choice.

Straightening, he put his phone in his pocket. He walked to the coffee machine, turned it off, and left the full mug on the counter. Then he grabbed his car keys and left.

••••••••••

An hour later, he signed the visitor log at the jail where Allison was being held, showed his badge, and relinquished his weapon. His fingers shook as he held the pen, and he waited until a guard arrived and guided him to a room with various sitting areas separated by narrow wooden slats with sheets of plexiglass dividing the prisoner and visitor sections. A phone hung beside each chair.

The officer left, and Rem was left alone. Apparently, no one else was visiting. He took a seat and waited, trying his best to remain calm. The conversation would be recorded, so Rem wondered why Allison wanted to talk, other than to convince him to reconsider his testimony, or to make it look like he was a liar, so he reminded himself to be careful.

He'd called Lozano, telling him he had an appointment and would be late to work, but Rem understood that eventually this encounter would reach the captain's ears. Imagining his captain's booming yell when he learned about the meeting, Rem almost winced, but if it meant protecting Lozano and Daniels, then Rem had to take the risk.

A few minutes passed, and Rem almost got up and left more than once, when he heard a clang. A door opened on the other side of the plexiglass, and then he saw her.

Ushered in by a guard, she wore an orange jumpsuit and no makeup. Her long hair was pulled back in a ponytail and her full lips smiled at him while the guard brought her to her seat, and she stared at Rem through the glass.

An image of her on the first day they'd met flashed in his head. She'd walked into the bar in her slim red dress that had emphasized her trim figure, her hair cascading down her back and her red lips gleaming. He'd barely been able to take his eyes off of her, as had the other men in the bar. Chastising himself, he regretted not walking out of the bar as much as he wanted to walk out of the jail right now.

Staring at him, Allison took hold of the phone and lifted the receiver. She put it to her ear and waited for Rem to do the same.

Steeling himself, and telling himself he could do this, he took hold of his own phone, lifted it, and put it to his ear. His heart pounded, and he tried to breathe normally, but images of the last time he'd seen her popped into his mind, and he remembered her straddling him, the knife in her hand, and the torches blazing.

"Hello, Rem," she said.

The guard had turned and left, and Rem wished he'd stayed. Rem didn't trust his voice, so he didn't answer.

"I see you got my message," she said. Her eyes glittered, much like they had in the torchlight.

"I'm here," Rem said. "What do you want?"

"I want to talk." She shifted in her seat. "I've missed you."

His stomach lurched. "You've got two minutes and then I'm gone."

"What's the hurry? Haven't you missed me, too?" Her voice crackled through the phone. "We had some fun together. Remember?"

Rem swallowed the bile in his throat. "Your time's running out."

"I'm in no hurry. And neither are you, unless you're willing for people to see the real you."

The image of himself wobbling down the hall pissed him off. "You threatened me in order to get me here. Now I'm here. What do you want?"

"Scared the truth will come out?" Her heavy breathing traveled through the phone. "It's inevitable, though. Once the trial starts, everyone will know your true colors."

Rem refused to be baited. "And they'll know yours. They'll learn what you did to me, and what you did to Victor. You're going to prison, Allison, for a long time, and no amount of disgusting tactics by your lawyer or whoever you use to frame me is going to prevent that."

She studied him through the glass. "You and me. We belong together."

"The further apart we are, the better. It makes me sick being this close to you."

"But you came, didn't you?"

"You didn't give me much choice. You're threatening to drag my name through the mud." Rem suspected his theory was true. Allison wanted him to say something incriminating. "And my partner's and captain's. Maybe this visit is stupid, but I care about the people in my life, and if making this one effort to protect them helps, then I'm willing to try. But I know you want to discredit me, which is why you drugged my coffee and used Rudy against me, and now Measy is involved. There's no stopping the depths of depravity you'll go to get what you want."

She smiled, and a chill ran up Rem's spine. "You're very eloquent, which I'm sure a jury will love, but it's more than that, Rem. There's a reason I needed to talk to you." She leaned closer to the glass. "You and I shared something special, whether you want to admit it or not."

"The only special thing we shared was a piece of pie. Beyond that, I've been trying to forget your existence."

"But you can't, can you?" She whispered. "I'm in your dreams, both awake and asleep. I follow you wherever you go. You can't escape me." She paused, her gaze lingering. "You never will."

"Try me," said Rem. "After today, I'll see you in court, and after that, I'll never see you again." He checked his watch. "You've got one minute."

She flicked her gaze over him, and Rem thought of a serpent ready to strike, but waiting for the perfect moment. "Listen to me, Remalla," she said. "Maybe I made a few mistakes and took things too far, but you made a few of your own. You liked me and I liked you, but it went too fast, and the flame burned too bright. We crashed and burned and now I'm taking the fall. I get it. I screwed up. Little ole' me can't compete with the fierce detective just doing his job. Victor was evil and did evil things. To me and to others. I don't deny that. He used me, and I let him. But I can't just sit back and let everyone take advantage because I've been weak in the past. I have to do what I can to survive. I've been sitting in a cell for three months now, and I've had some time to think." She hesitated. "Plus, I've come to terms with something you need to know. Something that may make you think twice before you use your clout to send me down the river."

Rem fidgeted in his chair, and he couldn't wait to get out of there. "Thirty seconds."

Her eyes widened, and she hesitated before she leaned up to the glass and spoke low into the phone. "I'm pregnant, Remalla, and before you ask, you're the father."

Rem stiffened in his seat, gripped the receiver, and almost laughed. "You're lying."

"I'm not."

Rem tried to formulate a thought, but struggled to comprehend what she was telling him. "You're something else. Trying to fake a pregnancy to get out of jail. Good luck."

"I'm not faking. Check with the jail's doctor. I gave permission for him to confirm it."

The room began to close in on Rem, and his chest tightened. "If it's true, then there's no way in hell I'm the father. I know you were with Victor, and God knows who else."

She blinked, her sharp gaze never wavering. "Victor didn't want children. He'd had a vasectomy. It's yours Rem. We're going to have a baby."

Struggling to suck air into his lungs, Rem shook his head. "No, we're not. I don't believe you."

"Take all the time you need, but when the trial starts and I walk into that courtroom nine months pregnant, you'll have no choice but to admit the truth." She paused. "And a jury will know it, too."

Rem shook with anger. "That's your and Measy's plan? To sway a jury because you're carrying a child?" He pounded a fist against the wood in front of him. "You're disgusting. And you think by telling me it's mine, that I'll, and maybe a jury, will go easy on you?"

"It is yours. If you take a second, you'll realize I'm telling the truth."

Rem closed his eyes, determined not to let this woman get to him.

"And what happens to our baby if I go to jail?" she asked, her voice melancholy.

Rem opened his eyes. "We're not having a baby."

"It's a girl. I can feel it." She sighed. "You know I can sense things. I can sense this as strongly as remembering your body against mine. It's a girl, and she's ours. I know you feel it, too."

"Stop it," said Rem, his stomach rolling.

"The question is," she said, "what are you going to do about it? Are you going to let your child's mother rot in prison? Make her visit her mommy once a month in a place like this?"

"Don't," said Rem.

"Are you going to raise her while I'm in here? Because that's what I want. If I go away, I want you to take her, but I want to be a presence in her life. I want her to know I'm her mother. You can't deny me that."

Rem's vision spun, and he struggled to breathe.

"But if I'm free, I'll raise her. I'll take care of her and if you want to be a part of her life, I'm fine with that. I'd welcome it. Either together or apart, she should know her parents love her...and each other.

Rem's world tilted. "I have to go."

"Think about it, Rem. Think about what's best for our daughter's future."

Rem hung up the phone and stood, his mind and body reeling. He grabbed the barrier between the stations, trying not to falter. Allison continued to talk from the other side of the plexiglass, her words muffled, but he could still hear them.

"She's your daughter. Don't make her go through this. It's your responsibility to take care of her."

The guard on Allison's side opened the door and ushered Allison out. She dropped the phone and yelled louder as the guard pulled her by the elbow. "You know what you have to do."

Rem turned, feeling sick and defeated, and walked out of the visitor's area. His mind a blur, he returned to the front, signed out, took his weapon, and with his emotions swirling and moving on autopilot, he stumbled out of the jail.

The bright light of the sun made him squint, but he kept moving. If he stopped, he'd collapse, and he couldn't do that. Not here. Not in front of Allison, with cameras everywhere, filming his shock and devastation.

Doing his best to put one foot in front of the other, he got to his car and found his keys. Starting the engine, he stared at nothing, knowing she'd won. Allison had pulled the ace, and he had nowhere to go but straight down the path she'd made for him. Thinking of the baby, he held his stomach. Was Allison telling him the truth? Was he going to be a father?

If so, he felt the odd excitement of it, but also the dread of the inevitable thought that he would be forever linked to Allison, whether she remained in prison or not.

Panic bubbled up when he realized he didn't know what to do next. He couldn't return to the station, and he couldn't go home. His whole future spun in his brain like a hurricane, and he hung his head, desperate to find some release. He couldn't help but think of all he'd been through with Jennie. He'd fought hard to find his way back after her death and learning the cause of it. He recalled meeting Jill, their instant connection, and their eventual breakup. And he groaned when he remembered meeting Allison, how stupid he'd been to think he was getting back to normal, and how he'd thought he was falling for her.

Rem squeezed his temples and thought of the note he'd received at the station. Its ugly words flashed in his mind. *Maybe you should put a gun to your head and pull the trigger.* His breath catching, he reached and took his gun from his holster. He stared at it, his mind racing and his stomach churning. Gripping the handle, he thought of his mother and Daniels, and Mikey and Lozano, and moaning, he tossed the gun into the passenger seat. He took a deep breath and tried to stop his downward spiral, but emotionally, he was in a tailspin.

Banging on the steering wheel with his palm, he bit back a sob, frantic to get out of there. Dazed, he pulled out of the parking space, and having no idea where he was going, gazed at the darkening clouds in the distant sky, said a small prayer for help, and tires squealing, sped away.

What's next?

Find out what happens next as Rem copes with Allison's disclosure. Here's a hint...he's not going to handle it well. Get ready for Daniels' and Remalla's return in the next book in the series, *Of Mind and Madness*. Rem's in a dark place and he and Daniels find themselves chasing a murderer and a hellhound. Enjoy an excerpt below.

And, if you're keeping up with *The Redstone Chronicles*, Lost Dreams (book two) follows the events of *Of Body and Bone*. Mason and Mikey's brother is accused of murder, and Mason must confront his demons, literally. An excerpt from *Lost Dreams* follows. Learn more about *The Redstone Chronicles* below.

Want more from J. T. Bishop?

Subscribe at jtbishopauthor.com to get the Daniels and Remalla prequel novellas, *The Girl and the Gunshot,* and *The Magic of Murder*, plus future books, for **free**, in addition to extra content.

Follow J. T. on her Amazon author page to be notified of new releases.

A Daniels and Remalla Prequel Novel?

Murder Unveiled, the highly anticipated prequel novel to *Haunted River,* is now available. A prominent art dealer is found murdered after the unveiling of a famous, but cursed, painting. When Daniels and Rem are assigned to investigate, they'll learn that a curse may prove more deadly than a killer and they could be the next targets.

How did it all begin?

Check out the *Family or Foe Saga* where we first meet the detectives. This four-book series focuses on a murderer with a mysterious background and unique abilities who's out for revenge against the family he believes wronged him. Can Daniels and Remalla stop him before he seeks his vengeance?

Discover *The Redstone Chronicles*

Did you know the Redstones have their own series?

Meet Mason and Mikey Redstone, introduced in *Of Breath and Blood*, book two in Daniels and Remalla.

Mason, a former Texas Ranger turned medium and paranormal investigator, along with his sister Mikey and partner Trick, take the cases others won't and risk their lives in the process. In *Lost Souls*, Mason's estranged partner returns and asks for Mason's help to solve a murder, but can he be trusted?

Chronologically, *Lost Souls* follows *Of Breath and Blood*, but can be read on its own.

Note: Because the Daniels and Remalla books and The Redstone Chronicles are a spinoff and crossover series, they share an overarching story, and the characters from each are mentioned or appear in all the books, so reading both is ideal. The books published alternate between both series. A list of books in chronological order follows below.

Fan of Paranormal Romance, Urban Fantasy, and Light Sci-Fi?

Discover Bishop's first series, *The Red-Line Trilogy*. Yanked from her predictable world, Sarah Randolph learns she's the key to unlocking a secret that will ensure the existence of a hidden community. One man, assigned to protect her from a dangerous adversary, will risk everything to keep her alive, but when he falls for her, will their destiny be enough to save them both?

In *The Fletcher Family Saga*, the four-book sister series to *The Red-Line Trilogy*, a distant but deadly threat risks the lives of three unique siblings, but life can't stop because of who they are. They'll endure love, loss and a dangerous enemy determined to destroy them all.

Either series can be read first. Take your pick. Boxed sets are available, too!

A Note From J. T.

I love to hear from my readers about their experiences with my books, and I'd love to know what you thought about *Of Body and Bone.* I wasn't quite sure where this book would lead me, but I found myself unable to leave the events of *Of Breath and Blood* behind. I had to dive deeper into the world of Victor D'Mato and his potential victims and cronies and the effects he had on their lives. There were too many story possibilities calling out to me. Plus, Rem's still making his way back and I like exploring his recovery and how it affects his and Daniels' partnership and his relationship with Mikey Redstone.

Rudy was especially fun to write. While he's grieving over the loss of his son, he's become a murderer who justifies his actions at the same time. His abilities make him even more dangerous, and I had to wonder, how do you kill a man who can't be killed? Thus, the ending. I had to do some fancy thinking and loved the thought of Daniels and Rem backing each other up in an extreme situation. What are friends for?

There's more to discover in upcoming books and in the spin-off/crossover series, *The Redstone Chronicles,* so check that out if you're curious. This has been an exciting journey, and I hope you're enjoying it as much as I am.

And as a note to Lone Ranger fans out there, I always heard him yell "Hi-ho, Silver" when I watched the show, but imagine my surprise when, after a little research, I realized he was actually saying Hi-yo. Mind blown. So, if you thought it was Hi-ho, too, now you know the crazy truth.

Reviews are a huge plus and big help for an author and potential readers. I would love it if you could please take a couple of minutes to leave a quick review for *Of Body and Bone* . And if you'd like, please leave a few comments, too.

As always, thank you for your time and readership. It is deeply valued and appreciated.

Now, on to the next book!

Books in Chronological Order

Although recommended but not required, in case you prefer to read in order...

Prelude to The Shift, a short story (free at jtbishopauthor.com)
Red-Line: The Shift
Red-Line: Mirrors
Red-Line: Trust Destiny
Curse Breaker
High Child
Spark
Forged Lines

....

The Girl and the Gunshot, a novella (free at jtbishopauthor.com)
A Hamburger Christmas, a novella
The Magic of Murder, a novella (free at jtbishopauthor.com)
First Cut
Second Slice
Third Blow
Fourth Strike
Murder Unveiled
Haunted River
Of Breath and Blood

Lost Souls

Of Body and Bone

Lost Dreams

Of Mind and Madness

Lost Chances

Of Power and Pain

Lost Hope

Of Love and Loss

Lost Lives

Dominion

Lost Time

Illusions

Lost Love

Vendetta

Acknowledgements

ANOTHER BOOK IS COMPLETE, and again, I have many to thank. This doesn't happen alone, and I am indebted to family and friends for their help, support, and encouragement. It is truly appreciated.

I love writing about the bonds between loving family, deep friendships and the ties that hold them together. Plus, my fascination with the unknown thrown into the mix makes for a satisfying story and hopefully, adds a little more thrill for my readers.

I especially want to thank my fans. Hearing from you and knowing that you're enjoying my books makes all the hard work worthwhile. None of this would matter without your tremendous support. If I can help you escape from this crazy world for a short period each day, then I've done my job.

Here's to more stories, more fun, and more time for yourself. If you can have a little of that each day, you're on the right track.

Enjoy an excerpt from Lost Dreams, Book Two in The Redstone Chronicles.

Mason Redstone walked through the old farmhouse that had recently been renovated into a beautiful two-story ranch-style home. High ceilings and big windows gave the house a light and airy feel and the gorgeous view of the rolling hills reminded Mason of his grandparents' home in the hill country of Texas.

The owners had contacted his agency, SCOPE, the previous week and had asked Mason to investigate their property. They'd bought the farmhouse a year earlier and had envisioned it as the place where they would enjoy their eventual retirement. But once construction had begun, they'd had nothing but issues. Workers came and went, never staying longer than a couple of weeks. They'd say the place had a vibe, or that they'd seen or heard something they couldn't explain. Renovations had come to a halt more than once until new workers could be employed. Eventually, the home had been completed, although eight months behind schedule, and the owners, an older couple in their mid-sixties, had moved in a month later. Having had no experiences themselves during the renovation, they were unconcerned about the activity, believing it to result from overactive imaginations and superstitious beliefs.

They'd made it three months before calling SCOPE.

SCOPE stood for the Study of Cryptids or Paranormal Entities, and Mason had thought it was the perfect name for his agency, although his sister Mikey had disagreed. After a two-year stint as a Texas Ranger, several talks with his brother Max who lived in San Diego and listening to the advice of his best friend Victor, Mason had taken the leap and left the Rangers, moved to California, and had become a private investigator hoping to use his gifts to help others. Mikey had followed soon after.

It had been a rocky start, especially after his estrangement from Trick, his partner in the Rangers, his falling out with Victor, rescuing Mikey from Victor and his cult, the murder of his cousin, and the gut-wrenching loss of his mother. But, as the saying went, life went on. As paranormal investigations became more mainstream, his business had picked up, resulting in Mason inviting Trick to join SCOPE.

Mason had been reluctant at first, especially after working a recent tough case with Trick in which they'd investigated Trick's sister-in-law, Cissy, for murder, and Mason and Mikey had barely made it out alive. But that case had led to repairing their fractured friendship, and now that Trick was here, Mason could see the benefit of a second investigator. One who could handle the non-paranormal cases, which also seemed to be on the rise despite the agency's name. Trick had completed the requirements for his P.I. license and had started work that week. He already had a client coming in later that day, and Mason was eager to hear about it once he returned to th e office, but right now, he had some spirits to clear from the old farmhouse.

The minute he'd walked into the home, he had sensed two souls who still wandered the property. One was an older man and the other a young child, a girl, maybe ten years of age. The owners had been confronted with odd noises and spectral voices, footsteps on the stairs and in the hallways, and objects falling from the shelves. They'd installed cameras and had caught an apparition moving past a door frame, and the wife had called Mason the next day, telling him they needed help, and threatening to sell if the activity continued.

Mason had arrived two days later and had investigated the house, sensing the two presences who he now felt sure had lived here before. After spending some time on the property and reaching out to the entities, he'd learned it had been a father and daughter. The daughter had died in the home after a long illness, and the father had grieved for her and had died himself years later from a heart attack, likely brought on from the long period of grief. The strange part of the visit, though, was why they remained.

Mason had discussed the problem with the homeowners, and they'd asked him to encourage the spirits to move on and let them live in their house in peace. He'd agreed, believing he could do some research, prepare, and would return to move the father and daughter on and into the light.

Now, a week later, as he walked through the main hallway, he opened himself up to the energy of the space, sensing the spirits. He'd communicated to them, telling them the situation, and letting them know it was time to leave. Honesty was the best policy with both the living and the dead, and Mason trusted that once the father and daughter understood their situation, they would happily move on. But as Mason continued his walk, he sensed another presence, one he hadn't felt on his earlier visit, and realized that the father and daughter remained not only because they felt a connection but also because they were being prevented from leaving.

Mason paused at the entry to a guest bedroom and eyed the closet. In his research, he'd found little to justify any lingering evil spirits, but he could never rule out the land itself. He could only go so far back in his search. Most history was lost to time and would never be known. Mason began to sense that there was more to this property that had nothing to do with the home itself.

Stepping into the small room, he eyed a bed, a sitting table with an attached mirror, and a bureau with a chest of drawers. Nothing seemed out of place, and Mason studied his reflection in the mirror. He wore his boots, jeans and pressed long-sleeved, forest green shirt. His groomed handlebar mustache dusted his cheeks, and not having shaved that morning, he sported a slight five o'clock shadow on his jawline. He'd left his cowboy hat in the front room and noted again when he saw his longish hair reaching his ears that it was time for a cut.

But now was not the time to worry about his appearance, because in the reflection, he saw and heard the closet door creak open behind him.

Mason turned, his heart thumping. Curious, but also careful, he approached the closet door, and nearing it, he reached out and pulled on the knob, opening the door more, and peered inside. The closet contained little more than a few items of clothing hanging from the bars and a couple of boxes on the floor.

Taking a steady breath, he moved closer, mentally asking who was present, but received no response. Reminding himself that fear never solved anything, he took slow steps and entered the small space, asking again for the presence to make itself known. He sensed that whatever had beckoned him held the answers as to why the father and daughter remained. Mason wanted those answers, and he asked again.

A cold breeze brought a sudden drop in temperature, and an icy chill ran up Mason's spine. His body tingled, and Mason had the sudden understanding that perhaps he'd made a mistake. Whatever had lured him into the closet had not done so in kindness, but in malevolence. Realizing his error, he turned to leave, when a low growl penetrated the silence, the light went out, and the closet door slammed shut.

Enjoy an excerpt from Of Mind and Madness, Book Four in Detectives Daniels and Remalla

Captain Frank Lozano sat at his desk and eyed his laptop. Detective Mellenbuehl sat across from him. "What do you think, Mel?" asked Lozano. "You think he's guilty?"

Mel sipped from a cup of coffee and chewed on a donut. "I think he's dirtier than O.J. We just need to prove it. His girlfriend's his only alibi. I say Garcia and I push her a little harder. See if a little pressure gets her to open up. I don't think she quite realizes what lying to us could do to her if we catch her."

"She might also clam up and protect him. We've seen it before."

"Yeah. I know. But it's worth a shot."

"You talk to his mother?" asked Lozano. "She might have something interesting to say, too."

"Going today. Just waiting for Garcia."

Lozano nodded. "Go on, then. Let me know how it goes." He checked his watch. "I've got a meeting. Keep me posted."

Mel nodded and stood. He tossed his empty coffee cup and napkin in the trashcan beside the door. "You got it." He took the last bite of his donut and left.

Lozano closed his laptop and sat back in his seat. His blinds open, he looked out the glass portion of his office wall into the squad room. Various detectives sat at their desks, and he observed the usual comings and goings of his men and women working. Spotting the empty desks of Daniels and Remalla, he wondered about each of them, and considered calling when the outer squad door swung open, and Detective Gordon Daniels walked in. He looked around and then saw Lozano through the glass. Lozano waved him over.

Daniels, his blonde hair gelled back and perfectly in place, strode toward him. He wore his usual casual, but ironed, slacks and a long-sleeved collared blue shirt. His attire stood in stark contrast to his partner Detective Aaron Remalla's, whose clothes were usually wrinkled, his jeans worn, and his shirts stained. While Daniels had the book smarts and the look of a wrestler, Remalla resembled more of a track and field athlete and had the street smarts. Together, they were a formidable team, had forged an indelible friendship, and were two of his best detectives.

Daniels opened the door to Lozano's office. "Hey, Cap."

"Come on in. Have a seat."

Daniels shut the door behind him and sat. "How are you?"

"Good. The crazies are a little more settled at the moment, so there's a brief lull."

"Glad to hear it."

"How're Marjorie and J.P.? You been enjoying a little time with the family while you're on leave?"

Daniels propped an ankle on his knee. "We actually took a couple days and got out of town. We needed it."

Lozano nodded, recalling Daniels' and Remalla's last case and how it had ended. Daniels was currently on leave, pending an internal investigation after firing his weapon with deadly force. "I know you did. You guys have been through a lot. I'm glad you could get away."

"Any news on my current status?"

"I spoke to the chief a couple of days ago. You should hear something soon about getting back to work. Everything's looking good, so hopefully, you'll know something next week."

"That would be great. As much as I've enjoyed getting some time off, I think I'm ready to get back. Relaxing isn't my strong suit."

"Funny, isn't it? You have a hellish case, wonder how you do this job, but then get some time away, and you miss it."

Daniels chuckled. "We're all a little crazy, aren't we? Otherwise, how else could we do what we do every day?"

"You got that right." Lozano sat up and tossed a folder on his desk into a pile. "How's Rem doing? You talk to him?"

"I was about to ask you the same thing."

"You came at a good time. I'm actually about to meet with Kate Schultz, the prosecutor on the Allison Albright case. Said she learned something and wanted to talk to me. She should be here any minute."

"Kate's coming?" Daniels frowned. "Is it something serious?"

"I don't know. Said she didn't want to discuss it on the phone."

"Did she talk to Rem about whatever it is?"

"I didn't interrogate her, Daniels. I figure if she needed to talk to Rem, she has his number."

Daniels rubbed his jaw. "Has he been okay while I've been out? He hasn't said much, but I know he didn't want to bother me while I was gone. You know how he is."

Lozano tipped his head. "Why are you asking me?"

"Because you've seen him more than I have." He sat up and looked out the glass. "Is he here? Don't tell me you paired him up with Silvers. Rem will be bitching like an angry cat, and I'll never hear the end of it."

"What the hell are you talking about?" asked Lozano, confused. "Remalla took some time off. I haven't seen him in four days."

Daniels swiveled in his seat, his face serious. "What?"

"You heard me. He took some time off."

"When?"

Lozano scowled. "Are you suddenly deaf? I told you. Four days ago. Didn't he tell you?"

Daniels shook his head. "Cap, he didn't say a word. He told me he's been here, either doing desk duty or helping with various cases. Are you saying he hasn't been here at all?"

"I think that's what taking time off means. No. I haven't seen or heard from him."

Daniels pulled out his phone. "Shit. Why in the hell wouldn't he tell me?" He dialed a number and put the phone to his ear.

"He's your partner. You tell me."

Listening, Daniels set his jaw. "He's not answering." He waited and then left a message. "Rem? I'm in Lozano's office. Where are you? Call me." He hung up. "What did he say when he asked for time off?"

Lozano shrugged, thinking back to his last phone call with Remalla. "He said he'd gotten word that his aunt was sick. He wanted to go see her. I told him to take the time he needed. Considering what he's been through, he needed to get away as much as you."

"His aunt? Which one?"

"Hell if I know, Daniels. I'm not his mother. I expected him back at the end of the week."

Daniels texted. "Well, he's not in hiding anymore. I'm on his trail now and he better damn well tell me where he is." He sent the text. "I don't get it. Why□?"

A knock sounded, and Lozano saw Kate Schultz through the glass. He raised his hand and waved. "Come in."

She entered, carrying a briefcase and wearing a two piece, fitted dark green suit. "Captain," she said. She eyed Daniels. "Gordon."

"Hi, Kate," said Daniels, standing but holding his phone.

Lozano raised a brow at their familiarity. Daniels tipped his head at Kate. "Kate's aunt and uncle lived down the street from my parents when we were kids. We used to ride our bikes around town during the summer when she was visiting."

"Small world," said Lozano.

"It is," said Daniels. He looked back at Kate. "How are you? How's the case?"

She looked between the two of them. "I've been better. I'm glad you're here. I can kill two birds with one stone." She set her briefcase on the chair beside Daniels. "I don't suppose you know where your partner is?"

Daniels lifted his phone. "I'm trying to find out right now. Why?"

"Something to do with the Albright case?" asked Lozano.

"You could say that," she said. "But just how much, I can't say. Not yet anyway. I've been trying to reach Remalla, but he's not returning my calls."

Lozano could see the shift in Daniels' posture. Something was up, and Daniels could sense it just as fast as Lozano could. "How can we help?" asked Lozano.

She opened her briefcase. "I became aware of something this morning. Allison's attorney contacted me."

"You mean Greasy Measy?" asked Daniels. "That guy's a toad. What'd he want?"

"He kindly informed me that your partner," she pulled out a file folder and opened it, "visited Allison Albright in jail four days ago."

Lozano tensed, and Daniels' jaw dropped. "He did what?" asked Daniels. "There's no way. He wouldn't go near her in a million years."

Kate pulled out a sheet of paper. "I didn't believe Measy either, so I contacted the warden. He sent me this." She handed the paper to Lozano.

Lozano studied it, his heart racing.

"What is it?" asked Daniels.

"Copy of the visitor log where Allison is being held," said Lozano. "Remalla signed in at nine sixteen a.m. and signed out at nine twenty-four, four days ago." He handed the sheet to Daniels.

"That's not possible," said Daniels. He read the paper.

"Oh, it's possible," said Kate. "I've requested the video to see what was said. He better pray he didn't do something stupid. Measy was almost salivating on the phone, so it doesn't bode well. Any of you talk to Remalla because I sure would like to."

"Has Remalla texted back?" asked Lozano.

"No. He hasn't." Daniels handed the paper back to Kate. He paused for a second and then headed for the door.

"Where are you going?" asked Lozano.

Opening the door, Daniels barely stopped to answer. "I'm going to find my partner." He walked out, passed his and Rem's desks without a second glance, and left the squad room.

www.ingramcontent.com/pod-product-compliance
Lightning Source LLC
LaVergne TN
LVHW010638110826
845149LV00014B/2869

* 9 7 8 1 9 5 5 3 7 0 1 2 7 *